BALFOUR,

STRANGER AT
STONEWYCKE

Books by the Phillips/Pella Writing Team

The Journals of Corrie Belle Hollister

My Father's World
Daughter of Grace
On the Trail of the Truth
A Place in the Sun
Sea to Shining Sea
Into the Long Dark Night
Land of the Brave and the Free

Grayfox

The Stonewycke Trilogy

The Heather Hills of Stonewycke
Flight from Stonewycke
Lady of Stonewycke

The Stonewycke Legacy

Stranger at Stonewycke
Shadows over Stonewycke
Treasure of Stonewycke

The Highland Collection

Jamie MacLeod: Highland Lass
Robbie Taggart: Highland Sailor

The Russians

The Crown and the Crucible
A House Divided
Travail and Triumph
Heirs of the Motherland
Dawning of Deliverance

HAMPSHIRE BOOKS®

STRANGER AT STONEWYCKE

MICHAEL PHILLIPS
JUDITH PELLA

BETHANY HOUSE PUBLISHERS
MINNEAPOLIS, MINNESOTA 55438

Stranger at Stonewycke
Michael R. Phillips and Judith Pella

Cover by Dan Thornberg,
Bethany House Publishers staff artist.

Library of Congress Catalog Card Number 87–6605

ISBN 0-87123-900-0 (trade paper edition)
ISBN 1-55661-581-7 (Hampshire Books edition)

Published by Bethany House Publishers
A Ministry of Bethany Fellowship, Inc.
11300 Hampshire Avenue South
Minneapolis, Minnesota 55438

Printed in the United States of America

Dedication

With love and thanks to my parents
John and Norma Pella

The Authors

The PHILLIPS/PELLA writing team had its beginning in the long-standing friendship of Michael and Judy Phillips with Judith Pella. Michael Phillips, with a number of non-fiction books to his credit, had been writing for several years. During a Bible study at Pella's home he chanced upon a half-completed sheet of paper sticking out of a typewriter. His author's instincts aroused, he inspected it more closely and asked their friend, "Do you write?" A discussion followed, common interests were explored, and it was not long before the Phillips invited Pella to their home for dinner to discuss collaboration on a proposed series of novels. Thus, the best-selling "Stonewycke" books were born, which led in turn to "The Highland Collection," and the "Journals of Corrie Belle Hollister."

Judith Pella holds a nursing degree and B.A. in Social Sciences. Her background as a writer stems from her avid reading and researching in historical, adventure, and geographical venues. Pella, with her two sons, resides in Eureka, California. Michael Phillips, who holds a degree from Humboldt State University and continues his post-graduate studies in history, owns and operates Christian bookstores on the West Coast. He is the editor of the best-selling George Mac-Donald Classic Reprint Series and is also MacDonald's biographer. The Phillips also live in Eureka with their three sons.

Contents

Introduction

To man's undiscerning eye, the generations come and go, fading one into the other, ultimately passing from the face of the earth. As the march of history progresses, only the land remains, while men, women, and children grow, live, and die and then return to the earth from which they came, seemingly swallowed into nothingness by a vast uncaring universe.

In reality, however, the land is the stage upon which a drama of unparalleled eternal significance is played within the hearts of every man and woman who sets foot upon it. Unseen by those around us, often uncomprehended by ourselves, the choices and values of our earthly lives mold and determine the character we take with us into the next life.

From the time the Picts settled in northern Scotland in the seventh century, until the region was overrun by the Vikings in the ninth, and then settled throughout the following centuries by the Scots, the estate known as Stonewycke became a symbol of the enduring quality of the land. When the castle of that same name was built by Andrew Ramsay in the 1540's, his prayer was that the estate would stand as a sentinel in the north to God's goodness. His prayers for the generations who would follow him in the Ramsay line resulted in blessings and prosperity to the family throughout the next two and a half centuries, finding special fulfillment in the righteousness of his descendant Anson Ramsey in the early nineteenth century. (The spelling of the family name was changed in 1745 to Ramsey.)

But as the blessings of God follow generational lines, so also do the consequences of wrongdoing and ungodly choices. The self-will and personal greed of Ross Ramsay, brother of Adam de Ramsay, baron of Banff, also became an intrinsic factor in the family bloodline—a black stain which, unknown to Andrew, his descendant, was too strong to be rooted out entirely by the prayers that followed the stigma.

Hence, though Andrew's blood was strong in Anson, Ross's found fertile soil in Anson's sons, whose father suffered the tormenting fate of watching his own offspring turn away from the God of their fathers. The family continued to be infused by new blood; while the choices and prayers of each succeeding generation breathed new life into the heritage of godliness, at the same time self-interest strengthened the forces which opposed those prayers. The grafting into the family of James Duncan in 1845 threatened to eradicate altogether by greed and ambition what Andrew and Anson had prayed so diligently for.

Yet in the mystery of God's purpose, in James's own daughter rose the strong desire to give her life to the Almighty plan. Such yielding, however, never comes easily. Battle raged within the soul of young Maggie Duncan—the conflict found in her Ramsey bloodline was illustrative of the essential human condition. Indeed, the future of the family's heritage was at stake. Her laying down of self, and her prayers for the future of the Ramsey/Duncan lineage, rekindled for a new era the prayers begun through her ancestors, enabling the blessings of God to pass to new generations through her granddaughter Joanna.

Thus the legacy continued into the second millennium of settlement on the northern Scottish coast. And with the passage of time the tempo of life accelerated. The twentieth century brought many changes to the inheritors of the once-magnificent estate known as Stonewycke. In Great Britain the twentieth century brought the end of the Victorian Era with the Queen's death in 1901. Monarchies had come and gone countless times before, but this transfer of power was more far-reaching in its impact on the world than a mere changing of the guard from mother to son in London. A thorough-going transfiguration, the roots of which had sprouted during Victoria's lifetime, was in the process of turning society inside out.

Not only was the entire political framework of the world being revamped; cataclysmic social change, affecting every level of society, was sweeping through the once-proud center of the mighty British Empire. The growth of the Labor Party overhauled Parliament's decision-making process. Morals and literature changed dramatically. The spiritual foundation-stones of Victoria's administration eroded. Socially, economically, politically, and spiritually old norms were being thrown out. Technological breakthroughs, given momentum by the Great War against Germany, found their way into the daily lives of countless millions on both sides of the Atlantic— automobiles, electricity, airplanes, radios, urban growth, new factories, and the wild music and fashions of the 1920's.

These were profound changes. The world in the first two decades of the twentieth century was a world rushing to modernize itself. The world of Maggie's childhood was a world as distinct from that in which Joanna would raise her daughter, as the horse was distinct from the automobile. Between 1900 and 1930 stretched a gulf, not of decades, but of centuries.

Perhaps most significant for the northern shires of Scotland during this time was the final demise of the old feudal and manorial systems of land management, which had been dying a slow death for centuries. Once-proud estates gradually were sold off in parcels, were apportioned and split between heirs, or went bankrupt as their owners desperately tried to keep vast holdings together with insufficient capital. Not only economics, but social outlook had changed. While titles and nobility still mattered a great deal in Britain, they were coming to matter less. The working classes could now vote and buy land and improve their lot. The separation between the workers and the aristocracy was much narrower. No longer were the fortunes of the workers solely bound up in their dependence on the landowners and lairds who owned their houses, their lands—sometimes, it seemed, their very souls.

With such total dependency gone, the economic benefits to local lairds of the surrounding crofters and poor tenant farmers was also gone. Only the landowners who were able to cope with the changes time had brought survived in their positions of stature. They forged new, more equitable relationships with their subjects, and found

11

other means to support their estates rather than by the blood and toil of the peasantry.

Many estates were not able to survive intact. Others, like Stonewycke, faced the new times by adapting to them rather than trying to stem the tides of change. With a wisdom supernaturally inspired, Anson Ramsey drew up a transfer document for a time which would come years after him, transferring a large portion of the Stonewycke estate to the people who lived on the land. Anson's transfer turned out to be the salvation of the proud Ramsey heritage. For in that magnanimous act was solidified a bond between the people of Stonewycke and its nobility, unique among such estates—a bond of mutual love that would see mighty Stonewycke, and all those bound to it, through years of change and regeneration.

Quietly, invisibly, the hand of God is always at work. Although we may see only a narrow individual perspective of His actions, the purpose of God goes on far beyond our limited understanding. In the Old and New Testament, God works through the generational flow of family and nation; both sin and righteousness sow seeds and harvest fruit into succeeding generations. Jesus himself came, not as a mere individual, but as a man born into the uninterrupted flow of the history of God's people. Son of God, Son of Man, Son of David, He brought God's salvation to the world through the heritage of family, through the legacy of man's ancestry and ancient birthright as the creation of our Father in heaven.

Twentieth-century mentality is often based on the present; we live in a vacuum of *now*. Yet every life is the result of a series of choices and crossroads—not only ours, but those of our ancestors for generations behind us. In the present, as in the past, each individual holds a key to the future. We stand at the crossroads of our personal histories, and the decisions we make set into motion values and attitudes that affect not only our own development as men and women made in the image of God, but the choices and decisions that will face our descendants for generations to come.

The Stonewycke saga, then, as it passes into the middle of the twentieth century, is a saga of those human choices, of the struggles of men and women to yield to the godliness to which all are called, while resisting the stain of evil that is passed down through the blood of our ancestors. It is a saga of the land, of a family, of righteousness and blessing passed down through the years as, in certain generations, the forces of good or the forces of evil gain the upper hand. And always the prayers of righteous men and women who have come before stand in the balance.

The Stonewycke saga is the story of God's work through the generations of one particular family. As the prayers of godly men and women from early in that family's history weave their way silently into the lives of future descendants, new strains of life (through such men as Ian and Alec) are grafted into the family tree just as the Gentiles were grafted into the family of God, further strengthening and solidifying God's purpose.

Stonewycke—as a home, as an estate, as a family seat—symbolizes that eternal quality of continuing life through the generations of the Ramsey and Duncan clan. Through the righteous prayers of Andrew and Anson Ramsey, and then Maggie Duncan, followed by Joanna MacNeil, the life of God moves through the generations like seeds which fall to the ground and are covered up and lie dormant—perhaps for many years—yet retain their power of growth and inherent life, waiting for the moment when the proper combination of sun, rain, and warmth sprouts them to life once more.

Though that essential life all but disappeared from the Ramsey clan during some of its darker years, the life hidden below the surface was waiting to sprout. That seed of righteousness, Anson Ramsey's transfer document, was unearthed by Anson's great-granddaughter Maggie, whose spiritual eyes were opened largely through the influence of a humble groom named Digory MacNab. Even then, the transfer document, and the very inheritance of Stonewycke itself, disappeared during the years of Maggie's lonely sojourn in America. However, the purposes of God are never lost, and through Maggie's own granddaughter Joanna, the life of Stonewycke blossomed and came to fruition once more.

The heritage continues, passing gradually from one generation to the next, with the hand of God infusing life through the answered prayers of the righteous. Man can never tell what methods God will use, nor when the fulfillment of prayers long silent will come. But God's purposes are always accomplished. The prayers of the righteous resound through the heavens, awaiting the moment when their fulfillment is at hand.

Thus, the Stonewycke legacy lives on, and moves into the future. And as it does, those of a new generation in the Ramsey/Duncan clan, and those who will be grafted into it, are imbued with a life which is given strength through the prayers and obedience of those who have come before. The only question remains: to which of the strains of their heritage will they yield their allegiance?

As the decisions surrounding that question are daily made, the future of the Stonewycke legacy is determined.

"The kingdom of heaven is like a treasure hidden in the ground. When a man found it, he hid it again, and then in his joy went and sold all he had and bought that field."

—Matthew 13:44

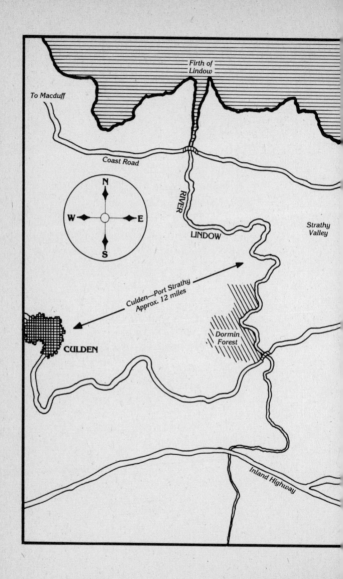

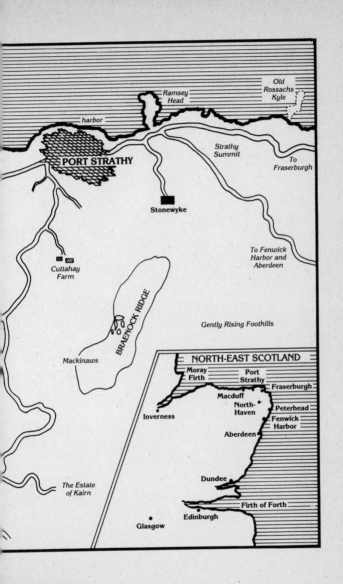

Old
Rossachs
Kyle

Ramsey
Head

harbor

Strathy
Summit

To
Fraserburgh

PORT STRATHY

Stonewyke

To Fenwick
Harbor and
Aberdeen

Cuttahay
Farm

BRAENOCK RIDGE

Gently Rising Foothills

Mackinaws

NORTH-EAST SCOTLAND

Moray
Firth

Port
Strathy

Fraserburgh

Macduff

Peterhead

North-
Haven

Inverness

Fenwick
Harbor

Aberdeen

The Estate
of Kairn

Dundee

Firth of Forth

Edinburgh

Glasgow

1 Lady Margaret

The recent rains lent an invigorating sparkle to the clean northern landscape. White caps on the lapping dark green waves sharpened into crisp focus, and on the horizon the sapphire of the sea and the azure blue of the sky met like a narrow line on an artist's canvas.

Lady Margaret Duncan, heiress and matriarch of the centuries-old Scottish estate of Stonewycke, took a deep breath of the tangy salt air as if she fully expected it to rejuvenate her aging form. In reality, however, she cared little to push back the years. That process was reserved for those whose memories harbored discontent. She had come to savor the years as treasures, quietly at peace with the flow of her life, and with the aging it brought. The passage of time added a richness nothing else could possibly bring, the fulfillment of all that had come before. How could she ever want to go back?

She paused for a moment in her casual stroll along the beach to watch a white-winged gull swoop swiftly down toward the water. It skimmed the glistening surface for a mere second, then arched again into the sky, its quest unsuccessful. Yet it seemed not to mind. The silvery-white bird winged in a widening circle overhead until it once again spotted a potential prey.

But Lady Margaret did not witness the conclusion of the hunt. Her attention instead skipped northward, toward the horizon, where two fishing boats had appeared and were now heading in the direction of the harbor. They must have sailed immediately after yesterday's storm had abated. After a night at sea they were now on their

19

way home. She wondered if the catch had been a good one.

Ah, yes, she was content, at home on the beach she had loved since childhood, the place she delighted in more than anywhere else. This was her Scotland, the country of her ancestors; her Stonewycke, the beloved land of generation upon generation of her own family. It was, she sometimes thought, as if God had created them just for her. Perhaps in a sense He had. For had she been the only human being in existence, He would just as fully have lavished upon her the beauty of His boundless creation, the wonder of His love.

That thought, as it had many times in the past, brought a tear to Lady Margaret's eye. The tears flowed more easily now than when she was young. A hard shell had surrounded her heart then, a shell which God had been able to break only by sending her miles from her homeland. The wilderness years across the sea had been painful, not only for her but also for her husband; the forgiveness that God had sought to implant within their hearts had not taken root easily in the soil of their independent spirits. But throughout the years of their sorrow, confusion, and aloneness, the Lord's hand upon them had never faltered.

How faithful He had been to her and Ian! If only they had been able to grasp the larger scope of God's plan for them sooner! Yet how could they, in the midst of their temporal suffering, perceive that often God's infinite answers to our finite prayers reach their victorious fulfillment only through His work in generations yet to come? As His ways are higher than our ways, so is the inexhaustible depth of His plan for reconciliation beyond the limited vision of our earthbound eyes.

Margaret and Ian now viewed their past, both the years apart and these blessed past two decades they had been allowed to share, not as one of earthly happiness, but of eternal gain. It had been a saga of God's unrelenting pursuit after the heart of man and woman, a chronicle of healing. And as the heritage of their experience continued through the lives of their grandchildren and great-grandchildren, they gave God thanks for the work He had wrought. How grateful they were for Joanna, the treasured granddaughter who had been the instrument in God's hand to bring about their reunion, and for Joanna's husband Alec, whose grafting into the family line had immeasurably strengthened the old Ramsey strain. And now, through their young children, the legacy continued into the third decade of the twentieth century.

Yes, the tears flowed more easily now, but they were tears of great joy which fell from the aged face. If Lord and Lady Duncan had known pain in their youth, it had been well-compensated for in their present contentment. *Twenty-one years ago,* she thought, *I found my husband again. But actually I found much more.* She had rediscovered the friend who had first come to Stonewycke as a mere lad of twenty. Those who knew the old couple only in passing marveled that they had not been together all their lives. Without speaking, they each knew the other's thoughts and feelings, and continually communicated with each other through the simplest gestures and glances. Though both the Lord and Lady of Stonewycke were past their mid-eighties, almost daily they could be seen upon the grassy hills about the estate, occasionally on the beach west of town, and up until recently even once or twice a year upon horseback. The companionship their heavenly Father had seen fit to deprive them of during their middle years of life had been amply restored, and a vitality and strength of body gave them back at the end of their lives the friendship and love each had stored away for so long.

Always they were deep in conversation—but not about the past, nor what might have been. They were too vitally caught up in the glories of the present to dwell long on times gone by. Every day was a new challenge. For the growth of God's life within their hearts had not stopped on that day they were reunited. If anything, it had accelerated. Often Ian now, it seemed, took the lead in spiritual matters, for with the bondage of his past finally shed, he had soared like a bird into the realms of heavenly truths. He often laughed when he thought how good a thing it was that they who wait upon the Lord could run and not be weary—especially for a man his age!

Yes, he had laughed!

These days his laughter—*their* laughter!—rang frequently within the once-somber granite walls of their beloved home, Stonewycke. But it was not their laughter alone. God had given them a wonderful family with whom to share their love, an added dimension of the old couple's joy. The marriage of Joanna and her fine man of faith had given proud old Stonewycke something it had not enjoyed in more than fifty years—the infectious sounds of childish exuberance and life reverberating through its walls. The youngest was May, and Lady Margaret often wondered if even the solid sixteenth-century castle could contain that ten-year-old girl's vibrant energy. Twelve-year-old Nathaniel was, except for his fiery red hair, most like his father. Tall and solidly built, he possessed Alec's easygoing and friendly nature, which made him an immediate favorite with whomever he met. Young Ian, at fourteen, could not have been more unlike his namesake at the same age. Slender and fine-featured, he was the scholar of the family. Margaret knew he was happy where he was—at one of Scotland's fine boarding schools for boys, showing promise for the university. His hunger for learning had never yet been satisfied, and wondrously that hunger served only to deepen his young but growing faith.

Allison, the eldest, had been reserved for last on this day in the gallery of her great-grandmother's thoughts, but not because she was the least. On the contrary, Allison at that moment weighed heaviest on Lady Margaret's mind.

With the very thought of the girl's face, a shadow passed over the old lady's countenance, encroaching upon the peacefulness of the splendid shoreline scene. *Dear Allison, what have we done wrong?* she said to herself. Perhaps too much responsibility had been placed on her as the eldest; or could it be she had not been given enough? Or was it nothing anyone had done at all, but simply the fact that she had been born into the nobility of the Stonewycke heritage?

When Lady Margaret attempted to analyze her great-grand-daughter, any lasting insight into the true nature of the girl always seemed to elude her. Allison, for some reason, wore her ancestry like a shield—a shield to protect her from what, or to hide from what—that was difficult to tell.

At seventeen, Allison was not a great deal unlike her great-grandmother had been at the same age—stubborn, headstrong, willful, and independent. But there was an element present that had never been part of young Maggie's makeup. Somehow Allison seemed to take her position as heiress to a noble Scottish lineage more seriously than any of the rest of the family—too seriously. Where she had come by this strain of haughty pride, no one knew—least of all her own mother and father; no one in all the northeast of Scotland would accuse them of anything except too much humility for their high station. Allison's look of disdain revealed, without words, that she considered her family's casual mingling with the commoner elements of society to be deplorable. She kept her feelings silent for the most part, however, not wanting to be reminded that her own father, notwithstanding that he was probably the most loved and respected man in the neighborhood, had come from this so-called "common" strata of the community.

How interesting it is, thought Margaret, *that in this proud family line, the estate of Stonewycke has been passed down for four generations through the women of the family.* Each of those women, it seemed, had a unique and individual story to tell—with the possible exception of Margaret's own daughter Eleanor, who had never seen the land where her life had begun. Yet even Eleanor's contribution to the eternal plan could not be disregarded, nor could the full scope of her portion of the story be grasped this side of the life that was to come, where all stories will be made complete with the endings God purposed for them.

And now young Allison, representing the fifth generation in the continuous female line of Ramseys spanning more than a century, stood on the threshold of her own womanhood. What would the coming years bring for her?

Margaret thought of her own mother Atlanta—proud, silent, a sentinel of Scottish fortitude in the midst of what had not been a happy marriage. Had Allison inherited a high percentage of Atlanta's blood? More likely the pride—if indeed it *was* pride—so evident in her great-granddaughter, had come from Margaret's father James, if it came through the veins of the family blood at all.

Lady Margaret sighed wearily, revealing for the first time a hint of her true age. *Lord,* she prayed silently, *protect Allison and keep your loving hand upon her, and upon those who come after her. Draw them all to you, Lord, as you did me, and as you did Ian. Reveal Yourself to Allison, in your way and in your own time.*

Margaret took in another deep breath of the warm salty air and glanced about her. Unconsciously her gaze had been fixed on the hard-packed expanse of white sand as she slowly walked along. Now she looked toward the rocky cliffs in the distance. Around the swirling eddies of ocean windrafts, twenty or thirty gulls glided up and down, in and out, cavorting in the sea currents. Even from this distance she could hear their screeching calls, grating perhaps to the ear of the musician, but melody in motion to anyone in love with the sea. *What a glorious place you have given me, oh, God,* she thought, *to live out the remainder of my days! How I love this coast of Scotland with its majestic and jagged coastline, the powerful cliffs dotted with the green of heather and a dozen other wiry shrubs! There was no sight I missed so greatly in America, and no sight is more impossible for me to tire of now that I can see it nearly every day. Thank you, Lord, for bringing me back! You have been better to me than I deserve!*

She turned back toward the village. The sigh that came next was one of contentment, and the smile which accompanied it, whether she sought it or not, was a smile of rejuvenation and peace. A chuckle momentarily passed her lips. *I'd better not stray too far! The days are long past since Raven and I could gallop wherever we wanted. If I get too far from Port Strathy now, it could take me the rest of the day to get back!*

With the thought of her own youth, Allison again came to Lady Margaret's mind. But this time she felt that there was a sensitive side to her great-granddaughter, which was struggling to break free more than she allowed anyone to know. This part of her nature was no doubt at battle with the personality she opened for public view. But it would slip out unexpectedly, and the perceptive aging matriarch was quick to notice, saying to herself, "Now *there's* the real Allison. I knew she was in there!" And this hidden self had in recent months become the focus of Margaret's prayers for the girl. *Show her herself, Lord,* she prayed. *When the time is right, give her insight. Let her know you, and let her come to know herself.*

The prayer brought with it the recollection of Walter Innes's death six months earlier. When Allison took her position too seriously, the factor had never been afraid to look her in the eye and tell her exactly what he thought, even if the blood of gentility flowed through her veins. He was perhaps the only one who could hoot at her attempted arrogance, and say, "Whether ye be a leddy or no, lassie, I expect ye're none too noble t' fit o'er my knee."

The two antagonized each other whenever their paths crossed, yet loved each other no less for it. When Innes died, Allison wept the entire day, though she never allowed a soul to see, and only her puffy red eyes and solemn face gave away the depth of her feeling for the man.

Was it pride which caused her to hide this part of her nature? Sadly Lady Margaret shook her head. For if it was, it frightened the old woman to consider what humbling it would take to heal the girl.

Suddenly a shout broke the deep silence imposed by Lady Margaret's thoughts.

"Grandma!"

She turned and looked away from the sea. It was Allison, waving her hand just as her head broke over the top of the great dune bordering the shore. She ran toward her great-grandmother almost as if the latter's thoughts and prayers had drawn her. The wide and lovely smile, lighting her pretty brown eyes, hardly seemed in harmony with what must lay within, if the old lady's estimation and grave concerns were correct. To all appearances she gave every indication of being an energetic young lady who would disregard such glum notions concerning her character with a hearty laugh.

Lady Margaret returned her greeting with a wave and began walking up the dune to meet her. She returned the girl's smile and hugged her warmly. For no matter what else Allison MacNeil thought about life or herself, she must know above all things how greatly she was loved.

2   Stonewycke

Joanna MacNeil sat at her mahogany desk in the dayroom pouring over the accounts one last time.

After a few more moments she set down her pen, propped her chin in her hand, and sighed deeply. Operating an estate like this had never seemed difficult in the fairy tales. Their family had moved up the hill to the castle after eleven years in a little cottage, just as she and Alec had dreamed. They had now been here nine years. Joanna loved Stonewycke and was no less happy than she had been in her homey cottage. She in no way regretted the move, especially knowing that her grandparents could no longer live here alone.

It was just that at times it could be such a burden.

The requirements of her position still surprised her, and she occasionally found herself lapsing back into her midwestern American timidity. Though she had been here twenty years, had picked up the local dialect noticeably, and thought of herself as a true Scot in every sense of the word, it still usually took her aback when one of the local women curtsied to her in town, or made way for her to pass in a crowd. At such times it was with a jolt that she had to remind herself who she was and of all the people who depended upon her.

Is this really me? she found herself asking. But then she reflected on how the Lord had led her to Scotland, and how she and Alec had met. What changes God had worked within her own heart for her to become the confident woman He had made! He had miraculously healed her grandmother and reunited her with her husband, and Joanna's own grandfather Dorey. When she remembered these things, her heart was filled with thanksgiving—even for the tedious paperwork which lay upon her desk.

Thank you, Lord, she said softly. *And teach me greater thankfulness of heart for these details which keep Stonewycke going.*

Suddenly the door behind her burst open.

"Mother, I've found it!" exclaimed Allison, hurrying toward her mother.

Joanna turned, smiled at her daughter's enthusiasm, and before she had the chance to say a word, found a magazine thrust onto the desktop before her. With obvious satisfaction the girl opened it to a full-page advertisement of an extremely pretty, not to mention a very expensive, evening dress. Most certainly made of satin, though the sketch made it difficult to tell, it was rather simple in design with a draped neckline trimmed in sequins, and a fitted bodice and skirt. Simple, that is, until it reached the knees, where it flared to remarkable fullness. Joanna had the good sense to keep to herself the first impression that such a dress was much too mature for her seventeen-year-old daughter.

"It's beautiful, darling," she said.

"It will be *perfect* for the Bramfords' ball!" replied Allison in high-pitched excitement. "Oh, Mother! please say I can have it!"

"Well, perhaps with a few adjustments," Joanna replied diplomatically. "We can show this to Elsie and see what she can do."

"Elsie . . . adjustments!" exclaimed the girl. "Mother, I want *this* dress—just like it is. And I don't want Elsie to make it!"

"What do you have against Elsie?"

"Mother, *please*! You wouldn't make me go to the Bramfords' in a homemade dress?" Allison's pleading tone sounded as if such would be a fate too horrible even to contemplate.

"Elsie does very professional work."

"It would be different if she were a designer," argued Allison. "But she is only a dressmaker, hardly more than a common *seamstress*."

"Allison, have you bothered to notice the price of this dress? It's fifty pounds. For many of our people, that's half a year's wages! In these times when there are so many who are suffering, I simply can't condone such frivolity—"

"I knew you'd say that!"

"It's true, dear."

"But when the nobility display their wealth, it gives the common people hope that things aren't really so bad."

Joanna had heard that worn excuse so often she didn't know whether to laugh or cry when the words came from the lips of her own daughter. How many in the aristocracy used just such an argument to justify their unnecessary opulence, and to waylay their guilt when their eyes could not disregard the widespread poverty around them? Times were hard throughout all of Britain, even all the world. But those in a position to help often did least of all.

"Allison," said Joanna after a moment's reflection, "I sincerely pray that you will give your words deep thought, and that the day will come when you will realize how empty they are. When we transferred the land to the people of Port Strathy twenty years ago, *that* was the thing which bound the nobility to the people who looked to them for guidance and sustenance. Giving our wealth, not displaying it, is our calling. In the meantime, we cannot pay that kind of money for a dress. These are hard times not only for the working class, but for us as well. Elsie can make the same dress for a third the cost."

"Without adjustments. . . ?" queried Allison who, seeing the war inevitably lost, hoped she might still reap a small victory.

"I'll have to give that more thought."

"I *am* seventeen."

Joanna smiled and took her daughter's hand in hers. "I know that, dear. And you are a lovely seventeen, with or without the dress. But I will keep it in mind."

"The ball is next month."

"I'll let you know in a few days."

Allison scooped up the magazine and exited, leaving Joanna once more alone. Unconsciously she found herself praying for her daughter. *She is so young, Lord, and has so much to learn...*

Her thoughts trailed off with no words to complete them.

Sometimes she wanted to shout at Allison out of her pent-up frustration: "Why can't you see! Why must you do everything your own way? Why can't you listen to what we have to teach you?"

Usually she refrained. But the unsettling realization that her daughter did not share the beliefs and priorities of the rest of the family was never far from Joanna's mind. And the older she grew, the more the distance seemed to widen between the mother and the daughter she loved so deeply.

Allison had always been the kind of girl who had to figure things out for herself. Her methods were, therefore, often fraught with obstacles and unexpected curves. When the first bicycle had come to Stonewycke, as a seven-year-old she had insisted on learning to ride it on the steepest path on the estate. Two years earlier, despite repeated warnings, only by sticking her entire hand into the hive did she learn the dangers of the bee. But as her adolescent years began to teach Allison the ways of life on more profound levels, the perils became far more hazardous and long-lasting than skinned knees and bee stings. Though Joanna firmly believed that the values of her childhood were still rooted deep inside her daughter, they became increasingly difficult to observe on the surface. One by one she seemed to be holding these values up for scrutiny, examining them, testing them, doubting them, suspicious that anything appropriate for a child could possibly be strong enough to hold her up now. Like youths in all ages, it never occurred to her that many men and women, older and wiser and with problems and anxieties more severe than hers, had discovered in those timeless principles sustenance and hope to carry them through all the dark valleys of life. Allison's young eyes seemed blinded to all but Allison herself. This fact did not so much hurt Joanna's motherly pride as it made her ache for the distance it placed between Allison and her Maker. And to make matters worse still, Allison kept such a close wall around her true self that even her mother could often no longer venture within. In fact, Allison's alienation, when displayed, seemed more directed toward her mother and Lady Margaret than anyone else, even though she had always been close to these two older women.

The girl was a paradox, that much was certain! At times she could be so warm and loving and affectionate, especially toward her great-grandmother. Then suddenly, without warning, an altogether different mood could sweep over her, during which she was cold, even embittered, toward those she loved most.

Joanna rubbed her eyes as if finally noticing the headache which had been threatening for the last two hours. Well, a new dress for Allison was simply another burden to add to the steadily growing pile. And was there a small twinge of guilt because she didn't have the money to buy her daughter the dress she wanted? Would the dress perhaps convince Allison that...?

No! Joanna quickly put a stop to that seductive train of thought. Even if they had the money, she could never allow it to be spent irresponsibly. And it was a moot question regardless. There was absolutely no room in the present accounts for such a costly dress.

Indeed, the fairy tales never specified just how much money it took to run a castle. Of course, there were no Depressions in fairy tales, either. The color red was showing more and more often in the ledger these days, and last year they had begun opening the House for public tours to bring in a little additional cash. To further conserve funds, without at first realizing the consequences, they had stopped maintaining the little-used east wing of the house, with the result that it had practically gone to ruin. A carpenter had recently informed them that if something was not done—and done soon— to save the roof, it would be lost and could bring down a good portion of the adjoining wing with it.

When they had enacted Anson Ramsey's Transfer Document twenty years ago, turning over a large part of the estate to the people of the valley and drastically reducing their yearly cash income, they had never foreseen what a problem money would one day become. However, the people of Port Strathy, and the sons and daughters who had inherited the good fortunes brought upon their families by the current two generations in the Ramsey line, had never forgotten. They loved Lady Margaret and Lord Duncan and Lady Joanna and Lord Alec with a love enjoyed by few in their position. Consequently, when the net of hard times began to draw itself about the valley, the people pulled together—commoners and landowners alike—to help see one another through. Many were the small offerings of fruit and produce and fish brought up the hill "t' the Hoose," as it was still called. And with the first news carried to the village that the east wing of the castle was in need of repair, a hundred men were on hand shortly after daybreak the following morning.

Perhaps, sighed Joanna as she reflected on it, *the loss of Stonewycke would work for Allison's ultimate good.* Perhaps it was because she had always had too much that she now came to think wealth and privilege a right.

Yet at the mere thought of losing Stonewycke, a deep pang of despair swept momentarily through Joanna. She could not imagine life without Stonewycke. For good or ill, the place was woven deeply into her very being. Homeless and alone she had come to Scotland that day so long ago. Now she had been grafted into the years of her family's heritage and was an intrinsic part of the ongoing flow of Stonewycke's history. Yet times were hard, and growing harder every year. Who could tell what they might be called upon to do?

If only they could hang on to the estate until the old folks were gone! She and Alec could be happy anywhere. She knew that. She sometimes wondered if Alec would prefer living the simple life of a country vet rather than as the laird of a great property. He still refused to let anyone call him "the laird" in his hearing. He would always be just plain Alec to the people of Port Strathy. *Could it be for the best to let Stonewycke go?* Joanna wondered. *Could that be what God wanted?*

"Dear Lord," Joanna murmured aloud, "you mean more to me, to any of us, than this parcel of land and trees and stone. I would gladly give it all up to do your will, to serve you and these people you have given us more fully."

Joanna paused. Whenever she turned to the Lord in prayer, her thoughts unconsciously strayed to the daughter who tugged so constantly on her heart.

"Oh, God!" she cried out, "I would give up Stonewycke, even my own life, if somehow by it you could reach Allison!"

Joanna bowed her head, but no more words came from her lips. Only her heart silently cried out, interceding where her tongue and conscious mind could not.

"You have it in your hands, don't you, Lord?" she said after another few moments of silence. "In my mortal mind I am unable to see how you will work it out. But somehow you will provide for my daughter's needs, and also for this land. Somehow, you will bring an answer..."

How fortunate it was that Joanna depended on her Father in heaven! The eyes of her infinite God saw beyond the contrite woman praying at her desk, beyond the teenage girl poring over a fashion magazine, beyond the aging matriarch lying down for a rest after her afternoon's walk on the beach, beyond the inanimate granite walls of an ancient castle. His all-seeing eye did not stop there. It reached beyond the expanse of the quaint northern village of Port Strathy and the valley surrounding it. It reached beyond the rugged highlands and grassy glens, to the lowlands of Scotland, and farther down, to the very heart of that chief of all cities hundreds of miles to the south.

God's faithful answer, as so often is the case, would come from a most unlooked-for source, from a place that Joanna, even in her most wildly imaginative mood, could never have suspected. And if she could have had a glimpse of the provision of God in answer to her prayer for her daughter and for her beloved Stonewycke, she would not have recognized it as from Him.

Joanna's silent cries did not float into an empty universe to dissolve into nothingness. Even before the plea had left her aching mother's breast, it had taken root in the loving heart of God, who heard, and whose answer was already on the way.

31

3   The Sinner and the Serpent

An ominous London fog drifted slowly in over the city from Southend as dusk made its appearance. Before another hour had passed, the streets and sidewalks would be slippery wet from the drizzle; residents walking home from their day's employment brandishing their trusty umbrellas, all the while flatly denied that this heavy mist was actually rain.

The young man striding purposefully down Hampstead Road behind Euston Station seemed unconcerned about the weather, for he was nearing his destination, a pub known as Pellam's, about a block away. He did, however, touch the rim of his new felt fedora a bit protectively, hoping he'd escape the drenching which was inevitable on nights such as this.

Looking across the street, he hailed a lad selling newspapers, removing a coin from his pocket as he did so. A newspaper should serve the purpose as well as an umbrella, which he did not happen to have.

"Here you go, lad," he said, flipping the coin to the boy, who caught it deftly as he ran toward him from the street.

"Thank'ee, sir," he replied with a grin as he handed him the paper. "Lemme gi' ye yer change."

"Don't trouble yourself," said the older of the two magnanimously. The boy grinned again and skipped off to peddle more of his wares. He clearly believed himself to have encountered one of London's elite, and would repeat many times over how a lord had given him a shilling for a newspaper.

The generous Logan Macintyre would be the last to refute the lad's misconception. And, dressed in a well-tailored cashmere pinstripe suit, silk necktie, and expensive wool overcoat, and, of course, the new fedora, he looked less the son of a ne'er-do-well Glasgow laborer than of a London lord. It was a ruse he was content to perpetuate as long as there were folks naive enough to accept it.

He also liked to pass himself off as thirty and, though in reality but twenty-two, he was usually as successful with this chicanery as with the other hoaxes he had pulled off in his young life. His boyish features, softly rounded about the chin with a slightly upturned nose and a thick crop of unruly brown wavy hair, might have helped dispel doubt as to his age to the more discerning. But most were fooled by his finely honed air of sophistication.

Logan paused at a corner to allow an auto to pass, then crossed the street. Glancing at his watch, he decided it was just about time. He'd soon have his shilling back—nearly the last bit of cash he had to his name, except his stake for the game—and much more along with it. For by now his partner Skittles would have everything set up to perfection.

Logan thought of his friend with an unmistakable touch of pride—like the devotion of a son for his father, though in truth he had never harbored similar feelings for his real father who had been in and out of one Glasgow jail after another. Whether Logan resented him because of what he was, or because he wasn't good enough at it to elude the police, would be difficult to determine. For his friend and mentor could hardly lay claim to an upright life of veracity and virtue. Somehow though, Logan admired him, even loved him.

Old Skittles—whose given name was the less colorful Clarence Ludlowe—was recognized in the circles of those who knew such things as the best sharp in the business. He had earned his peculiar nickname some thirty-odd years ago, before the turn of the century when the old Queen, as he called her, was still on the throne; he ran the most lucrative Skittles racket in London. He had been able to maneuver the pins with such nimble precision that even the wariest fool could not tell he was being taken. And if the game of skittles was somewhat outmoded in this modern and sophisticated era of stage plays, talkies, cafeterias, and high fashion, the old con man still maintained the status of a legend among his compatriots.

But the Depression had hit the confidence business, too. People were now more reluctant than ever to part with their money, and it took a more astute strategy to make a scheme succeed than in the old days. You had to choose not only your mark but also your partners with caution. But with the right decoy in place, it could still be like taking candy from a baby when a master such as Skittles went to work.

Perhaps it was due to their mutual respect for each other's finesse at the game that allowed Skittles and Logan to work so well together. Logan's one regret in life was that he hadn't been with his old friend in his early days. "What times we would have had!" he remarked more than once. For in his later years, Skittles had legitimized his enterprises somewhat, earning most of his income bookmaking, a practice—as long as he kept to the rules—that allowed him to operate inside the law. He was, however, known to take cash bets upon occasion, a procedure forbidden by law. For the most part the local constabulary did not scrutinize Skittles' improprieties too closely, although Logan had been stung a time or two by carelessly getting too close to a couple of cash deals. Cooling his heels twice in the neighborhood tollbooth and once in Holloway for several days taught him more than all Skittles' remonstrations about keeping his eyes open in front of him, and guarding his flank as well. At twenty-two, he had begun to learn that important lesson and had not seen the inside of a jail in more than a year. He now left the cash bookmaking to others who might want to risk it. For himself, he would stick to what he enjoyed most. And besides, swindling another man was not strictly recognized as a criminal offense. Most magistrates based their lenient decisions on the old adage, "A fool and his money are soon parted," believing that the world will never be purged of dishonesty or swindling, and that a victim had only himself to blame for his folly. Thus, Logan committed to memory the famous quotation of eighteenth-century Chief Justice Holt—"Shall we indict one man for making a fool of another?"—to be pulled out and recited should he encounter any unenlightened bobbies who gave him a hard knock, and in the meantime he went about his activities with relish and spirit.

In another five minutes Logan reached Pellam's, and he turned into the establishment now crowded with workmen having a drink or two before boarding trains home. The setup was perfect! He glanced quickly around with pleasure. Not only was the swelling crowd suitable, but in addition, many appeared to be businessmen whose fat wallets and large egos concerning their intellectual prowess would play right into their hands. They would, no doubt, egg each other on in the emptying of their pound notes onto the bar better than Logan himself could.

Skittles, with his slick-combed hair, bulbous nose, florid cheeks, and altogether friendly countenance, sat at the bar with a frothing pint of ale in his hand, his workman's trousers and grimy leather vest completing the illusion that he was just off a hard day's work on the job. The checkered cap sitting far back on his head seemed about to topple off as a result of the animated discussion in which he was engaged with one of his neighbors. Logan passed by, and without so much as a side-glance or the least hesitation in his voice, Skittles knew he was there. The only indication he gave of his friend's presence was a momentary flash in his eyes which his companion took for the prelude to one more intoxicated tale of dubious factual content. Logan ordered a pint and seated himself in an adjacent booth.

Soon Skittles' voice rose slightly above the general din of the place. His cockney accent contained a purposefully noticeable drunken slur, but Logan knew the man was as sober as an undertaker. For far from laboring in London's streets all day, Skittles had only just now begun his night's work.

"Gawd's troth!" he said, lowering his glass to the counter with a resounding thud to emphasize his words.

"The Queen herself?" asked the man seated to Skittles' right, half incredulous, half concealing a laugh at the lunacy of the thought of this old drunk at Buckingham Palace.

"Dear old Vicky—Gawd rest 'er sowl!" exclaimed Skittles. " 'Course I were but a lad then, an' much better lookin', if I do say so m'sel'."

"Incredible!" said another.

"Why, 'tis as true as Jonah slayin' Goliath!" returned Skittles in a wounded tone, but hardly had the words had time to sink in than a great laugh broke out behind him. He turned sharply around, glaring toward the source of the merriment being made at his expense.

"Hey, young fella!" he called out with feigned anger. "Are you dispargin' the word of a gent'man?"

Logan dabbed the corners of his eyes with his handkerchief and tried to look apologetic. "I'm terribly sorry," he said at length. "I couldn't help myself."

"An' you think I'm lyin', or maybe too drunk t' know me own words, is that it?" he challenged.

"In actuality I did not hear your story at all but only caught your last remark."

"An' wot of that?" Skittles had just the right edge to his voice and Logan was reminded once more of what a true pro his friend was. By now those in the immediate vicinity had begun to turn their heads in the direction of the conversation, which was steadily increasing in volume.

"Well, sir, it was, as a matter-of-fact, David who slew Goliath. Jonah was swallowed by the whale."

"He's right there, gov!" chimed in one of the men behind Logan, who was now listening intently.

"Ow, is 'e now?" said Skittles with animated gesture. "Excuse me! I must say I didn't know as we 'ad a bleedin' *parson* in our midst!"

His barbed ridicule of the dapper young know-it-all pleased the crowd, whose chuckles now began to spread out in increasing ripples throughout the room.

Unperturbed, Logan humbly shored up his defense. "I am by no means of such lofty repute, my good man. I have only a layman's knowledge in matters of a religious nature."

"Then you don't claim t' know *everythin'*?"

"Well . . ." and here Logan looked away for a moment and tried to show interest in his ale, "it would be a bit foolish of me to make such a claim, wouldn't you say?"

"So you don't know everythin'," probed Skittles further, "but you think you're a lot smarter than me, is that it?"

"I did not say that, nor would I, old man," returned Logan, taking a sip of his brew. "And as I have been something of a student in these matters, it would hardly be fitting for me to boast of my knowledge over a man who's already had—"

"*So!* We gots a prodigy in our midst!" declared Skittles mockingly.

"What's the matter, old man?" interjected Skittles' neighbor, himself a good pint past what was good for him, and still thinking about the sharp's churlish claims before Logan happened in, "Are you afraid this young man knows more'n you, an' you bein' Queen Vicky's friend 'at ye are?"

"I 'appen t' be a church-goin' man," boasted Skittles, "an' I been doin' so longer'n this wee laddie 'ere's been alive."

"Here! here!" chimed in someone from across the room.

Another laughed.

"I didn't mean to imply—" began Logan, but Skittles brashly interrupted him.

"Why, if you're such a knowin' young fella," he said, "I gots five quid in me pocket 'ere that says you can't tell me the name o' who it was wot gave Adam the apple t' eat."

"I wouldn't want to take your money so easily," replied Logan. "And besides, everyone knows it was the—"

"Say nothin' without puttin' your money on the table!" interrupted Skittles.

Logan hesitated a moment, seemingly mulling the proposition over in his mind. Then he reached a hand inside his coat, and saying, "All right, you're on, you old fool! Here's my five pounds that says it was the serpent!" he slapped a five-pound note onto the table in front of Skittles.

"I didn't ask *what* it was," said Skittles, reaching out to take Logan's money. "I bet you couldn't tell me the *name*!"

"Not so fast," returned Logan. "His name was Satan. There's the answer to your question! Satan ... the devil ... the serpent—whatever you want to call him. I think the ten pounds is mine!"

"Keep your 'and from off the table!" said Skittles. "My five quid still says you be wrong!"

"He's beat ye, old man!" cried someone from across the room. "He's beat ye at yer own game! Give 'im the note an' don't be a sore loser."

"Who's talkin' about losin'?" cried Skittles, spinning toward the voice. "I got another fiver I'll lay 'gainst yours wot says you're both wrong!"

The owner of the voice strode forward, placed his own note in front of Skittles and said, "The serpent's name was Satan, like the young fella said. Everyone in this room knows it. But if ye be givin' yer money away, then I'll be happy t' oblige an' take it from ye."

"Any other takers?" screamed Skittles, as if in a fit of passion.

"Why can't any of you dull-witted blokes tell me the right name?"

A momentary shuffling ensued, during which several near Logan looked to him with questioning glances as if to ask, "Are ye *sure* ye got the right name, mate?" His confirming nod of self-assurance and confidence sent several hands in search of wallets. One by one, pound and five-pound notes began accumulating on the table in front of Skittles, who continued to drink his ale and act more inebriated all the time. When the table contained some twenty or twenty-five pounds, suddenly Logan jumped up.

"Wait just a minute! Something's not right here. We've put our money on the table and have given our answer. But we still haven't seen anything but that first five-pound note of yours! I don't think you've even got this kind of money to cover these bets!"

A murmur of agreement and approval went through the crowd. By now the attention of everyone in the pub was focused in the drama with Skittles right in the middle of it.

Without saying a word, Skittles reached into his pocket and pulled forth a handful of notes, holding them aloft in a clenched fist that hid the fact that most of the bills were only flash notes. "Fifty quid, me doubting frien's!" he said. "One month's labor fit t' break the back of any son of Adam!" Then as if producing his bankroll were tantamount to winning the questionable wager, with a self-satisfied expression of well-being, he raised his glass to his lips and swallowed down the remaining third of the pint.

Looks of amazement accompanied low whistles and "ah's" as Logan slowly returned to his seat, looking around as he did so with glances to those around him which conveyed, "This old duffer's loonier than I thought!"

"Now!" concluded Skittles, "I'll put me whole wad up t' prove I'm a smarter man than the parson here!"

Within ten minutes the table was piled with the full fifty pounds in bets.

"And now," said a well-dressed man whose investment happened to be six pounds, "just where do you intend to find your proof? I don't have all night to wait for my twelve pounds!"

"Proof ... get me a Bible," said Skittles.

A roar of laughter went up. "In this place!" yelled someone.

Logan stood and approached the bar. "My good man," he said

to the pubkeeper, "would you by chance have a Bible on the premises? I need to show this well-intentioned but ignorant man where he is in error."

"The wife'll have one up t' the parlor," the man replied.

"Would you be so kind as to let us borrow it for a moment?"

The man hesitated, but immediately received such prodding from his patrons that he turned and hastened up to his flat on the second floor. In two or three minutes he returned, and handed the old, black, leather-bound volume to Logan.

"Thank you," said Logan, who immediately began flipping through the pages toward the beginning of the book.

"The Book of Genesis!" called out Skittles. "Who's name were it wot gave Adam the apple?"

"I told you before," replied Logan, all eyes upon him, "that the serpent's name was Satan. Now, if I can just find it ..." he added, almost to himself, continuing to turn over the leaves of the Bible.

"Chapter three ... verse twelve," said Skittles.

Logan turned another page, stopped, read for a few moments in silence, then sank back to his chair looking as one stunned. By now the room had grown quiet.

"Well, what does it say?" asked the six-pound investor.

"Tell 'im, parson!" said Skittles, a grin of fiendish delight spreading over his face. Then he burst into a great peal of riotous laughter. "Read it, laddie!" he taunted. "Or shall I tell 'em wot it says?"

Slowly and deliberately, and in measured tones so that there would be no mistaking his words, Logan began to read: "And the man said, The woman whom thou gavest to be with me, *she* gave me of the tree, *and I did eat.*"

"It were *Eve!*" shouted Skittles with triumph. "*Eve* gave the bloke the apple, not the serpent!"

"You said *he!*" objected one of the many victims.

"I said, 'I say you can't tell me the name o' who it was wot gave Adam the apple.' That's wot I said, as the Lord an' Queen Vicky be my witnesses. Your young frien' there, the know-it-all parson, *he* said it were the serpent, an' then I said, 'I bet you couldn't tell me the name.'"

Again Skittles burst out in uproarious laughter, then stood, clutching at his head; though the drunkenness was all part of the deception, he had still had a bit more ale than he was accustomed to.

With the pub about equally split between the gloomy set who had taken the bait and followed Logan into the trap, and those who were now congratulating themselves that they had kept out of it, Skittles gathered up his winnings, with the humility of a peacock in full feather. He gave Logan a condescending pat on the shoulder, and a smug, "Sorry, old chap . . . you should stick t' your preachin' an' stay out of dens o' iniquity like this," and with that he half-strutted, half-staggered out of the pub.

Logan sat on for some time longer, ordering another pint and turning his dejected stares silently into the amber glass. His momentary newfound friends gave him cool glances, and the wan smile of apology on his lips whenever he did happen to look around did little to alleviate their reproachful looks. "Oh, well," he said to himself, "a fool and his money are soon parted. You gullible dolts should have known better than to believe a good-for-nothing like me!"

This was always the most difficult part of this particular dodge—knowing the right time to make an exit. Natural instinct urged him to hurry out on Skittles' heels. But that would be too obvious. However, if he waited too long, someone might eventually put two and two—or in this case five and five—together.

Therefore, he drained his drink in a leisurely fashion, glanced tiredly at his watch, and casually announced to no one in particular, "Just about time for the seven-ten." He then rose, gathered up his newspaper, set his fedora back on his head, and exited. A number of stares followed him, but no one said anything or attempted to stop him. They all appeared glad enough to let him go.

He found Skittles at their preappointed rendezvous in front of a newsstand about four blocks away. He ran forward, slapping his old friend on the back.

"You did good, lad!" laughed Skittles.

"I can never believe how they fall for it!"

"They do every time," replied the experienced sharp as he dug the wad of money from his pocket. As he did so he moved away from the stand to the darkness of an overhang at the edge of an alley. "An' this time," he went on in a subdued voice, "t' the tune of fifty quid!"

Logan could hardly restrain the whoop he felt like making as Skittles began counting off from the stack of bills. " 'Ere's your 'alf, Logan. You earned it!"

Logan took the money and stood for a moment just admiring it. Most men had to work a month, sometimes two or three, at dirty, grueling labor for this kind of cash. He had gotten it all in less than an hour! *Not bad*, he thought as he pocketed the loot.

Business out of the way and the exchange settled amiably, the two men began walking, unperturbed by the darkness and the deepening foggy drizzle. Their conversation turned to what they'd do with their new-found wealth. Skittles mentioned a new dress or possibly that ornate plum hat he'd seen his wife Molly admiring in a store window the other day. Logan figured he'd better pay his long overdue rent.

Skittles stopped and laid an earnest hand on Logan's arm. "Wot you need, my young frien', is a good woman t' spen' your money on—that is, a good wife like my Molly."

Logan laughed. "That's just like a married man—wanting to wish their misery on everyone else."

"I been with Molly thirty years now, an' though there may 'ave been a bad day or two, there n'er were a bad week in the lot," replied Skittles with a tone and look in his aging eyes that was deeply sincere.

"And there's the point!" Logan slapped the newspaper he had been holding against his hand for emphasis. "How many gems like Molly do you suppose there are in this world? Not many, I'll wager! No thank you," he said, shaking his head. "I don't care to take my chances."

"Well, you're a young strapper yet," said Skittles, looking dreamily into the fog. "I 'spect the day'll come when you'll fin' yoursel' someone you'll want t' settle down with."

"I doubt I'll ever become an upstanding businessman like yourself, Skits."

Now it was the older man's turn to chuckle. "There are them wot consider certain aspects o' my so-called upstandin' *business* illegal, e'en though they're pretty good about lettin' you lay out bets if you do it all properlike."

"Well, at least you run it like a gentleman."

" 'Ere's where I turn for 'ome, Logan," said Skittles as they reached a broad but deserted intersection. "Come with me an' say 'ello t' Molly. 'Ave some stew an' tatties with us."

"Another time, Skits."

"Plans?"

"Nah. It's just too early for me to be in for the night."

"Suit yoursel'."

"Good night, Skits."

"You did good at Pellam's, lad."

4 Skittles

That night Logan spent a bit more of his booty than he intended. Cards, dice, more ale, and a rather foolish sense of false invulnerability all combined to leave him penniless by the time he returned to his flat in the early hours of the morning. He had often been in this position and it caused him no great concern. A new day would bring new opportunities! He did, however, take special care as he passed his landlady's door; he would just have to avoid her for a few more days.

It was almost ten when he woke from a sound sleep. The dreary March clouds showed signs of trying to break up, allowing a few rays of sun to push through. But a steady north wind blew as if to warn that the lull in the weather would be short-lived.

As Logan swung his feet out of bed, his first thought was of food; his stomach was sending out reminders that he'd have been wiser to do more eating than gambling the night before. But even a cursory glance about his flat would have told anyone that the last thing they'd expect to find there was a decent meal. It boasted but one room, which was reasonably tidy if only because there was so little present to clutter it up. Save for sleeping, Logan did very little in these quarters. His meals he either took with Skittles and Molly or in any of a dozen public houses of which he was a frequent visitor.

His prospects for breakfast were slim if he remained where he was. In fifteen minutes he was dressed and on his way over to Skittles' place. Besides the thought of a cup of tea with something solid to go with it, he wanted to confer with his friend on a new money-making scheme, made all the more imperative by his imprudent behavior the night before after they had parted.

Skittles' flat in Shoreditch was a hearty walk for a man with benefit of neither cab fare nor breakfast. And when he reached it, the climb up the tenement's three steep flights of stairs left him panting as he gave several short raps on the door. The exercise had sharpened his appetite more than ever, but the moment Molly Ludlowe opened the door all thought of food vanished.

"Molly, what is it?" Logan exclaimed.

"'Tis Skittles," she replied. "He got 'imself beaten an' robbed last night—Ow! He's all right," she added quickly, seeing the look of panic that crossed Logan's face. "Came in about midnight—dragged 'imself all the way up these curs'd stairs!"

"Has he seen a doctor?"

"Ow, he'd 'ave none of that—stubborn bloke that he is! He'd 'ave t' be at death's door t' let a doctor go pokin' aroun' 'im—an' that's a fact!" Logan could see the pain hidden in Molly's face behind her helpless outburst of frustration.

"Did he talk to the police?"

"An' when might he 'ave done that, I ask you, Logan? He just come 'ome last night an's been in bed ever since."

She paused a moment and looked toward the floor, averting Logan's gaze, embarrassed for her shortness with her husband's friend. But she was afraid for her man, and could not help thinking that perhaps it was because of his association with Logan and others like him that Skittles got into these jams.

"Well, don't just stand there," she added at length, "come on in."

Notwithstanding the occasional rough edges around Molly's demeanor, the interior of her cheap little flat gave ample evidence that beneath her gruff cockney exterior beat the heart of a lady. Here was the kind of room anyone would count it a privilege to call home. Without the least hint of affluence, it was, even through the unmistakable signs of poverty, a place where the love that had gone into its arrangement could be felt. Crochet doilies lay on the threadbare arms of the sofa. A shelf of nic-a-bric and a few books sat against the far wall. And the pictures on the other walls—a few photos and a print or two of idyllic country scenes—had all clearly been chosen with care. It was hardly surprising that Logan felt more comfortable here than in his own flat.

"Did he lose much?" asked Logan after Molly closed the door behind him.

"Won't say. He's bein' close about the whole thing. Said the bla'arts got away clean so wouldn't do nothin' to call a bobbie."

"That's not like Skittles," replied Logan, pondering Molly's words. His friend loved a good story. And if it was true, all the better. Even if he had to embellish the actual facts, it gave him no less pleasure in the retelling. A good street mugging, especially if it was his own personal adventure, should have provided him with story material for weeks and be worth all the temporary pain. There must be some reason why he was being so tight-lipped. The moment the thought crossed his mind, Logan suspected what that reason undoubtedly was.

"Can I see him?" he asked, glancing in the direction of the closed bedroom door.

"He might be sleepin', but you're welcome t' try. He'd no doubt like t' see you."

"I won't wake him."

Logan walked to the door and opened it slowly. He could do nothing to silence the squeak of its rusty hinges, however, and even before he poked his head inside he heard a moan from the direction of the bed. He approached slowly, and even in the subdued light of the room, Logan could tell that Skittles had endured more than an ordinary mugging. His friend looked more like a prize-fighter the morning after a rough ten rounds than an aging bookmaker. His usually florid complexion had taken on a bluish-gray hue, his thick nose was cut and battered, and his eyes—nearly swollen shut—made his friendly features appear almost sinister. Without his cap he looked much older than usual, somehow shrunken from his usual stature.

At the sound of the door opening he turned his head, his eyes as wide as the swelling would permit. He glanced at the clock on the sideboard, tried to rise, then winced and fell back in pain.

"Wot does the woman think?" he bellowed—or rather snarled, for the actual sounds which emerged from his pain-thickened lips were subdued and forced. "The day's nigh gone—I'll end me days in the poor'ouse if I sleep away the bleedin' day!"

"You're feeling a mite better, I see?" said Logan hopefully.

"'Course I'm better!" And as if to substantiate the truth of his words, Skittles struggled to work his way into a sitting position, and thence to his feet. But before he could complete the undertaking, he fell back against the pillow once more. "Blimey!" he hissed in frustration.

"Won't hurt you to take a day or two off, Skits," said Logan, and as he spoke he reached down to try to rearrange one of the pillows.

"No need t' make such a fuss!" he replied, trying to shove Logan's hands away. "I'm not a baby! The only real loss is me 'at, wot fell off in the close by the shop where the bla'arts jumped me. Now," he added, trying to clutch at Logan who was still trying to fiddle with the pillows, "just give a 'and. That's all I need, an' I'll be up an' out of 'ere!"

"You just lie there!" said Logan firmly. "You should talk to a bobbie, Skits. Are you sure you didn't see the blokes?"

"I'm sure," Skittles mumbled, and turned his head away.

"Not a clue?"

Skittles only shook his head in reply.

"You're sure?"

There was still no answer, and in his friend's silence Logan perceived the answer he had suspected from the first.

"It was Chase Morgan, wasn't it? Tell the truth, Skits."

"Leave it be, Logan."

"We *can't* leave it be! Don't you see—"

Logan cut off his words sharply as Molly entered carrying a tray.

"Thought you might be able to use some food," she said to her husband. "An' there's plenty for you, too, Logan," she added.

"Breakfast in bed!" grumbled Skittles. "Now, that's takin' it a mite too far!"

"An' 'ere's a cold damp cloth for that eye," she went on, ignoring his grousing. "It'll need stitches, I shouldn't wonder."

Skittles said nothing to her last remark, but appeared to soften as he detected the concern in her voice. He reached up and gave her hand a squeeze. The look which passed between them belied their verbal sparring and was filled with tenderness. A moment or two longer Molly fussed about the meal. Then, with a gentle admonition to Logan not to overtax the patient, she departed.

The moment the door closed, Skittles turned to his young friend and said, "Don't you breathe so much as a word about Morgan t' me Molly."

"What do you take me for?" Logan replied. "But don't you see, Skits? We can't let him pull here what he did in America!"

"I've tried," said Skittles. "But wot are a couple of no-account blokes like us goin' t' do? It's cost me o'er fifty quid this week t' try t' resist 'im."

"Fifty quid!"

"I 'ad me receipts from the shop with me besides what we picked up at Pellam's," explained Skittles. "All he wants is five quid a week for 'is so-called *protection*. Look at 'ow much I'd already 'ave saved if I'd paid 'im from the start."

"It's highway robbery, Skits!"

Skittles managed a hoarse chuckle at the words.

"An' just wot do you call wot *we* do for a livin', lad?" he queried. "I s'pose I'm gettin' no more'n I deserve."

"'Tis different with us," argued Logan. "We don't hurt anybody. And we don't take from anyone who can't willingly spare it."

"An' the blokes at Pellam's? I'm sure we didn't ask t' see any of *their* bank balances."

"We didn't *force* so much as a farthing from any of them. We never even asked for their money. They took it out of their wallets and laid it on the table on their own. They were just as greedy to take your money as we were!"

Logan paused, frowned momentarily, and scratched his head. "Are you delirious or something, Skits? I've never heard you talk this way before."

"I s'pose as a fellar gets on, he starts t' give 'is life a bit more thinkin'..."

"Well, there's no comparing the likes of Chase Morgan with you," said Logan intractably, brushing aside the more philosophical aspects of his friend's pensive comment. "And," he added hotly, "he's not about to get away with it!"

"Just calm that Scottish blood of yours, Logan. You're not going to—" His speech suddenly broke off as he was assailed by a fit of coughing.

This only intensified Logan's rising anger.

"I'll get your money back, Skits! And I'll make sure—"

But at that moment Molly returned and Logan checked his tongue, for the present at least. Still simmering inside, he strode to the window so she wouldn't be able to observe his distress.

Parting the curtains, he pretended to occupy himself with interest in the activities in the street down below, but in truth he was listening as Molly continued to stew over her husband, while the old con man persisted in telling her he was fine.

They were the best people Logan had ever known, except perhaps for his own mother. Hearing them now—her gentle, caring tone and his tired voice growing weaker with each word he uttered—only heightened his determination. They didn't deserve any of this! As he looked out on the dingy alley below, a resolve began to grow within him.

He was not going to let them get hurt, ever again!

It was no more than they would have done for him, and *had* done for him, when, seven years ago, he had appeared practically on their doorstep. He had been fifteen and pretty cocksure of himself. But growing up in the Glasgow Gorbals, a street urchin from the time his father died when he was ten, Logan had learned to take care of himself. And even before his father's death, the older Macintyre had been in and out of Barlinnie Prison so many times that his impact upon his son's life had been minimal. His mother did her best by Logan, but her work as a cleaning lady to keep even the scant food they had in the cupboards from dwindling to nothing left Logan running free and wild, learning from a tender age to steal and pilfer food to augment his sparse diet at home.

From there it had been a short enough path to picking up the various street games—marbles, dice, cards—where he soon discovered he had some skill. He thought he fooled his mother by telling her that he had earned the money she found him bringing home by doing odd jobs in the neighborhood after school. But she had been married to one swindler too many years and knew her son was being caught in the gambling net at an early age. And she wanted no part of it.

"I'd be prood t' take an honest shillin' from ye, son," she would say. But "honest money" was much more difficult to come by, and Logan was not exactly a patient young man. Besides, he rationalized, gambling wasn't actually dishonest, just unreliable. And if he did occasionally slip in a loaded die or a marked card in the middle of a game ... well, the other fellow would just as soon have done the same if he had been good enough to get away with it.

For all his rowdy lifestyle and bad company, however, Mrs. Macintyre's son did manage to maintain a certain good-natured air and easygoing grin, which, combined with his cocky bravado, made it difficult for people to readily dislike him. Shopkeepers in the Barrows might shake a halfhearted fist his way as he occasionally dodged away from their stands with a bulging pocket. But somehow they always found it in their hearts to forgive him. After all, they said, look what a father he had. It was a wonder the boy turned out to be as nice a chap as he was! And his gambling friends were always willing to loan him a few shillings when he was down on his luck, for he was never stingy with them.

Then he had encountered the earl's son, and from that point on everything seemed to go downhill.

Logan was a mere fifteen at the time, and the spoiled, arrogant Charles Fairgate III but a year older. The card game had been completely honest. Unfortunately for Logan, however, he was in the middle of a legitimate run of good luck. Fairgate insisted the game was rigged, and went so far as to bring his adversary up before the magistrate. With his father's support, the young heir seemed likely to win his case, especially once Logan's reputation and own paternal pedigree came to light. While Logan sat in custody awaiting the outcome, he would never have guessed the agony his mother was suffering as she saw her son on his way down the same path his father had taken. But children in the midst of their own growing pains and struggles rarely have any depth of insight into the feelings of their parents on their behalf. It takes their own parenthood, perhaps ten, fifteen, or even twenty years later to open their eyes to the true inexhaustibility of a parent's love.

For his part, Logan would have disdained any remark pointing out a similarity between himself and his no-account father; the last thing he wanted to do was follow in his footsteps. But when the magistrate finally dropped the case with a "not proven" verdict, he did pause to rethink a few things—not so deeply as his mother may have liked, perhaps, but sufficiently to realize that his life in Glasgow was going nowhere, at least toward a destination of dubious result. Nor was his announced solution to her liking, but she wisely kept her own counsel. These things took time, she tried to console herself. Perhaps he *would* find a better life in London.

The first thing to come Logan's way upon stepping off the platform in Euston Station was a crooked back-alley dice game. He should have known better, but his cocky Scots independence thought he could beat the slick London sharpies at their own game.

He soon discovered his folly; he was fleeced for all he had.

Few things are worse than finding oneself friendless and penniless in a strange city—especially a city as huge and insensitive as London. But even there, one can find occasional pockets of warmth and human kindness if one is persistent enough.

It was quite by accident that Logan stumbled upon just such a place, drifting through just the sort of neighborhood he should have been trying to avoid. From time to time he had done some running for a Glasgow bookmaker, so he was familiar with at least the rudiments of the business. Hearing his dice-playing companions mention a street in a place called Shoreditch, he decided to try his luck and see if he might find something to alleviate his desperate need of cash. There were two or three list shops on the street. Without much reason, he picked one, and walked in—trying to assume his most confident manner. It was a tiny place, hardly larger than a cigar box, and in fact had originally been used in conjunction with a tobacconist's, where one could still get a fairly decent Havana to enjoy while placing his bets.

Skittles was hardly in a position to afford another assistant, especially one as green as this kid, who looked like he would have to be reminded to wash behind his ears. But he didn't have the heart to turn the poor Scottish lad away; something inside the old man's heart took an instant liking to the runabout. Thus the seven-year friendship had begun. It had proven mutually beneficial in a number of ways. But deep inside, Logan knew he owed more to Skittles

Ludlowe than he could ever possibly repay.

Molly's voice broke through the silence of his thoughts—

"Logan, we better let the ol' boy 'ave his bit of rest."

"Ol' boy is it now!" broke in Skittles. "Wot kind of thing is that t' say about your man?" The labor behind his irrascible tone only made his weakness the more pathetic.

"Come along, Logan," Molly continued, adding to her husband in the same unruffled tone, "An' you take care, or you'll fin' me callin' you worse than ol' boy!"

An hour later Logan and Molly sat together at the table, having just finished with tea and a few biscuits. Molly rose to clear away the plates and cups, and as Logan watched, his thoughts returned to his conversation with her husband the previous day. She was indeed the kind of woman men in their sometimes shady profession dreamed of having, but seldom encountered. Despite her long involvement with Skittles—and in her early years she had participated more actively in his schemes and ploys—there had yet remained a certain purity about her. She never developed the hard core that so often formed around the hearts of women in her position. Perhaps it was because her motive was a deep and abiding love for her husband rather than personal greed. Perhaps, too, it had to do with the kind of man Skittles himself was toward her.

Suddenly his eyes came back into focus on the present. He jumped up from his seat, saying, "Here, let me give you a hand, Molly!"

"Just fancy such a thing!" she replied, laying a restraining hand on his arm. "You're a well-meanin' lad, but I shudder t' think 'ow many of my dishes I'd lose afore you 'ad done with the job."

Then she paused in the midst of her efforts, with the teapot still in her hand, and turned to Logan with a grave look in her soft, brown eyes.

"He's real sick, he is, Logan," she said, setting down the teapot and sinking back into her chair.

"Oh, the old cove'll be fine," Logan assured confidently, his tone almost good enough to convince himself. "He'll be jumping out of bed and roaring like a lion by tomorrow."

"You've got t' promise me somethin', Logan," she said, her voice serious.

"Anything, dear girl."

"I don't want you gettin' yersel' 'urt too," she said.

"What in the world makes you think I'd get hurt?"

"Ow, Logan! I know all about 'at bloke Chase Morgan," she said flatly. "That Skittles may be one of London's best sharps, but he can't fool me. I 'ear the talk. I knew somethin' was goin' on. But I ought t' crown 'im for not tellin' me wot it were."

Logan knew it was no use persisting in the ruse. "You couldn't have done anything, Molly," he said.

"That may be," she replied, "but if a woman's 'usband's goin' t' come home lookin' like a piece of steak, well, she'd just like t' have some warnin', that's all."

Logan opened his mouth to reply, but she quickly cut him off.

"But the point I was tryin' to make is that I don't want anyone else gettin' 'urt. An' that means you, Logan Macintyre! I've ne'er 'ad the good fortune t' meet your mother. But so long's you're 'ere in London, I gots me own responsibility to you. An' I'd ne'er be able t' forgive myself if anythin' was t' happen to you, nor could your mother forgive me either."

"Ease your mind, Molly," he replied with a great show of earnestness. "I'm not fool enough to go getting mixed up with Morgan." He probably wouldn't have bothered lying to the wise old woman, but he had already forgotten her previous declaration that she could not be so easily misled. And the habit of trying to cover his tracks with defenses and excuses was too deeply ingrained by this time to allow any sudden changes in what were already conditioned responses.

Molly was no less fooled by Logan than she had been by her husband. Yet what more could she say? If he intended to try to get even with Morgan on behalf of his old mentor and friend, she doubted anything she might say would make him change his mind. Besides, if she pursued it he'd vehemently deny his intentions anyway, thinking all the while that he was protecting her. *Well,* she thought, *maybe it's for the best. At least he won't be worrying about me.*

Walking home that afternoon, Logan became more sure of what he had to do. Like Molly, he wanted no one else to get hurt. But his conception of how to eliminate the problem was drastically different than hers. The specifics may have still been blurry. But he was certain of one thing—Chase Morgan had to be stopped.

He took a brief detour to the neighborhood of Skittles' shop. He searched each of the back streets until suddenly he stumbled upon just what he was looking for, his friend's black and white checkered cap, hardly visible between two cans of garbage. He reached down and picked it up, dusted it off, and then before tucking it into his coat, ran his finger affectionately along the visor.

Yes, something had to be done about that low-life scum Morgan!
And Logan figured he was as good as any man to do it.

For the remainder of the day he wandered aimlessly about the streets, concentrating his thoughts on a plan which he had been toying with now and then for some time. Now, with his mark chosen, the pieces began to fit into place more quickly. His mind continued to work most of the night as he lay awake in bed. By morning he was ready to jump to his feet, hardly feeling his lack of rest.

He was ready to do what had to be done.

5   A Scheme Takes Shape

Logan had little difficulty finding Billy Cochran. Though it was eleven o'clock in the morning, Cochran was still sound asleep in his tiny room in the ramshackle boardinghouse on Bow Street. Pounding on the door, Logan could not keep back a twinge of guilt knowing the wiry little man had likely been up all night at his favorite occupation—pub crawling. But he pounded nonetheless, for he brought important business.

After some minutes, a raspy voice snarled at him through the closed door. "Who's there? An' wot's yer blamed rush?"

"It's me, Billy, Logan Macintyre."

"Wot ye're doin' bangin' me door in at such an hour?" As Billy spoke Logan heard the click of the bolt and other fumbling noises. Then they ceased, and the door opened a bare crack. Two of the smallest eyes Logan had ever seen peered out at him, opened to no more than tiny slits, like the crack in the door out of which they were gazing, as if daylight were a mortal offense to all that was decent in the world.

"I hain't decent." The thin, unshaven face gave credence to his words.

"And I ain't the blamed king!" shot back Logan impatiently.

A bony hand reached up to scratch a sparse crop of salt-and-pepper hair. "No need t' get snappish," said Billy Cochran in a semi-wounded tone. "This better be mighty important, Logan. I was—"

"Sleeping away the day, I know, Billy! Now come on, open the door!"

There were more fumbling sounds at the chain lock, after which the door at last swung open to reveal a complete view of the odd little man behind it, now shielding his eyes from the glare of the morning's light as if it would wound him by its very brightness. In actuality the morning fog protected him from what he avoided even more—direct sunlight falling on the earth before one o'clock in the afternoon!

Only a fraction over five feet tall, Billy was thin and bony all over, with a slight hump in his back that caused his face to jut alarmingly forward. The overall effect was rather birdlike, emphasized especially by the small slits for eyes and the disproportionately large nose.

Logan stepped inside and shut the door behind him. The room had a threadbare look, not at all unlike its occupant. Somehow the small living space seemed a perfect reflection of its owner. The sparse furnishings included an iron-railed bed, chipped and rusting, a metal bedside table with a shadeless lamp on it, and a scratched and worn unpainted pine table with two unmatched chairs. Billy motioned Logan into one of the chairs, as he himself finished fastening his trousers and pulling the wide red suspenders up over his shoulders.

"Well, now as you gots me up, you better make it good, Macintyre!" The voice remained sharp and gruff, but it was as harmless as the impertinent but toothless bark of a twelve-year-old beagle.

"Skittles was attacked a couple of nights ago," Logan began gravely.

"An' is the ol' bloke okay?" Billy let go of his last suspender with a resounding snap; new wrinkles furrowed into his already creased brow. "I wondered why he 'adn't been around."

"He was battered up good. But he seems on the way up."

"Wot kinda dirty bla'art'd do somethin' like that t' ol' Skits?" exclaimed Billy, slamming his fist down on the rickety table.

"Chase Morgan, that's who!" replied Logan with conviction.

Billy sank back in the opposite chair. "I tol' Skits not t' try t' fight the man. But he 'ad some notion 'at mebbe if he stood up t' 'im, all the others'd follow 'im."

"Maybe he did have the right idea after all," said Logan. "He just went about it the wrong way."

"There hain't no way, Logan. Morgan's got ten or more of the biggest an' meanest thugs I e'er seen workin' for 'im. An' everyone knows who he's connected with in the States."

"Capone's five thousand miles away," argued Logan. "I doubt he even remembers Morgan exists. But none of that matters anyway, Billy. I've got a plan!"

"You've gots a plan...?" Billy repeated, rubbing his stubbly beard skeptically. "You hain't thinkin' of pullin' some dodge on Morgan?"

"I know I can do it, Billy!" Logan's eyes flashed with enthusiasm.

"Lad," said Billy in a more cautious tone, "hain't you 'eard the ol' sayin', 'Ne'er con a con.'?"

"Sure, Billy. But I like the saying better—'It takes a thief to catch a thief.' "

"Humm..." was Billy's noncommittal reply.

Logan needed no further encouragement to outline his plan in detail.

"I spent the morning at the library, Billy, reading some American newspapers. Morgan has a little hobby—more like an obsession— which I'm going to make his downfall. Seems he's a dabbler in counterfeiting. He's been run out of half a dozen states, and when he finally slipped from the FBI's reach in Florida, an agent was quoted as saying that Morgan wouldn't quit till he found the perfect plate. When he was forced from the States, he went to Cuba for a while, then to South America, and after that Paris. He was almost arrested in Paris again—for counterfeiting."

"You'd think he'd learn 'is lęsson," replied Billy.

"That's just it! He figures somewhere out there he's going to find the perfect plate and be set up for life. And that's where I'm going to get him!"

"An' do you 'ave the perfect snide note?" Billy's single cocked eyebrow indicated he would not be easily convinced.

With a great flourish and a smug grin to match, Logan whisked out a brand-new five-pound note from his pocket. He handed it to Billy.

"See for yourself," he stated.

Billy held the note out at arm's length, shook his head in frustration, then, pulling himself out of the chair, hobbled over to the bedside where he found a pair of spectacles. He shoved them on carelessly, grumbling, "Can't see for nothin' th'out these blimey things."

He then proceeded to examine the note, first holding it close to his eyes, then at arm's length again, and finally up in the air over his head. "Well, I ne'er," he mumbled. At length he shuffled over to the only window in the room and held it up to the sunlight. He turned it over several times, and when he turned back toward Logan there was a perplexed scowl on his face.

"Where'd you get this?" he asked at last.

"The Bank of England," Logan replied, slapping his knee and laughing heartily.

"I knew it were too perfect," said Billy, unperturbed by Logan's laughter.

"Admit it, Billy! I had you fooled and you know it."

" 'Course, but I'm blind as a curs'd bat!"

"I've seen those spectacles of yours! They're practically clear as glass."

"An' so wot do all your tricks prove? Nothin' is wot I say!"

"It's the perfect counterfeit note!" said Logan triumphantly. "Morgan would pay a bundle for the plates to that note."

"An' I doobt the Bank of England's sellin'!"

"You know what I'm getting at, Billy."

"Aye, an' 'tis plumb harebrained! Don't be a fool, Logan."

"You're the best, Billy, and it fooled you."

"You set me up! 'sides, I knew it couldn't be real. One look'll tell any sane man as much."

"Morgan will want to believe it so bad, it won't take that much to convince him. We'll set him up, too! When he sees this, he'll think he's found the best counterfeit notes in the world. I'll sell him the plates, slipping some real counterfeits into the package, making sure he walks right into the waiting arms of the police. I'll get all Skittles' money back, with a nice profit to boot. And the bobbies'll have a dangerous criminal off the streets."

Logan paused, the fire of anticipation still burning in his eyes.

"You're mad as a March hare, Logan."

"I need your help."

"I hain't done no snide pitchin' since I done two years in the chokey for it," Billy replied.

"You won't have to make up any bogus notes," Logan quickly assured. "I just need some help putting together a press. And..."—here he hesitated once more before going on—"...I need a real plate."

"You're crazy, Logan, I tell you. He'll see you comin' all the way across the city! He puts young scamps like you in the bottom of the Thames!"

Now it was the older man's turn to pause. Logan held his peace. He was as sure of Billy's allegiance to Skittles as his own.

"Logan," Cochran went on at length, "you can get yoursel' into real trouble doin' somethin' like this." For the first time the older man's voice carried a note of deep concern. "If they fin' you with the plates or the notes."

"They won't!"

Billy scratched his large nose and rubbed his hands over his scraggly face again. "I knew I should've burned all that hardware last time I were sent up," he muttered.

"Then you'll help."

" 'Tis pure craziness. But then I guess wot more could you expect from a deranged Scot..." He paused, shaking his head. "An' 'sides, someone's got t' keep an eye on you that you don't get yoursel' locked up, or killed by Morgan."

Logan grinned and slapped the little man on the shoulder.

" 'Sides," Billy added, "I s'pose I owe it t' Skittles."

It was now Logan's turn to grow serious. "There isn't a man on this side of London, leastways who knows old Skits, who doesn't owe him something."

"Okay, Logan," said Billy, "tell me wot you was thinkin'."

Logan spent the next fifteen minutes outlining his plan in more detail, after which Billy proceeded to poke a hundred holes in every careless aspect of it. Then the veteran counterfeiter set about reshaping Logan's original strategy, adding dimensions to it that Logan had scarcely considered. By the time they were through, even Billy admitted that there might be a slim possibility the harebrained scheme could work. One problem remained to be considered.

"We'll need cash for operatin' expenses," said Billy.

"There is a bit of a problem there," Logan conceded. "I sort of had t' 'borrow' that fiver there."

"I 'ave the feelin' that when word gets out about Skittles, we'll find no shortage of contributors."

"How much do you think we'll need?"

"I'll need parts for a press an' you need enough new notes t' be convincin'—a couple 'undred pounds."

"We could do it with less if we had to."

"Mebbe. But I'll start collectin' the funds regardless. I'll tell you wot t' get for the press—I'd get picked up sure if I tried it! You ought t' go out of town for wot we're needin', just in case."

Then Billy dug into his pockets and pulled out an assortment of coins, along with a fine gold pocket watch. "This ought t' get you started."

"Not your watch, Billy!" Logan knew it was the only possession of any value the man had these days, and he had many times seen him hold it up in the midst of his cronies at the pub and announce the time.

"Hain't nothin'," Billy replied carelessly, " 'Sides, you can get it back for me with those so-called profits."

Logan left Billy's more convinced than ever that his plan would not fail. He was anxious to get it in motion, and yet Billy had demanded much more preliminary work than Logan had anticipated. It was going to take considerably longer to come to fruition than he had at first thought. But the first order of business was to drop by to see how Skittles was getting on.

He knocked on the door several times, but there was no answer. Everything seemed unusually quiet inside. He set his ear to the door but could not make out the slightest sound. Puzzled, he slowly descended the stairs, and as he stepped out onto the landing of the first floor, he encountered the landlady.

"Ye lookin' fer Molly an' Skittles?" she asked.

"Yes," he answered. "I wanted to see how Skittles was. He wasn't feeling too well yesterday."

"'Tis a fact!" affirmed the lady. "An' worse t'day. Molly took 'im off t' the 'ospital this mornin'."

"Hospital!" exclaimed Logan, turning pale.

He waited only long enough to find out from the woman which hospital his friend had been taken to, then flew down the remaining several stairs and out the door into a freshly falling rain.

6   A Festive Evening at Stonewycke

The lowering black clouds seemed oblivious to the fact that it was the first day of spring. Allison sent one final glance toward the sunless sky, then yanked her drapes shut. Well, it wasn't her celebration the weather was threatening. At least she could be glad for that. Still, several of her friends would be attending, and it would have been so much nicer if the sun had shone.

The family had decided that Port Strathy was due for a holiday. Since Dorey's birthday came so near the outbreak of spring, it provided the perfect opportunity to commemorate not only his eighty-ninth birthday and the coming of spring but also the apparent easing of the hardships that had held everyone in its grip for the last two years. The winter had been a relatively mild one and everyone was optimistic, both with regard to the fishing and the crops of the

Strathy valley, that the coming spring and summer seasons would be the most productive in years.

All Allison had to say about the plans was that it was about time everyone stopped acting as if life had ended because of some depression going on in London and New York. She was glad to see that her mother was dressing up the family home in a manner that showed off their position in the best possible light. They were, after all, the Duncan clan of the celebrated Ramsey stock—the closest thing to royalty, if not in the whole of northeast Scotland, then certainly for miles around. Her mother always seemed to downplay that important fact; Allison for one was delighted that on this occasion, at least, they would put on their true colors.

The whole town had been invited, as well as three prominent families from out of the area: the Arylin-Michaels from Aberdeen, the Fairgates of Dundee, and of course the Bramfords from nearby Culden. Alec had originally proposed the event strictly for local folk, but Allison had ardently argued that if they were going to have a party, she ought to be able to invite some of *her* friends, and in the end her parents consented. Thus the three families, all of whom had daughters at Allison's boarding school, were included. The fact that each of these particular friends also had dashing older brothers only slightly colored her choice. Or so she told herself, though she said nothing about this reason for her insistence to anyone.

Allison turned from the window and walked toward the mirror. She paused, smoothed out her lace dress as she took one last look, and smirked with disdain—but not without a sigh of satisfaction—that she had been able to make it turn out as well as she had. Her mother made her dress like such an absolute *infant*. At least she had extracted what was nearly an ironclad promise that she could wear the dress of her choice to the Bramfords' ball next month.

She left her room and made her way down the hall. Many of the guests had already arrived and were milling about below, for, in deference to the threatening storm, the inside of the house had also been opened to the festivities. Outside, large tables had been set up where the factor, nervously glancing toward the sky every few minutes, could not seem to make up his mind whether to continue preparations for the food and drinks that would be served, or to repair inside and there make the best of it he could, despite limitations of space.

As she approached the top of the main stairway, Allison stopped at the railing and looked down. Just then she saw Olivia Fairgate's brother entering. *There couldn't be a better moment to make my grand entrance,* she thought to herself, smiling. She glided down the stairs with all the grace that could be taught in Scotland's finest boarding schools, a noble smile on her face as if to imply, *I am the queen, come to greet my subjects.* And as intended, at least one set of eyes looked up admiringly.

"Why, Lord Dalmount, how good of you to come," she said demurely, holding out her hand with feigned timidity. And true to his breeding, the young man took the soft, dainty hand and kissed it lightly.

"The estate is hardly mine—yet," he replied in a soft voice and a chuckle, with a tinge of anxiety lest anyone should have heard Allison's flippant remark. "You must have been talking to my sister, and she sometimes says more than is good for her." Then, resuming a more relaxed countenance, he added, "But in the meantime, please just call me Charles."

"Why of course, Charles. As I said, it is nice to see you."

"I couldn't possibly resist an invitation from Stonewycke—notwithstanding the distance. They come so seldom."

"Yes, we are socially buried up here," she replied. "It has always been so. And I'm afraid large estates with old-fashioned castles on them are hardly in vogue these days."

"Going the way of the dinosaur, I suppose."

"I can't help but think it might be good to kill the old place off, and get on with the times. It is the thirties, you know."

"It has a certain provincial quaintness about it, though," he replied glancing about. And though his tone could not have been more polite, there was a certain undetectable upward tilt of his nose that indicated he shared her disdain for the ancient relics of the past. "However," he added, "I do see what you mean. Just think what could be done if the whole thing was modernized."

As they talked they had slowly made their way toward the large open parlor, where several tables of light refreshments had been laid.

"Will there be dancing later?" asked Dalmount as he lifted two glasses of punch from the tray of a passing servant.

"I think there is some kind of entertainment planned."

"*Real* dancing?" he queried, "or will we have to don our kilts and pick up our knees to the screeching sounds of the pipes?"

Allison laughed—a very musical, grown-up, and bewitching laugh. "I'm afraid you are right there! Just as with everything else about this place, my father is a traditionalist when it comes to dancing too."

"No Jan Garber or Fred Waring?"

She laughed again. "Don't I wish! But I'm afraid we will be lucky to kick up our heels to a *Gay Gordon.*"

"No ballroom dancing where I might be favored with a spin around the floor with you?"

"Surely you jest. This little fete is for the fishermen and crofters. You don't think any of them know how to jitterbug or waltz, do you? My father and mother are going to lead a round of *The Rakes of Glasgow* and *De'il Amang the Tailors* and maybe even *The Dashing White Sergeant* if they can get together enough sets of people who know it. But that's all. Do you know any of the folk dances?"

"Never bothered to learn. You?"

"Some of them. I always liked *Dee's Dandy Dance* when I was a girl, but at school we've been—oh, look!" exclaimed Allison in mid-sentence, getting more caught up in the festive mood of the day now that she saw some acquaintances from her own crowd in the midst of the local peasants, "there's Eddie Bramford outside! We must say hello." It might not exactly be the kind of party Allison would have chosen, but with Olivia's handsome, eligible brother by her side, she could overlook that fact. She linked her arm through his, and led him out through the French doors.

The garden, protected on three sides by the walls of the house and a low hedge, was rather pleasant considering the cold borne in on the winds of the gathering storm. With old-fashioned lanterns strung overhead and garlands of flowers and draped tartans of the various clans represented all about, it could almost have been a summer afternoon. But the precariously swinging lanterns and the flapping edges of the blankets served as a constant reminder that the weather would soon have its way even in this secluded spot. The children playing tag, most dressed in what seemed to Allison mere rags, had long since donned their coats.

Edward Bramford, a florid, fleshy twenty-year-old, possessed an athletic kind of attractiveness, unlike the lean, debonaire appearance of Allison's temporary companion. He lumbered up to the approaching pair and held out a thick hand to Charles.

"Grand party, Allison," he said with a good-natured grin of ridicule on his heavy face, glancing around knowingly at the other guests whom he considered beneath the dignity of his position.

"It is now that the gang's all here," Allison replied.

"I didn't realize the local gentry was going to be so well represented," he said with another sarcastic laugh. "Eh, Charles?"

"Well, Bramford," said Charles, not willing to take the bait of the joke and risk losing Allison's favor over a remark in poor taste, "will Oxford make the finals this year?"

"As long as they've got me on the offense."

"Rugby, rugby, rugby!" said Allison in mock frustration. "Is that all you men can talk about?"

"I imagine you would be more at home if we took up the subject of the lastest fashions?" rejoined Charles.

"Of course. But I hardly know when something new's out before it's two years behind the times. It is just too frustrating being stuck in such an out-of-the-way place!"

"Now really, Miss MacNeil," said Bramford, not to be diverted from a discussion of his true love, "what's wrong with rugby?"

"Nothing, I suppose . . ." replied Allison, tapping her chin thoughtfully. "That is, if I understood a whit about the game."

Thereupon Eddie Bramford launched into a description of the game detailed enough to put even an enthusiast of the game like Charles to sleep. Fortunately they were soon joined by Clifford Arylin-Michaels, the third bachelor of the little group whose presence had been secured by Allison's contrivances with Joanna and Alec. Allison was clearly the chief attraction for each of the three, and no doubt the only reason they consented to accompany their parents to an event that would otherwise bore them past endurance with all its local, boorish color.

The appearance of Arylin-Michaels fell somewhere between those of the other two men. His face was rather plain and nondescript, as was his soft-spoken voice. He also knew little about rugby, but the moment the conversation lagged, he was ready with a political expostulation about the situation on the Continent, for his father was a Conservative M.P. in the House of Commons.

Allison cared little that the conversation was dull. It was enough for the moment to be surrounded by these three young men. When her three school friends migrated toward the circle and aroused virtually no interest on the part of any of the young men, she could hardly keep her inward exhilaration from spilling onto her face. She purposefully took no notice of their hostile glances throughout the remainder of the evening.

It was difficult to tell exactly when the sun had set, for the dark afternoon had passed gradually into evening. Still the rain had not come. Though a number of guests had to leave to attend to their livestock, and a few to their fishing boats, those who remained were at last led into the ballroom, where Alec, true to Allison's prediction, marched into the center of the crowd in full Highland regalia, extemporizing an ear-deafening rendition of *Scotland the Brave* on his bagpipes, much to the delight of all present. Only Allison's small group of friends standing toward one corner was indifferent to the proceedings. The rest of Port Strathy's inhabitants whooped and clapped and sang along to the most familiar of all Scotland's tunes.

"An' noo, my friends," Alec called out when the drone from his pipes had died away, "I wad like t' invite any o' ye adventurous enough fer it, ont' the floor. Ye are the evenin's entertainment yersel's!"

Suddenly a rousing *Reel* began from the small local contingency of fiddlers and accordionists. In an instant all hands were clapping and feet stomping to the beat, and soon Alec had again filled his bag with air and was searching in wailful tones for the melody.

The *Reel* lasted about five minutes, after which Alec announced, "Let's start with *The Gay Gordons*! Men, bring your ladies onto the floor and take your positions in the center of the circle!"

But his last words could hardly be heard. No sooner had the words *Gay Gordons* left his lips than the small band had again struck up the music with their instruments and the shuffling of many feet on the hardwood floor made momentary chaos of the room. Nor did anyone present require Alec's instructions, for every native Scot—fisher, crofter, or laird—had known the favorite dance from childhood.

Soon the couples, led by Joanna and Alec, were circling the room rhythmically to the lively music. With every new stanza the men advanced to a new partner, and thus progressed around the room. Alec's laugh seemed loudest of all, and with each of the fisher or farmer wives he came to, he appeared to enjoy himself still further. The men, on their part, when they took Joanna in their arms, did so with a timid grace that was wonderful to behold. The humble pride on the faces of the hard-working men of Port Strathy told the story—for them, this was like dancing with royalty itself!

The mood was infectious. Even Allison's so-called sophisticated friends could not resist the invitation to share in the gaiety, even when it came at the hand of a crusty and red-faced old fisherman. No amount of expostulation, however, on the part of the future laird of Dalmount, could get Allison onto the floor. She stood watching the festivities in moody silence, trying occasionally to cover the mortification she felt at having her family seen mingling with such people, with snide and haughty comments intended to be witty. How could her father, *the laird,* degrade himself so!

Out-of-breath, laughing, and perspiring freely, the thirty or forty persons left on the floor burst into spontaneous applause as the music came to a loud and triumphant conclusion. No one could remember when they'd had so much fun!

"An' noo, what would ye all say t' seein' Lady Margaret an' Lord Duncan favor us wi' a sight o' their nimble feet?" said Alec above the noise, at which the clapping and shouts of encouragement grew louder still.

Knowing the futility of trying to argue, Maggie and Ian came slowly forward from where they had been standing clapping their hands and tapping their toes. Ian beamed with pleasure as his wife gently took his arm and allowed him to lead her into the center of the room. Then, as the small band softly took up the melancholy strains of *Lochnagar,* Ian tenderly slipped his hand around Maggie's waist and their aging feet began an improvisation about the floor, now a waltz, now a quick shuffle-stepping reel. Suddenly they were young again! All thought of the watching eyes were gone. The wind was on their faces, blowing down upon them from across the heather hills over which they had ridden together. Raven and Maukin stood close by, their sides heaving from the strenuous ride. For music, the birds and the breeze and the nearby rushing burn in the trees supplied more than enough. Maggie gave herself up to Ian's strong and loving arms. He swung her around, lifting her feet from the ground as she laughed as only young Maggie Duncan could laugh. *Oh, Ian, I love you!* she thought, and with the words the dying melody once again penetrated her consciousness. As her mind came back to the present, Maggie was gazing deeply into Ian's chestnut brown eyes, still thinking the same words. As if he knew her thoughts, he returned her gaze with the deep love which only two who had been through such trials as they could share. Oblivious to the music, which had by now stopped, the aging couple continued to dance a few moments longer, content in each other's arms, until the broken sounds of applause, growing steadily louder, at last awakened them. They looked around at their friends, laughed, and then Ian said, "Weel, I guess we're jist a couple o' auld lovesick fools!" That brought laughs all around, for everyone in the village knew he spoke the most perfect London-English in the entire valley.

Joanna's laugh, however, could hardly hide the tears streaming down her face at the sight of her grandmother and grandfather so happy and content together. *Thank you, Lord,* she sighed, *for bringing them together!* And indeed, as the women of Port Strathy looked on, especially those old enough to remember, Joanna was not the only one in whose eyes stood tears of joy for the lady they loved.

"An' noo, let's see if we canna get the white sergeant t' dash aboot a bit!" said Alec. "We need a set o' six—as many as we can weel fill up the floor wi'."

As the band plunged vigorously into a lively introduction to *The Dashing White Sergeant,* once again there was a great scurrying about as four or five sets of six tried to arrange themselves in lines of three, forming a great wheel about the room, with its spokes pointing toward the center. But no sooner had the dance gotten underway when suddenly Evan Hughes burst into the room, out of breath, with his hat crumpled in his hand. Mrs. Bonner, the housekeeper, trailed Hughes through the door of the ballroom.

He ran straight to Alec, who was jovially winding his way

through the dance's first figure-eight, and stopped him with an urgent hand on his arm.

"There's been an accident," he began. "The schooner's run aground!"

Immediately the dancing in Alec's group came to a halt as he turned to Evan for details. One by one the other groups wound down also, and at last the music ceased, as gasps and exclamations around the room gave evidence to the severity of the news, especially for those with relatives or friends aboard.

"We'll need all the help we can git fer the rescue!" shouted Alec, and no sooner had the words fallen upon the ears of his fellow townsmen than once again the room became alive, now with no preparation for a dance but rather in preparation to battle the wind and a surly sea to save their kinsmen. The local folk never had to be told twice. Before Hughes was through with his news, a full half of them were already out of the ballroom and on their way down to the harbor.

Those remaining, however, heard as Evan continued: "Tim Peters were mindin' the helm" he said, "an' when his wife heard . . ."

He hesitated, then went on, turning toward Joanna who had joined Alec, " . . . weel, ye know her condition, my leddy."

"Yes," Joanna replied with concern in her voice, "she's had an unpleasant pregnancy—"

"Aye, she has!" broke in Hughes, "an' Doc Connally's over t' Culden."

"You don't mean. . . ?"

"Aye, my leddy!"

"She's gone into labor?"

" 'Tis what I come here t' tell ye. I figured Alec here, ye know, might be a mite sight better'n nae doctor at all—that is t' say— weel . . ." And, flustered, he broke off his speech.

"I know yer meanin'," replied Alec with a smile. "But nae doobt I'll be needed at the wreck too. Hoo bad is't, Evan?"

"Can't alt'gither tell. 'Tis fearsome dark oot there! But it could be bad, my laird."

"Please, Evan, 'tis no time fer formalities! Joanna," he said, turning to his wife, "can ye see t' Mrs. Peters? Ye've had mair experience wi' human births than I."

Joanna nodded, adding, "She may not be in any real danger. Sometimes these things come and go."

"Thank ye, lass!" replied Alec with a grin. "I'll organize the men at the harbor. We'll hae t' send a fleet o' boats oot t' pick up the men, I'm thinkin'. Meantime, Evan, jist in case it *is* her time, are ye up fer a hasty ride t' Culden?"

Hughes nodded his assent and hurried away with Alec close behind him.

Now it was Joanna's turn to spring into action. She walked quickly toward Maggie where she stood anxiously watching the developments. After a few moments of hurried conversation, Lady Margaret nodded. She would take charge of the house and what guests remained. Most, however, even of the out-of-town guests, had joined the throng on its way down the road to the town, if not to help, then at least as spectators. In the meantime, Joanna turned and her eyes, flashing now in anticipation of what lay ahead, sought her daughter.

Allison felt dizzy. This was not at all how she had envisioned the conclusion of the evening. Two of her three young men had trooped off to watch the rescue efforts, while the third was even now plying his skills in an attempt to persuade her to accompany him along with the others. Her three school friends, in a group by themselves a little way away, were observing Allison's every move with jealous eyes while pretending to be completely unaware of her presence. Allison at length resigned herself to following along, that prospect being more desirable than the boredom of remaining behind listening to Clifford expound on the dangers of German rearmament, when from behind her she heard her mother's voice.

"Allison, would you come with me?"

She turned to see Joanna approaching with a determined stride.

"Uh . . . where?" she asked nervously. Now this really was too much, to have her mother speak to her like a child—and in front of her friends!

"Mrs. Peters—she may be about to have a baby."

"But—but . . ." Allison faltered, shrinking back from Joanna's penetrating eyes and the urgency in her voice.

"Allison, I may need you."

"Oh, Mother! My good dress . . . I'll spoil it!"

"*Allison!*" returned Joanna imperatively. "I need your help! Now, please—come with me!"

"But the guests—" attempted Allison lamely.

Lady Margaret, who had slowly come up to the two, now laid a hand gently on her great-granddaughter's shoulder. "I will see to everything here," she said. "You may go with your mother." Her words were gently spoken, but there was an immovable firmness to them at the same time which Allison could not refuse. Further resistance would be pointless. She only hoped her friends weren't watching, even though Clifford would probably recount every word to all of them!

With a sigh of martyred resignation, Allison took the coat that Mrs. Bonner held out to her and wrapped it around her shoulders. If her great-grandmother had only stayed out of it! She might be able to argue with her mother. But Lady Margaret was like a rock. No matter how kind and gentle she appeared on the outside, down inside she could be so determined. Whenever Allison tried to withstand the old lady, somehow her voice always caught in her throat. Was she afraid of her great-grandmother? She doubted it. How could anyone be afraid of one like Lady Margaret? What was it, then? Was she intimidated by the sheer age and eminent standing of her great-grandmother, both in the family and in the community? Or was it simply an awe, a deep respect? But if that was its proper name, it was never a direction in which she allowed her thoughts to travel for long. And on this occasion she hardly had time to reflect on these things at all, for events began to sweep her along in their train.

Joanna brought the Austin around front from the garage, sounded an authoritative blast on the shrill horn, and Allison ran out into the night and climbed in beside her without a word.

As the automobile flew rattling down the hill, Allison glanced back. The last thing she saw before a bend in the road obscured her vision were several of the lanterns swinging above the courtyard garden, more agitated now in the rapidly brewing storm, a fine mist giving the lights an ethereal appearance, as if to punctuate the disastrous climax to the evening's events.

7 Allison

The room spun around and all the blood rushed from her head. Allison's hand trembled as she tried to grasp the edge of the coarse oak table nearby. But that was not going to help.

She was going to be sick.

I've got to get out of here, she thought.

Allison turned toward the door, threw a hasty glance back into the room, then stumbled out of the cottage into the biting rain. They were all still busy. They would never even notice that she was gone.

She tumbled forward down the incline, unconscious of the rain beating on her body, not feeling the fierce wind on her face, twice nearly twisting her ankle on the rocky ground. On she ran. The direction hardly mattered. Only that she put as much distance between herself and that hateful place as possible.

The baby had died, only moments before.

There had been nothing her mother could do. There had been nothing anyone could have done. Even if Dr. Connally had been there, the outcome would doubtless have been unchanged. The labor had suddenly come two months premature after what had been a very difficult pregnancy. Perhaps had there been a hospital nearby, there might have been a chance. But how could an infant struggling for its life hope to survive under such primitive conditions? Aberdeen was sixty miles away. Her mother might be the best midwife in the area, but some things were impossible even for Joanna Mac-Neil. And perhaps as Allison stumbled alone into the night, she managed to dull the sting of her own sense of failure with the realization that no one else had been able to save the child, either.

Who wouldn't get sick in that hovel? she thought, with the stupid peat smoke clogging the air so they couldn't breathe, and the disagreeably intimate proximity with all the noisome neighbor women who turned out to lend a hand to the blessed event. Some blessedness! Now they were all in there crying and praying and trying to comfort the pathetic Peters woman.

But Allison knew what had really sent her reeling from the cottage was the pitiful sight of the dead baby. She had never actually *seen* death before. The infant had scarcely been larger than the two hands of her mother that had frantically tried to pump the life back into it. And now, a quarter mile from the Peters' cottage, wind in her hair and rain streaming down her tear-stained face, Allison could not blot the sight of that tiny, limp, bluish body from her memory.

Oh, why had her mother forced her to witness such an awful thing!

Allison stopped for a moment and forced her eyes tightly shut. But it did not help. The death-child still loomed larger than life before the eyes of her mind.

She should have known better than to bring me, thought Allison, forgetting how many times in the last month she had pleaded with her mother to treat her like a grown woman rather than a child. *All those other women . . . they've seen it before. It's part of their life. But not mine. That's what people like them have to face as their lot in life. But not me! Why does my mother insist on being one of them? It's not our place! We're meant to be above—*

Her self-centered and confused thoughts were suddenly cut short as her foot snagged on a protruding scraggly heather bush. She stumbled and fell, hands and knees landing in the muddy dirt. It was not until that moment that she became aware of how cold she was. Or that she'd left her coat behind. Slowly she picked herself off the ground. Her party dress was not only soaked, now it was splattered with mud. It would serve her mother right, she thought! Now she would *have* to buy her a new dress, and it was no fault but her own. And after what she had been through this evening, Allison considered herself well-deserving of the fifty-pound dress in the magazine.

The icy cold was penetrating. But the thought of returning to the cottage for her coat never entered her mind.

Allison stood and looked about her, realizing for the first time that she had no idea in which direction she was headed. Yet above the din of the wind she could hear the faint sounds of the sea. The Peters' place was located three miles east of town, about half a mile inland on the large bluff that spread out toward Strathy Summit.

Glancing about her, she realized she must have gone north from the cottage, down the slope, toward the sea. Fortunately she had gathered her wits just in time. Inching ahead, she made her way forward until before long she came to the rocky ledge atop the cliffs overlooking the sea some ninety feet below.

It was well she did not suffer the same reaction to heights as she had to blood and death. Below and to her left, Ramsey Head—now shrouded in fog and rain and nearly too black to distinguish clearly—loomed so close she could have tossed a rock onto its southern slope. She shuddered, as many would to find themselves so near the Head on such a wild night as this. Children were warned away from the place. Local folk had tale after tale of strange and mysterious sounds and disreputable doings associated with the promontory. An evil man—a murderer, they said—jumped from the top of the Head, plunging to his death in the treacherous shoal below. His body had never been recovered, undoubtedly carried far out to sea by the strong tides of the North Sea. But even after seventy years, no one cared to linger long in a place where—so the old-timers like to point out—a body might surface at any moment.

Allison did not shudder on this night, however, because of the eerie tales of past evils. Or even at this moment from the cold which had now pierced to her very bones. Rather the quiver which went involuntarily through her spine as she stood looking down on the faint white-tipped waves resounding against the rocks below was from the sight of several dozen dim lights bobbing up and down in the water offshore.

This must have been where the schooner went down, on the most hazardous stretch of coastline for miles. Growing accustomed to the darkness, she could now begin to make out lights of the rescue party on the shore as well. Now and then a muffled shout from below could be heard. But they'd have little success tonight, it seemed, with the rain and fog and high seas impairing their every effort. Turning her eyes again toward the lights from the daring fishing vessels bobbing up and down like corks in the angry waves, she thought, *They must be crazy! They'll end up in the same fix as the schooner!*

So intent was she upon the playing out of events on the water and on the shore below her that she did not hear the approach behind her until the snap of a twig revealed that she was not alone.

She started and let out a little cry.

"I didn't mean to frighten you, dear."

Composing herself quickly, almost reluctantly Allison turned. Though she was relieved, at that moment she wished the voice had belonged to almost anyone else.

"I brought your coat," Joanna continued. "You must be freezing."

"Yes . . . thank you," replied Allison, taking the coat and slipping it over her soaked dress.

"Dear," Joanna began, reaching out to her daughter not only with her hand but also with the yearning tone of her voice.

"Look!" Allison broke in with a light voice, pointing toward the sea with the arm her mother would have touched, "the schooner must have gone down off the Head."

"Allison," continued her mother, not to be deterred despite her daughter's apparent reluctance to hear her words, "forgive me for making you come tonight."

"You needed help," replied Allison coolly.

"If I had known what was going to happen . . ."

"Mother, I'm a big girl."

"You left so suddenly. I thought—"

"It looked as if you had enough help," said the daughter quickly, " . . . and I was curious about the wreck."

Joanna simply nodded, making no mention of the hurriedly forgotten coat. "Would you like to talk about what happened?"

"I don't see what there is to talk about, Mother. A baby died. There's not much we can do about that. It happens all the time. But really, the conditions these people live in are deplorable." She turned abruptly and began a brisk walk back to their car, which was waiting at the cottage.

Joanna sighed, and followed.

Nothing more was said about the experiences of the evening, except a passing comment on Allison's part about her desperate need for a new party dress.

8   Grave Words

The antiseptic odor stung at Logan's nose. This bleak hospital ward gave him the chills, and he especially didn't like seeing his friend lying between those stark white sheets. He suddenly looked so old and vulnerable.

He approached Skittles' bed with uncharacteristic timidity, his damp fedora in hand and an uncomfortable look on his face. He attempted a smile, but his eyes lacked their usual lively glint. The doleful effect could certainly not have been much of a comfort to the patient.

"How are you, Skits?" Logan's voice started to crack. It was all he could do to sound cheerful.

"I must be a goner, lad, t' 'ave landed in a pokey joint like this," replied the old bookie.

"Not a bit of it," answered Logan, still standing stiffly while nervously fingering the rim of his hat. "These days they put folks in the hospital for every little thing. Modern medicine, you know."

"I s'pose time'll tell."

"You'll be out of here before tomorrow's first race at Epsom."

Skittles gravely motioned his head to one side. "Get a chair, lad. I 'ave something t' talk o'er with you."

Logan found a chair on the other side of the ward, carried it to Skittles' bedside, and straddled it with his arms folded across the back.

"If you're worried about the shop," Logan said, "there's no need. Billy and I will take care of it. And he swore he'd do no drinking while he was in charge."

" 'Tis not the shop I'm worryin' about." Skittles paused to cough, a deep wrenching cough. "But I s'pose the shop's got somethin' t' do with it," he began once more.

"Just tell me what it is, Skits. Anything I can do to help."

"Laying 'ere, a man's got time t' think. An' I been wondering wot I could give t' you after I'm gone . . ."

Logan opened his mouth to protest, but Skittles held up a hand to quiet him. "Just listen t' me, Logan," he said. "I thought about leavin' you the shop. But I just can't bring myself to it. I'm going t' leave it t' Billy. He'll do good by it, and give a percentage of the profits t' take care of Molly—not that you wouldn't do the same, lad. I know you would. But . . ."

He sighed, reached for a glass of water by his bedside, and took several long swallows before continuing. "I just wouldn't feel right bein' responsible for keeping you in this business—"

"What do you mean, Skits? I'm happy enough with what I do."

"Just let me finish." As he spoke, Skittles' voice was becoming more labored. Therefore Logan obeyed, albeit reluctantly. " 'Tis a rotten business we're in, Logan. Oh, maybe we ain't villainous to the core like Morgan an' 'is bunch. But when was the last time you made any *honest* money? You're a bright boy, an' you can make somethin' better of yourself. There! That's wot I wanted t' say!"

"I've made just what I want of myself," answered Logan, both in defense of himself and to try to put his friend at ease.

"You say that only because you don't know nothin' else. Get out of it!" pleaded the old man, "before it's too late. Before you wind up goin' the way of Chase Morgan."

"You can't really think that could ever happen to me?"

"I've seen many a good lad turn cold and 'ard with greed."

But even as he spoke Logan shook his head with a stubborn look which said he had stopped listening. Skittles exhaled a defeated sigh. "Guess it'll take more'n the words of an ol' reprobate like me to make you understand."

"Don't go on talking like that, Skits—" Logan's words faltered and his voice nearly broke. Steadily he bit back the rising emotion in his throat. "You're the best man I've ever known and . . . well, you just better get out of that bed in a hurry, because I need you, you crotchety old windbag!"

Logan jumped out of his chair and strode over to the window where he looked intently out as if something of great interest had suddenly caught his attention. In truth, he did not want anyone—least of all Skittles—to see the moisture filling his eyes.

"You don't need me, lad," Skittles replied with deep affection. He too brushed a hand across his misting eyes, for Logan was the son of his later years that he and Molly had never had in their youth. "Though your sentiment does me old 'eart good to 'ear it, I can't say for certain wot it tis you're needing, but it ain't the likes of me."

Logan did not reply. He knew his voice would betray him.

Silence filled the room for a few moments, each of the men struggling to maintain the long-practiced street tradition of keeping emotions well buried. When Logan again felt certain of his control, he turned and walked back to the bed.

"I almost forgot," he said, forcing a light casual tone into his words as he took the checkered cap from his pocket. "I got your hat back for you." He held it out and Skittles took it, new tears rising in his weary eyes at the sight.

"I figured you might be needing it soon," Logan added.

"Molly bought this for me ten years ago," the old man said tenderly, "to replace one just like it I lost in a—you might say in a little skirmish at Ascot. I only take it off to sleep."

He lay contemplating the cap for a minute, then held it back out to Logan.

"All I do in this place is sleep. 'Ere, Logan. Would you take care of the cap for me . . . until I need it again?"

Logan said nothing.

He reached forward, clutched the cap in his hand, and turned to leave the room.

"You'll think about it, lad . . . wot I said?" Skittles called out after him.

Logan stopped, turned, looked one last time at his friend where he lay, then nodded. "Yeah, Skits," he said. "Promise."

9 To Catch a Thief

Logan spent the remainder of the day in consultation with Billy. The next two days were devoted to train rides, some long, some short, to various towns on the outskirts of the city. Each time he returned with several packages which he carried to a dirty one-room flat he had rented in a tenement across town from his own place.

With rising impatience to get on with the plan, Logan next submitted to Billy's habit of practicing with "dry runs" until everything was timed to perfection.

"There can't be no hitches!" Billy kept saying. "Morgan's no blimey pigeon. One whiff of a setup, Logan, an' we're dead men!"

"Why can't I just go into his place, spread a few bills around, talk it up, boast a little about how I can get as many as I need, drink a few pints, and wait for Morgan to make a move on me?"

"Oh, he'd make a move on you all right!" replied Billy mockingly. "He'd move you right int' the Thames in a lead box! Think, man! He'd see through a ruse like that five minutes after you walked in the door. We gots to make 'im come to you. The man's got to *want* that plate so bad that he's taken the bait before he e'er set 'is eyes on you. That's the key to any con, lad. Hain't Skits taught you nothin'? We gots to make 'im *want* to believe in those plates! Then he's eating out of our 'ands, not us out of 'is."

"And just how do you propose to manage such a thing?"

"That's where the rest of the boys come in. We spread a few bills round town. Discreetly. Slowly. None of your wild, fool shenanigans. We let the news of a new plate sift slowly along the grapevine. We gradually connect you with the 'earsay. Very subtle. So's no one gets the idea we're lookin' for a deal. An' we keep spreadin' bills, throwing in a few bad 'uns so the thing gets talked up."

"But how long's all that going to take, Billy?"

"Doesn't matter how long. Mebbe a week or two, mebbe six months."

"Six months!"

"Settle down, Logan. Patience is the most important ingredient to this scheme. You 'ave to wait it out, dangling the hook e'er so gently, waitin' for Morgan t' get 'ungrier and 'ungrier. If we make a move before he's ready, like I said before—we're dead men! But if we can wait 'im out—no matter how long it takes—then when he pounces, we'll be ready t' reel 'im in. By then we gots 'im where we want 'im. He'll *want* to believe so bad we can slip in an amateur's plate and he'll jump at it. An' we hain't going' t' stick no amateur plate in front o' his nose. No siree! When Morgan's moment comes, he's goin' t' be feastin' his eyes on the most perfect plate I ever made. 'Course, we'll make sure the light in the place hain't too good, just in case. But e'en in broad daylight I could 'ardly tell my plate from the real one. No, Logan, if we bide our time and don't rush 'im, he'll come to you. You can be sure of that."

"And what do I do in the meantime?"

"You'll do just as I tell you," replied Billy. "I'll get the boys t' put the word out, real casual-like. And you just 'ave a good time. Don't go into Morgan's place at first. Then mebbe once or twice, then disappear for a few days. And don't say nothin'! You just keep your young mouth shut, do you understand? You don't do no talkin' till Morgan comes t' you. And then you say only what I tell you!"

The bait took three weeks to take. But then, exactly as Billy had predicted, it was Morgan who initiated a move in their direction. Logan had not been in Morgan's plush nightclub pub in four days. Billy had begun to step up the tempo and warned him to stay away. But by this time he had well coached his young protegé in what to say, for the bite on the part of Morgan could come at any time, he said.

It came about ten o'clock one evening as Logan was leaving *The Purple Pig* pub some three blocks away. Without even a word, he was suddenly sandwiched between two very large and very insistent colleagues of Morgan's who brusquely thrust him into the backseat of a waiting limousine. In less than five minutes, without a word having yet been spoken, he was escorted into the big man's office.

He had never before even seen the underworld hoodlum, and was momentarily stunned to see that he was a short man—probably no more than five foot six. Though solidly built, he had a thick appearance with little sign of a neck, and a round face that might have lent a boyish air to his overall look had it not been for his dark, glaring eyes.

Logan glanced around quickly, taking stock of his surroundings. The room in which he found himself certainly was impressive, giving every indication that Morgan's brief sojourn in the British Isles had been highly profitable thus far. Though Logan's trademark on the streets of London was his smooth tongue, his talents were stretched to their limits before the wary American gangster. And

Morgan's first words immediately dispelled any further thought of his *boyish* face. He was anything but a neophyte.

"I understand you got a five-pound plate," he demanded.

"Maybe I have ... maybe not," answered Logan, as per Billy's instructions.

"Don't play coy with me, Mr. Logan!" snapped Morgan. "For twenty pounds I can have you dropped in the river!"

Just what Billy said he'd do! thought Logan to himself. *First a vain, angry outburst, followed by a threat. "If he does that,"* Billy had said, *"he's playing right into our 'ands!"*

"Now, Mr. Logan, is the plate for sale?"

"Stall him a little longer," were Billy's instructions. *"Take it cautiously. But string him along until it begins to look dangerous."*

"Say, who are you?" Logan replied, avoiding the question.

"Who I am is none of your concern. Who I am is the man who just asked you a question. Now tell me, is—"

"And how do you know my name?"

Suddenly Morgan's fist slammed down on his desk and he jumped to his feet.

"You interrupt me again, Logan!" he shouted, "and I'll ..." Apparently he thought better of himself. He paused, then continued. "Look. I know all about you. I've had you followed for a week. I know your name, where you drink, how badly you gamble, and where you live. And I also know about the plate. I've never heard of you. You look like a punk. But they say it's the best plate ever seen in this town, and I want it. Do you understand? Now, I'm only going to ask you nice one more time—is the plate for sale?"

"When he gives you no more choices and 'as your back to the wall, then give 'im a little more line. Not much. Just enough for us to 'ang 'im with." Okay, Billy, thought Logan, *I think this is it!*

"I ... I hadn't really thought of selling it. I suppose I could think—"

"I don't want you to think about it. I want you to do it!" replied Morgan angrily. "Don't you understand, you little creep of a street punk? You either sell me the plate or I'll kill you. If you do it my way, I just might let you live. What do you say to two thousand pounds?"

Logan laughed outright. *"Show a cocky confidence,"* Billy had said. *"He'll 'ate you for it. But it just may save your life at the same time. No con man likes a wimp. Stand up to 'im. It's the only way to keep 'im honest at a dishonest game. Laugh at 'is first offer. He'll go at least twice as 'igh, maybe even more."*

"Two thousand!" he repeated. "The plate's worth at least ten."

"Ten thousand! What kind of a fool do you take me for?"

"Perfect five-pound notes. And you want it for a song?"

"No note's perfect!"

"And maybe mine aren't, either. But they're good enough to pass off as the real thing. And that's really all that matters, isn't it now, mate?"

"I'll give you three thousand."

"And maybe I'll just keep it. Why should I give away the golden goose for t'pence? I still ain't said the plate's for sale."

"And I said it *is* for sale!" replied Morgan, growing heated once more. "Now you look, Mr. Logan. I'll give you five thousand pounds for the blasted thing. One more word out of you and we'll put you out of your misery tonight and ransack your flat till we find it."

"You won't find it there, mate," laughed Logan.

"Then maybe we'll kill you just for the fun of it and make our own plate. Now, five thousand it is. Take it, or take your last look around at this world."

"And how do I know you'll keep your part of the bargain?"

"You don't. But you got no choice, kid. But don't worry. I don't want the word out that Chase Morgan welches on his deals. Too many people know about you already. You're safe. That is, unless you try anything stupid!"

Logan was summarily dismissed with a wave of Morgan's hand and found himself brusquely escorted through the front of the club and shoved out the door with a curt, "Mr. Morgan'll be in touch!" from one of Morgan's bouncers.

The moment he was alone Logan looked around, rippled his shoulders once or twice to figuratively dust himself off from the disquieting encounter, then exhaled a long sigh. "Whew!" he said under his breath, as he turned and walked away. "That's over!"

He walked on, turning the events of the past ten minutes over in his mind. "*Mister* Logan!" he thought, then laughed aloud. "Why, the sucker doesn't even know my real name!"

He headed immediately for Billy's, but did not reach him till after eleven, having followed the most circuitous route imaginable to shake off any potential tails.

"It was just like you said!" he exclaimed excitedly. "I didn't have to convince him of a thing."

"I tell you, Logan, if your setup's right, he's a believer long before you 'ave t' spin out your song t' 'im."

"It's going to be like taking candy from a baby!"

"Hey! Not so fast. That was the easy part," cautioned Billy. "The real game is still t' come. If he doesn't buy it all the way, and makes you demonstrate the plates, we're goners."

"He seemed ready enough to believe in it tonight."

"Threatening a kid comes easy for blow'ards like Morgan. Parting with five thousand quid in cash—that's another matter. You just don't get too smart for your own good. A little cocksure, but don't get patronizing or presumptuous. A guy like 'im 'ates that! He's got t' think you're a nitwit all the way—one with nimble fingers and a sharp eye, but still a nitwit. He's got t' think *he's* taking *you*! That's the only way a big score like this can work. And the second it's over—man, you gots t' disappear! When he finds out he's been 'ad, 'is eyes'll be flaming with vengeance! What comes next?"

"He just said he'd be in touch. What should I do?"

"Just 'ang around the neighborhood. Keep spending money."

"I'm almost out, Billy."

"Wot! Already?"

"You said to spread the bills around."

"Yeah. I guess there's no other way t' bait the hook. 'Ere's another fifty. But that's got t' last you!"

"Fifty! Sure . . . this'll last fine. But, Billy—where do you get all this money we're using?"

"Don't ask. I got it, that's all. It's part of the cost. A big setup always takes plenty of cash. Now, get outta 'ere. I gotta get some sleep. I'm not as young as you. I'll meet you at the other place tomorrow and we'll make sure everything's ready."

It was the afternoon of the third day when Logan was sent for again. The same two thugs were similarly talkative, and once more Logan found himself facing Morgan.

"I want to see the plate," he said without introductory pleasantries.

"You got the five thousand?" replied Logan.

"You're an impertinent twit, I'll say that much for you. Yeah, I got the five thousand! That is, if you can back up what you say."

"I never said anything. You gave me no choice, remember?"

"What of it! If the plate's the genuine article, you'll be on easy street for a long time. Now let's get going!"

"We can't go now."

"What do you mean, we can't go now!"

"My landlady's onto me, watches me like a hawk. I think she's put the bobbies onto me, too. The streets have been crawling with them lately."

"You never told me that!"

"You never asked!" Logan knew he was pushing Morgan to his limits of patience, but he hoped, as Billy had said, that if he demonstrated just the right amount of cheek, it might save his life.

Morgan was silent a moment, clearly in thought. "Okay, you good-for-nothing shaver, when can we go?"

"She goes into her place for the night about eight."

"Then be here at seven-thirty."

Logan turned to leave. But just as he reached the door, he heard Morgan's sinister voice behind him. It sounded more evil and threatening than it yet had.

"And, Mr. Logan," the racketeer said slowly in a menacing tone, "you better be on the level or you're a dead man. Do you understand me? I'd like nothing better than to put a hole through you if I find out you're playing games with me."

Logan turned back toward the man where he still sat behind his desk. Trying to give his voice the balance Billy had spoken of without betraying his fear, he replied: "Look, Morgan, if you want out of this deal, just say the word. I never wanted to sell in the first place. I'd be just as happy to—"

"Get him out of here!" shouted Morgan angrily. "You just be here at seven-thirty, Logan! You understand?"

Before he had a chance to say anything further, he was shoved out of the office and the door shut behind him.

At a quarter to eight that same evening, Logan was shoved into the backseat of Morgan's shiny new 1932 Rolls Royce between Morgan and one of his henchmen. The driver was the same man who had driven the limousine twice before. The other thug in the front seat Logan had not seen before. The sinister bulge in the coat pocket next to him hardly escaped Logan's attention. He knew there would be no room for mistakes tonight. The dress rehearsals were over. Billy would even now be out of the room, having perfectly set up the last details for authenticity, right down to wet ink and a couple of drying notes.

The flat was located near the shipyards, and a drifting fog was swirling about the place. It was eight thirty-five when they arrived, and most of the side streets were reasonably quiet, all the dockside action taking place in the row of pubs along the Thames. As Logan fiddled with the lock on the door, he found himself worrying again about the unthinkable consequences should Morgan insist on an actual demonstration. Despite the fact that the plates were Billy's best, the notes themselves could not compare with the authentic workmanship of the real thing—a fact for which Billy had been compelled to spend some time in one of London's grimy prisons. But if a demonstration was required, it might still work. It would just depend on how closely Morgan felt like scrutinizing the end result.

They went inside and Logan switched on the light, his signal to Billy waiting in the alley below to make his call to the police.

"There she is," said Logan, proudly indicating the press.

Everything was perfect, looking as genuine as the detailed preparations of an experienced artist like Billy could make it. Beside the press were several crisp, new notes, mixed in with a few smudged ones, and a couple of fakes on which the ink was still wet. Under the table a box contained crumpled paper, trash, many attempted notes, some crooked, some with smeared ink, even a couple of genuine notes on which smears had been added for effect. Billy had considered the tiniest detail.

Morgan immediately approached the table and reached for one of the notes.

"Careful," Logan warned. "The ink on those top ones is still wet."

"Why didn't you warn me!" said Morgan, pulling back his hand, two of his fingertips smudged.

"I did warn you," replied Logan testily, keeping up the bravado. "Try one of these," he said, reaching toward one of the legitimate bills. "These are from yesterday. They should be dry." Of course the ink was as dry as on any of the notes issued by the Bank of England.

Gingerly, Morgan took the note and held it up by a corner to the bare light bulb hanging from the ceiling.

"Nice," he muttered. "Yes ... very nice." He turned and again approached the table, sifting through the contents on its top with a prudent finger. "Not so good here," he said, looking at one of the fakes on which Billy had intentionally double-stamped the image.

"I'm still getting the hang of the mechanics of the press," said Logan. "Kind of a temperamental old thing."

"What about this one?" asked Morgan, pointing to a genuine note on which Billy had judiciously added two or three splotches of ink. "Looks like it should have been a good one."

I botched it taking it out of the press," said Logan.

"Well, that'll be a problem we won't have," replied Morgan. "My men have considerably more experience at this kind of thing than you do."

A satirical response jumped to Logan's lips, but he thought better of it and held his silence.

Morgan gave the press a thorough going-over, peering in to see the plate where it sat in position. "There's ink all over the thing!" he said. "Don't you know a clean plate's the secret to a good run?"

"I was working on it today," said Logan. "Didn't see any reason to clean up. I try to run a few notes every day, so I can keep ahead."

"Idiot!" said Morgan under his breath. He was hardly aware of Logan by this time. He had swallowed the bait now, without knowing it, and was slowly being reeled in.

Next he stooped down to examine the throw-aways, fishing through the paper and trash, looking now and then at one of the rejects. As Billy hoped he would, a genuine note with some added streaks of ink caught his attention. He held it up to the light, mumbled some inaudible words to himself, then crinkled it back into a ball and threw it on the floor.

"I'd like to see the press in action," stated Morgan.

"Sure," said Logan without flinching. "But the press makes an awful racket. That's why I located here by the shipyards. You can hardly notice it in the daytime with the noises outside. More'n likely my landlady's in bed by now anyway. I doubt she'll cause us any trouble." As he spoke, Logan proceeded to make some adjustments to the press, smeared some new ink on the rubber roller and rolled out the excess on a sheet of blank paper. Then as he reached for the crank handle, he turned to one of Morgan's men who was standing by the window, and said, "Hey, mate, look down there and see if that bobby's still standing down at the corner. He's been a mite trouble-some lately . . . I think the old lady put him onto me."

The man peered out into the darkness, then turned back to his boss rather than Logan, "Can't see nothin', Mr. Morgan. It's too foggy."

"Never mind," said Logan. "Just one of you keep an ear to the door. If you hear him coming up the stairs, we'll shut it down and stuff everything in the closet." With the words Logan put his hand to the crank and gave it a swift turn. An immediate grating screech filled the room, but before Logan had the chance to give the handle another full revolution, Morgan's sharp voice stopped him.

"Shut it down!" he yelled.

Logan obeyed, feigning a look of puzzlement.

"Just take out the blasted plate so I can look at it!" demanded the hoodlum. Logan did so, not once betraying his relief. Disengag-ing it from the press, with ink all over his hands, Logan handed the bogus plate to Morgan, who, with a look of disgust at its messy condition, took it and examined it intently. *Good thing,* thought Logan, *that the ink obscures any defects he might be able to spot. I wonder how long it will take for the police to show up.* He hoped too that they would take Billy's advice and wait for their quarry outside the building. It would never do for them to raid the room and pinch him along with Morgan.

Morgan's raspy voice broke into his thoughts. "I believe our deal was for five thousand," he said, handing the plate back to Logan.

"Deal? As I recall, you left me little choice. I would still—"

"Don't get smart with me, kid!" snapped Morgan. "I offered you five thousand. I could take that plate for nothing if I wanted. But I expect you to come up with a plate for a ten-pound note real soon."

"If you're good for your word and it's worth my while, I might be willing to deal with you again."

"You're pretty sure of yourself for a baby-faced punk!"

"I'm sure of my *merchandise*, Mr. Morgan," Logan replied evenly.

Morgan eyed Logan steadfastly, squinting slightly as his eyes seemed to probe Logan's face one last time to find any involuntary twitch that would reveal the chink in his armor. Logan returned his gaze with determination, fully aware that the next words he heard could very well be, "Kill him!"

After what seemed like an interminable period, Morgan slowly reached into his coat pocket, took out an envelope, but instead of giving it directly to Logan, he handed it to one of his men. "Give it to him, Lombardo," he said—either because he felt he was too good to make the exchange himself or from long years of keeping his own hands off the actual dirty work.

Lombardo represented the stereotype of the underworld thug. He was well over six feet tall, muscular, with a deep scar over his right eye. Morgan could not have chosen a more picturesque companion had he fabricated him according to preset specifications. He handed Logan the envelope with a scowl that seemed intended to say, "Just you wait till I get my hands on you, you little creep!" With one final gesture of cocky impudence that nettled Morgan to the very edge of his endurance with this young upstart, Logan opened the envelope and counted the notes inside. Then, as an added insult, he removed one, held it up to the light, and examined it closely.

"Can't be too careful in this business," he said.

Lombardo took a menacing step forward, but Morgan restrained him.

"Well, I guess you're as good as your word," said Logan at length, reaching into a nearby drawer as he spoke, and taking out an envelope in which he had earlier secreted several counterfeit notes. "I'll put it in here so the ink won't smear all over," he said, dropping the plate into the envelope, licking the flap and sealing it shut.

"And the other plate," said Morgan. "You weren't going to send me out ready to do only half the job, were you now, Mr. Logan?"

"Would I do a thing like that?" laughed Logan, removing the reverse plate and depositing it into a second envelope. "Here you are—two plates as agreed."

He held out the two envelopes to Morgan. Lombardo stepped

forward to take them, but Logan drew in his hand, looking directly at Morgan. Morgan scowled, swore under his breath, grabbed the two plates, jammed them into his coat, and made for the door without another word. Logan exhaled an almost audible sigh of relief. It would never have done for the police to nab Morgan, with the plates and counterfeit notes in Lombardo's possession. For no doubt the hoodlum would swear complete ignorance, even backed up by his pigmy-brained flunky, who would then be trotted off to jail in his stead.

The moment the roughnecks had exited and their footsteps had died away on the steps, Logan rushed forward, caught up a screwdriver, and began to disassemble the press with all the haste he could muster. Billy had been over this phase of the operation with him many times. Time would be of the essence here. If the police were already waiting outside, he would have but a matter of minutes—probably five at most—to rid the place of every shred of evidence by the time Morgan, claiming to have been duped by a London mobster, led the constables back up the stairs to his flat.

Logan hurriedly filled the three burlap sacks he had stashed in the closet with the pieces of the press, all notes, ink, trash, and other bits of paper. He walked to the back window and gingerly opened it. He had planned to let down the bags to the ground with a rope he had already tied outside the window. But there was already a constable positioned at the end of the alley. He should have known they would surround the building! *Why didn't Billy think of this?* he muttered, tiptoeing back from the window to take quick stock of the situation. He was trapped. But he couldn't panic. There was always a way out, if not by fast talking, then by wit or sheer daring. But there was always a way!

He could already hear the thudding of heavily booted feet on the stairs below. Morgan had wasted no time telling his story of being taken. He had probably claimed he didn't even know what was inside the envelopes. No matter what became of Morgan now. He had to get out of there!

He'd have to leave the sacks. There was no way he could be connected to anything. And who could tell, maybe they'd incriminate Morgan all the more. It was just a shame Billy would have to lose all that hard work.

He set down the bags, ducked out the window onto the fire escape, and pulled the window shut behind him. Keeping one eye on the constable below, whose back was to him, and keeping his ear atuned to the approaching police inside, he ascended the steep metal steps. Glad it was only a four-story building, he swung onto the roof just as a uniformed bobby raised the window he had just left and peered out. All his attention, however, was focused downward. Seeing nothing, and not thinking to look above him, he whistled to his companion guarding the entrance to the alley below.

But Logan could not rest yet.

With great caution he crept across the rooftop, hoping all the while that the police didn't decide to press their search. If they did, he'd have to make a run for it across the rooftops of London, and that would mean several jumps he'd rather not have to negotiate.

He sat down in the darkest corner he could find atop the building, his jump to the adjoining building well settled in his mind should it be necessary; and there he waited. Occasionally a shout broke the silence, some muffled sounds came from inside the building, and about ten minutes later he heard loud and angry protests from what he was sure was Lombardo's voice coming from the street below.

Then a police wagon roared off, followed by two automobiles, sirens piercing the night air as if to announce to all the world their capture of Al Capone's dangerous associate who had thought to find easy pickings in London.

Then all was quiet.

Still Logan sat. For two hours more he waited.

But this was indeed his lucky night. For if the police even believed Morgan's story of some phantom swindler pulling a masterful con on him, they didn't seem inclined to press it. They appeared well satisfied just to have their hands securely on Chase Morgan, with ironclad evidence to back up their arrest.

10   Flight

Logan lay stretched out on the bed in his own flat. Once more he began to count out Chase Morgan's money.

The temporary ecstasy of the feel of the notes in his fingers and the smell of more money than he had ever had in his hands at one time took his mind off the stark and dingy walls surrounding him, although it was only occasionally that he wondered what it would be like to have a real home like Skittles. But he never allowed such thoughts to progress seriously in his mind. His was not the kind of life where a man could really consider having a home or a family.

There were a few women who had been passing parts of his life. But he had never been genuinely in love. He had not been willing, or even able, to give a relationship what any kind of lasting love demanded. Besides, he was much too young to get himself "imprisoned," as he liked to phrase it. Whenever Molly heard him use the term, she acted affronted. "Wot a way t' speak of something so loverly as marriage!" she would protest, turning to Skittles with some comment like, "Is that how you think o' it too, old boy?"

Skittles would always reply wisely, and truthfully, " 'Course not! But then there ain't many men as can lay claim to such a fine ol' girl as you, Molly!"

Nothing less than a discovery so fortuitous as Skittles' could alter Logan's less than idealized attitude toward the institution of marriage. But he sincerely doubted he'd ever find someone quite like Molly. Forthright and honest, but at the same time gentle, she could be stubborn and gruff enough to keep things interesting. And how she could laugh! He knew Skittles always had a good time with Molly—which was probably why, in all their thirty years together, he had never strayed. Logan well knew that in the kind of life they led, there were sufficient opportunities.

However, at this particular moment, marriage was the furthest thing from his thoughts. He lay there, in his run-down flat, gloating over his victory. He had just completed the most successful con game of his young career. And on top of that, had fleeced the famous American gangster and sent him to jail. This could boost his reputation to the heights! For the moment Logan had entirely forgotten his original intent. Intoxicated with his success, he could not keep himself from dreaming about the prospects that might now be open to him. Who could tell—might he not even be able to take over Morgan's operation himself? Of course he'd put an end to that dirty protection racket. And he'd clean up lots of other things in the process. But that posh club, with its classy clientele—why it would be enough to set up an enterprising man for life...

The insistent pounding at his door suddenly woke Logan from his reverie.

"Come on in," he called.

The door opened and Billy Cochran walked in. He always seemed to have a disgruntled air about him, but his face now showed displeasure.

"Why don't you 'ave this door locked?" he reproved without preamble. "I could've been anyone!"

"Who's going to bother me?" answered Logan airily. "Morgan's on his way to prison, isn't he?"

"I saw them take 'im off with me own two eyes, bad as they may be," said Billy. "But you can't be too careful," he added, squinting and looking about, the lines in his face accentuated in the dim light.

Ignoring his cautions, Logan stuffed the money he had been holding back into its envelope and, tossing it to Billy, said, "See if this doesn't cheer you up!"

Billy caught the envelope effortlessly despite his reputed bad eyesight, and looked inside, emitting a soft whistle.

"I'd say Morgan's debt with Skittles is cleared," said Logan, grinning.

At the mention of their friend's name, Billy's hardened expression dropped and he slowly shook his head. "You 'aven't 'eard . . . I thought as much."

He walked to the bed and sat down heavily on its edge. "I just 'eard mysel'. I guess I thought you might already know."

"What is it, Billy?"

"This hain't so easy, Logan," sputtered Billy. "Skittles . . . well— he died earlier this mornin'."

For a moment Billy thought Logan had not heard him at all. For when he looked over toward him, Logan was staring blankly at the wall in front of him. The words had come too abruptly, like a fist out of nowhere, striking him senseless. As his glassy gaze gradually came back into focus, Logan slowly turned back toward Billy, his eyes filled with helpless appeal that somehow Billy's thick accent had distorted his words and that he had mistaken what he thought he heard. But the old man's small, narrow orbs—grim and filled with an agony even more pronounced because he had forgotten how to shed tears of remorse—dashed the younger man's flimsy hope.

It was true. Poor old Billy's eyes told the story. Skittles was gone.

Logan jumped off the bed. "I'll kill him," he breathed, almost softly in his wrathful distress.

It was the very quietness of his tone, the clenched understatement, that frightened Billy the most. "Logan," he began, as one entreating a child, "now don't go runnin' off an'—"

But Logan quickly cut him off, the hot blood of passion now rising in him that the dreadful news had at last sunk in. "I'll kill him!" he repeated, louder this time. "I'll kill Morgan, I tell you!"

Billy stood and caught Logan's arm, the little man holding Logan's agitated form fast in his grip.

"Hain't no way that's goin' to 'elp ol' Skits now," he said quietly, but with determination.

"Morgan murdered him!"

Billy closed his eyes, seeming to fight against his own passion for revenge, for he also loved Skittles. He, too, would have squeezed the life out of Morgan if it lay within his power. But he was old. Whether that gave him a little extra dose of wisdom, or whether it had made of him a coward, he didn't know. In any event, he understood the futility of revenge. But to assist him, Billy had something Logan had never made use of. Billy Cochran knew he had his bottle to turn to for the easing of the pain and hatred. He didn't know what Logan could do instead. Perhaps revenge was his only way to get rid of the ache inside.

"Don't stop me, Billy!" yelled Logan, and with a sudden burst of strength, he shoved Billy from him. The old ex-convict stumbled backward, lost his balance, and fell against the iron bedrail.

The shock of his temporary violent outburst, unintended though it had been, seemed to clear Logan's head. He rushed forward to assist his friend.

"Billy!" he cried. "Billy ... I'm sorry!" Logan stooped down, stretched his arm around him, and helped him to his feet. As he did so, something deep within Logan began to crumble.

A strangled sob broke from his lips. He fought hard to bite it back, but another quickly followed. Billy reached up to pat his young friend's shoulder in sympathetic gesture. His caring action wrecked all further attempts at holding his distraught emotions in reserve. Tears started from Logan's eyes. He tried to brush them away, but the more he did so the more steadily they flowed. Hardly knowing what he was doing, Logan sagged against Billy, and his body shook as the older man laid a comforting arm on his shoulder. Neither had felt such an embrace of comfort since childhood.

Slowly Billy led Logan back to the bed, where he sat him gently down.

"Take it easy, lad," he said in a voice unaccustomed to gentleness. " 'Tis a rotten shame, it is ... but you can see, lad, can't you? Why, you're 'most a son to Molly, and it'd break 'er 'eart if somethin' was t' 'appen t' you too."

"Molly!" Logan exclaimed with renewed emotion. "I forgot about Molly. I've got to go to her!"

But Billy held him back once again. "You'd better not," he said. "Least not now. 'Tis best no one has the chance to connect you with Molly."

"But Morgan's in jail."

"E'en if he stays in jail—which hain't at all certain he will, an' you know it—but e'en if he does, he's still got boys to take care of things for 'im. I thought you understood before you got into this that you'd 'ave t' leave town for a while—"

"You said disappear. You never said get out of town," Logan interrupted, dismally shaking his head. "I hadn't thought about that."

"Well," declared Billy emphatically, "losin' five thousand quid's one thing. But landin' in jail's another. Morgan's goin' to be mad—and he's goin' to be on the lookout for you. You might 'ave t' stay away for a couple months, mebbe longer, till we see wot 'appens."

"But—"

"There hain't no other way, Logan—that is, if you value your skin."

Logan stood again and paced the room. Some sharp he was! His great scheme had accomplished nothing more than to make Morgan more dangerous than ever. Not only to himself but to Molly as well, should Morgan ever discover their connection. Skittles was dead. Molly was alone. And he could not even go to her to offer what small comfort he could—and after all she had done for him over the years.

He kicked at a chair in his frustration, sending the flimsy wooden thing flying across the room. Much as he wanted to see Morgan pay for what he had done, he felt impotent, and such a childish action was the only violence of which he was capable. He could lie, he could cheat, he could steal. But he could not murder. To do so would put him in the same class as Morgan himself. But there was something else besides, something he couldn't quite put his finger on, something inside him which told him a murderer was somehow less of a human being than any other, no matter what other crimes one might have committed. All at once he remembered what Skittles had said to him in the hospital. *"Get out,"* his friend had pleaded with him, *"before it's too late . . . before you end up going the way of Chase Morgan."*

He was different from the likes of Morgan. Wasn't he? He knew where to draw the line. He would never . . .

His thoughts drifted off to an indistinct end. Well, he *was* different! And he wasn't going to let Skittles down. Never!

Slowly he turned back toward Billy, still seated on the edge of the bed anxiously watching him pace back and forth.

"Square everything with the lads that helped us," Logan said, nodding toward the envelope which Billy still held. "Keep some for yourself and get your watch back. Then give the rest to Molly."

It seemed that abruptly Logan had resigned himself with what must be done. His voice now took on a determined tone.

"Don't worry about a thing, lad," answered Billy. "I'll take care of it. But wot about yoursel'?"

"Guess I'll need a bit for traveling."

Billy handed him two hundred pounds.

Logan recoiled. "I don't need *that* much!" he exclaimed. "I'd only lose it gambling, or doing something else just as stupid."

"Take it," insisted Billy. "You earned it. An' Molly wouldn't want to be thinkin' of you headin' off to who knows where penniless."

Logan hesitated a moment longer, then reached out and took the notes from Billy's hand. After an awkward embrace, during which even the crotchety old counterfeiter's eyes glistened with a hint of moisture, Billy left to deliver the money, and more bad news to Molly.

Through the dirty pane of his flat's only window, Logan watched him head up the mostly deserted street, sighed a long sigh when he was out of sight, then turned back into his room. He went directly to the closet, pulled a brown leather suitcase from it, and hoisted it onto the bed to begin packing. His possessions were few, so the activity occupied little of his time. When all his other worldly belongings had been stuffed inside, he laid on top the fine cashmere suit he had worn to impress Morgan, along with the silk necktie and linen shirt. Who could tell when he might need them again? Instead of such finery, he dressed himself in clothes more appropriate for travel—a brown tweed suit, with an open-collared shirt, sturdy shoes, and his well-worn dark overcoat. He picked up Skittles' checkered cap and set it rather reverently on his head. It hardly went with the rest of his attire, but at such a moment Logan could think of wearing nothing else.

"I'll never live up to it," he said to himself, "but maybe it'll bring me luck."

The new fedora—well, there just wasn't room for it. And somehow it reminded him of things he'd just as soon forget at present. He laid it on the dresser, hoping it would come by a worthier owner than Skittles' cap had. Next to the hat he placed a few notes to cover his back rent. He didn't want a disgruntled landlady setting the police on his tail, too.

As he stepped outside, the wind and rain pelted him. He pulled his overcoat tightly about his neck, looked back and forth along the street, then headed out into the nasty weather. It was no day to be traveling.

He cast a backward glance at the building where he had lived for the past year. It had never meant much to him, but now it was all he had to represent those many things that did mean so much to him in London. The falling rain, the dreary tenement, the deserted street—it all seemed such a sad ending to his seven years in the city of cities, a city he had grown to love in spite of its size and occasional filth and squalor.

I'll be back ... and soon! he told himself, then turned away and walked down the street, not looking back again.

An hour later he found himself looking up at the entrance of Euston Station. He had arrived there almost without thinking where his steps were leading him. He still had no idea of his ultimate destination as he walked inside and strode to one of the lines.

He gradually made his way toward the front, wondering what he would say when he reached the booth. Standing before the ticket seller at last, the single word *Glasgow* seemed to come out of his mouth of its own volition.

11   Home Again

The train ride was a long one.

And tedious. Despite whatever resolve he may have felt while staring out the window as the buildings and streets of London gradually gave way to the countryside of Chilterns, by the time they reached Northampton, Logan was embroiled in a heated game of cards. And as he had predicted, he had lost nearly everything before the train reached Carlisle. He had been a wealthy man in Leeds, but by the time the train had pulled into Cumberland, he had lost his shirt, just as the Duke by that same name nearly had against Bonnie Prince Charlie not far from that very spot. He built his fortune up once more by Moffat in his own homeland. But Logan had had no Culloden like the famous Duke, and by the time he reached Glasgow, he was a poor man once again.

"Just like when I left," Logan mused as he stepped off the train.

He straightened his silk necktie, buffed the toes of his black dress shoes on his pant cuffs, and made one last attempt to brush the wrinkles from the cashmere suit he had donned in honor of his homecoming. Even without the fedora, he cut a rather striking figure strutting down the street as if he owned that portion of the soot-blackened industrial city. The two days on the train, and the outbreak of sunshine eight hours north of London had served to heighten Logan's enthusiasm for life once more. Never one to stay down for long, he walked along feeling as optimistic as if he *did* own the city—and the world, if he chose. Having no money in his pockets was only a minor inconvenience to Logan Macintyre, though certainly one he would not want to advertise in his hometown. But temporary setbacks, as he always called his losses at cards and dice, in no way diminished the possibilities for the future. Though he remembered his friend fondly, and indeed, over the last two days the image of the old man's dying face had scarcely left his mind, Skittles' final words to him had yet to be driven into his heart. It would take more than a friend's death to penetrate his superficial existence with a deeper and more lasting vision of life's true values.

As he passed a public house where he had spent many an idle hour during his youth, Logan's brisk pace slowed to a stop. Through the sooty window he spied several faces he thought he recognized, sitting, as it seemed, in the very spots where he had left them seven years earlier. He turned inside, wondering if he had changed as little as they. His question was answered in short order; he sauntered toward the bar unrecognized.

He removed Skittles' cap, kept his eye on the table where three old friends sat, and waited. It took but a moment or two longer before a dawning stare of recognition began to spread over one of the faces. Logan grinned.

"Be that Logan Macintyre?" exclaimed the man.

His two cronies glanced up and peered across the room.

"Ain't no wiseacre kid no more!" said another.

Slowly Logan approached, laughing at their comments.

"Hoots! Jist look at ye!" cried the first.

"Didna anyone tell ye there was a depression on?" asked the third man, speaking now for the first time. "Where ye been, Logan, 'at ye can dress in sich fine duds?"

"London," replied Logan.

"An' hoo lang's it been since ye left Glasgow, lad?"

"Seven years."

"Ye still haen't told us hoo ye came by sich a suit," jibed another. "Hasna the Depression hit auld London yet?"

"Or maybe oor frien' here has finally found himsel' a lucrative"—with the word the speaker winked at his two friends knowingly—"line o' work!"

Logan laughed again, wanting to dispel no fancies for the moment, at least until he could once again get a feel for the lay of the land.

Drinks were bought all around, and no one so much as thought of allowing Logan to lay out a penny toward them. The fact that he *looked* wealthier than all of them put together only made them the more determined that they should finance this festive afternoon of his homecoming.

"Where's old Bernie MacPhee?" asked Logan.

"Oh, he's doin' a drag up in Barlinnie for stealin' a automobile."

"An' Danny?" tried Logan again.

"Got himsel' killed a year ago. Seems a feller didna agree that his full house were on the up-an'-up."

Logan exhaled softly at the news, somewhat deflated.

"An' what hae ye been up t' in Lonnon, Logan?"

"Me?"

But before he had the opportunity to frame a response, one of the others at the table answered for him.

"Why look at him, ye dunderhead," the man said, fingering the fine fabric of Logan's suit. "Anyone can see he's doin' jist what he set oot t' do. Ye run one o' them fancy night clubs, nae doobt, don't ye noo, Logan?"

"Well ..." Logan began, thinking how best to answer the question. But before he had said another word, the innkeeper had shouldered his way into the group to pour refills, and the conversation was sidetracked, leaving Logan still thinking what might have been his reply. But he did not appear anxious to correct his friend's miscalculation. And when the second round was finished, he took his leave, promising to return soon to try out his London luck on them. In high spirits the three sent him on his way, sure enough in their own minds that their former acquaintance of the streets had indeed made it into the big time in London.

A light rain, never far away even on the sunniest of days in Scotland, greeted him as he left the pub. He threw on his overcoat and pulled the checkered cap down over his unruly hair. He had thought about walking around the old neighborhood for a while, but the rain forced him to turn his steps directly toward his mother's home.

Yet even as he did so, he realized for the first time that he was actually reluctant to face her. *Well, who would blame me?* he rationalized. After all, this was hardly the homecoming he had always fantasized for himself—penniless and practically running for his life. The picture his mind had usually conjured up of the event always included a Rolls Royce, a mink-clad lady on his arm, and an armload of gifts for his mother—in every way the epitome of the son who had made good. He thought fleetingly of the five thousand pounds he had handed over to Billy in London. Of course if his mother had known how he came by the money, all the outward show of success and sophistication in the world would not have impressed her. And besides, knowing the money was now in Molly's hands was worth ten Rolls Royces.

Well, tomorrow his luck would change! It was bound to—because it could hardly get much worse.

In thirty minutes he had arrived. He came to the front of the old gray granite building (he avoided calling the place a tenement, which in fact it was) where his mother lived. The front door squeaked on its hinges as he opened it, and the fifth step still had a loose board. *One's old home should always appear changed after a long absence,* he thought, but at first glance everything here was exactly as he remembered it. Everything was supposed to look different, because *he* had changed—hadn't he?

He glanced quickly down at his fine clothing as if to reassure himself. He certainly hadn't had apparel like this when he left seven years ago. Even the blokes at the pub hadn't recognized him. For the moment he forgot, as he was prone to do, that he was nothing but a lad seven years ago.

One thing he knew for certain: the three flights up to his mother's flat had never seemed this fatiguing. He was panting heavily when he reached the final landing, and had to pause a moment to catch his breath. He raised his hand to knock on the door. That seemed the strangest sensation of all.

Suddenly his mind flooded with visions of a dirty-faced, ragamuffin boy racing up and down the steps, bounding through the door. Or more often than not, when that same youngster reached the age of thirteen or fourteen, creeping up the steps in the middle of the night and sneaking through the door so that his mother would not hear.

The temptation seized him once more to try to sneak into the flat, but he gave a mature chuckle at the idea and rapped sharply on the door instead.

His mother opened the door.

A brief moment of utter stillness ensued, like some of the moving pictures Logan had been to in London when the film had jammed and the action momentarily had ceased. Then all at once the film began running again, and Frances Macintyre smiled and took her son's hands in hers.

Logan mused that she was indeed another of the fixtures of his home that had not changed. She was nearly as tall as he, and still displayed a certain poise, though it was difficult to discern properly, covered as it was by a poorly fitting housedress of drab green.

For an instant Logan wanted to flee. Was it childlike embarrassment to once again stand in front of his mother? Or was it the manly disappointment of wanting to hang his head in shame for neglecting her all these years? How many times does a man possess five thousand pounds—right in his very hands! Yet he had not once thought to keep a little back for his mother. She had seemed so distant, almost a nonexistent memory out of his past, when he was back in London. Molly and Skittles had been everything then. But suddenly it was different. He had flown back in time and now here she was, part of his life once more. And how desperately he wished he had a few quid to buy her a new dress.

"Evening, Mum," he said, kissing her lightly on the cheek, as if he hoped the gesture could substitute for all the other things he could not do.

"Ye sure know hoo t' surprise a woman," she replied in an even contralto voice he remembered always finding so soothing. She led him inside and he noted that most of the old furnishings were still in place.

"I guess I never was one for letter writing."

"Two letters in seven years," she said without reproach. "I'm thinkin' it must be a record o' some kind fer makin' yer kin wonder whether ye be alive or dead."

As they gravitated toward the kitchen, Mrs. Macintyre set a kettle of water on the stove.

"Ye haena had supper yet?" she asked. Logan shook his head. "Weel," she said, "I got a bit left from my own. I always make more'n I need. Tomorrow I'll go t' the market an' get some real man food fer ye."

"I don't want you to make a bother for me."

"Seven years I hae been waitin' fer jist sich trouble, son! Leave me t' enjoy ye while I can."

Logan sat back and studied her as she set about her tasks, and he realized he was seeing her in a completely different light than he had before. Perhaps the years apart and his own maturity helped him to view things more objectively. At any rate, he unexpectedly noticed that his mother was still an attractive woman. But then, she was only forty-one. And even after years of hard work and poverty, Frances Macintyre could still hold her own beside the women of the world he had seen daily in London. He wondered why she had never remarried. Somehow, he had been the reason. Maybe she hadn't wanted him to turn up one day and find a new surrogate father in his home.

Before many minutes she set a dish of steaming potatoes on the table with a plate of brown bread and sliced cheese. He hadn't eaten anything all day due to his lack of funds, and fell to it with a relish that warmed the mother's heart. After he had finished everything in front of him and the second helpings that followed, she poured them both cups of hot, strong tea. It was then that he noticed her hands. They looked old. Like nothing else about her, they showed the life of toil. It seemed as if all the years of hardship and heartache had drained to those two appendages. Even old Molly's hands had never seemed so worn and wrinkled. But perhaps they were noticeable because they contrasted so sharply with her attractive, almost youthful appearance otherwise. Something about that made it all the more pitiable.

Impulsively Logan reached out and touched one of the hands which had so attracted his gaze.

Puzzled, his mother stopped with the kettle in midair. He looked up at her, and smiled—a bit embarrassed.

"It's good to be home," he said, as if he felt some words were appropriate. But he wasn't at all certain those were the exact words he wanted to say.

" 'Tis good t' hae ye home, Logan."

"Don't you wonder why I've come?"

"I figured ye'd tell me when an' if ye had a mind fer it."

"I wish I'd done more for you, Mum."

" 'Tweren't yer responsibility, son," she said gently, "so dinna get it int' yer mind that it were."

"I don't have any money."

Mrs. Macintyre's lips curved up into a smile—a nice smile too, considering the few occasions in her life when she had been able to practice it. "Knowin' ye as I do," she said, "I doobt that'll last fer lang."

"That's not why I've come back," he said. "But I thought you should know."

" 'Tis fine wi' me, fer whate'er reasons ye came. An' noo there'll be not anither word aboot it. Ye can help oot when ye can."

She set the kettle once again on the stove. When she turned back toward him, from her wan smile Logan thought she might be on the verge of tears. She quickly sat down and took a sip of her tea. "Mr. Runyard'll be needin' some help in his restaurant," she suggested. And if her voice carried a note of hopefulness, she could perhaps be forgiven for wishing against hope that her son was at last home to stay.

"I don't know how long I'll be staying," he answered evasively.

"Oh?"

"But I'll bring some money in—"

"That weren't my meanin', son," she added hastily. "I jist knew ye'd be wantin' t' keep busy."

"I never had trouble keeping busy before."

"I know. But ye was yoonger then. An' perhaps what was keepin' ye busy wasn't the best o' things fer a grown man t' be doin'."

Then came a long silence.

They each pretended that their tea was consuming their complete interest. But a half-empty teacup can serve that purpose only so long. At length Mrs. Macintyre rose and began to clear away the supper things.

Logan jumped up to help.

"Sit doon," she said. "Ye must be tired after yer trip."

"Not a bit," he replied. "At least, not after that feast. I even thought I'd take a walk around the old neighborhood and reacquaint myself."

" 'Twill be late soon—" she began, but then stopped herself. "I'll get ye a key t' let yersel' in."

"Thanks, Mum. I won't be too late. And thanks for the supper and tea."

She merely smiled as he gathered up his coat and cap. Then she walked over to a ceramic jar by the sink and took out two one-pound notes. These she pressed into Logan's hand. He began to protest, but she shook her head.

"Ye're my son," she insisted. "Let me do it fer ye."

He took the money and left, knowing all the while that his whole reason for wanting to walk about the neighborhood was simply to escape the intimacy he was so unaccustomed to—and he hated himself for it. She wanted to make up for the years of his absence by giving to him of the little she had, yet he knew it was he who should be doing for her. But because he couldn't, he found it difficult to look her in the face. At this moment he found it hard even to face himself honestly. How much easier it was to duck out into the familiar streets where every promise seemed available, especially to a man of his wit and skill.

He had little difficulty finding a back-room card game, and the cronies of his youth welcomed him with gusto, treating him with the eminence of a returning hero. Logan had no reason to doubt that tomorrow would bring changes, and there was no reason for those changes not to be for the better.

12   A New Scheme

Logan awoke the next morning some time after ten. He had been out much later the previous night than he had anticipated.

He ambled into the kitchen where he discovered oatcakes and cheese laid out on the table for him alongside a note from his mother telling him when she expected to be home from work. Munching one of the crunchy biscuits, he wandered back into his room and set about getting dressed, this time in the tweeds, not the cashmere.

Then he began to consider his prospects for the day.

Last night's efforts had put ten pounds in his pocket, half of which he had deposited in his mother's ceramic jar. He felt much better about himself now than when he had left the evening before. Things indeed had begun to look up, despite that the light mist had turned into a distinct downpour. The weather certainly didn't beckon him to step out, though how long he could remain cooped up inside would be hard to tell. After thirty minutes he could stand it no longer. He grabbed an umbrella, not pausing to think that his mother had gone to work without hers just so that her son would have use of it, and decided to chance the storm.

The streets were nearly deserted, and his favorite pub was still empty. He bought a pint, but didn't enjoy it much without company. Feeling rather dejected he picked up a copy of yesterday's *Daily Mail* from the stand across from the pub, and returned home.

He sank down on the timeworn couch in his mother's small sitting room, propped his feet up on a low table, and tried to interest himself in London's happenings. Perhaps the paper might suggest something as to future possibilities. Dominating the front page was an account covering the opening of the trial of the Rector of Stiffkey, the clergyman whose lifestyle had lately scandalized Britain. Reading further, he learned that Britain had sent troops to Singapore to defend British interests there against the rising threat of the Japanese. On page two he read a brief account of the upcoming election in Germany and the fears of some that a former army corporal by the name of Hitler might soon take over the reins of power there. Logan recalled that Winston Churchill had once sung Hitler's praises; now it seemed that English leaders were changing their tune.

So far nothing seemed either to concern or to interest Logan very much, though it would have been a lark to have been in London for the Rector's trial. All the other news was too far removed. Singapore, Germany—even the accounts of the flagging economy failed to arouse him. His own personal financial depression seemed far more pressing, and neither the Conservatives nor the Laborites could offer him relief.

He tossed aside the paper and stood to stretch his legs. A small shelf of books caught his eye and he wandered listlessly over to it. His mother was not much of a reader, and these books had sat here untouched as long as he could remember, for he, too, had never read much. Today, however, almost without even thinking what he was doing, he found himself standing looking at the spines of the dozen or so volumes that sat here as a reminder of literacy in the midst of Glasgow's working district.

Sheer boredom led Logan to reach toward a volume and take it down—Dickens' *Bleak House.* After not much more than a moment, he replaced it with a bit of a smirk. *No wonder I never read any of these*, he thought with a droll smile. Still he removed another and then another, giving each a cursory perusal, until he came to an extremely aged black volume. The moment he took it in his hands, he could feel that this was an altogether different kind of book, bound as it was in dark, limp leather. It was a Bible, but try as he might Logan could not recall ever seeing the book on this shelf during his childhood. He was sure his mother had never mentioned it, and he certainly had never seen her read from it. If it was a recent acquisition, it was a curious one, for the book was clearly of great age. He had a friend who had dealt in old and rare books—or more precisely in *bogus* old and rare books. *I wonder what it's worth*, he thought as he unconsciously flipped through the pages. *I should probably show this to old Silky. It might be just the thing to—*

"Hello!" he exclaimed aloud as a sheet of paper fell from between the pages, "what's this?"

He stooped down, picked up the folded and yellowed paper,

opened it, and saw that it was a letter, handwritten in a most illegible scrawl.

His interest piqued, he carried the Bible, along with the mysterious letter, over to the couch, where he sat down once more to attempt to decipher it. This proved to be no small task, for judging from the many misspellings and archaic expressions, the writing had obviously come from the hand of an uneducated man. The date on the letter, however, encouraged him to persevere. He was bored with nothing better to do, and one in Logan's line of work tended to look for fortune to smile upon him at every turn; through the years Logan had grown accustomed never to look the other direction no matter how unpromising the opportunity may have appeared at first glance.

March 19, 1865, he read, then continued on, making his way through the body of the letter a single word at a time.

Dear little Maggie, it began, *I dinna ken where to send this, but I pray daily that ye will write to them what love ye at Stonewycke. I write this noo because I must explain to ye what I hae doon and why. Ye see, the treasure has weighed heavily on my heart . . .*

Logan sat up right on the couch, suddenly coming fully awake.

Yer father almost stumbled upon it one day, before his illness, that is. Weel, it set me to pondering, and I couldna keep frae thinking as hoo much trouble that treasure has already brought to this world. I thought aboot tossing it into the sea, but always I was reminded that tisna mine to destroy. I didna want to be a thief, especially from yerself, Maggie. Yet I feared lest another discover it and begin again the chain of terrible greed and violence. So I hae moved it, Maggie, and hidden it where I pray none will discover that evil horde, unless ye come back yerself, and then I'll tell ye where I had put it, 'cause 'tis yers to do with as ye see fit.

By now Logan was nearly perspiring, and reading as rapidly as the aged writing would allow.

But be assured, at this moment, Maggie, 'tis no treasure we lang fer—but 'tis only to hae ye back in oor midst once mair. To see ye with auld Raven riding upon lonely Braenock or the sandy beach would be worth all the gold in this world. But in yer memory I hae put it in a spot I thocht ye loved, hoping that'll please ye. For 'tis the

Lady of Stonewycke ye'll be someday. And I'll always think of myself as yer servant.

Do ye remember when ye were a wee lass with Cinder, and ye tried that cliff and ye both got stuck? Ye were always so free upon hill and sand that I didna miss ye too sore fer some time. But then when I did, I kenned just where to find ye in the other direction. Ye loved that path to the rock bearing yer name. And I hold sich memories of ye, dear. I pray one day ye will read this and return to us. But 'tis all in oor dear Lord's hands, and his will be doon.

The letter was signed *Yers very truly, yer servant, Digory MacNab.*

Logan leaned back and let out a long, low whistle.

This was indeed a find! He might just have fallen on his feet at last! And without a hint of any illegalities connected with the case. Maybe he would make his fortune on the up-and-up after all!

Of course, he reasoned with himself, this letter was sixty-seven years old and who was to say whether this Maggie might not have long since returned to claim her prize? But no, she could clearly never have received this letter, for here it still sat after all these years. Thus, if she had returned, with the only clue tucked away in a Bible out of sight, she would never have found it anyway.

Hmm! This held promise! The infinite possibilities to a mind like Logan's were intriguing, to say the least.

But then, he reflected further, in that many years countless things could have intervened in the disposition of this MacNab's treasure—excavations, building projects, erosion of the ground. To even think that it might . . .

Well, it was preposterous!

But what if it *were* still there! Could this be the change in his fortunes he had been waiting for?

A treasure hunt! He had participated in more harebrained schemes in his time. But this would be a first.

Yet he had hardly a clue to start with.

Or did he? Hadn't he seen a motion picture last year where the clues were hidden in just such a note as this? And where was this Stonewycke place, anyway?

That would be a beginning. Perhaps his mother would know something about all this. He glanced at his watch—it would be hours before she returned from work.

He stood and paced around the small room, his boredom completely dissolved by now, thoughts tumbling rapidly out of his active brain. Now here was a project worthy of his most diligent efforts! If it led to a dead end, what had he lost but a little time—of which he had an abundance, anyway. But he did not want to waste a minute of that valuable time waiting around for his mother's return. There must be something he could do in the meantime. In a city like Glasgow, there must be scores of places to begin his research.

He turned back to the small table where he had lain the Bible, picking it up—more gingerly this time, now that it had suddenly become so valuable in his eyes. Tiny black flakes of the crumbling leather along the edges of the spine came off into his hand. On the ornately decorated nameplate page were inscribed the words in a florid, feminine hand:

> *Presented to Digory MacNab*
> *On his tenth birthday*
> *July 15, 1791—Port Strathy*

Blimey! thought Logan. *This book is one hundred and forty-one years old!*

Running the figures quickly through his head, Logan did some further calculating. MacNab would have been eighty-four at the time of the writing of the letter. It seemed an odds-on bet that the old man went to his grave taking the secret of the treasure with him.

Logan sat pondering this turn of events another minute or two in silence. Then he jumped up, nearly forgetting his coat and cap, and hurried out.

————

Later that evening he scarcely gave his mother a chance to unload her basket of groceries before he began plying her with a barage of questions.

"Where did that old Bible come from?" he began.

The words sent a small spark of hope flickering in her mother's heart, until she quickly discerned that the gist of his interrogation was not spiritual in nature at all.

"It's been in an old trunk," she answered. "I finally decided t' get it oot an' put it up on the shelf with the other books."

"What trunk?" he queried.

"Jist an auld trunk o' family things."

"Who is Digory MacNab?"

"My goodness! What's sparked all this curiosity?" Mrs. Macintyre asked as she began preparations for their supper.

"Have you ever heard of a place called Stonewycke?"

"Up north, isn't it?"

"Yes," replied Logan quickly. "I did a bit of asking around today," he went on, "and I visited the library, read some old newspapers. You're right, there's a Stonewycke on the northern coast. Used to be a rather substantial estate."

"An' what's anythin' got t' do with this Stonewycke?" she asked as she cut up a few vegetables on the counter.

"Look at this," said Logan in place of an answer, thrusting the Bible in front of her, along with the letter. She scanned it hastily, gave him a noncommittal nod, and returned to her work.

"Don't you see, Mum? It must be the same Stonewycke. It was the biggest estate in those parts; then some twenty years ago most of the land was parcelled off to the tenants—given to them outright!"

"Generous lords, I'd say," commented Frances.

"Maybe. But more likely daft."

"There *are* good folk in this world, son."

"I know," conceded Logan. "But we're talking about thousands of acres of land. Why would anybody just *give* it away!"

"Maybe they cared more aboot their people than their ain wealth."

"Like I say—daft!"

"An' so who's the laird noo?"

"Is no laird, least none whose name I could find. The present heir is a Lady Margaret Duncan."

"There's yer Maggie, then."

"Could be . . ." he replied thoughtfully, sitting down at the table. He pulled several scraps of paper from his pockets and pored through them again. "The age would be about right," he mused, almost to himself.

"What's that ye say, son?" asked his mother, her interest in the matter growing.

"She turned up twenty years ago to claim the estate after having been in America some forty years. That would have put her in the States about the time this MacNab wrote his letter. The pieces all seem to fit."

"I dinna ken why ye're askin' me all these questions. Seems as if ye know more'n yer auld mum already."

Logan chuckled. "I couldn't help myself from finding out what I could. It caused some stir twenty years ago. The Aberdeen papers were full of it. Not only giving away all the land, but because there was some fraudulent scheme going on at the same time that the whole transfer exposed. Couple of big shots even did some time for it. And the laird before this Duncan lady had been murdered, it seems by the greedy family lawyer who was part of the fraud hoping to get his hands on the estate. The thing's positively fraught with intrigue!"

"I don't understand, son. Hoo could the lawyer hae seized the estate if there was still a living heiress?"

"That's the beauty of it, Mum!" Logan beamed triumphantly, as if he had single-handedly solved the mystery of the century. "No one knew this Margaret Duncan was alive. She had dropped completely out of sight forty years before. Don't you see? She couldn't possibly have received MacNab's letter. She probably doesn't know a thing about the treasure!"

"What's all this leading up to, son?" asked Logan's mother with just that tone in her voice which revealed that she knew all too well the answer to her own question. The gleam in her son's eye told more than any words he had spoken. " 'Course ye're plannin' on informin' these Duncans o' their good fortune...?"

"Of course ... eventually." With a flourish adroitly designed to change the subject, Logan opened and spread out the letter on the table, perusing it again in detail. "I'd really like to know who this MacNab fellow was."

"He'd be some kin o' yers, nae doobt," his mother answered simply.

"Kin!"

"Why, what'd ye 'pect wi' a name like MacNab? Great Uncle maybe."

"Kin of mine?"

" 'Tis my maiden name. Surely ye haena forgotten so soon?"

In fact, Logan had not forgotten. It was just that he had so little interest in his own background in his younger years that he had never taken the trouble to learn his mother's maiden name in the first place. All at once Logan's blood ran hot with exhilaration.

"My own relative," he said, continuing to ponder the implications of this latest surprising piece of information. "I should have guessed—the cagy old fox!"

"Seems ye're missin' the point o' that letter." Frances paused long enough to dump the vegetables in a kettle of bubbling water that contained six or seven potatoes, then sat down with Logan. "He says that the treasure, whate'er it be, caused nothin' but trouble an' he hid it t' spare the family more heartache. Digory MacNab didna want it t' be found again."

"Unless it was by the girl Maggie," added Logan.

"Aye. Noo the Lady Margaret o' the estate. But ye said yersel' that ye weren't plannin' t' tell her—least not at first."

"Let's consider for a moment the possibility that MacNab's motives *were* pure," said Logan, once more diverting the track of the conversation away from his *own* motives. "I still don't think he would have left his letter if he truly wanted the treasure forgotten forever."

"Then he would hae wanted his Maggie t' have it."

"Or one of his own relatives," suggested Logan cautiously.

"Ye're stretchin' it a bit there, son. Ye know he intended nae sich thing."

"But once a man's dead, whatever he leaves behind comes into the hands of those of his own he leaves alive, whatever he may have intended. That's the law, Mum."

"An' ye're a fine one t' be keepin' sich a straight line!"

"The law's the law, Mum," said Logan with a tongue-in-cheek grin. "If MacNab passed on, leaving no other heirs—well, me being his nearest relation, that would make this Bible and the letter and whatever else mine, don't you think?"

"The judge might place me ahead o' ye in that line," replied

Frances with just a note of offense in her tone.

"And whatever's yours is mine, right, Mum?" rejoiced Logan cheerily, ignoring the flash of her eye. "And the letter's written quite familiarly," he went on. "I wonder if he couldn't have been related to Maggie also. An uncle perhaps, or a grandfather. That would make me—"

Here Frances laughed outright—a deep, soft laugh, not one overly filled with merriment, but pleasant to hear nonetheless.

"Believe me, Logan," she answered, dabbing her eyes on the corner of her apron, "if we had sich family connections, I'd know! Why, that'd make us kin t' lords an' ladies! 'Tis outright nonsense! This Digory was more'n likely a family servant—they got mighty attached t' those noble families back then."

"And how'd you come by the Bible?" asked Logan.

"Was in the family chest. I jist never paid it no heed till I decided t' put it oot a while back."

"I wonder if there isn't some way to confirm my relationship with the shrewd old boy."

Frances sighed, her safest reply when she knew that to say more to her son would only lead to strife. Seven years ago she had made frequent use of the habit, and it was amazing how quickly the old habit returned. For of all things, strife with her son was the last thing she desired at this moment in her life.

"Ye can look through the bureau that came t' me when yer gran'daddy passed on," she replied. The statement came somewhat grudgingly. She wanted no part in his scheme, and certainly didn't want to encourage him, but she knew he'd get to the bottom of it eventually anyway, so there was no use resisting and prolonging the inevitable. "He took great store in his family line. I never paid it much heed, but ye may find somethin'."

He was away from the table before the words had died out on her lips.

There was something in all this. Logan could feel it! It could be something big, so why shouldn't he take full advantage of such a splendid opportunity? He had no better options with which to occupy his time. And with Chase Morgan still to worry about, a trip to the north of Scotland, placing the wild Highlands between himself and his hometown, might be the perfect solution to that thorny dilemma. He doubted he could remain long in Glasgow without being traced there. If Morgan's cronies asked around Shoreditch, they were certain to discover his identity. And didn't most of his friends know of his Glasgow past? But who would think to search for him in the untamed and barren country above the Grampians?

Already the decision to go north was planted firmly in his mind. But first he had to possess all the facts possible about this estate of Stonewycke, the Duncan family, and Digory MacNab. The whole prospect was exhilarating! Who could tell what one might run across while unearthing ancient history?

Who could tell, indeed! For if Logan could have guessed what sleeping giants he was about to stir into wakefulness, a few second thoughts may have crept in with regard to the scheme hatching in his brain.

But he did not. Thus the next two days he spent—discreetly, he thought—asking more questions and stirring dust into corners that might have been better off left alone.

13   A Suspicious Caller

The gentleman sitting at the desk in the darkened office leaned back in his chair as he picked up the receiver of the phone. The only light in the room, coming from the street lamps outside, revealed a fashionably furnished place, though intimating that days had once been better. The man sat in shadows; his hair occasionally caught a ray of light, revealing substantial streaks of silver gray.

"I was just on my way out," he said into the phone in a low, hard tone.

He paused to listen to the voice on the other end of the line.

"Is that so...?" he replied to the unseen voice, drawing out his words thoughtfully. "Inquiring about Stonewycke, you say?"

More listening.

"A treasure ... then the rumors we heard are true...?"

He leaned forward, grabbed a pencil, and drew a pad toward him.

"What was the name. . .? Macintyre . . . from London, you say. . .? No, no, don't do anything just yet. We don't want to scare him off. I'll make some inquiries here. For now we'll let him do the footwork for us. But don't let him out of your sight."

Another pause followed.

"He did?"

The man rubbed his chin reflectively. "Well, you do the same. Just remember, it's a sleepy little burg. Make sure he gets off at Strathy; then you go on to the next town and double back. I want no one to know of our interest in the matter. Report back to me regularly."

Another question interrupted him. After a brief pause he resumed: "Use that code we used in the last project we worked on together. Is that all, Sprague? All right. Just be sure he doesn't get on to you."

Without another word he replaced the receiver.

Notwithstanding the periodic raising of his eyebrows during the course of the conversation, if he was in any way excited over the prospects raised by the phone call, he did not show it. Instead, he continued to sit at his desk, absently tapping his pencil against the solid walnut top.

In fact, though his surface appearance seemed perfectly nonchalant, inside he was more than enthusiastic over this turn of events. He had been looking for just such a break. At this point he had no idea where it might lead, but he felt certain that he would somehow be able to use these tidings to his advantage. He had carried out some research of his own through the years and had heard a local legend about some ancient horde from the Pict era over a thousand years ago supposedly connected with the Stonewycke property. Intriguing though it was, he had always considered it nothing but a straw in the dark. Perhaps he had been wrong. A fellow from London asking about a treasure, then heading north by train—certainly bore looking into!

He picked up the phone receiver once more, hastily looked for a number in the card file on his desk, gave the operator the city and number, then sat back to wait. After about a minute he sat forward attentively.

"Hello," he said, in a different voice this time. "Yes, yes—it's me . . . I know, it's been a long time . . ."

He tapped the pencil impatiently while he listened for another minute to the man he had called.

"I—I certainly will," he said, finally getting a word in. "But perhaps until then, you might help me out . . . No, no!" he laughed, "I only want a bit of information. Yes . . . Do you know of a young fellow by the name of Macintyre, early twenties, I'd say, likes to hang around where there's some action in the back room, if you know what I mean?"

The voice on the line rambled on again for some time, with an occasional question or comment interspersed on the part of the listener.

"A sharp . . . can't say as I'm surprised . . ."

More listening.

". . . a bookie? . . . oh, an old counterfeiter. Hmmm . . ."

All at once the gentleman's impatience with his talkative informant changed to rapt interest. "He did what?" he exclaimed. "To Chase Morgan. . . !"

After another pause the man chuckled, the first crack in his otherwise steely demeanor. "It's a good thing Morgan can afford clever lawyers. Three months in jail isn't much, but for a man like Chase it's enough. I should think he'd want Macintyre! . . . How much? . . . I'm sure some low-life goon will take him up on his offer and try to collect, if Morgan doesn't find him first . . . My interest? A different matter altogether. A friend of mine was making inquiries—didn't think he was on the up-and-up, but the deal he offered sounded too good to pass up . . . Yes, you're right there," he laughed. "Morgan should have been as smart. Certainly, I'll come by next week . . . Thanks for your assistance."

The thing was becoming more fascinating by the moment, thought the man as he hung up the phone. A confidence man like this Macintyre was bound to be up to something . . . something shady, no doubt! It was lucky for him his man in Glasgow had stumbled into the middle of it. Well, *stumbled* was not exactly the right word, he reflected further. After all, Sprague had been hired for the express purpose of gathering information. And he had definitely hit the jackpot in Glasgow!

14   Errand Day in Port Strathy

Allison tapped her foot impatiently as she leaned with folded arms against the parked Austin.

She and her younger brother had driven their great-grand-mother into town for several errands; she did not mind so much waiting for her, but Nat had run off just as Lady Margaret was due to be finished. He had probably gone down to the harbor to pass the time with those fishermen whom he seemed to adore, would lose all track of time, and she would be forced to go all the way down there to fetch him.

As a child she had not really noticed. But now that she had grown into a refined young lady of seventeen, it became clearer to her worldly-wise eyes with each passing day that there was absolutely nothing in this provincial town to interest her. The main street of Port Strathy had not changed in fifty years, possibly even longer. The chandlery, Miss Sinclair's Mercantile, the office next door—now occupied by Strathy's first resident doctor—all were as staid and static in their appearance as ever.

The fish processing plant was the town's newest addition, having been built not long before Allison's birth. But it wasn't much to boast about for one like Allison MacNeil. Nor was the "New Town" which had sprung up around it. The entire vicinity was permeated with the distasteful odor of fish, and if it had swelled the population of the town by some two hundred, they were of an even more undesirable breed than the fishers and farmers. The rows of company houses they occupied were in many cases as poor as the abandoned crofters' cottages in the Highlands, and a rowdy district had grown up alongside them, with two new pubs where loud music and heavy-fisted brawls were not uncommon.

Allison looked about and sighed heavily. Still no sign either of her great-grandmother or Nat. But what was there at home for her to hurry back to? She doubted she'd ever be able to forgive her parents for taking her away from school; it had been her only touch with civilization. As much as everyone else in the family might enjoy the company of those dull fishers and ignorant crofters, she certainly had more respect for her own position than that. If her father was from that class, he was different. He had struggled to get an education, to better himself, to rise above the station of his birth.

And Allison intended to do the same. That is, she did not intend to be dragged back to those depths by remaining buried here in Port Strathy all her life. Let her mother prattle about the merits of the simple life; Allison wanted no part of it. What she wanted was the life her family's position and standing entitled her to. She should be wearing silk and fine linen, not this outlandish checkered shirt with dungarees. But she had no reason to dress up;—she would never run into Charles—or even Eddie Bramford here.

She glanced up again, this time noticing a plain girl about her own age crossing the street. *If I remain in Port Strathy much longer,* she thought to herself, *I will be certain to end up like Patty Doohan.* Of course, Patty had no choice. She was a commoner, an orphan raised by an older sister who worked in the plant. Watching the girl approach, Allison could hardly believe they had been childhood friends. But there had been so few girls her age in the area, and Patty had seemed, at the time, the best of the lot. She could have been pretty, with her rich chestnut hair and large dark brown eyes. But she let her hair hang in a most unfashionable manner, and her eyes seemed to droop like the eyes of a sad, tired bassett hound. What they could have had in common back then, Allison couldn't even imagine. Fortunately, she had now grown beyond such juvenile relationships. If Patty had no choice about her direction in life, Allison did, and she intended to make use of it.

Or did she? Allison sighed once more. Well, maybe not for the time being. But one day she *would* be able to make her own choices, and then she'd show everyone!

"Hi, Allison," said Patty rather shyly as she came close. Perhaps she, too, was remembering the days not so long ago when they had played and laughed together.

"Hello, Patty," replied Allison. "How are you?" she asked, as a matter of course, in a tone that implied that it did not matter.

"Jist fine." She held out the basket she was holding. "Been shoppin'. Miss Sinclair's got some real fine apples this week."

"Oh, has she? I'll have to tell the cook so she can purchase some for us." Allison emphasized the word *cook* heavily. She wouldn't want Patty to think she did the shopping herself.

"I thought ye was away at that boardin' school."

"Oh, I was, but I'm rather old for school now." As she spoke Allison was not the least aware of the upward tilt of her nose. "I'm just biding my time here before I go to London for the season."

"Oh," said Patty flatly. Then as if an afterthought, she added, "How nice."

What an awkward conversation, thought Allison. *If only I had some excuse not to just stay here, or if Patty would be on her way.*

An uncomfortable moment or two of silence followed. At length Patty said goodbye, and turned to go.

"It was good t' see ye, Allison," she called back with a smile.

Allison forced a smile in return, but no words of farewell would come. She had not particularly enjoyed seeing her old friend, for more reasons than she could even name or understand.

Not many minutes after Patty's retreating figure had disappeared in one direction, Nat appeared ambling casually toward her down the street in the other. He was munching an apple and seemed to be thoroughly enjoying the first fine spring day since the storm the night of the celebration when the schooner had gone down.

"Well, it's about time!" Allison snapped when he was within earshot. "You're lucky I didn't have to come fetch you."

"What's your rush? Grandma's not back yet."

"She'll be along," replied Allison defensively. "I just didn't want her to have to wait on you."

Nat grinned good-naturedly, but before his sister could retort with another caustic remark, she saw her great-grandmother emerging from the mercantile carrying a small parcel. Nat hurried to her side, relieving her of the package, took her arm, and led her across the street to the car.

For all her frail appearance, the old woman walked with a sure, steady gait, hardly requiring the assistance of her young great-grandson. But she patted the boy's hand and smiled her thanks to him.

"Well, children," said Lady Margaret rather breathlessly, "I think I've finished with everything. I do appreciate your carting me about."

"Glad to do it, Grandma," replied Nat, while inside Allison wondered what he meant by the words. It was *she*, not Nat, who was doing the carting.

"Your great-grandfather thinks I should take up driving one of these," she said, tilting her head to indicate the auto. "But," she chuckled gaily, "I'd sooner take to horseback riding again."

The younger folk laughed with her. Whether she could have mounted one of the spritely coursers in their stables was a question their father, Alec, would not allow to be answered. But both of them had heard many times of the three wonderful mares, Cinder, Raven, and Maukin, which Lady Margaret and Grandpa Dorey had ridden all over this very countryside in their youths.

Nat proceeded to help his great-grandmother into the front seat of the car. He then walked around in order to climb in behind the wheel, leaving the rear seat for Allison. But she put out her hand to prevent him from opening the door.

"What do you think you're doing?" Allison inquired pointedly.

"Aw, come on, Ali," pleaded Nat. "I can do it."

"That may be. But you can practice with Daddy, not with me."

"Aw, Ali!"

"The car is my responsibility, and I won't leave it in the hands of a child. And don't call me Ali!"

Brushing past him, Allison climbed into the driver's seat, and Nat into the back. She turned the key in the ignition, but the engine only turned over limply, then made not another sound. The Austin seemed to have no intention of moving from the spot where it sat. Again Allison tried to coax it to life, this time pumping furiously on the accelerator. Still there was no response. Slapping at the steering wheel, she opened the door and climbed out, with Nat on her heels. Wrenching up the bonnet of the car, she stared at the jumble inside. Nat elbowed her aside, and she had no choice but to defer to him. He had, after all, learned something about the workings of engines from Mr. Innes before his death.

Nat reached in and began tapping and wriggling various parts that he considered the most likely offenders.

"Here, hold this back," he said, indicating a greasy hose.

Allison wrinkled her nose distastefully, then plunged her hand into the grimy mess. In a moment Nat seemed satisfied with his work.

"Go around and try it again," he said.

She laid the hose down according to her brother's instruction, then brushed her hair from her eyes, smudging her nose as she did so, and climbed in once more behind the wheel.

But despite Nat's efforts, nothing happened. She rejoined Nat, who had procured several tools from the boot and was about to take a wrench to what he thought might be a loose connection.

"Mr. Innes would know what to do," he said, almost to himself and with a hint of sadness in his voice.

For the first time of the afternoon, Allison's expression softened. Each of the MacNeil children, in their own way, had been attached to the kind old factor, and Allison knew what her brother must be feeling to miss him at such a moment. They exchanged a rare, momentary, tender look.

But just as quickly Allison's expression resumed its look of superiority, and she barked out rather gruffly, "Maybe you've hit *something* this time . . . I'll try again."

But the Austin continued to make the same obstinate protestations. And since automobiles were few in Port Strathy, and the nearest automobile mechanic more than twenty miles away in Fraserburg, the options before the three stranded travelers looked to be rather limited.

Allison jumped out of the car a third time, angry by now, looked around helplessly, and gave the tire a futile, surly kick.

15   Stranger in a Strange Land

Logan had stepped off the schooner that morning a bit shaky in the knees and even more so in the stomach, wondering why he had abandoned the train in Aberdeen in favor of the sea route. He had never been attracted to the sea-faring life—and now he knew why. Even worse, he had not been able to interest a soul onboard in a friendly little game of poker. He had reached the conclusion that if these fisher types were all so intent upon hanging on to their money, it would be dull sojourn indeed in this place called Port Strathy.

For his stomach's sake, and in an attempt to disprove his first impression of these northern folk, the first thing Logan did upon touching firm, dry land was to spy out the local pub. Had he been seeking only a drink and a round or two of cards, he would no doubt have ended up at one of the establishments of the New Town, where his enterprising nature might have been more fully satisfied. However, as he was in need of a place to stay as well, he was directed to the only respectable inn in the place—the Bluster 'N Blow.

The fact that the history of the establishment dated back nearly two hundred years impressed Logan very little. Always looking ahead, to him anything that old was a step backward rather than into the future where real life was to be lived. He had had quite enough of old buildings—mostly the rat-infested tenements of Glasgow and London. The ultimate dream, to Logan Macintyre, would be to take up residence in one of the fashionable new West End apartment complexes, complete with every modern convenience.

He thus viewed the Bluster 'N Blow as neither quaint nor respectable. But since it was the only available hostelry, he'd have to make do. If he, however, was unimpressed with the inn, the innkeeper was quite taken with his new customer. For though Logan was dressed only in his tweeds, he appeared every inch a dapper gentleman, and Sandy Cobden knew a man of means when he saw one.

"Afternoon, sir," said the innkeeper. "An' what might I be doin' fer ye?"

Logan strode jauntily to the counter and perched himself on one of the tall stools. "I'd like a room, my good man," he said, "and something to soothe my sea-tossed insides."

"Ah, ye must hae jist come in on the schooner."

"That I did," replied Logan. "I should have waited for the train, but then I'd have had to finish the last of the trip overland, and I was anxious to get here."

Cobden laughed. "Ye see why we dinna get many visitors," he said, and as he spoke the innkeeper brought a bottle of his best Glenfidich Scotch up from under the counter. "Ye're lucky e'en t' hae a schooner t' ride after the accident several weeks ago. But take a drap o' this. It'll be jist the thing fer yer stomach," he added, pouring out a dram for his guest. "So, ye've come from Aberdeen, have ye...?" queried Cobden, drawing out his tone in order to elicit some response. He took what he considered his "position" in the community with the utmost seriousness, and was therefore ever vigilant for whatever bits of gossip he might stumble across.

"Farther than that, I'd say—London, actually."

"I thought so!" declared Cobden, "the moment I heard yer accent."

In reality he had thought no such thing, for even after seven years in London, Logan had not entirely lost his Scottish tongue. He spoke with just enough mixture of the various dialects to which he had been exposed that his speech readily would have confounded the most experienced British linguist. Without revealing a thing, Cobden's curiosity was more than aroused by this well-dressed Londoner with the Scottish brogue. But he restrained himself from further questioning for the moment. He preferred to gather his information by more subtle means.

Instead, he busied himself with buffing the counter and wiping several glasses, while Logan sipped his Scotch and wondered that such energy could be summoned from so huge a bulk of a man. At length Logan finished his drink and took a coin from his pocket.

"Are you a sporting man, Mr.—?" Logan paused, as no introductions had as yet been forthcoming.

"Cobden's the name—Sandy Cobden." The innkeeper laid down

his cloth and thrust a hand toward his visitor, shaking the smaller man's hand vigorously.

Logan, smiling a bit wanly, recovered his hand and introduced himself. "Well, as I was saying, Mr. Cobden, might you be a sporting man?"

"I'm na too sure if I take yer meanin'."

"I thought we'd lend a little interest to our tête-à-tête and toss a coin for my drink. Tails, I pay double, and heads, it's on the house."

"Why not?" agreed Cobden.

Logan flipped his gold sovereign high into the air, catching it crisply on the back of his left hand with his right over it. When he uncovered it, the face of George the Third leered up at them. "Sorry, old chap," he apologized, pocketing his coin.

"Not a bit o' it!" grinned Cobden in his most congenial manner. "Yer drink would hae been on the house anyway, ye bein' all the way from London, an' all."

"That's mighty friendly of you."

"We're a friendly little toon, Port Strathy is." Cobden resumed his labors, then after a moment's pause, in an off-handed way, asked, "So . . . hoo lang will ye be stayin' wi' us?"

"It's hard to say just how long my business will detain me," replied Logan noncommitally.

"Business, ye say . . ." Cobden mused, half to himself, half hoping his puzzled expression would draw something further from the stranger. He was remembering the last time such a dapper-looking fellow had come to Strathy on business some twenty years ago. That time it had meant nothing but trouble for the town. He hoped it would be different this time. But this young man certainly looked friendly enough, Cobden decided. And if there was one thing Sandy Cobden prided himself on, it was his keen ability to judge character.

"I thought I'd have a look about the place before dinner," Logan went on, ignoring Cobden's query. He was not quite certain how he was going to proceed on his quest, and he wanted to make sure he had a good feel for the town before he said anything. "Would you be so kind as to take my suitcase up to my room? I should be back in an hour or so."

Logan strode confidently from the inn.

He might not know how to begin this latest project that had

brought him so far off the beaten path. But one thing appeared certain—it was going to be a breeze. These cuddys wouldn't know a good dodge if it jumped out and kissed them. Why, that Cobden fellow still had no idea he had been fooled by the most elemental of cons—a double-headed coin!

Yes . . . he felt instinctively that his luck was taking a turn for the better. It only remained to find old Uncle Digory's treasure and hop aboard the next schooner or train back to civilization.

The first order of business, therefore, was to locate these Stonewycke people. They might prove his most difficult obstacle, however, for if they were of the cultured aristocracy, they were likely to be far more worldly-wise than that Cobden or the sea-folk he had encountered on the schooner. But notwithstanding whatever potential snags lay in his path, Logan's confidence was running high as he walked along the cobbled street, noting the rustic buildings of gray granite and the coarsely clad residents he met along the way.

Ambling past Sinclair's Mercantile and looking in the window, he heard a shout from farther down the street. He glanced up just at the moment when an animated young lady had aimed a fierce blow to her Austin's tire.

He took in the scene with amused interest. The girl in blue jeans and sandy blonde hair with a smudge across her nose was certainly in keeping with the general motif of the town, though the auto was somewhat out of place, despite its antiquity and obvious state of disrepair.

All at once, without really thinking, Logan turned and started toward the Austin. His best ploy in a place like this would be to ingratiate himself with these country folk. And what better place to begin than with these stranded wayfarers?

16   Introductions

Allison had ducked her head into the car to explain the situation to her great-grandmother; she did not, therefore, immediately notice the approach of the stranger. When she did look up, he had gone past her and was greeting Nat in a cheerful tone.

"Good afternoon," he said.

Nat wiped a grimy hand across his sweaty forehead and grinned.

"Having problems?" inquired the stranger.

Nat nodded, and the man continued, "I've some small skill in mechanics. If you like, I'll have a look."

"Sure," replied Nat eagerly. "I'm not doing much good."

He stepped up to the bonnet, affording Allison a closer view of his features. No doubt he was a stranger, she thought, not only in the unfamiliarity of his face, but also because of his general carriage and the polished finesse of his actions. No fisherman would have removed his jacket with such care, even if it had been a well-tailored tweed such as this man's. Folding it neatly, he laid it on the car, then proceeded to roll up the sleeves of his fine linen shirt. He definitely did not possess the brawny physique Allison was accustomed to seeing on the fishers and farmers around Strathy. She might have taken him for a scholar, but the tone of his voice and a peculiar look in his eye did not quite concur with that conclusion. There was a boldness about him, as if he feared nothing and, in fact, invited challenge with relish.

The fact that the newcomer was young and good-looking was not lost on her, but for the moment she could not help feeling perturbed that she had thus far gone completely unnoticed as he concentrated on the more practical aspects of the situation. *And however bold and confident his appearance,* she asked herself, *how much does he really know about automobiles?* Her doubts along that line were preempted when he called out to Nat from under the bonnet.

"Give her a try."

Nat brushed past Allison and slipped in behind the wheel. Then miraculously came the sudden roar of the engine.

Nat whooped and hopped out. "Thanks, mister," he said.

"Glad to be of assistance."

"What was wrong with it?"

The man replied with a technical explanation involving wires and sparks, connections and cylinders, which greatly impressed Nat, whose budding love affair with things mechanical had been cut short by Mr. Innes's death. Allison, however, could make little of it.

"Where'd you learn all that?" asked the youth with admiration.

"Oh ... here and there," replied the stranger, a bit evasively, thought Allison. Though she could not possibly have known, her misgivings were sound, for he had in fact gained most of his knowledge of cars from his involvement in a rather lucrative, albeit illegitimate, auto racing enterprise some two years earlier. This, of course, he wisely kept to himself.

"Our factor knew all about cars," said Nat, "and he was teaching me all he knew, but ... he died a while ago, and no one in Strathy knows more than I do."

"That's too bad." The man brushed his hands together, then held one out to Nat. "I'm Logan Macintyre. I may be here a while, if you'd ever like a few pointers."

"Thanks." Nat took Logan's hand and shook it awkwardly. He was hardly used to being treated on equal terms as this man was now doing. "I'm real pleased t' meet ye. Nat MacNeil's my name."

Finally Allison could no longer stand to remain in anonymity. She stepped boldly forward, clearing her throat daintily.

"Oh, that's my sister, Ali," Nat added, almost as an unnecessary afterthought.

"Allison," she corrected with a disapproving cocked eyebrow directed at her brother. "We are very much in your debt, Mr. Macintyre," she added in her most mature tone, smiling prettily.

It was a pleasant smile, and ought to have had a very positive effect on the stranger, even though it was tinged with an indiscernible trace of haughtiness, which Allison could not have helped even had she wanted to. The smile did, in fact, largely make up for her appearance in his mind, though as he looked fully upon her, Allison was acutely aware of her old clothes and messy hair. Had she known

of the smudge of grease across her cheek, she would have turned a
bright shade of pink.

But after a moment or two Allison began to gain the distinct
impression that this man was looking at her as if she were a little
girl, and might at any moment reach out and pat her condescend-
ingly on the head. At last she thought she knew what the peculiar
look was that she had noted earlier—it was the unmistakable air of
superiority. It was a wonder she had not drawn the conclusion
sooner, as familiar as she was with that very bearing. And she found
it especially distasteful in someone who treated Nat as more his
equal than herself. However, her hastily formed judgment was confused by his congenial reply.

"Don't think of a debt to me," he said. "Actually, I haven't been
able to tinker with a car for some time, and I rather enjoyed myself."
Had Allison been able to read deeper into the truth of his statement,
she would have known that after his close brush with the law two
years ago he had sworn never to touch another automobile in his
life.

Maybe I misjudged him, Allison thought. *He might deserve Port
Strathy's best welcome after all.*

"Now that you've managed to get our car running," she offered,
"can we give you a lift anywhere?"

"Oh, no thanks. I'm staying at the inn down the street, and don't
have anyplace else to go."

"Then you *are* new here?" Allison observed.

"Just arrived today."

"What brings you here?" put in Nat.

"I'm sure it's none of our business, Nat," reproved Allison.

"You must be visitin' friends, though," ventured Nat, ignoring
Allison's remonstration.

"I don't know a soul in town," answered Logan, apparently not
as disturbed by the inquisitive nature of the youth as his older sister
assumed he might be. "Except you folks," he added.

"Then we can repay you by having you to our place for dinner,"
declared Nat.

"That's not necessary," answered Logan, taken aback momentarily by the unexpected display of hospitality.

"Sandy Cobden's cooking leaves a great deal to be desired since

Mrs. Cobden died," came a new voice from inside the automobile. Logan had not at first realized there were other passengers. He stooped down and tilted his head to have a look at the new speaker.

A brief silence ensued as the two surveyed one another. Before he spoke, Logan cleared his throat, somewhat nervously Allison thought, and as he did, she noted a slight sagging of the cool composure he had thus far assumed.

"In that case," he said, recovering himself as best as he was able, "perhaps I had better take you up on your kind offer."

"Jolly good!" exclaimed Nat.

"We shall be pleased to have you, young man," said the woman in the Austin.

"Mr. Macintyre," said Allison in a rather lofty tone, "may I present my great-grandmother, Lady Margaret Duncan."

17   The Lady and the Sharp

Logan sat back in the rear seat of the Austin as it left the small town and headed up the steep coast road.

If he hadn't been one who had trained himself to take in stride whatever life chanced to throw him, he might have been knocked off balance a bit with the sudden turn of events. As it was, he sat back and reveled in his good fortune.

His fortuitous stumbling upon the very people he sought had momentarily been lost upon him as he and the old lady had first exchanged glances. For when his eyes met those of Lady Margaret, a very odd and unfamiliar sensation passed through him. Even if he had tried, he couldn't have explained what it was he felt. He might have made a faltering attempt to describe it as like being suddenly stripped naked before one who knew you better than you knew yourself, as if the lady had been able to perceive to the very depths of his being. It seemed in that passing moment of time as if she had possessed the ability to read him more accurately than if his whole life had been boldly printed upon his shirt front—better than Skittles, better than his mother, better even than himself. He had an unnerving premonition that possibly he had opened the door to more than he bargained for.

But just as quickly the sensation passed. Logan was not of the temperament to ponder such things deeply. He was content to allow it to pass without further reflection. And if there was any truth to the unsettling foreboding, if she did know of his motives or his duplicity, the pleasant smile which followed immediately made clear that she would never have held any of these things against him. The only acquiescence he gave to the uncomfortable feelings her penetrating eyes had elicited was an unconscious and barely perceptible faltering of his self-command.

It was only the beginning of an afternoon filled with unexpected sensations. But at the moment Logan climbed into the automobile, the remainder of this landmark day still lay ahead of him. As he settled into his seat, he took a few moments to regather his equanimity. And now as Allison maneuvered the Austin up that oft-trod road southeast of town, Logan's eyes took in the wonders of the rugged seascape terrain on his left.

In a few more minutes they turned off the road to the right, away from the sea, through a slight wooded area, still climbing, until suddenly looming before them was the great, gray-brown ancient castle known as Stonewycke. They sped through an ornate open iron gate, and for a moment all his worldly savoir-faire fled. Even a modern sophisticate such as Logan could not help being awed by the four-hundred-year-old ediface.

And with the awe came a fleeting sense of defeat. Suddenly things were happening he hadn't planned on. Who was he, a mere mortal, to think of pitting his puny wiles against this place? Here for the first time an impression of history came over him. The walls of this fortress had withstood storms and armies and revolutions, and the lives and deaths of hundreds of mortals no better nor stronger than he. Yet here it stood, outlasting them all. Logan had faced up to many obstacles in his life—poverty and failure among them. But here was something he could never hope to conquer—inanimate, yet commanding.

He struggled to clear his head. These kinds of thoughts would never do.

But then a voice, soft and dreamy, seeming to float down from the heavens, caught his attention as if his very thoughts had been read:

> *"Child of loud-throated war! the mountain stream*
> *Roars in thy hearing; but thy hour of rest*
> *Is come, and thou art silent in thy age:*
> *Save when the wind sweeps by and sounds are caught*
> *Ambiguous, neither wholly thine nor theirs...."*

Logan glanced around and saw that the words had come from Lady Margaret. The peculiar feeling he had had when he first met her in town tried to intrude upon him once more. But this time he shook the spell away, and looked back toward the castle.

He was himself again. He had to be wary. Something about this place, and especially something about that lady, was unnerving him. He couldn't let that happen. This was business. This was his big chance. He'd just have to call to his aid all those years on the tough streets of London. Why, this place couldn't throw anything at him in a year like what one day in the big city did. He had to keep his head about him.

"Nice poem, m'lady," he commented, in a tone perceptibly more distant than he had thus far used.

"William Wordsworth wrote it about another castle," Lady Margaret replied. "But to me it has always captured the soul of our Stonewycke."

"That's what you call the place?"

"The name goes back to the time of the Picts. But the castle's only been here less than half that time."

Suddenly Allison braked to a jerky stop at the doorstep of the great mansion.

"How does it stand after four hundred years?" asked Logan.

"You are familiar with the history of our home I see, Mr. Macintyre," said Lady Margaret, evidently pleased.

Only then did Logan realize his blunder. "Oh, no more than most," he quickly replied, hoping to repair his error. "You said it had been here less than half of the last thousand years, so I naturally figured—"

"I see," she replied.

I had better be more careful, thought Logan. *I don't want to arouse any suspicions this early in the game.* It had been a lucky break to stumble upon the Duncans as he had, even if it was a small town. But he couldn't trust to luck, not with something this important at stake. He had to use his wits and his brains. And he needed to think of something fast, some reason for being here, for no doubt at dinner there would be questions flowing his way.

His hosts ushered him into the mansion through huge oaken doors, which were easily twice his height and seemed as thick as his head. *I'd better not have to make any quick escapes,* he thought wryly.

The larcenous side of Logan's nature could hardly help noting the finery that greeted him as he stepped across the threshold. Some of the pieces in the entryway had to be nearly as old as the house itself. That hall tree, for example, if it was authentic, might be worth a thousand pounds. And nestled on a shelf in the middle of the ornate antique piece stood a gilt-edged vase—he couldn't even venture a guess as to its probable value. Then there was the artwork. While they passed down a long corridor, he glanced into several rooms to his right and left. In one his eyes focused on a magnificent portrait of a highland chieftain that reflected a distinct Raeburn touch. Logan had a passing knowledge of art, for in his line of work one usually managed to acquire at least a cursory knowledge in a wide variety of potentially useful fields. If that painting was an original . . .

He did note, however, from the very moment he entered the place, that it was not opulent in its display of finery. Now that he looked around further, in fact, everything was quite simple. And that very simplicity convinced him that what he did see could be nothing but the real thing. The place had no hint of anything fake about it. And these people must be the real thing, too. People didn't have to flaunt their wealth or position when the blue of their blood ran as deeply as the Duncans'.

From the corridor they stepped into a large parlor, and all at once it seemed to Logan that they had stepped again back into the twentieth century. The room was furnished with several low comfortable sofas, three rocking chairs, a couple of slender-legged tables, and three electric lamps in two of the corners and against a third wall. Magazines and newspapers were strewn about, and a large console radio stood along the adjacent wall. This was clearly where the family spent a great deal of time. A roaring fire blazed in a huge hearth that occupied nearly the entire far wall.

"Some digs," said Logan with a low whistle.

"Please make yourself comfortable, Mr. Macintyre," said Allison. "I'll go and find my parents." Then turning to Nat, she added in what the young boy thought was a snooty tone, "Nat, you go tell Claire we'll have a guest for dinner."

None too pleased at having to leave Logan, whom he considered his own personal discovery, and even less pleased at being ordered about by his big sister, Nat nevertheless complied. Then Allison followed him from the room.

After the departure of the young people, Logan found it extremely difficult to make himself comfortable as Allison had encouraged him to do. He was not quite ready to spend an extended amount of time alone with this intimidating lady, despite the fact that it was she he had come to Port Strathy to find. He would no doubt be able to like her; she seemed pleasant enough. But her effect on him thus far had been disconcerting and he could not help being—he hated to admit this—just a little afraid of her.

Had he been alone and at liberty to do so, he would probably have laughed outright at the very suggestion of such a thing. Why . . . she was just a frail old lady, after all! There could not be a sinister fiber in her entire being. On the contrary, she struck him as thoroughly kind, gentle, and compassionate. He had no doubt imagined the whole thing—probably a hangover from his seasickness! Had he given the matter deeper consideration, he might have discovered that it was these very qualities of virtue which caused his inner self to squirm. But Logan did not consider such things deeply, least of all introspective matters to do with his own emotions. Instead, he strolled toward the hearth and pretended to be engrossed in the procedure of warming his hands.

"For all her grandeur," the voice he had been hoping not to hear said, "we do have a time keeping this old place warm."

"I can imagine," replied Logan, hoping the conversation would drift to topics no more threatening than the weather. "Installing central heating would be rather a difficult task."

"We have done so in the sleeping quarters," she said. "It would have been too hard on the children without it. I don't know how I survived it as a child."

"Then you've been here all your life?" He knew he might regret this line of questioning, but he couldn't help himself.

"Not exactly. I had a sojourn in America. A rather long sojourn, actually. But I shan't easily forget my childhood here."

"You sound as if you love the old place."

Lady Margaret laughed a bright, merry laugh. The tones were almost musical, and obliterated all sense of her great age in a single instant.

"The love of Stonewycke is rather a family inheritance," she said, in the same melodic voice, which sounded cheery and youthful. "You've heard of some families which inherit a family curse? Well, we Stonewycke women pass along a deep regard for this home, this estate, these people, and this land. At least—" she paused momentarily, and the hint of a cloud passed rapidly across her brow as Allison's face suddenly came into her mind. She left the sentence unfinished, glanced up at Logan, smiled, and just as quickly the momentary shadow disappeared and she resumed. "It runs in the blood, like genes and chromosomes and personality traits. But do forgive me; I laughed only because your comment struck me as so understated."

"I suppose having a place where you belong is pretty important," offered Logan, suddenly feeling a hint of the discomfort returning.

"Yes it is. But in all the places I've been, sometimes almost beyond memory of this, where my sense of belonging began, I've learned over the years that there is something even more important . . ."

She paused thoughtfully, then walked toward one of the rocking chairs and sat down, rocking gently back and forth as she continued to speak. "And where might be such a place for you, Mr. Macintyre—if it's not too forward of me to ask?"

He didn't mind her asking. What he minded was the feeling that she must certainly already know the answer.

"I should have said," he replied, "that belonging must be important to *some* people. In my case, I prefer to keep my options open, so I'm free to move about. I suppose I haven't found a place where I *want* to belong yet."

"I detect a Glasgow ring to your accent, and even, strange as it may seem, a bit of cockney."

This lady doesn't miss much, thought Logan. She'd make an *honest* fellow nervous. He was going to have to be *very* careful.

"Born in Glasgow," he answered. "Been in London the last seven years."

"But still no roots?"

"I've plenty of time."

"Yes . . . I suppose you do," she answered thoughtfully. Had she felt a little freer with their new acquaintance, she might have added, "But time, Mr. Macintyre, is a fickle commodity. It can deepen the hurts, or it can heal them, depending on what you do with it." As it was she said nothing.

The tone of her words disturbed Logan, but he was saved from having to ponder it further by the arrival of Allison. At her side was a lovely woman whom Logan immediately took for her mother. She was three inches taller than Allison, slim of figure, and carried herself in a manner worthy of her station. Her auburn hair, streaked lightly with gray and pulled back in a simple bun, framed a face of delicately chiseled features. Though there was a youthfulness about her, delicate crowsfeet at the corners of her eyes hinted at her forty-two years. She was dressed simply in a navy woolen skirt and pale blue sweater. Logan was again struck by the understated simplicity of this family. But Mrs. MacNeil required no ornaments to announce her breeding. It flowed unmistakably with her every move and proclaimed to anyone perceptive enough to notice it that she had been born to the grandeur of Stonewycke. Had Logan read his Glasgow newspapers more closely, of course, he would have realized that things are not always as obvious as they appear.

She stepped toward him and held out a hand, smiling, "Mr. Macintyre, I'm so pleased to meet you. Allison has told me how you helped them on the road today. It was very kind of you."

Logan stepped awkwardly forward to take her proffered hand. The American accent which spilled fluidly from her mouth came so unexpectedly that, when coupled with the easy grace of her manner, the sophistication which had seemed so refined in London among the Ludlowes and Cochrans fled him.

"I . . . well, it was no real trouble," he stammered. "I had nothing better to occupy my time."

"We'd still be stuck in Port Strathy," put in Nat, who had come back into the parlor behind his mother, "if you hadn't come along."

"Well, we couldn't have that," laughed Mrs. MacNeil. "And we are certainly happy you have accepted our hospitality."

"I'm sure the honor's entirely mine, ma'am," answered Logan, recovering his possession.

"Dinner won't be for some time," she added. "Perhaps you would enjoy having the children show you about the grounds in the meantime."

Logan replied enthusiastically to the suggestion. Allison, however, begged to be excused from the excursion.

So Nat, who could not have been more fully pleased with the turn of events, led their guest back outside. Breathing in a great draught of the country air, Logan disguised his sigh of relief as a delight for the out-of-doors. More relieved than he would have imagined for the respite from the conversation, he decided this would be the perfect opportunity to question the youth away from the scrutiny of the adults. Thus he could better prepare himself for the more formidable assault of the masters of Stonewycke.

18 Disclosures

Allison scrubbed her face until it shone.

Of course all the while she told herself that it actually *needed* scrubbing and that her great-grandmother would not have approved of her coming to dinner, especially in the presence of a guest, with a dirty face and dressed in worn denim. In no way, she tried to convince herself, did her present actions have anything to do with the guest in particular.

But it wasn't every day a handsome young man ventured to set foot in Port Strathy, even if he was arrogant and treated her like a child. Although she had to admit that was partly her own fault, for she hadn't exactly presented her best side today, what with grime on her face and dressed in old clothes.

She'd make up for it at dinner. She'd make certain he wouldn't be able to neglect her. *I wonder how long he's staying?* she thought. *And what could have brought him to Strathy?* He had been rather vague about it. She laid down her washcloth and tapped her lips thoughtfully as she tried to place his name. There were the banking Macintyres down in Edinburgh. They were quite wealthy and had weathered the banking problems in '29 better than most. They'd had a daughter in one of the schools she had attended. A year behind her, as she recalled. She wished now she'd been friendlier with her.

Yes, that must be it. He had something of the look of a financier, although she could hardly picture his youthful face in a pinstripe suit and vest sitting behind a desk. The thought brought a laugh to her lips. But he did carry himself with the refinement of someone with breeding. There was a certain worldliness about him too, and she liked that. Of course it made his condescension toward her all the more grating.

Well, she would command his interest tonight, and it would be no child that he saw.

She looked fully into the mirror on her wall, turning her head back and forth to gain her best advantage. She did not have to lie to herself when she concluded that the face which met her gaze was a pretty one. Picking up her brush, she began to arrange the silky golden waves that fell to her mid-back. She twisted and turned her hair in many styles and shapes, some absolutely goulish, some rather alluring. In the end she left it to hang in its most natural manner, which was becoming in its own way. But she did wish she could do something about the paleness of her skin. Next year—she didn't care what her mother said!—she was going to wear lipstick.

She pulled open the vanity drawer where she had secretly laid a tube of pale pink, called "passion flower." They might not even notice if she wore some tonight. And even if they did, they would never embarrass her in front of a guest. And later ... they could do what they chose.

Slowly she lifted off the cap, and with the painstaking effort of inexperienced and nervous fingers, attempted to dab the color onto her lips.

Leaning back, she surveyed the effect. *Hmmm ... not bad at all,* she thought. She pinched her cheeks till they matched the color on her lips. Too bad she was cursed with that infernal Duncan pale skin! A hundred years earlier it might have been in vogue. But modern women preferred to glow with health and vitality. They were not frail and helpless as were their predecessors. *Today's women,* thought Allison, *are capable and independent, able to stand on their own two feet.*

Allison thought she carried the effect off rather well, and if she lied about anything as she completed her toilette, it was the worldly maturity of the girl seated at the vanity. No amount of lipstick or verbal prattle about self-sufficiency could hide the lingering child within seventeen-year-old Allison MacNeil. As the eldest of the family, a great deal of maturity had been expected of her, and she had grown to expect it even more so from herself. She refused to be less than the adult woman she hoped to become, and if childish insecurity tried occasionally to surface, she repressed it beneath a veneer of grown-up hauteur. The facade, however, was only skin-deep, though she protected it well—protected it especially against the comparisons with the two women who had raised her in the Duncan heritage. At such distinctions she steadfastly refused to look. The time of her unmasking had not yet come.

The selection of a dress proved to be more difficult than the choice of hairdo. She pulled open her wardrobe door and began sorting through the clothes hanging before her. The white eyelet was too frilly, the navy organdy too grim, the tartan too ... well, too gauche.

Allison walked over to her bed and flopped down upon it. Even if he *was* one of the banking Macintyres, he could hardly be worth all this trouble!

Then sighing, she rose, and once again lifted her eyes to survey the wardrobe. At length she settled on the pink and white floral cotton with its A-line skirt and flared elbow-length sleeves. Her father had once commented on how grown-up she looked in it. His opinion on most things mattered next to nothing to her, but on this particular occasion she hoped maybe he was right. It was a calculated risk she was willing to take.

After slipping the dress on her trim figure, she decided the choice had been a good one. She walked to the door, refraining purposely from taking one final satisfied look in the mirror. She opened the door, then hesitated and turned back into the room for that one last look.

She looked pretty, indeed. This Logan Macintyre would take notice tonight!

She descended the main stairway as gracefully as each of the Duncan women had before her. But when she passed the portrait of Lady Atlanta Duncan that hung on the wall where the staircase curved around, Allison's step faltered momentarily. The austere face, looking as if it had been chiseled in white marble, seemed to stare down upon her in mockery. "How do *you*," she seemed to be saying, in that proud, restrained voice she knew her great-great-grandmother must have had, "presume to carry the mantle of your Duncan heritage?"

Allison puckered her mouth stubbornly at her fancy, hitched her shoulders as straight and tall as her regal ancestor's, and proceeded on her way, giving a defiant backward glance at the portrait.

———

A pleasant fragrance, emanating from several bowls of flowers, filled the dining room. Logan wondered if they always ate this way, or if today marked some special occasion. Surely the finery had not all been laid out for the benefit of a guest they had just picked up on the road and invited home for dinner. Sterling, crystal, expensive china, and fine linen all graced the long flower-bedecked table. It was quite a spread, indeed.

Seeming to anticipate his silent question from his puzzled gaze, Mrs. MacNeil spoke. "Perhaps you would have preferred eating in the kitchen," she said. "We usually do, to be quite truthful. But we so seldom have guests to entertain that before we knew it . . . well— we had the dining room all opened and dressed."

Logan commented that he'd enjoy himself regardless, but asked them to forgive him if he chanced to pick up the wrong fork. While his hostess chuckled over his pleasant-natured humor, the rest of the family began to enter. Lady Margaret appeared on the arm of an elderly gentleman whom Logan took for her husband, Lord Theodore Duncan. Logan recalled having read that he had recently inherited the family title, Earl of Landsbury, from an older brother who had died. He noted that though the white-haired old man carried himself with dignity, there was a marked self-effacing humility about him. When Logan referred to him as "Your Lordship," he had demurred, almost bashfully, saying something about how meaningless such titles could be at times. And indeed, everyone but his wife referred to him simply as *Grandpa Dorey,* and thus Logan settled on "Sir" as the safest appellation.

Lord Duncan sat at the head of the table, and Lady Margaret at the opposite end. Logan sat to Lady Margaret's right, and Mrs. MacNeil and her eldest daughter flanked him. He did not fail to observe the change in Allison. *She'd be quite attractive,* he thought, *if it wasn't for that smug self-centered manner of hers.* Across the table sat Nat and a younger sister, Margaret, whom all simply called May. A vivacious ten-year-old, she looked more like her mother and great-grandmother, despite her age and dark curls, than either of the other offspring Logan had yet met. She had apparently been very aptly named. Next to May sat an empty chair.

For some time Logan was spared the grilling he had feared by the constant jabbering of little May. There was no end of information which poured forth concerning neighbors, house pets, events at school, and a hundred other trivialities. The two older people, especially Lord Duncan, encouraged her along, and laughed merrily over her endless anecdotes.

About fifteen minutes into the meal, they were interrupted as a man poked his head into the room.

"The Johnsons' mare had a lovely filly," he announced as he entered and walked toward the table. From his coarse dress, tousled pale hair, and sweat-streaked face, Logan assumed that he must be one of the workmen.

"Oh, can we see her, Daddy?" chimed May.

"Of course ye can, lassie," he replied. "We'll go oot t'morrow mornin'."

So, Logan mused to himself, *the elegant, highbred Mrs. NacNeil is married to a common country fellow.* The prospects for amusement here became more and more interesting by the moment. However, as he surveyed the man further, Logan concluded that he'd be best to reserve any hasty judgments regarding this powerfully built man until he was better acquainted. He could see at a glance that it would not do to cross the fellow.

"Alec," said Mrs. MacNeil, "this is our guest, Mr. Logan Macintyre. From London."

"Pleased t' make yer acquaintance, Mr. Macintyre," said Alec, approaching the table with outstretched hand. Logan stood and shook it. The big man's hand seemed to swallow his own as it wrapped around it in a firm grip, which was followed by a vigorous and friendly shake. "Ye're most welcome in oor hoose!"

Oh, Daddy, for heaven's sake! thought Allison as her father brushed past her. *Coming into the dining room smelling of the barnyard! And with a guest, too!* She tried to ignore the proceedings by directing her interest toward her plate, but Allison could hardly hide her embarrassed displeasure. Her father's country ways, untamed by position, title, modest wealth, or the fact that he lived as laird in a prestigious mansion, was a constant source of chagrin to her elevated sensibilities. *Why can't he act befitting his station,* she thought, *instead of always having to play the country bumpkin!*

"Dinner is still warm, Alec," said his wife.

"I'll be along directly," he replied.

He disappeared, only to return ten minutes later, washed, with hair combed, and dressed in corduroy trousers, an open-collared cotton shirt, and a slightly worn Eaton jacket. Even with the improvements of his attire, he hardly seemed to befit the station of a country squire.

MacNeil took the empty place which had been reserved for him. His presence at once added a distinctive energy to the atmosphere in the room, not unlike that provided by young May, but on a higher level, more substantial, the incidents related with more meaning. By his speech and mannerisms he revealed himself even more as a country-bred man than before. Yet that appeared to in no way affect the attitudes of the others toward him. They all deferred to him; even the earl spoke in a deferential manner when addressing the younger man. He was the obvious master of Stonewycke, but it was not an authority he demanded or required. It was simply there, without anyone's having thought about it, given unconsciously simply by virtue of the person he was. Logan noted, however, a considerable cooling on the part of Allison the moment her father sat down across the table from her.

This crowd is most unusual! thought Logan. *I wonder what other surprises are waiting behind these ancient stone walls.*

He had not been looking forward to the inevitable moment when he should become the central topic of conversation. But when it came it took him almost by surprise, for it came more like the whisper of a breeze than the hurricane he had expected.

The main course had been served—a steaming, juicy salmon—when Nat, no doubt feeling himself the resident expert on the stranger, opened the discussion in Logan's direction.

"Mr. Macintyre knows all about cars," he said to his father, the only one at the table not yet informed of the incident in town.

"Do ye, Mr. Macintyre," said MacNeil. "Weel, if ye intend t' stay here in Port Strathy, ye'll find nae dearth o' work in that area."

"I haven't seen many autos about," said Logan.

"There be only a handful o' autos, t' be sure," replied Alec, "but we hae oor share o' tractors, threshers, an' the like. All needin' repairin' e'en more than the auld oxen an' draught horses."

"Maybe *you're* in the wrong field," suggested Lady Margaret playfully.

MacNeil gave a great laugh.

"Hoots! I'd sooner wrestle wi' a stubborn Gallowa' or a huge Clydesdale any day than wi' one o' them mystical engines."

"You work with animals then, Mr. MacNeil?" asked Logan.

"Aye, do I! I'm a veterinarian."

"And what do you do for a living, Mr. Macintyre—that is, when you're not tinkering with autos?" It was Allison who spoke.

Fortunately for Logan he had spent the afternoon giving that very question considerable thought. For he had known it would come sooner or later, and he wanted to be ready with a well-formulated response. He may not have been eager for an inquisition with himself at the center. But at least if it came, he would be amply prepared for it.

"I'm in finance—investments, mostly," he replied. "However, at the moment I'm on an extended leave from my firm."

"Ye willna find much in that line aroun' here," said MacNeil.

"Looking for new investment opportunities?" suggested Allison, ignoring her father's comment.

"I'm really not at liberty to divulge anything," replied Logan, content to maintain the charade, but Allison thought she detected the hint of a knowing look in his eyes.

"Can't imagine what could interest anyone aroun' here whose business was bankin'," insisted Allison's father.

"But it is a lovely spot for vacationing," said Lady Margaret, entering the discussion for the first time. As she did so, her eyes drifted to Logan's. Somehow he picked up the impression that he was being rescued, spared the ordeal of answering any more uncomfortable questions.

Well, I don't need rescuing, lady, he thought stubbornly. *And I won't be intimidated either!*

Out loud he said, "I'm here neither strictly for business nor pleasure." His tone held a hint of defiance, as if he would not be daunted by their questions and would maintain a sense of his own strength of presence in spite of these very unexpected surroundings. "Mine is, you might say, an errand of . . . well, I suppose you might call it an errand of sentiment," he went on, now opening the door shrewdly in the direction of his choice, and hoping that someone would take the bait and lead him where he wanted to go. "My mother has a keen interest in our family heritage, and I am now in the process of tracing a branch of our family that seems to have led me to this area. You see, my mother is quite aged now."—he silently hoped his mother would forgive him for coloring the facts a bit, and was glad none of those present would ever have occasion to meet his mother, who could not have been a day older than Mrs. MacNeil—"and she resorts to using me as her feet, so to speak."

A butler began clearing away the dishes while a maid, who also doubled as the cook, set bowls of berries and cream at each place.

"How very fascinating!" said Mrs. MacNeil, smiling in a most mysterious way. "My own introduction to Port Strathy came as a result of a very similar purpose . . ." She glanced toward her husband with a twinkle in her eye. "However," she went on, "I got much more than I would ever have anticipated."

The whole family seemed greatly amused, and enjoyed a merry laugh over her statement. Logan stirred a lump of sugar into the coffee the maid had just poured for him. He was considering an appropriate response to Mrs. MacNeil's humorous remark, when Lady Margaret spoke.

"Please excuse us, Mr. Macintyre," she said. "We don't mean to leave you out of our family jocularity. It is a long story, though interesting. I'm sure one day any of us would be happy to relate it to you."

"I shall look forward to it," exaggerated Logan diplomatically.

"Perhaps," offered MacNeil, "we can be o' some assistance t' ye in yer quest."

"Thank you, sir, but I'm sure folks like yourselves could not have known *my* relatives," answered Logan, skillfully allowing himself to be led down the very path he had hoped to steer the conversation from the beginning.

"This is a small town," said Mrs. MacNeil, "and being in our position I daresay we know just about everyone, especially the families that have been here a long time."

"I haven't a great deal to go on," he replied unpretentiously. "There is, of course, the family name, and we have record of an uncle—a great-great-great uncle, to be exact—who may have lived in this area."

"If I may ask, Mr. Macintyre, what was the name?"

"Why certainly," replied Logan. "My mother's maiden name, the one we are in the process of tracing, is MacNab."

"MacNab . . ." repeated Lady Margaret, her interest clearly piqued. When Logan nodded, she continued in a faltering voice, obviously attempting to call up remembrances from a past that was growing all too hazy from the march of years gone by. "And this uncle of yours . . . do you know his name?"

"Why, yes," replied Logan. "It was Digory MacNab."

The words had but left his lips when he saw that Lady Margaret had turned suddenly pale.

"Grandmother, what is it?" asked Joanna, alarmed. "Alec, hand me that pitcher of water."

But before her husband could comply, Lady Margaret appeared

to regain her composure. "No, no, Joanna . . . please. I'm fine." Then turning to Logan, she smiled weakly and went on in a soft voice. "I have not heard that name in years. It rather took me by surprise."

"Who is he, Grandma?" asked May, unabashed.

But seeming to ignore the question, Lady Margaret reached across the table and grasped Logan's hand in hers.

"You are related to him . . ." she said. It was not a question, but rather a statement spoken deliberately and with a touch of wonder. "*You* are Digory's nephew!" Again the words were in the same tone, her face gazing at him as if she wanted to weep, or laugh, or gather him into her arms. After a moment, she recovered herself, released his hand, straightened herself in her chair, and smiled. "Forgive me for taking on so. But this is like meeting a ghost—a most welcome and pleasant ghost!—from the past."

"I didn't intend to shock you."

"Only a shock in a most gratifying and wonderful way," she assured.

"Then you knew him?"

"He was groom, right here at Stonewycke, when I was a girl. He made quite an impact on me."

"No!" exclaimed Logan. "Why, that's positively uncanny! I mean that I should chance upon you in town as I did, then be led to this very spot!" Logan judged it best that he verbalize the coincidence before anyone else thought of it and had their suspicions aroused.

"We dinna believe in coincidences aroun' here," said MacNeil.

His statement, unprepared as he was for it, startled Logan to such an extent that he had difficulty maintaining his own composure. It sounded almost threatening.

"What my husband means," interposed Mrs. MacNeil, "is that we believe in a Lord and God who is the great Master Planner of life. With Him there are no accidents, no events without deeper meaning, no coincidences."

So that was all he meant! Logan exhaled a sigh of relief and almost broke out laughing. For a moment he had feared they were on to him. But now, he hardly knew whether to laugh or stiffen up his defenses all the more. On top of everything else, he found he had landed in the middle of a bunch of religious zealots!

19 Conversations in the Bluster 'N Blow

In the middle of the night the weather turned stormy and violent. The winds off the North Sea pelted the coast with such force that three trees on the bluff east of town were uprooted and crashed into the sea below. By morning the sky was still so black that sunrise offered only a whimper of protest against the dark, a pathetic streak of light swallowed up in minutes by the fierce, gray, rolling clouds.

By noon Logan had had all he could take of the vacant, deathly quiet inn, and of Sandy Cobden's company. What he wouldn't have given for an evening with Skittles at some pub like Pellam's! It looked as if the weather might be trying to break up a bit, so he donned his overcoat and cap and made his escape.

He wandered over to the New Town, but the place was all but deserted. He engaged one of the innkeepers in a game of cribbage, but when Logan won two games and several shillings, the innkeeper lost interest in any further contests of luck and wit. He was heading back toward town when the storm, with redoubled force, opened up once more upon Port Strathy. In minutes Logan was drenched through to the skin. Any notions of further exploration were firmly quelled.

He opened the Bluster 'N Blow's stout door, but it was the wind which forced him inside. Cobden was busy as always, this time sweeping the floors.

"Looks as if the storm ootraced ye, Mr. Macintyre," said the innkeeper.

"There wasn't even a warning," replied Logan, then looking down at the puddle he was making on the clean floor, added, "Sorry about the floor. Looks like I've made a new mess for you." He stripped off his overcoat and jacket and cap and hung them on a rack to dry.

"Canna be helped . . . 'tis the wettest spring we've had in years."

Without missing a stroke of his perpetual labor, the innkeeper continued. "There's a good blaze in the hearth where ye can dry off."

Logan thanked Cobden and was turning gratefully toward the warmth of the fire when he heard some commotion. Someone had entered from the kitchen, and the swinging door had clattered shut behind him.

"Tabby ought t' be jist fine in a day or twa," said the newcomer.

Hearing a familiar voice, Logan turned and saw the broad hulk of Alec MacNeil, at the moment rifling through a black valise.

"Good afternoon, Mr. MacNeil," said Logan.

Alec looked up from his search with a friendly grin on his face. "Logan! Good t' see ye again!"

All over again Logan was stirred by the vibrant energy that seemed to flow from this unlikely landed gentleman. Who would possibly have guessed his position and esteem in the community from seeing him in his manure-caked rubber boots and working clothes? "Been makin' some house calls," he added before returning his attention to his valise. "Ah, here we be!" He held up a small pill box. "She should be better afore ye finish these, Sandy. But use them all onyway." He gave the box to the innkeeper.

"Thank ye kindly, Alec," said Cobden. "I hate t' admit it, but auld Tabby's been a right fair companion since the missus passed on." He set his broom against a wall and wiped his hands on his dingy apron. "Let me fix ye gents a pot o' tea ... or a hot toddy, if ye'd rather?"

"Tea would be wonderful, thank ye, Sandy," said Alec. "I dinna like the idea o' goin' back oot in that storm. Ye'll join me, willna ye, Logan?"

They found seats as near the fire as possible. "That is," said Alec with a touch of jovial gruffness, "I'll let ye join me if ye'll leave off the *Mr. MacNeil* wi' me. Everyone in the toon calls me Alec, an' I'd be pleased t' have ye do the same!"

Logan smiled his assent and sat down opposite his unlikely companion. They exchanged conversation as Cobden served them their tea and then retreated to his labors. Logan meanwhile tried to fathom this Alec MacNeil, Doctor of Veterinary Medicine. It had come out in the conversation the previous evening that his father had been a fisherman; yet here was Alec, as he insisted on being called, married into one of Scotland's ancient titled families. Logan had known men in similar positions, common men who had married money and position. Though they lived well and were able to draw upon certain advantages as a result of their appropriated position, there yet remained a sense in which they maintained a subordinate place in the scheme of things, especially in the eyes of their peers. Logan had never met such a man he did not disdain; it seemed as if they had forfeited the pride of their manhood for wealth.

But Alec MacNeil fit no such pattern. What had seemed obvious around the dinner table—the deference of his family toward the authority of his character—was no less apparent here with Cobden, who, though their exchange was as of equals, nevertheless treated Alec with a visible respect. MacNeil had relinquished nothing of his manhood in his marriage, and instead seemed to command the totality of the Stonewycke prestige and whatever else may have gone along with it.

"That auld Austin's been runnin' like a top since ye tinkered wi' her, Logan," said Alec, taking a gulp of his steaming tea.

"Glad to hear it. But you've got to watch that magneto and especially keep the spark plugs clean. Otherwise it won't crank."

Alec held up his hand and laughed good-naturedly. "I'm afraid I dinna ken one end o' an engine from the other. But I'll pass yer instructions on t' Nathaniel—he's likely goin' t' be the mechanic o' the family."

"He did seem to have a knack for it." Logan cupped his cold hands around his steaming cup and drank deeply. "I offered to give him some pointers," he added, "and the offer still stands whenever he's free."

"That's kind o' ye," replied Alec. "So ye think ye may bide a wee wi' us here?"

"I'd like to learn more about my uncle Digory and the place where he spent his life. Possibly I might be able to meet one or two old-timers who knew him."

" 'Tisna many yoong folks these days who hae such an interest in their family histories."

"I'm doing this for my mother," stated Logan. "But I have to confess that since I've discovered who Uncle Digory was, I am growing more and more intrigued with him."

"He seemed rather a simple man, from what little I've heard," commented Alec.

"Perhaps that's the very thing that interests me. There must be more under the surface, and I wouldn't want to miss it."

"Could be. It'd be Lady Margaret who'd help ye best. We'd all be pleased fer ye t' take up her invitation to speak with her further on the subject. I suppose she was too tired last night t' help ye much."

"I don't want to put a strain on her."

Silently Logan wondered if it indeed had been fatigue which had restrained her conversation last night at dinner. At times she could be most ebullient, then suddenly would draw back as if the conversation had approached shaky ground. Once he had asked an innocuous question about her parents. All at once the tables were reversed and it was as if she were being discomforted by him. Her eyes darkened for a flickering instant, a look had passed over her face which he couldn't identify, and then just as quickly she had laughed lightly and said there must be more interesting topics to discuss. The conversation had then moved into a different track, but before he left she had promised him another interview regarding Digory. He knew it would have been unwise to press further just then. Whether he was anticipating seeing her again with fear or with eagerness, Logan couldn't really tell. It all would depend on which aspects of her mysterious nature presented themselves to him.

"Oh, she's hale an' hearty enough," Alec was saying. "But at that age, I suppose some days are jist better than others."

At that moment the door opened and a new face entered the room. Logan, seated facing the door, saw her first. She was a tall woman, and though not exactly fat, bore a muscular frame uncommon in women. Her storm-tousled thick brown hair, streaked with gray, framed a hard-working but not entirely unattractive face. She had a healthy glow about her and a certain liveliness in her sea-blue eyes that made it difficult to fix her exact age, though it was nearer forty than fifty. She was dressed in worn dungarees with wide navy suspenders hitched up over a chambray work shirt. She had already hung a heavy red-and-black checkered coat and battered wide-brimmed hat on Sandy's coat rack. In her arms she carried a sleek, silky-coated Irish setter.

146

"There ye are, Alec MacNeil!" she said in a voice as husky as her physique.

"Why, Jesse . . . hello!" exclaimed Alec, turning. "What have we here?" He had risen and was now giving the dog a friendly pat. The animal gave a pathetic wag of her tail. Then first Logan noticed a thick rag wrapped around her forepaw.

"Luckie got tore up pretty bad," replied Jesse. "I saw yer car parked oot front an' thought I might save a trip up t' yer surgery."

Alec took the setter called Luckie into his arms and carried her over to the rug in front of the hearth. Logan watched closely as the doctor cleaned the wound, all the while speaking in soothing tones to the animal. Luckie did not protest, hardly whimpering at what must have been a painful process. It seemed that Alec MacNeil's uncanny charisma extended even to the animals of Port Strathy.

The woman apparently noticed Logan's rapt interest in the process and sidled toward his table. In hushed tones, as if she did not want to disturb a master at work, she said, "Wouldn't trust my Luckie t' no one else."

"He appears to know what he's doing," commented Logan, following her example and speaking in a subdued voice.

"Mind if I take a load off?" she said, and without waiting for a reply, plopped rather ungracefully onto the bench opposite Logan. "Ye're new here, aren't ye?"

"Yes. Came yesterday. The name's Logan Macintyre." He held a hand out to the woman.

"Jesse Cameron here," she replied, grasping his hand firmly and shaking it vigorously. She then proceeded to fill Alec's abandoned cup with hot tea, taking a long, satisfied swig. "Ah! That warms the body good! 'Tis a muckel storm oot there! Nae doobt the mercury's dropped twenty degrees since yesterday." She took another drink of Alec's tea. "We may as weel scrap the season completely. I doobt it'll let up fer days."

"Bad for the crops, is it?" offered Logan, feeling bound to hold up the other end of the conversation, though he had the distinct impression that she would do just fine without him.

"Crops!" she rejoined, as if the word were an insult. "Rain in spring doesna bother the farmers! 'Tis the draughts in August that sen's them t' an early grave. Oh, a flood might slow things up a mite.

But as far's the weather goes, the farmers haena a thing t' worry aboot. But a fisher! The slightest ruffle on the deep blue surface o' life, is enough t' louse things up fer him fer weeks!"

"You're a fisher . . . ah, fisherwoman?"

"That surprises ye? Ye canna hide't from me, young man! But 'tisna so odd as ye may think. Womenfolk aroun' here are as hearty as their men, ye ken." Her tone contained no defensiveness, but she spoke firmly, as if she had made the statement so many times it had become a fact from mere repetition at the mouth of Port Strathy's resident thick-skinned and opinionated expert on women's rights. "Women hae always worked alongside their men aroun' here. The fact that my man's dead an' gone doesna mean I should let the best trawler in Strathy go."

"By no means! I agree completely," said Logan. This was quite some woman, he had to admit. "I meant no offense."

"O' course ye didna, lad," she answered without guile or sarcasm. "There's many strangers, city folk mostly, who might. Lord knows, I've had my troubles, companies in Aberdeen no wantin' t' contract oot t' a woman. Had t' prove mysel' o'er an' o'er."

"I understand. It must be difficult," said Logan. "My mother supported my family since I was a child, so I know what you mean." Actually, it was only at that very moment that Logan had ever given so much as a thought to what his mother had been through all those years. But he'd make up for it when he found old Digory's treasure, he told himself.

"I'm no complainin', mind ye," Jesse went on. "An' I've done right weel. 'Course e'erybody's havin' a struggle these days. An' these storms dinna help neither."

By now Alec had rejoined the two. " 'Tis a muckle storm, Jesse!" he said. "I hope no one was oot when't struck?"

"The only casualty I know o' is poor Luckie there," replied Jesse. "E'erybody's been more fearsome careful since the schooner cracked up. We were o'er haulin' some equipment—'bout the only thing ye can do in the rain—when a hook flew back an' grabbed hold o' auld Luckie."

"You take your dog onboard your boat?" asked Logan.

"Ye heard o' sea-farin' cats, haena ye? Well, we hae oorsel's a sea dog. Couldna keep her off, if the truth be known!"

"Weel," put in Alec, "this storm may be a blessin' fer Luckie. 'Tis best she stays in fer a day or twa. She lost some blood, so keep her warm. I'll send doon some powders tomorrow fer ye t' put on the wound. I sewed it up with some stitches I had in my bag. I think it'll do fer her. Bring her aroun' t' the hoose in aboot a week so I can remove them."

"Thank ye kindly, Alec. I dinna ken what I'd do wi'oot Luckie."

She slid her frame off the bench, gathered Luckie into her arms and made ready to leave. She paused at the door. "Will we be seein' more o' ye, Logan?" she asked across the room. But then, as was her custom, she waited for no reply, and continued, "If ye're o' a mind t' bide a wee in Strathy, come doon t' the harbor an' I'll show ye hoo a real fishin' boat is run."

Logan laughed and said he'd be sure to look her up.

When Jesse Cameron and Luckie had gone, Alec turned to Logan and said. "That is a remarkable woman. Lost her husban' t' the sea ten years ago. She refused t' give up everythin' they had worked an' died fer, so she took it o'er. Operates two trawlers noo an' pulls a man's weight in a man's business, so they say of her doon in the New Town. Each an' every person in Strathy hae nothin' but respect fer her. But when she first started, none o' the men fer miles wanted t' work fer a woman. There was no blamin' them, I suppose—'tis a dangerous business, fightin' the sea. But she's made't work an' is noo one o' the most successful fishers—man or woman—in all o' this part o' the coastline."

"How'd she get on her feet if no one would work for her?"

"She's tenacious," answered Alec. "At first she went oot by hersel', an' all the others thought she had gone crazy o'er the death o' her man. But she was determined not t' lose the business. When they saw what she was doin', one or two that needed the work took a chance wi' her. An' noo, when they're oot on the sea, they hardly know she's a woman. One thing she is, she's the boss! An' she runs her boats like any tough man'd have t'. She takes nothin' from no one. Ye ought t' take her up on her offer—ye'd find it a grand learnin' experience. I went oot on the sea one night wi' her. I'll never forget it as long's I live."

Alec drained the tea which Jesse had left behind, and then rose.

"Weel, rain or no, I best be gettin' back t' my work. Was nice t' visit wi' ye, Logan."

Logan rose and shook his hand.

"An' dinna ye forget," said Alec, tossing the words over his shoulder as he exited, "ye're welcome at the hoose any time!"

Logan leaned back against the hard support of the wooden bench. No, he would hardly forget that invitation. But he'd have to be judicious in his steps so as not to appear over-anxious. He had to contrive some way to make frequent comings and goings to and from Stonewycke seem quite natural. As intimidating as she might be, he had to get close to Lady Margaret. And he was certain he'd be able to handle her once he had his bearings a little more solid. He'd been in tighter jams. Her penetrating eyes were no match for Chase Morgan's thugs, and he'd outwitted them.

Yes, he thought, the old lady was the key. She had known Digory. If there were clues to where the old boy had hidden whatever treasure he'd been talking about, she would be the one to put him on the right track. Somehow those clues were locked in Lady Margaret's head, though she might not even realize it—especially if she'd never received any communication from old Uncle Digory. He first had to find out if any other letter had been sent. If not, then the clues he sought might lie in some altogether obscure thing the old boy had said to her, or in a place they may have gone together. Though the treasure may be hidden, he was certain it was still here. He could feel it!

Too bad she wasn't younger; he could charm the answers from her. As it was he'd have to use some finesse to entice her to open up to him. He had already noticed that there were some areas of her youth at Stonewycke she was reticent to speak of—but those might be the very things he needed to know about.

Well, he did have time. But he would like to find the loot while he was young enough to enjoy it.

20 On the Sea with Jesse Cameron

By Friday it had rained almost solidly for two days. It wasn't the rain so much as the fact that he had lost all his cash in a card game on the first evening that caused the time to drag slowly for Logan. There was nothing to do, and the rain forbade any casual exploration. The weather notwithstanding, he had toyed with the notion of a walk up the hill to Stonewycke. But he ruled out the idea on the grounds that a man doesn't brave a severe storm merely to enjoy casual conversation about a virtually unknown relative who has been dead some sixty-odd years.

Around midmorning, however, the clouds began to break up. Logan hurriedly finished his breakfast, grabbed his coat, and headed outdoors. That afternoon, if the weather held, he would walk up to Stonewycke. He'd simply excuse himself on the basis of needing to stretch his legs after the storm had forced him indoors for so long—a perfectly acceptable excuse. And he would time his visit so that he might be able to wheedle a dinner invitation in the process.

Until then, and with his encounter with Jesse Cameron in the back of his mind, he wandered down toward the harbor. Some thirty or forty boats, ranging from six-foot dories to hundred-foot vessels, were tied up to the docks, gently rocking up and down in the decreasing swell. Apparently he had not been the only one to notice the changes overhead, for the whole place was a bustle of activity, the fishing community apparently determined not to let this lull pass them by and go to waste. Shouts from dozens of fishermen, the clatter of gear being hauled aboard the boats, and the purring from some and the sputtering from other engines warming up filled the salty air. A few of the sailors who had been involved in the card game shouted friendly greetings to him. They had every reason to be friendly, thought Logan; they had each profited greatly from his foolishness. He would not underestimate their acumen at cards the next time.

Just then a more feminine call, though by no means softer, rose above the others.

"Weel, Logan!" called out Jesse Cameron. "So ye decided t' give us a look. Welcome t' ye!"

"Thank you," replied Logan. "Trying to squeeze in some fishing between storms?"

"We got t' make a run when we can," she replied. "But they say it may hold fer a day or twa."

Jesse was perched aft near the wheelhouse of a 50-foot double-ended craft called the *Little Stevie*. She momentarily turned from Logan and shouted to a crewman who was bent forward, with a frustrated scowl on his lined and weathered face, over the winch.

"Hoo's it goin', Buckie?" she called. "We dinna want t' be the last ones oot."

"I got it," he drawled uncertainly. "But I dinna ken if it'll hold wi' the weight o' the fish."

"You're about to be taking off?" interjected Logan.

"Aye, that we are!" answered Jesse. "We got t' take advantage o' e'ery minute possible." Then swinging back toward Buckie, she said, "I'll do it. Let's get underway."

Suddenly there was a flurry of activity as the crew of three sprang into action. "Hurry up, yoong fella!" Jesse called to Logan.

"What?" replied Logan, puzzled.

"Ye're comin' wi' us, arena ye?"

"I . . . I don't—"

" 'Tis what ye're here fer, ain't it?"

"I hadn't really intended—" began Logan, feeling very uncharacteristically like a tenderfoot whelp.

"Come along!" Jesse interrupted, and reaching out a sturdy arm, hauled Logan aboard the *Little Stevie* before he had a chance to object. Logan looked about him, feeling altogether useless and out of his element—and not enjoying the sensation. Even Luckie, favoring her injured foot but otherwise appearing none the worse for the wear, was scurrying about as if she were an invaluable member of the crew.

Jesse quickly took up her position in the wheelhouse, Buckie cast off the remaining lines, and Jesse began maneuvering the boat out of the narrow mouth of Port Strathy's harbor. Logan braced his body against the starboard rail; he hoped he had not let himself in for more than a day at sea; he had heard of these boats spending days, even weeks, on the water before returning. But never one to brood over the lot life might cast him, if he was going to sea, he would enjoy himself.

The sharp, pungent sea air proved invigorating, as if it could scrape clean the cloudy residue of a spotted city life. The sight of the great wave of fishing boats was moving indeed. Within twenty minutes they had broken free of the neck of the harbor and found themselves surrounded only by the white-capped azure sea below, and above, a blue sky, marked heavily with white and gray clouds which still seemed uncertain about their future. With the wind tossing his hair and beating against his face, Logan found that he could appreciate just such an outdoor life, however alien it was to him. There was the same freedom and challenge here that he relished on the streets of London.

He turned and watched Jesse through the window of the wheelhouse. Yes, he could see it in her eyes, that same flash of enthusiasm which he'd seen pass through old Skittles' eyes as they embarked on their con in Pellam's. It was a thirst for adventure, the love of the chase, the pursuit of the quarry with nothing to rely on but daring, wit, and skill.

Yes, he and Jesse Cameron could hardly appear more dissimilar on the surface. Yet down inside, they were the same. Her life was spent chasing the fish, and fighting against those who would take her self-respect and personhood from her because she was a woman. He, on the other hand, sought more elusive prey. But they were each driven in the same way, though perhaps toward different ends.

His thoughts were shattered as the mistress of the vessel shouted out several more orders. He could feel the excitement even in her voice. He could almost imagine that she was old Skits, setting up a con to lure the fish into their nets. In another couple of minutes Buckie replaced her at the wheel and she joined Logan where he stood.

"Ye're a city fella, ain't ye?" she asked.

Logan nodded.

"Weel, ye look as though ye can take the water. There canna be another life like it!"

"I half believe you," replied Logan, laughing.

"Ye'll be a believer by the time we dock this evenin'."

"We'll be out only a day?"

"Aye. We're only rigged fer a short haul. What do ye ken aboot boats?"

"Very little," said Logan. "I have gathered that this is a *fishing* vessel, however," he added with a grin.

Jesse let forth a great, booming laugh, as hearty and invigorating as the crisp air. "Ye're a good sport, mate!" she said.

"What kind of fish are we after?"

"We'll take what we can get," replied Jesse. "After a storm like this, wha knows what'll blow oor way. The *Little Stevie* is a drifter, an' we used t' gill net the herrin' wi' her. But I converted her into a side-trawler so we can fish fer cod or haddock in the spring."

"What's the difference?"

"Doon in Aberdeen they're findin' trawlin' t' be more productive. I'm thinkin' that after twa centuries or so, the herrin's gettin' wise. Some folks'll keep gill nettin' till they drop. But I've always kept my eyes open t' new advances." She paused and rubbed her hands together. "Come on in oot o' the wind fer a spell, an' I'll pour ye a cup o' hot coffee."

They went into the wheelhouse where a wooden bench large enough to seat two or three was strung against the aft wall. Jesse found a large thermal flask and poured out three tin cups of steaming brew.

"I drink coffee at sea," she said, handing one of the cups to Buckie at the wheel and the other to Logan. "These flasks are handy inventions, but they jist dinna do justice t' tea. I'll brew ye a proper pot o' tea after we cast the net, if there be time." She took a large gulp from her cup, apparently impervious to the burning of the liquid. Logan felt rather dainty by comparison as he cautiously sipped at his.

"I'm curious," he said at length. "Most boats seem to have feminine names. How did yours come by such an unusual epithet?"

A soft smile enveloped Jesse's lined mouth as a tender look filled her eyes. Logan would have thought from her expression that they were sailing on a glassy sea under a warm summer's sun. And perhaps it was just such a day that now filled her memory. "My husband closed the deal on this boat the day after oor son was born. So we, o' course, named it 'Little Stevie' after the boy."

"And your husband was *big* Stevie?"

" 'Twas the boy's grandfather ... my own father, Stevie Mackinaw." She said the name almost dreamily, and with a touch of sorrow.

"Have you been in fishing all your life?"

"Oh no," laughed Jesse. "I'm new at it compared t' most o' the folks ye find hereaboot. My daddy came from a long line o' crofters. They were tenants right on the Stonewycke lands fer generations. They herded sheep an' scratched oot a few bushels o' oats a year on the poorest piece o' moorlan' ye could imagine. Hoo they did I'll ne'er ken. Finally when my daddy was but a lad an' orphaned at that, the laird turned him oot."

"Just like that? After generations?"

"Wasna a crueler, more arrogant man than James Duncan, the laird then. Figured he couldna turn a profit w' jist a lad workin' the land—an' wha kens but maybe he was right. It might hae killed my daddy had he kept workin' that rocky groun'. As it was he wandered aboot, homeless an' penniless, an' near t' starvin' 'cause he was too prood t' take handoots. Finally, na that lang after James Duncan died, the Lady Atlanta found oot what had happened, an' gave my daddy a small piece o' land o'erlooking the coast, atween Strathy Summit an' the toon."

"These are the same Duncans that inhabit the estate now?" asked Logan innocently.

"Aye. But they're a different breed, these are." Jesse refilled the tin cups, then handed the flask to one of the other hands out on deck. Coming back inside she took up the end of the conversation where she had left off. "They love the land as much as the rest o' us. An' Lady Margaret always did care. Somethin' different aboot that lady. Why, my daddy used t' say that when he was a lad—"

"He knew Lady Margaret back then?" Logan nearly spilled his coffee, but struggled to keep up the nonchalance of his exterior.

"Only as weel's a crofter could know the daughter o' the laird. There werena all the mixin' then like ye see nowadays. But Lady Margaret took a special likin' t' my daddy's mother, an' the family in general. He always said 'twas 'cause o' her that he taught me the ways o' the Lord as he did. T' tell ye the truth, I always fancied that my daddy was a mite in love wi' Lady Margaret. I think that's why he married so late in life. But I guess fate was against him, though I'm sure the Lord's hand was in't as weel, 'cause a year after he married, his wife died havin' me. I brought him sorrow from the day I was born."

"You must be exaggerating," said Logan, intrigued.

"I ne'er took t' the land. I always sat on the cliffs an' looked oot t' sea. He shouldna hae been surprised when I married a fisherman. 'Course I was only a bairn, hardly sixteen at the time, an' it meant me leavin' home, 'cause Charlie was one o' them itinerant fishers, hirin' himsel' oot fer seasonal work. My daddy was none too happy an' I left wi'oot very frien'ly feelings atween us."

"I'm sure he's very proud of you now."

"He's been dead some four years noo," said Jesse. "Luckily we patched it up when I came back after my Charlie died—that was in 1919, after the war, ye ken. We had some good years t'gether, Daddy an' me. The Lord used the loss o' my husban' an' son t' mellow me oot some—made me learn t' appreciate all the things a yoong girl used t' scoff at."

"You don't mean you went back to a farming life like your father?"

"Na, na," replied Jesse. "I meant the things my father used t' tell me when I was yoong that I had nae use fer then. Things aboot God an' nature, aboot God's love fer His children, things we've all heard from oor mothers an' fathers, but which we pay no attention t'. Till we get older an' wiser, perhaps—an' then we start rememberin' an' seein' the truth o' it. Or until some catastrophe smacks us in the face an' makes us listen. I don't know why we willna listen till we get oorsel's int' trouble. But it took the loss o' my Charlie an' my boy t' wake me up."

"And even after what happened to them, you stayed in fishing?" asked Logan, trying to change the direction of the conversation off this uncomfortable subject.

Jesse rose and crossed the small open space of floor to the wheel where she stood next to Buckie, looking out on the vast expanse of blue all about them.

"It grows on ye, Logan," she said wistfully. Her gaze out toward the open sea, and her contented sigh said the rest.

Some time before noon the *Little Stevie* crept to a stop. Jesse told Logan they were ready to shoot the net over the side.

He found a place well out of the way, then watched as the crew expertly lowered the trawl, by means of rope suspended on gallows hitched to the starboard side of the boat. Jesse and Buckie were giving particular attention to the troublesome winch located amidship. To Logan's untrained eye everything appeared to be going smoothly, but Buckie looked none too pleased. Once again he attempted some adjustments on the winch, this time with screwdriver in hand.

When the net was finally in place, Jesse disappeared and Logan guessed by the steam emitted from the smokestack that she was firing up the engines. When she rejoined him, the *Little Stevie* was again underway, this time with one of the other crew members at the wheel.

"Noo we can relax a wee," she said. "We'll trawl fer three or so hours afore we haul in the catch. Time t' give oor attention t' the galley—I hope ye're hungry."

Logan had hardly thought about food until that moment. But with the suggestion of a meal he realized he was starving. At the same time it dawned on him that the undulating sea had in no way affected his insides as it had on the schooner. Mentally he patted himself on the back and began to wonder what fortunes a man of his unique talents might make aboard luxury ocean liners.

Jesse set a fine table, even in the cramped galley, which was located directly under the wheelhouse. Smoked fish, oatcakes, and fresh tea heated over the engine boiler, at that moment tasted as fine to Logan as any meal he had taken in London.

He liked the company too. If Jesse had an occasionally overbearing nature, her warmth and forthrightness softened any other rough edges. Perhaps she was just a coarse version of Molly Ludlowe. No doubt that was why he had in this short time felt such an attachment to her. He found himself talking to her as he would have to Molly or Skittles, and a time or two caught himself just as he was about to reveal too much of who he was and what he was about in Port Strathy.

And when he slipped back into his familiar ruse of hypocrisy, he could not keep back a surge of unfamiliar guilt, as if he were—

of all things!—actually *lying.* The experience was novel to him, and most disconcerting. But he managed to salve these pricks of conscience by telling himself that when he found Digory's treasure, he'd buy Jesse Cameron a new boat—one with a modern diesel engine and motorized winches and even radio equipment. She had talked about them, and had gone so far as to show him a picture of one she had clipped from a magazine and pinned up in the wheelhouse.

"Dinna ken what I'd do wi' a radio, though," she had laughed. "Don't know who else in the fleet'd be able t' talk t' me. Not a single one o' them has radios neither, except the *MacD*, an' he's never oot when the fish are runnin', anyway."

But Logan thought to himself, *I'll get the whole fleet radios!*

That morning he hadn't given the welfare of Port Strathy's fishing fleet a moment's thought. But now he felt oddly bound up in their well-being. Shortly, that bond was to grow yet stronger, as the invisible forces working upon the soul of young Logan Macintyre zeroed in on him ever more closely.

It came about two hours after they had eaten.

Buckie had earlier noted that the wind seemed to be picking up, though at the time all had agreed they still had time for another hour or two's trawl. And the few other boats they could see in the distance seemed to be holding. But by half past two the sky had blackened and the *Little Stevie* was riding ten-foot swells. There was nothing else to do but haul in the net and head for home. Every hand was needed by this time, as the wind now suddenly whipped up to double its force. The battle of net, fish, and human strength pitted against wind, wave, and rocking boat was a torturous and dangerous one. As Logan lent his inexperienced hands to the task, he noticed for the first time in his life how soft they were.

Halfway through the job the rain began to fall. Now the ropes became twice as difficult to handle, and the decks too slippery to get a strong foothold. To seasoned fishers, such hazards were commonplace enough, and with one's wits firmly intact, presented no obstacle which could not be dealt with. Logan, however, was hard pressed merely to remain upright, and all the more to shoulder his share of the increasingly heavy and cumbersome load.

The foul weather had one positive point, though. The fishing grounds that day had been especially fertile, and the net was bulging. Logan had taken a position near the starboard rail, holding a rope fast while two of the other men swung the net past the starboard stanchion in order to lift it in—all the while the wind swinging it murderously overhead. At the very moment when the heavy load was at its apex over the deck, the winch gave way from the weight and added tension of movement.

Suddenly the rope gripped in Logan's hand lurched forward without warning.

"Let go!"

Scarcely hearing the shout, Logan found himself yanked off his feet; even the rubber boots Jesse had fitted him with could offer no traction on the wet deck to prevent him from altogether losing his footing.

In another instant he was flying overboard, then plunged into the icy sea.

As an angry wave engulfed him and pulled him under, his first thought was that now he wouldn't be able to get Jesse a new boat. His second was the realization that he couldn't swim. And the third, following almost instantly in succession after the others as his head broke through the surface only to be overwhelmed by another wave, was that he was going to die and never see his mother again.

Again his head bobbed to the surface. Logan gulped for air, but took in little more than a mouthful of the freezing salt water. Frantically he looked around for the *Little Stevie*, but could see nothing except water and sky. He tried to yell, but only a sputtering gurgle emerged; his panic-stricken lungs were already filling with the salty water. Another huge wave crashed over him, and all went black. Floundering and flailing to reach the surface, the only sensation he could afterward recall was the sense of being pulled upon by an evil force intent upon drawing him down ... down ... down.

Gradually the will to fight slackened. He could feel the downward force tightening its grip. He began to relax. It would be so much easier to give in ... to let it have its way with him. If only he could just go to sleep ... then he could be warm again ... then he could wake up and everything would be—

Suddenly a strong pair of arms wrapped themselves around him. These were not the arms of the downward force. These arms, though he barely felt them, were strong and were pulling him up . . . up . . . out of the sea!

Within seconds after he had gone over, Jesse had a life rope around her waist and had plunged over the side after him. And though Logan's benumbed senses told him he was not being rescued because he was still surrounded by thousands of fish, in fact he now lay on the deck in the midst of the catch of the day.

He must have lost consciousness for only two or three minutes, for Jesse was still pounding his back and pumping sea water from him when he awoke. He rolled over, then coughed and gagged for a few moments, but it was some time before he could speak. When words finally came out, they were little more then a weak wheeze.

"I'm sorry," he gasped.

"Hoots!" exclaimed Jesse. " 'Tis my own\ fault. I should hae known better than t' place ye there!"

The incident had given the toughened sea woman a scare as nothing else could. It had been many years since her husband and son were lost to the sea, but she still had occasional nightmares in which she pictured them floundering helplessly in the icy North Sea waters. Her son had been but ten at the time, and he'd now be nearly Logan's age if he had lived. The thought made her shudder, and also angry with herself for not taking better care of her young guest. Thus her gruff tone contained more hidden meaning than Logan could have guessed. As Jesse looked at Logan lying before her, in her mind's eye he was her own son. And it would be a sensation she would long remember.

She and Buckie helped Logan below, where Buckie found him some blankets and dry clothes, then poured him a cup of hot tea. After changing out of her own drenched things in the wheelhouse, Jesse poked her head in to see how he was doing. He looked up over his second cup of hot tea with a solemn expression he seldom wore.

"I owe you, Jesse," he said in a tone to match his look. "I'll repay you somehow. I won't forget."

"There'll be nae talk o' repayin'," she replied crustily. "At sea everyone gives their all—that's what's expected o' us. Couldn't survive no other way." But beneath her words, the voice of Jesse Cameron betrayed that she, too, had been touched by the emotion of the incident. To save a fragile human being's life, for the fragile human animal, may be just as awesome a thing as to see your own snatched from the very door of death. In any case, neither would Jesse soon forget this day. Perhaps the heartaches of her own life had prepared her for this moment when she would become a vessel in God's hands, instigating the purifying work of redemption in the heart of this boy who could almost be her own son.

Logan watched as she poured a cup of tea, recalling what Alec had said about her. He had to agree. A remarkable woman she was, indeed.

21   Allison in New Town

Allison parked the Austin on High Street, the main thoroughfare connecting Port Strathy proper with New Town, right across from one of its two public houses. The second stood at the other end of the street. She remained in the car, hoping that somehow Mr. Macintyre would make an appearance so she would be spared having to get out and go hunting around for him.

She had been shopping in the Mercantile when her mother had called. The tractor had broken down and neither the men, Nat, nor Alec could get it operational again as they usually managed to do. And since they could afford to lose no more time with the spring planting, she asked Allison to inquire about town and try to find Mr. Macintyre. Would he be interested, she was told to ask him, in being of further service to them, at a fair wage this time?

When the call ended, Allison slammed down the receiver and stormed out of the store without a single word of explanation to Miss Sinclair. Now she was a common errand girl! She had her own plans. It was early, her mother said, and there was sufficient time for her to deliver Mr. Macintyre and still meet Sarah Bramford. But the whole thing nevertheless upset her—even if her mother did promise to call the Bramfords to inform them she would be a little late.

The only hope was that this errand might afford her an opportunity to better acquaint herself with the mysterious Logan Macintyre. Though after the revelation of his common heritage the other night, she wondered why she even wanted to bother. The great-nephew of a groom! Really, she had better prospects than that!

But there was something incongruous about him ... an intriguing side. He was no dolt, however common his heritage. He carried himself with aplomb. If she hadn't known his background, she would have been rather proud to display him to her friends. And that unique accent, with just a hint of Scots tempered with the genteel London sound—it all came off rather pleasantly.

It was irksome how he all but ignored her. The rest of the family had, of course, monopolized him shamefully. Perhaps it wasn't his fault. Who could tell but that he had been attracted to her, had even wanted to speak to her, but had been unable to in the awkward surroundings of a family dinner?

Maybe she could turn this inconvenient request of her mother's to her own advantage after all!

At the Bluster 'N Blow, however, Allison's inquiries were met with a shake of the head. "Came in last night," said Cobden, "wi'oot e'en informin' me he wasna plannin' t' be here fer dinner. Came in late, passed the time wi' the few customers I had at the time, then went t' his room, an' a few minutes later was back in new duds, an' then was gone t' the New Toon—jist like that. I dinna think he e'en came back fer the night."

"That was last night, Mr. Cobden," said Allison impatiently. "What about today?"

"I' ain't seen him since."

"He hasn't left town?"

"Na, na," the innkeeper shook his head. "His gear's all still here."

Allison waited to hear no more. Without a word of thanks, she bounded from the inn and set out for New Town, where she now sat, growing more irritable with each passing moment. After observing the deserted streets for about as long as she could stand, she was about to get out and head for one of the pubs, when the door she had been watching opened and several figures ambled out.

There could be no doubt that one was the man she sought. That checkered cap of his was pushed well back on his head and his face sported a day or two's growth of beard. His suit, which might at one time have been a fine one, was wrinkled with a long night of wear. In his mouth he sported a cigar, which he appeared to be enjoying immensely. With him were three or four locals. They were all laughing, but with their eyes squinting against the glare of the sun, looking brashly out of place on a sunny Saturday morning.

Allison stepped out of the Austin and approached waving to him. "Mr. Macintyre," she called in a tight voice, taking no pains to conceal her contempt.

Logan looked up, removed the cigar, and smiled. Well, at least there was nothing wrong with his smile, thought Allison. Why did everything else about him have to be so entirely wrong?

"Why, Miss MacNeil," he said, "this is a pleasure. What brings you out on a fine morning like this?"

She could not tell whether his joviality was from being drunk or from simple high spirits. "I was looking for you," she replied coolly.

"Ah," he intoned, with a knowing glance and a wink to one of the other men, "can I be of further assistance to your family, or to yourself perhaps?"

Before she could answer, the men with Logan began to wave and call out. At first she thought the commotion was directed at her. But to her even greater chagrin, she then realized they had hardly noticed her at all, and were instead calling to a woman crossing from the other side of the street.

"Mornin', Liz," said one of Logan's cronies.

"Hello, Jimmy . . . boys," the woman replied. As she approached and greeted them, her eyes strayed to the newcomer as she appraised him with a thoughtful smile.

It took all the self-restraint Allison could muster to keep her snort of disgust to herself. Wasn't that just like Liz Doohan, Patty's elder sister? Dressed in a simple cotton frock and maroon cloth coat that clashed dreadfully with her red hair, she looked frumpy but may have been pretty a few years earlier. But working women aged faster than most, and it hardly became her now to flirt with men right out on the street. For all her caustic notions of superiority, Allison would no doubt have been surprised to know that Liz Doohan was but twenty-six.

A lively banter had sprung up between Logan's small group and

Liz, who was now being told by Logan's shipmates of the previous day and how well their young friend from London had taken to the sea, mercifully omitting his adventure in the water. Allison's presence had been altogether forgotten.

"Am I the only one who has t' work t'day?" asked Liz with a mock pout.

"Grounded fer repairs," answered Jimmy.

"An' the weather's so cockeyed," added Buckie, "that another storm could blow in on us afore noon."

"Mr. Macintyre," interrupted Allison, approaching with a huffy gait. "If you don't mind ..."

"Oh, Miss MacNeil. What was it you were wanting?"

He may not have intended for his tone to sound condescending, but in her present mood Allison could hardly interpret it as otherwise.

"There is trouble with our tractor," she answered, rankled even further by the turn of events, "and we would like to *employ* your services." She emphasized the word so there could be no possible mistaking her own patronizing attitude.

"Glad to be of assistance," he replied good-naturedly.

"It *is* rather pressing. Do you suppose you can tear yourself away?"

He turned to his friends. "Duty calls," he said. "I'll give you a chance to get even tonight."

"Ye deserve the win," said Buckie with a laugh. "Especially after yer day yesterday."

"But we willna begrudge ye yer offer," laughed Jimmy.

"It was nice t' meet ye, Logan," purred Liz; "maybe I'll see ye aroun' again...?"

"No doubt," he answered with a noncommittal grin.

Finally, with the fishers all slapping Logan fraternally on the back as if they had known him for years, they parted company.

Allison drove Logan back to the inn for a change of clothes, saying hardly a word. She dropped him off, then returned to the Mercantile for something she had forgotten as a result of her agitated departure from the store after her mother's call. Why she was so angry she could not exactly say. Was it because he had tramped about all night in the most disreputable section of town? Or because he persisted in humoring her as if she were nothing but a child? Or was the real reason that she wanted to be noticed like he had noticed Liz Doohan? That she could never admit! Liz was . . . a *nobody*. How could he pay more attention to her than to an heiress like herself! He must be blind to the way things really were!

And I had entertained ideas of presenting him to my friends. Never! He'll have to beg first!

At the thought, a sly smile crept across Allison's lips. Perhaps that was not such a bad idea. In fact, it would be rather splendid to have that arrogant southerner groveling at her feet. Of course, she'd turn him down flat. But what a pleasure it would be!

Returning to the inn, she found Logan outside leaning casually against a post, arms folded across his chest. The manner in which he surveyed the town gave every impression that he thought he owned the place. His face was shaven and one could hardly tell he had been awake all night.

All at once Allison realized that while his self-assured, I-don't-need-anyone manner irritated her, in an odd sort of way it drew her, too. One could not help being attracted to someone so independent. Wasn't that the very thing she herself wanted to be?

Considering the matter further, she decided that after she had him begging, she might grant him the privilege of her attentions—for a while, at least. There could be nothing permanent, of course. He didn't have the blood to match her breeding.

22   The Door Is Opened

An old clunk of a tractor was a far cry from race cars or street automobiles, but Logan determined to put on a convincing show that he knew what he was about. If Skittles had taught him one thing it was that man had been given a tongue to make up for what he lacked in actual skill. Logan had bluffed his way through stickier situations than this. Only this time he had to come up with a working tractor in the end. If he could do it, he knew this would be his ticket into Stonewycke.

Allison dropped him in front of a large stone structure behind the house that she referred to as the stable. The tractor was sitting outside. Allison spun the Austin around and sped off, leaving him coughing in a cloud of dust. If the family did not fit his expectations of the occupants of Stonewycke, Allison did, for she was out of harmony with the rest of the family. In fact, she was the only one who came close to matching his expectations. She paraded her position around like she was the daughter of the king. What a contrast there was between her looks of superiority toward Jesse Cameron's crew, and the manner in which her father had received Jesse herself! Maybe Alec was still one of the townspeople at heart. But Logan could not imagine even Lady Margaret treating the common folk with such derision.

Where, then, had Allison acquired such attitudes, he wondered, if not from her own family? One thing was sure—Allison MacNeil had something to prove. But he wasn't at all sure what it was. She had everything she could possibly want. Her mother and great-grandmother were the most respected women in the community, and thus she herself would surely have been accepted with a certain sense of stature by the townsfolk. Yet she seemed to disdain it all.

Well, he concluded, *Allison may be an enigma in a family full of enigmas, but it doesn't rest on me to try to figure them all out.* He had a hidden treasure to find, and then he'd be out of this place.

Even as he was still watching the Austin speed away, Logan found himself being hailed by Fergusson Dougall, Stonewycke's factor since the passing of Walter Innes.

"Ye must be Macintyre!" said the factor, moving as hastily as he was able toward Logan where he stood puzzling over his thoughts. To have described the man's movement would have been difficult; it resembled a waddle more than a walk, for Dougall was an extremely bulky man, whose weight over the years had settled mostly into his lower regions, the end result being a most unwieldly pear-shape configuration. His round, sunburned face with sagging jowls was friendly, and his voice carried an unpretentious, almost self-effacing tone.

"That I am," replied Logan, turning and extending his hand,

which was quickly engulfed in Dougall's beefy paw.

"Weel, I'm the factor," he said, his voice almost reminiscent of an apology. "Fergusson Dougall at yer service, but everyone jist calls me Fergie, an' ye're welcome t' do the same, Mr. Macintyre."

"Thank you. And it's Logan."

"I'm obliged t' ye fer comin'," said Dougall, relieved that the tedious formalities were dispensed with and anxious to get to the business at hand. "This here's the tractor—the troublesome beast!" he began, then chuckled, producing a great jiggling effect in the regions of his stomach. "'Course I needna be tellin' *you* that!"

Logan laughed at the factor's wit, but the humor which struck him was the irony of the man's words. For in reality, Logan had never before that very moment laid eyes on a tractor in his life.

"Well, let's have a look," said Logan, then hung back a moment hoping Dougall would take the initiative and open the engine's bonnet, for he was even uncertain how to go about that most basic of operations.

Fergie did so. Logan peered inside, discovering to his great relief that he recognized most of the basic parts, though their arrangement was somewhat bewildering at first. He turned back and picked up a couple of the tools that had been laid out on the ground in preparation for the arrival of the tractor "expert."

"Does she start at all?" he asked.

"Nothin' but a cough an' a sputter."

"Hmmm," pondered Logan. "Let's hear it."

The factor moved toward the tractor but apparently had not driven it personally on many occasions. His difficulty in climbing up into the high seat would have been humorous had the sight not been sadly pathetic, and he would not have accomplished the task without a helpful boost from Logan. It took him a moment to get the cantankerous shift lever into neutral. But when he did and the attempted start was made, his description of the result could not have been more accurate. Another look at the engine made Logan wonder that the thing had ever run at all.

"I shouldna wonder if nothin' can be done wi' it," said the factor. "We always left the engine work t' Walter—in fact, he wouldna hardly let anyone else touch his engines, 'ceptin' Nat. He treated them jist like they was livin' things, like he did the horses. I know farmin', but I neither ken nor do I like these contraptions."

"The time will come, Fergie," said Logan philosophically, "when you won't be able to survive without them."

Logan proceeded to tinker with the engine until it began to make sense to him. Gradually the puzzle of its operation came clear to him, not without several more attempts at starting it. Within an hour he had located the problem, and as he had feared, a new part was going to be needed. He was determined, however, to get the engine functional. Who could tell how long it might take to get the new part, if it could be obtained at all? He didn't have that kind of time.

He therefore unbolted the carburetor, then turned to Fergie and said, "I'm pretty sure she needs a new coil. If this one's not bad already, it will be soon. So you'll need to order one wherever you get parts around here. In the meantime I'm going to try to clean up the carburetor. If the coil's got any life still left in it, that might help to get it going."

Nodding as if he understood every word, Fergie followed each move of the young man who more and more appeared to him a mechanical expert with every moment that passed.

"Where's young Nat?" asked Logan as he rummaged through the tool box sitting beside the tractor in search of a certain tool.

"He an' Alec went oot t' the field after the tractor broke doon, t' check the state o' the soil after all the rain. Be back any minute noo, I shouldna think."

Logan proceeded to do what he could to clean up the carburetor, removing accumulated grime from the tiny valves and carefully scrutinizing every inch of it. "Probably hasn't been adjusted recently," he said, more to himself than anyone else, but Fergie responded quickly.

"Adjusted?"

"These carburetors have to be adjusted almost constantly. I take it Mr. Innes didn't pass on that bit of information? Well, I'll do what I can. I think we've got the tools here to do at least a workable job. In the meantime, do you have any extra diesel?"

Dougall scurried off into the stone building and in a few moments returned carrying a small red can.

"Ah, perfect!" said Logan, opening the can and splashing a bit of the oily reddish-gold liquid onto the offending mechanism. "I think with an adjustment here and there, and with all the cracks and crevices and holes and jets cleaned out, we just *may* get this thing running again—that is *if* the coil isn't altogether gone already."

In five minutes, after several final adjustments and another thorough cleaning, Logan bent over the tractor's engine and reinstalled the carburetor into position.

"That's it, my friend!" he called out at length, giving his back a stretch but remaining in front of the engine. "Time to give the old bucket of bolts a try . . . and keep your fingers crossed!"

Summoning both his pride and all the discipline possible for his overtaxed frame, Dougall managed to scramble up onto the seat without assistance and immediately tried the starter. Logan held his breath as the engine coughed once, then again, and at last kicked into activity.

"Give it a little more throttle!" shouted Logan above the racket, reaching in to adjust the carburetor.

The factor did so.

Within thirty seconds the engine settled down and began, if not exactly to purr, at least to chug rather steadily along.

Sensing victory over the uncanny beast, the free-spirited factor gave a whoop and stood to jump out of the driver's seat. In his excitement his portly leg knocked against the gearshift lever, sending the tractor into gear and suddenly lurching forward. His corpulent bottom side came crashing back into the seat and he barely managed to keep from falling off the tractor completely. Logan, still standing directly in front of it, wrenched his body to the side only missing by inches having the runaway vehicle crush his leg under its massive wheel. As he did so he tripped over the tool box, twisting his ankle in the process. He crumpled to the ground as the tractor rumbled dangerously past.

Fergie managed to grind the lever back out of gear and slam on the worn brakes, then laboriously catapulted his bulk off the tractor—a procedure which nearly cost him more damage to his entire frame than Logan, who was still lying on the ground, had suffered.

"Oh, dear Lord!" cried the factor. In the melee, he had been slammed to his seat at the moment Logan had jumped free, and he thought he had run directly over the young man. "I've killed him!"

"I'm nowhere near dead, man," replied Logan, turning onto his side. Fergie, however, refused to be comforted and continued to loudly bemoan his stupidity.

"I'm fine, Fergie," insisted Logan, in a voice intended to sound weak but brave. "Just help me to my feet."

Fergie put his thick arm around Logan and pulled him up, but as soon as Logan reached an upright position and tried to test out his own weight, his left foot slipped under him.

"Ye've broken yer ankle!" wailed the factor. "Dinna ye move a step," he said, taking firm hold of Logan again and easing him back to the ground. "I'll get ye help." The moment he had Logan comfortable, he ran off like a charging elephant, making more noise than speed, puffing laboriously.

His ankle did hurt, but it was certainly not broken. Logan knew that much. It was probably not sprained, either. He could walk on it right now if he wanted, and it would be fine in a couple of days. But if he had received this much sympathy from the factor, how much might he garner from the members of the family? Might they even feel duty-bound to nurse him back to health? This could be his key into the good graces of the family. He would be stupid to turn his back on such a fortuitous gift.

Within moments Joanna MacNeil, little May, and two farmhands came running from the direction of the house. Dougall was hobbling along at the rear, panting awfully, and mopping his brow with a huge red handkerchief.

Joanna was the first to reach Logan's prostrate form, and he smiled weakly at her.

"I'm terribly sorry for causing you this trouble," he said.

"It's certainly no fault of yours," she answered, kneeling at his side. "I should never have asked Allison to bring you here. May I have a look? I'll be able to tell if it's broken or not." She began to roll up his right pantleg.

"It's the left ankle," he corrected her, making a mental note that he was going to have to remember that fact as well.

Gently Joanna manipulated the injured foot, with Logan wincing at all the appropriate moments.

"It doesn't appear to be broken," she announced, clearly relieved, "but you must have sprained it badly. If you don't mind I'll have

Harry and Russell here carry you to the house. Then I'll call for the doctor."

"I don't want to put you to the trouble. If someone could just—"

"Nonsense! You're not going anywhere. Don't even think it. This is the least we can do." And without further argument, she instructed the two sturdy men to take him in hand.

He was carried into the house and upstairs to a guest room on the second floor. They laid him on top of a made-up four-poster, while Joanna remained downstairs to use the phone. When the men left him alone, he looked about, nodding his head approvingly. This would do quite nicely! The Duke of Windsor himself would find little to complain about in a setup like this. The room was Victorian and very expensive. But like everything else at Stonewycke, it was tastefully simple. He wondered how long a sprained ankle should keep one immobile, and what other symptoms he should display. The doctor could be trouble. But if he was like the rest of the rustics in this out-of-the-way place, he shouldn't be too difficult to convince. He couldn't remain on his back for long. But then if he played his cards right, by the time his *injury* was healed, he'd have another reason to stay at Stonewycke.

Soon a light knock came to the door and Joanna entered carrying a tray with tea.

"Forgive me for leaving you so long," she said, pouring the tea. "I've been trying to soothe poor Fergie."

For the first time Logan felt a pang of guilt at his subterfuge. The factor was a nice fellow, and well-meaning. He was sorry to put him through this. *But he'll get over his worry*, Logan told himself. When this was behind them, the man would be more beholden to him than anyone on the estate, which could prove a tangible asset later on. And he would make it up to the factor somehow, just like to Jesse. After all, it was Dougall who had inadvertently landed him right into the middle of the biggest opportunity of his life. Yes, he owed him too!

In the meantime, it felt rather nice to have the Lady MacNeil wait on him. He let her stir two lumps of sugar and some cream into his cup, then arrange his pillows while he painfully pulled himself up on the bed. He'd have to be careful not to overdo it, however, for these people would sympathize more with brave fortitude than with sniveling.

"Fergie tells me this all happened because of your good fortune with the tractor," she said.

He laughed softly. "Good for the tractor, that is," he said.

"You do seem to be quite a mechanical wonder, Mr. Macintyre."

"I guess I've always been handy in that way," he replied modestly.

She tapped her chin thoughtfully but said nothing more. To make conversation, Logan launched into an account of his experiences aboard the *Little Stevie*. When he laughed at his trip overboard, she laughed with him and commented that she had had a similar "baptism" into Port Strathy life, only hers was more figurative: midwifing in a barn with manure up to her knees. She related in full the story of the calf-birthing and how she had been reluctantly pressed into service by a very cross vet by the name of Alec MacNeil. The doctor arrived in the midst of their laughter over the story.

He complimented Joanna on keeping the patient in good spirits. When he examined the ankle he noted the lack of swelling, the only symptom Logan was unable to feign. But everything else met with his apparent medical satisfaction, and his final diagnosis was even somewhat more severe: there could possibly be a pulled muscle or torn ligament, injuries which might not produce overt swelling but could be even more serious than a sprain. He parted with the final instructions to apply ice and to stay off the foot for two days, calling him after that time if it was still able to bear no weight. He left a small bottle of pain pills, and upon taking two Logan immediately fell asleep, aided no doubt by the fact that he had not slept in well over thirty-six hours.

Dark shadows had begun to crisscross the bed when Logan awoke some hours later. His sleep had been a heavy one, yet somehow not entirely refreshing. Unaccustomed to the pull of conscience, he attributed the uneasiness he felt to the effects of the drug. He remained groggy and disoriented for several minutes, but by the time he heard the knock at the door, he had regained his full faculties.

Joanna entered, followed by Alec. She was carrying another tray, this one burdened with several steaming bowls and another pot of tea.

"I hope you've slept well," she said.

"Yes, thank you. I did. Those pills must've been strong."

Joanna reached over to arrange his pillows.

"Lady MacNeil, you don't have to wait on me like this."

Then Alec spoke for the first time. "Logan," he said, "my wife's a born nurse. She wouldna be happy wi'oot servin' others. So dinna try t' stop her—ye'll only end up wi' a fight on yer hands." He chuckled as he watched her, but there was an unmistakable look of pride in his eyes.

"Well . . ." Logan conceded reluctantly, letting her set his dinner in place.

"Ye worked more o' yer wonders wi' oor tractor, I understan'?"

"Nothing much," replied Logan. "I got her started, but she's going to need a new coil. I'm almost certain of that."

There was a slight pause; then Alec spoke again. "Logan," he began in a more businesslike tone, "I came up here, o' course, t' see hoo ye're farin', but also, my wife an' I hae been talkin'—"

"Please," interrupted Logan, "you have been more than hospitable, but I have no intention of taking advantage of your kindness. There's no reason why someone can't drive me down to the inn."

"We wouldna think o' na such thing, Logan," said Alec sternly, "an' dinna insult us by inferrin' that we'd sen' ye away in yer present state."

Logan was taken aback by the rebuke, and hardly knew how to react to it. But when Alec spoke again, his voice had softened perceptibly. "Noo, ye'll be stayin' here as long as it takes t' git ye on yer feet, an' we'll hear nae more aboot it. But that's not what Joanna an' I were talkin' aboot. Ye see, we hae a good bit o' machinery here, an' some o't it's gettin' rather auld, an' it's all been sorely neglected since oor auld factor died a few months ago. What's more, Walter made himsel' almost indispensable t' the crofters an' farmers and fishers, too. Everyone's been managin', I s'pose, like they'd manage wi'oot a vet if they were forced t'. But 'tis a lot easier t' have someone aboot wi' a special touch who can eliminate the headaches that come when ye hae t' do somethin' y'ere not trained fer. Well, that's a roundaboot way o' sayin' that we'd like t' hire ye here at Stonewycke, t' work fer us an' t' lend ye oot t' the others in Port Strathy that might be able to make use o' yer services. We know ye hae important work in London, but ye said ye was on leave, an' we'd be pleased fer ye t' consider it. We'd give ye room an' board an' ten pounds a month in salary."

Logan doubted that even his smoothest talking could have conjured up a better offer. Still, he did not want to appear too anxious.

"You don't owe me this, you know," was his reply.

"We know that, Mr. Macintyre," said Joanna. "We need your service, pure and simple. It has been a struggle since Walter left us. As much as Fergie has a heart of gold, there are just too many things he doesn't know yet. We understand that you did not come here intending to settle. But perhaps you could try it for a month or two, or at least long enough to teach Fergie some of what you know—"

"Oh, my lady," broke in Logan, "my reasons for coming here wouldn't be a factor in my decision. This is a wonderful place and you are all very kind. It might be nice to be away from the rush of London for a time." He took a long, thoughtful swallow of tea, and when he spoke again he sounded as if his decision were being made even as he spoke. "As I told you, I am more or less between assignments, and have no pressing date when I must be back, and . . ." Here he chuckled lightly as if an amusing thought had just occurred to him. "My mother would certainly be thrilled to hear that I was *plannin' t' bide a wee in the muckle toon o' my ain oncle Digory.*"

They both laughed at his attempt at the local dialect. "It sounds right fine on ye, lad!" said Alec.

"Yes . . . this might be just what I'm looking for."

"Then ye'll do it?" asked Alec, grinning.

Logan paused just long enough for effect, then nodded. Both men shook hands while Joanna poured her new mechanic another cup of tea.

Logan fell asleep that night feeling extremely satisfied with himself. Everything couldn't have gone more smoothly if he had planned each minute detail. Here he was, an employee of Stonewycke. He could now freely roam about the estate, and even more importantly, he'd have opportunity to work his way closer to Lady Margaret.

Suddenly a dark thought entered his mind. What if, as an employee, the family stood more aloof to him? It was only natural that they would keep their distance from the hired help. But, then, nothing thus far had indicated that these people did anything according to the book. Perhaps they treated their employees like family as well.

No matter. He had come this far. He would manage any further obstacles that presented themselves. Things were going perfectly. Almost too perfectly. If he had been back on the streets of London, Skittles would probably tell him to watch his backside; when things went this well, it was time to suspect a setup.

But Logan didn't follow that train of thought even for another moment. There was no one here who could possibly be setting him up. No one even knew he had come. Who could possibly be interested in him? No, he was in the driver's seat, and everything was moving just as he wanted it to. He lay back on the luxurious feather bed and smiled contentedly.

23   Another Stranger in Town

Roy Hamilton was not accustomed to taking in boarders.

His pub on New Town's High Street was a drinking establishment, nothing else. He did have the spare room next to his living quarters upstairs. But he used it for storage and, to tell the truth, he'd just as soon have kept it that way. The minute you started letting in boarders, you had nothing but headaches. The profit was in drink, and that's the way he intended to keep it.

He rinsed off another dish and dropped it in the drainer. It wasn't washing the extra dishes that was so bad. After all, he had to do that anyway, although it was mostly only glasses. But now he'd have to sweep out that room occasionally and maybe even change the sheets, not to mention cooking the man's meals. Hamilton was a bachelor, a thin man who ate only slightly more often than he washed himself, which was not three times a day by the remotest stretch of anyone's imagination. But then his customers did not expect cleanliness, only liquor, and a pretty poor grade of spirits it was that he served.

He would have refused the man outright. Started to, in fact, with a wave of the hand before he had even completed his question. But then the stranger had unfolded a thick wad of banknotes, and Roy Hamilton would have been a fool to refuse *them*. Maybe he *could* reconsider, he had said. The man had begun to peel several notes off the stack and hand them across the counter, and the end of it all was that now he had a guest. A most peculiar guest, to be sure, a man who guarded his privacy and offered few words. About the only thing he had said was what almost sounded like a threat, that the innkeeper was to say nothing about either his presence or his bankroll. But for this man's price, he could give him the room and keep his mouth shut.

Why he hadn't gone to the Bluster 'N Blow where visitors usually stayed in Port Strathy, Hamilton did not know. He had asked at the first, but the man had been most uncommunicative on the subject. And he remained untalkative. Last night he had done his drinking off in a corner, alone. He hadn't even been interested in giving the local folk a chance to relieve him of some of that cash he had stuffed in his pockets. At least that other stranger, the young fellow, had been free with his money—he lost a good deal the last time he was in Hamilton's place, though the innkeeper heard he won a bundle at MacFarlane's pub just down the street the other night.

Hamilton washed up the remainder of the dishes, flicked a cockroach off the drainboard, then dried his hands on his grimy apron. Well, with times being so bad, maybe he ought to give some more thought to this taking in of boarders. The man hadn't really been that much trouble. The room was just sitting there, and if it meant a little more work, it might be worth it if his guests paid him half as much as this Sprague bloke had.

———

Ross Sprague puffed at his Cuban cigar, then downed the last drink of his rum-braced tea.

It was not his habit to imbibe alcoholic beverages so early in the morning, but it was the only way to kill the taste of that garbage the innkeeper had called breakfast. He should have expected a hick town like this to have only one decent hotel. He had grown up in a town no bigger than Port Strathy. And his childhood in the dusty prairie town had taught him the limitations of little one-horse watering holes like this. That town had had only one hotel, run by Mae Wadell, whose reputation was none too sterling in Aldo, Oklahoma. He had learned a few things at Wadell's, but the most valuable lesson learned was the quickest way out of Aldo. When he left at seventeen, he swore he'd never go back—and he never did. He had come a long way since the Aldo days and Mae Wadell's wild place. Now he was forty-five, and liked fine cigars, expensive Scotch, and hotels that weren't crawling with vermin, like this fleabag.

Unfortunately, Macintyre had arrived first and procured the better establishment. Though when Sprague had looked in at the place called the Bluster 'N Blow upon arriving yesterday, it didn't appear to be much of an improvement over this sleazy joint. He supposed he ought to consider himself lucky that Macintyre was still here. If he lost him, it would be his head! He hadn't intended on giving Macintyre a four-day lead, but storms and a few other entanglements he'd just as soon forget had held him up. He hadn't been too worried, however, for if this Macintyre was on some sort of a treasure hunt, it was bound to take him some time. He doubted the fellow had much to go on, and from what he had been able to learn of Macintyre's activities since his arrival, he did not appear to have gotten much closer.

What puzzled Sprague more than anything was why his boss had been so adamant about his sticking to Macintyre. Sprague rubbed a hand over his thinning gray-blonde hair. Why would a successful man like his boss want to waste time on some rumors about a ridiculous ancient treasure—no doubt entirely mythical? Pure greed, he supposed. The man had nearly lost everything in the Wall Street crash, and that had made him more conscious than ever of retaining his old wealth and power. But he was already making his way back to the top, with a classy flat in London's West End and a business that boasted branches not only in London but also Paris and Berlin. He was never satisfied, and no doubt that's what would make him a success again. But the whole thing still seemed peculiarly out of his line, and Sprague could not help but think there was something personal involved, something more than business—

revenge, perhaps. Or did his boss know something more than he was telling?

Sprague was being paid well for his services, well enough not to ask questions. But things were beginning to get puzzling, and he could hardly keep from being curious. First, he was sent to Glasgow to make discreet—very discreet!—inquiries into various property owners, specifically of Scottish coastal property, and even more specifically into the holdings of what had formerly been the vast Duncan estate. He had been told to get the names of every property owner in the valley and along the coast. He figured his boss was looking to buy some country place with a view and wanted to make a killing by closing in on someone who had been particularly hard hit by the crash. It was logical. Everyone with a few bucks these days was scouting around for the chance to benefit by picking up the pieces.

Then he was suddenly told to drop everything and follow this Macintyre fellow. Sure that this so-called treasure was supposed to be located on the Duncan property, Macintyre had come here. There was a connection. But why would an intelligent man like his boss fall for what could be no more than a con game by a petty, small-time crook?

The best move, he thought, would be to stop Macintyre before he clued anyone in about the treasure—pay him off, do whatever it took. If there was any validity to the treasure fairy tale, and the Duncans were tipped off, it would put the lid on any possible sale. As it was, it seemed that the Duncan clan was in bad enough shape financially that they might be more than willing to sell if the price was right. Why didn't his boss just put Macintyre on ice for a while, move in smoothly and make the Duncans an offer they couldn't refuse? Then he could find the treasure later, without any need to hide a thing. If there was no treasure, then at least he had his beach house—or castle, rather.

But his boss was just that—the boss. If he wanted him to tail Macintyre till doomsday, Sprague would do it. But he personally felt they were wasting their time.

Sprague inhaled the smoke from his cigar two or three more times. No, they sure didn't have smokes like this in Aldo. Maybe in Muskogee, but even if they'd had them there, he hadn't had the money in those days to buy them. Thanks to a generous boss, he now possessed an unlimited supply—so who was he to question the man's judgment?

Stick to Macintyre. Keep a low profile.

Those were his orders. And Ross Sprague followed orders. That's how he got to where he was today. And he'd keep following orders until eventually *he* was the one *giving* the orders.

24 Visitors

Logan was restless.

Now that he didn't *need* this injured ankle, he was stuck with it. He couldn't very well hop out of bed and proclaim a miracle. The doctor had said two days off his feet, and that meant he couldn't get up until tomorrow. Even then, he'd have to remember to limp somewhat for a week or so.

Out of sheer boredom he picked up one of the three books Lady MacNeil had brought up to him. *After all,* he thought, *the last time I started flipping through books, I stumbled onto Digory's letter.* Maybe he'd find a further clue to the location of the treasure here, perhaps even a hint of what the treasure actually was. Who could tell? The events of his life seemed somehow ordered since he had arrived here. He would hardly be surprised at this point if a clue jumped right off the page.

Mrs. MacNeil had offered to have him carried down to the library or a sunlit dayroom where he might see better. But pretending an injury for business was one thing; letting people carry him around was quite another. He would just brave it out right here. He had taken the books, not having the heart to tell her he had no interest in reading.

But interested or not, he was going crazy just lying there. Not knowing his preferences, she said, she had brought a variety. Dickens' *Great Expectations,* however apropos the title, he quickly tossed aside. He remembered teachers trying to force it down him. A hasty flipping through the book revealed no notes or letters, and that was that. Next was Scott's *Guy Mannering*. Who could possibly plow through the small print, and all those anachronisms? He turned it upside down and let the pages hang as he gave it a shake or two. No clues there either. Of course the whole thing was absurd! What was he thinking, that right under her nose the proprietress of the estate was going to tell him where the treasure was so he could steal it from them?

He laughed aloud. The isolation had already made him come unhinged!

Finally he reached for the third book, a volume of poems by George MacDonald. Although the name sounded vaguely familiar, Logan couldn't quite place him—a Scot, he thought, perhaps nineteenth century. He wasn't sure. He had never been much on poetry, but these were short and uncluttered and at least looked more palatable than the other two books. He opened the book to the middle. One of the nice things about books like this was that you didn't have to start at the beginning and read to the end. And when someone asked you how you liked the book, you could spout off a few things about a poem—maybe the only one you read—and they'd never be the wiser.

Skimming the page, he noticed a reference to boats, and thinking this as good a place as any to start, he sought the beginning of the verse:

Master, thou workest with such common things—
Low souls, weak hearts, I mean—and hast to use,
Therefore, such common means and rescuings,
That hard we find it, as we sit and muse,
To think thou workest in us verily:
Bad sea-boats, we and manned with wretched crews—
That doubt the captain, watch the storm-spray flee.

Thou art hampered in thy natural working then
When beings designed on freedom's holy plan
Will not be free: with thy poor, foolish men,

Thou therefore hast to work just like a man.
But when, tangling thyself in their sore need,
Thou hast to freedom fashioned them indeed,
Then wilt thou grandly move, and godlike speed.

Logan stopped reading.

These were nothing but religious poems. There was no treasure here—just old-fashioned notions of piety! He should have known!

Actually, Logan had nothing personal against religion. His mother had been religious on and off, and went through bouts of dragging him to church when he hadn't made his escape fast enough on Sunday mornings. But never in his life had he felt any particular need for religion.

Bad sea-boats, we and manned with wretched crews. . . . Yes, he supposed that described him. At least he had been told as much on those few Sundays when he had ventured into church. "Ye're a bad apple, Logan Macintyre. Settle doon afore ye wind up in hell!"

No thanks, he thought. He had no use for such fanatical pessimism. If they wanted to be prisoners of that kind of fear, that was their choice. But he didn't need it. He was free. With the thought, the words came back into his mind, and he looked back onto the page to see exactly what the poet had said. *Thou art hampered in thy natural working then when beings designed on freedom's holy plan will not be free. . . .*

What did the man mean? What a strange thing to say?

He was free, wasn't he? He prided himself on that fact. Footloose and fancy free; he had always taken pleasure in being just that sort of man. Whatever freedom this old-fashioned writer was talking about, he certainly wasn't referring to someone like himself. Logan Macintyre was free, was on the track of a treasure which was going to put him on easy street, and nothing was going to stop him.

He closed the book just as a sharp knock came at the door, jerking him out of his momentary reverie.

It would be a relief to have some company. He had never been a deep thinker and had no intention of starting now. No old dead poet was going to start filling his mind with foolish fancies. Somehow he was sure it was the kind of thing Lady Margaret would know all about. The poem almost reminded him of that peculiar look in her eyes. It wouldn't surprise him if she knew the old bloke who wrote it.

"Come in," he called.

The door opened and Allison ushered in an entourage that appeared as out of place within the grand walls of Stonewycke as she had on the streets of New Town. With her were Jesse Cameron, Buckie Buchannan, and Jimmy MacMillan.

"It looks like ye're na havin' a run o' much luck here in Strathy," said Jesse, taking his hand and shaking it heartily.

"Ha!" laughed Jimmy who had been involved in the poker game at MacFarlane's. "Dinna be talkin' t' this bloke aboot luck. He's got plenty o' it!"

"Aye," added Buckie with a friendly grin. "He's got enough Port Strathy siller in his pockets t' stay in bed a month."

"What a surprise!" said Logan, laughing with the banter.

"Ye dinna think oor best crew member would get laid up an' rate no visit from his mates?" said Jesse with mock astonishment.

"If you don't mind," came Allison's cool voice, noticeably out of concert with the other congenial tones, "I'll be leaving you to your ... visitors, Mr. Macintyre." Then turning toward Jesse, "I trust you can find your own way out when you are through?"

"Yes, mem," replied Jesse, with the quiet respect of one who knew her place when she was put in it. "Thank ye, m'leddy."

Favoring those in the room with one final aloof glance, which left Logan with the impression that she was appraising how they would handle their temptation to carry out the family silver, Allison turned crisply and exited.

"Pull up some chairs," he said to his guests. When he saw Buckie glancing all about and then giving a soft whistle, he added, "Some digs, huh?"

"Who says the bloke ain't lucky!" said Jimmy as he straddled a delicate Queen Anne chair.

Jesse and Buckie took two other chairs, launching immediately into a conversation about the weather, fishing prospects, and the latest repairs being undertaken aboard the *Little Stevie*. A week earlier such topics would have held no meaning whatsoever for Logan, but now he found himself interested in even the most trivial details. From firsthand experience he now knew how vitally important the weather was to the fishermen, and since his "voyage," he had now and then found his eyes straying toward the sky with a concern he would never have felt before. Would those clouds bring rain? From which direction was the wind coming? Could the *Little Stevie* take another gale? Thus Logan found himself listening with more attentiveness than he could have thought possible.

Before anyone realized it, an hour had passed. Jesse was the first to rise.

"We didn't mean t' take all yer time, an' we still got plenty t' do today," she said.

"My time!" said Logan. "Time's all I've got!"

She laughed. "The soft life's gettin' t' ye already?"

"I'd sooner be out on your deck in a rainstorm than caged up in here," Logan replied.

A serious look passed over Jesse's face, one Logan had not seen her wear previously. "The Lord spared ye once, my frien'," she said, "an' it's no wise t' be temptin' the likes o' Him afore ye figure oot what He saved ye fer."

Logan's unresponsive stare apparently urged her to explain further.

"When we're oot on the water an' a squall breaks oot, sometimes a clap o' thunder'll break an' I'll swear we're all goners. Or sometimes a flash o' lightnin'll break almost from a clear sky. Weel, sometimes somethin' happens like that in life, too. Somethin' terrible will fall wi'oot warnin'. An' from that time on, everythin' is changed. Life can no more be what it was afore. Like when my Charlie an' my boy was lost. An' the result depen's on hoo ye respon' t' the invadin' storm o' trouble. What do ye do after the echo o' the thunder has died away? Is yer life better than it was . . . or worse? Do ye let Him use the bolt o' lightnin' t' open yer eyes, or do ye keep them shut?"

"I'm afraid I don't really understand what you're talking about, Jesse," said Logan in an apologetic tone.

"Weel, I'll see if I canna be a mite more plain-spoken, lad," she replied. After a short pause, she resumed. "I dinna believe in accidents. Everythin' is t' a purpose. Jist like yer comin' here, an' like yer accident on the boat, an' maybe like yer accident here, too, fer all I ken. Dinna ye see, lad? The Lord's tryin' t' get yer attention. 'Tis the bolt o' lightnin' in yer own life. He's tryin' t' wake ye up. An' that's what I said in the beginnin', that ye'd be wise t' figure oot what He's tryin' t' save ye fer afore He runs oot o' patience an' leaves ye t' yer own devices."

Logan was silent, trying to ponder her words, but in truth they barely reached past the surface of his mind.

"We almost forgot," put in Buckie in a lighter tone; "we got presents."

"Presents! It's not my birthday, Buckie!" laughed Logan.

" 'Twas Jesse's idea, but we all agreed 'twas a good one," replied the first mate, stuffing his hand into his pocket and withdrawing three cigars. "We thought ye might like a fine smoke," he added, laying them on the bed.

Logan picked one up and sniffed it lingeringly. "Ah," he said, "*that* is a good cigar!"

"I brought ye somethin'," said Jimmy, "but I left it wi' the cook. We smoked some o' the catch ye helped wi'."

"I hardly *helped!*"

"Ye was there, an' that's enough," said Jesse, and Logan could tell she meant it sincerely. Then she proceeded to take a small package from her pocket. "The lads thought ye might be able t' fin' some use fer these."

It was a deck of cards. Logan slipped them out of the box and fanned them out expertly; his fingers obviously had more than a passing acquaintance with the game. Suddenly he broke into an uproarious laugh. Each card bore a picture of a fish on its back.

He looked up at Jesse and noted a definite twinkle in each eye.

All at once he felt very odd. He bit his lip and looked hastily down, pretending to examine the cards more closely. He didn't know what this feeling inside him was, nor what he should say. When at last he did speak, his voice felt hollow. He couldn't say what he felt without saying too much.

"Thanks. You are all . . . you're good friends," was all he said, but when he ventured a glance at Jesse, he knew she understood.

Telling him to visit them at the boat again sometime, even though he was now an important man and working for the estate, they left, and again Logan found himself alone.

He lay quietly on the bed, feeling very strange—not a little deceptive, certainly ill at ease, and at the same time, very heavy. He fingered the deck of cards and sniffed at another cigar. Suddenly he knew what felt heavy—it was his blasted left foot, sound and whole as it was.

"So what was I *supposed* to do?" he half yelled to himself, throwing back the blankets and jumping out of bed.

Pacing back and forth over the Persian carpet, he continued to argue with himself. "They'd understand! They'd do the same in my shoes if they had the chance. These are big stakes! Friends or no friends, I've come too far to start getting wishy-washy now!"

Then, as if resolving his temporary ambivalence, he grabbed up one of the cigars, bit off the end, which he spat out on the floor, lit it, and puffed dramatically. It wasn't *that* great a cigar, anyway. It certainly wasn't as if they had spent their last penny on it. He puffed again and tried to blow the smoke into a ring. But despite all his efforts, that was one trick Skittles had not been able to teach him.

Poor old Skittles . . .

Why did things have to change? Why couldn't he be back in London where he belonged, among people he belonged with? Everything had been simple enough there. He had known what he wanted and how to get it. There were no deeper questions of life back there—at least, not many. Now here was Jesse trying to talk to him about thunderbolts from heaven, and some ancient poet yapping about foolish men who didn't want to be free! It was all such nonsense!

Suddenly he heard a noise outside the door.

Like a naughty child, he leaped back under the covers, his heart racing. The cigar had lost all its flavor. Never before had he felt so much like a common sneak.

25   The Greenhouse

Leaving Logan with his friends, Allison returned downstairs in a none-too-pleasant frame of mind. It was disgraceful how they were all treating the man—giving him the best guestroom, waiting on him hand and foot, allowing his coarse and smelly friends the run of the house.

Yet all those things had not irritated her half as much as her mother asking her to show the visitors up to Macintyre's room. They had servants for such tasks!

Her mother and father both knew what sort of person he was; Allison had made a point of telling exactly how she had found him in town the other day when they had mentioned they were going to hire him. If *she* had tried to befriend such a person, they would have objected strenuously.

When she reached the bottom of the stairs, she was carrying a taut, sour expression on her face, which Joanna could hardly have missed. The perceptive mother had a vague idea of the cause, for she had seen the protest in her daughter's eyes the moment she had been asked to escort Logan's guests upstairs. Joanna often doubted whether or not she was approaching her daughter's problems wisely, thrusting her into situations that would challenge and expose her arrogant attitude for what it was. She'd hoped that when Allison saw herself in her true light, it would have a much greater impact than a mother's preaching. Joanna told herself over and over to exercise patience and to stand faithful in prayer for her daughter—those would be her greatest weapons against this thing that was eating away at Allison. But sometimes it was so hard to keep from saying what sprang to her mind.

"Mother!" said Allison in a remonstrative tone, as a master rebuking a servant. "How could you? It's hardly suitable for a member of the family to be showing a mere employee his guests! How do you expect to maintain order around here? And *such* guests!"

The arrogant tone of her daughter's words taxed Joanna's resolve to the limit. *Perhaps what she needs is a good hard spanking!* Joanna thought to herself. But instead she took a breath, then answered calmly, "I hadn't thought of that."

"You wouldn't, Mother," replied Allison. "Sometimes you just let them walk all over you!"

"Do I...?"

Allison nodded, looking as though she were expecting a verbal attack from her mother on another flank. But then Joanna went on in the same controlled voice. "I'm on my way out to the greenhouse." With the words, Allison noticed for the first time the basket her mother was carrying. "Dorey said there were some lovely rhododendrons ready to pick. Would you care to join me?"

Allison hesitated.

There seemed no threat in the invitation. Still it was a little odd. Why hadn't her mother given her the usual sermon on treating everyone as equals? She and her mother used to take walks over the grounds all the time. Why had they stopped, she wondered? She was about to make some excuse for refusing when suddenly she found herself saying, "Yes."

It was not a day particularly conducive to a morning stroll. A steady wind had arisen and was now blowing in from the north, filled with portents of another rainstorm. It whipped Allison's hair in her face, and she pulled her sweater snugly about her. It would have been impossible to talk as they walked without yelling in one another's ears.

The moment they stepped into the greenhouse, they seemed to enter another realm altogether. The glass walls immediately cut off the roar of the wind and they were surrounded by a still, quiet, humid warmth.

Joanna smiled as she looked about.

"I remember the first time I came into this place," she said reflectively. "Your father and I had sneaked onto the grounds through a breach in the hedge. I was trembling when we came through this door, and with good reason, for I was a common trespasser—an unwelcome interloper."

"I've heard the story many times, Mother."

"Yes ... I suppose you have." Joanna took down a pair of shears from a hook on the wall. "I guess I'm telling you now because I hoped it would help you understand why I feel as I do toward the folk around here."

"Because you were one of them once?"

"Yes. I was an outsider too. A commoner. I have never *stopped* being 'one of them,' as you put it." She walked to several rhododendron bushes laden with large deep red blossoms. "I suppose it's my own background that made me realize there wasn't anything magical about being a *Duncan*. And when I began to learn about some family history, I learned there wasn't even anything very *desirable* about it."

"Mother! How can you say such a thing?"

"There's nothing special about us, dear, except in God's eyes— where every one of His children is infinitely special." Joanna clipped one of the blooms and laid it in her basket. "Several hundred years ago a man by the name of Ramsay happened to save a king's life, and the king gave him some land and a title for his reward. It could have happened to anyone."

"But it didn't."

"Andrew Ramsay, then, was special. He was a courageous man who placed another's life above his own. *That* was special and he deserved what he got. But the rest ... in a sense, they belonged no more to that reward than I belonged in the greenhouse that day."

"We've *earned* our place by faithfully administering the estate," argued Allison.

"You know," said Joanna, attempting a new train of thought, "your brother wants to go to America; he may decide to live there permanently. Nat has no interest in being a country squire—I think he'd much rather be a fisherman. Thus, the mantle of Stonewycke will no doubt fall to you, Allison."

Allison had never heard her mother talk like this. It was a little sobering, even frightening. Allison did not like fear, and she responded by trying to protect herself with a hard, cool shell. For the moment she said nothing.

"I agree with you in one sense," Joanna continued. "We do have a unique responsibility to the community. They look to us for a kind of stability and leadership, which is a good thing when wisely used. But it is not because of who *we* are, or even what we are, but rather because of what *Stonewycke* is, what it represents in the minds of the people and in the history of this community, what it has always stood for. Allison, *we* have been placed here as servants to the folk around us. To serve—that is the highest calling of all."

"I *knew* you would find a way to twist it around to that," retorted Allison angrily. "No one expects servanthood from us, least of all the people in Port Strathy. They like to flaunt their resident nobility, just like all common people do. I think it embarrasses them the way this family sometimes behaves, acting as if we were not better than they."

"And you do think we're better?"

"Maybe *better* was an unwise word. But yes, we're supposed to be set apart, higher in society. It's for their good too, don't you see? They *need* us to be above them."

"And you think we should lord it over them because of our position?"

"Do you know what the real problem is, Mother?" asked Allison, ignoring her mother's question.

Joanna simply raised her eyebrows inquisitively, knowing her daughter's answer was going to come no matter what she said.

"I think you're afraid of what your position really means, afraid you won't be able to measure up to *real* nobility." Joanna stared, too stunned by her daughter's reasoning to respond. "I think you're hiding behind all this servant rhetoric!" Allison added in one final outburst.

Joanna closed her eyes and let the shears slip from her hand. "Oh, Allison . . ." she breathed, the pain evident in her voice. "I . . . I can see we can't talk about this," she tried to go on, then stopped. Her lip trembled as she tried to hold back the tears, for she knew they would not draw Allison's sympathy, and might even induce her contempt.

Joanna could not utter another word. She was hurt, disappointed, even a little angry in a quiet sort of way, and afraid of what, at that point, she might say—what terrible things might lash out at her own daughter.

She turned, and still clutching the basket of Dorey's lovely flowers, hurried out of the greenhouse.

Allison watched, but her own fancied indignation on the side of truth shielded her from feeling her mother's poignant and heart-wrenching emotion. She hadn't noticed the soft shuffling sound behind her, and had no idea someone had entered the greenhouse by the back door while she had made her cruel speech to her mother.

"I didn't mean to intrude," came a soft, aged voice.

Startled at the sound, she jerked herself around, glaring at whoever had the gall to frighten her so. It was Dorey.

"Oh, Grandpa," she said, quickly rearranging her features into a look of deference, for he was one of her elders whose opinion she still respected. "You frightened me."

"You frightened me, dear," he replied in a calm tone, sounding not at all like one who had been frightened in anything like a normal manner.

"Me?"

Appearing to ignore her questioning tone, Dorey hobbled slowly over to the place where Joanna had dropped the shears. He inched his frame gingerly down and picked them up. "They'll rust if they lay there and chance to get wet," he said quietly. He laid them carefully on a worktable.

"Were . . ." Allison began hesitatingly, "were you here the whole time?"

"I haven't yet fallen into the habit of common eavesdropping."

"I'm sorry, Grandpa. That's not what I meant."

"When I came in, you and your mother were too intent on one another to notice me. I was rather at a disadvantage, and at the moment I tried to make my presence known, your mother walked out."

"She's impossible to talk to," said Allison with a defensive edge to her voice.

"A common malady between mothers and daughters, I expect," said the old man.

"I'm afraid she didn't understand me."

"I think she understands you only too well," replied Dorey, his brow furrowed with a rebuke his soft-spoken voice did not carry. "As I also understood you."

"What do you mean?" she asked. She really didn't want to ask the question, but somehow it almost seemed expected, and she could not help herself.

He came toward her and took her hands into his—gnarled old hands, coarse with their work in the soil and trembling slightly with age. But his grasp was firm and warm, filled with a love he knew his great-granddaughter was unwilling to acknowledge openly.

"I heard something in your voice," he said, his voice forever soft, as a man who gave little credit to his own wisdom. "I see it now in your eyes, and it does frighten me, my dear, dear Ali." He was the only one she permitted to call her by that name. "As much as we would like to, we cannot forget that *his* blood flows through your veins. But I saw it so clearly in your eyes just now. They were *his* eyes . . . I could never forget them."

"Whose, Grandpa?" Allison's voice trembled a bit now too. Her great-grandfather was as lucid a man as there ever was, but she knew he had suffered greatly and had had some mental disorder many years ago; and every now and then, not often, he said something that reminded her of that fact.

"James Duncan's," he replied tightly. The name would always be difficult for him to say.

"He was rather a scoundrel, wasn't he?"

"He was your great-great-grandfather," was Dorey's only reply. He brought her hands to his wrinkled lips and kissed them softly.

"Mother didn't get any pink rhodies," Allison said with a forced tightness in her voice. She blithely released herself from Dorey's grasp, picked up the shears, and flitted about the flowers like a butterfly.

Dorey shook his head sadly. "Will you apologize to your mother?" he asked.

"I don't see why," said Allison, frantically clipping blossoms.

"You hurt her terribly."

"I didn't mean to."

"We never mean to hurt those we love," he said as he let out a weary sigh. "But it happens only too often. You mustn't let such things fester between you."

"Well . . . I suppose I should have used a different tone," she conceded, though reluctantly, appearing to do so only to please her grandfather. "That should be enough pink ones, don't you think?" She dropped the shears on the table and skitted to the door. "Luncheon should be ready soon, Grandpa, so don't be too long."

She was out the door and gone before he could even reply.

Dorey sighed heavily. "Dear Lord," he prayed softly, "don't let her go that way—his way. Draw her to you early in her life, my Father, so that she may have that many more years to enjoy your love. She needs you so. Help her to realize her need . . ."

As he passed, he thought of a young man so many, many years ago, and what it had taken for him to acknowledge his need for God. The thought made him wince in pain for Allison. But the dread was even greater when he recalled James Duncan's terrible glint in his dear Ali's eyes.

"Do whatever you must, Father." They were hard words to say. And perhaps would have been impossible if he did not know he was saying them to a loving and merciful God.

26   The Stable

Logan gripped the cane and took a few tentative steps. He looked up and smiled at Joanna who was watching encouragingly.

"I should think it'll be taking my full weight in no time," he said, holding out his left foot.

"Don't rush it, Logan."

"I'm anxious to start work," he replied. And in his own context, the words were truthfully spoken.

"Believe me, we are anxious to have you, but the doctor did say that if the muscles have been damaged, another injury could recur more easily."

"I'll be careful."

It was now the third day since the "accident," and he at last had official permission to be up and about. The doctor had dropped by with the cane yesterday, just after his visitors had left, and fortunately discovered Logan lying in bed. After resisting the idea at first, Logan then decided that the cane would be a nice touch. It lent him rather a distinguished air, and even a bit of sympathy that might work to his advantage later. The old recurring injury ploy might play into his hands at some future time, who could tell? He recalled a crony in London who had his shoulder shattered during the Great War. He was as fit as anyone until he wanted to impress a lady or dodge a bill collector. Then, how he could favor that shoulder—it was masterful!

All Logan wanted right now, though, was to get some fresh air and exercise. Being waited on in this kingly room had been splendid for a while. But he couldn't take another day of it.

"Would it be in order for me to have a look around my new work area?" he asked.

"By all means," replied Joanna. "I'll accompany you if you like."

"You're too kind. But I can manage, and I'm certain you have other responsibilities."

"At least let me help you down the stairs. It might be a little tricky with that cane."

Logan simply smiled, and set off with her slowly down the corridor.

In five minutes they had reached the rear exit nearest the stable. There Joanna left him, pointing the way, and Logan limped—careful to continue favoring his left foot, though he could see no one watching him—the rest of the way alone.

The front section of the huge stone structure had been walled off to serve as a garage and workshop of sorts. He swung open the wooden doors, large enough to admit a vehicle—motor cars and farm machinery now, but in days past coaches and wagons must have passed through them. In the foreground was a large, open room, very old, with a floor of compressed dirt and cobwebby open-beamed walls and ceiling. Scattered randomly about were the machines of farm labor—some old and rusted, others still in use. A broken-down wooden wagon against one wall must have been fifty or more years old. He recognized a primitive threshing machine from a picture he had seen; it looked as if it might still be in working order. Several plows were on the floor, and a couple of other attachments whose purpose he did not know. Neither the Austin nor the tractor was present, but the room was large enough to hold them both. In the near corner to his right, the modern era clearly predominated with the presence of tools and equipment obviously intended for working on motorized engines. An old tire leaned against the wall; a rusted-out fender and containers of oil and diesel stood nearby. *This must have been Innes's niche,* thought Logan. He had a friend who ran a small automobile garage, and it looked just like that corner.

As Logan made his way into the depths of the room, the years seemed to slowly turn back the farther he went. A stone fire pit with an ancient bellows overhead spoke of times past when a blacksmith worked with the groom to shoe horses or mend a wagon wheel. Logan wandered toward it and reached out for the wooden lever which opened and closed the bellows. It was tight with age, but he managed to force some air through it, raising a small cloud of ash dust in the fire pit.

Suddenly it dawned on him that his uncle Digory must have worked in this place, walked in day after day just as he had done, even stood on this very spot, possibly maneuvering the bellows for a muscular blacksmith who stood over a roaring fire hammering useful shapes out of crude iron.

He looked around the enclosure. Now it was no more iron shoes and iron-rimmed wooden wheels, but rubber tires and inanimate machines. No more horses and oxen and hand-driven plows, but automobiles and tractors and the mechanisms of a modern age. An involuntary twinge of sadness pricked Logan's heart with the thought. He had never considered it before, but there was something appealing about the ancient methods, something melancholy about witnessing their passing.

He took a deep breath, as if searching for the faint, lingering smells of a time now past. Then with one final glance about him and an involuntary sigh, he continued deeper into the building, arriving at length to a wall which ran from floor to ceiling. It appeared to be of relatively recent date, erected some two-thirds of the way from one end of the structure to the other, no doubt to section off the modern garage from the originally purposed stables, for which there was an ever-dwindling need.

He pushed open the door in the middle of the wall and stepped inside.

The snort of a horse startled him, but then all was quiet again except for the shuffling feet of several animals. He seemed to have taken still another step backward in time, for here were the more traditional surroundings of agrarian life. No doubt this was the place where his uncle had spent most of his time. Flies buzzed about, the fragrance of sweet-smelling hay mingled with the odor of horse-flesh filled the air, and an occasional snort from the equine residents broke the stillness. How many worlds apart this was from the life Logan knew on the streets of London! Yet the spell that had come over him while standing at the bellows deepened. There was something vital and elemental in the air about him. Again he sucked in a deep draught of air, but this time it filled him with an intense pleasure rather than sadness. There was a quality of earthiness here, something wholesome, something basic, something invigorating—as if here, and nowhere else, one might discover the very foundation-stone of life. Here there was quiet. Here there was peace. Here one might actually shut out the world and settle into a calmness of spirit unknown on the busy streets and fast-paced thoroughfares of life.

He thought of the stately grandeur of the castle he had just left, which stood not a hundred yards away. Though the people occupying it might seem rather docile, the castle itself emanated a severe, even harsh sense of authority. There it stood, cold, immovable, unfeeling—a sentinel to times past, a reminder of turbulent and violent times in Scottish history. What had Lady Margaret quoted? "Child of loud-throated war. . . !" All the crystal and satins and velvets could not hide the grim undercurrent of stormy and self-motivated violence that had characterized so many eras of Scotland's past, giving birth to the many castles such as this one.

Yet in the midst of that formidable tower of unbending might, surviving alongside it, stood this stable—a soothing, protective element against the grimness of the castle itself. With the thought, Logan was reminded of the words Lady Margaret had spoken at dinner that first evening.

"I spent many hours in Digory's stable," she had said. "I loved horses, but perhaps even more I loved the peace and respite it offered me." Digory had been her only real friend, she had said, and she had longed for his world to be hers. But always she had been compelled to return to the sobering realities of life within the castle.

"But surely your family must have cheered the place somewhat?" Logan had asked.

At that moment a subtle change had momentarily come over

her—that darkening of her eyes and faltering of the conversation. She had quickly shaken off whatever the spell had been, and curious though he had been, Logan had felt restrained from pursuing any further.

Now here he was in Digory's world, that place which the young girl had shared with him and longed to be more a part of. Did the man himself somehow embody the very qualities of the place? The peacefulness and serenity and calm? Why had Lady Margaret as a child sought out his uncle?

Musing over these thoughts, Logan strolled past the stalls where the horses were kept. Many were empty now, a further reminder that the estate was not what it once had been; but there were five or six fine specimens: two grand bays, a black mare with three white socks, and a trim chestnut he knew must be a thoroughbred. He began to move on, then stopped at the chestnut's stall and reached in to rub her silky nose. She whinnied and stamped her hoof.

"I'd bet you'd turn a pretty penny at Epsom," Logan said aloud.

"We've only raced her locally," came a voice behind him.

Startled, Logan turned sharply. "Lady Margaret ... good afternoon."

"I'm sorry to have startled you."

"I must have been too absorbed to hear you coming."

"You have an eye for good horseflesh."

"I've spent some time at the racetrack." He patted the mare again. "What's her showing been?"

Before replying, she held out an open hand to the animal, revealing two lumps of sugar. The chestnut lapped them greedily and stamped her foot again. "She came off quite well," Lady Margaret continued, "a national champion. But I'm afraid the racing circuit is rather strenuous on both beasts and owners. Last year we decided to breed her instead. Come here."

Glowing with eagerness, she took Logan's free arm and led him to the next stall. "There's her foal. A beauty, isn't he?"

Still only a mangy colt, the animal nevertheless showed in every powerful sinew the evidence of noble breeding. The young stallion was a deep amber color with a pale tan star on his nose.

"He's magnificent!" said Logan, and the awe in his voice was genuine. "You really ought to race him!"

Margaret laughed with his enthusiasm.

"Why, you should hire someone to take him around. I'd beg for the job myself if I knew anything about horses."

"He's already been sold." She spoke the words sadly, even regretfully. Logan sensed that the animals meant far more to her than a mere business enterprise.

"Did Digory teach you to love horses so?" asked Logan. Had he been able to analyze the change, he would have been surprised to find that the question sprang from a real desire to know the answer rather than as part of his scheme. Subtly, he was being lured into an affinity for this life he had unwittingly become part of.

"Digory emanated such a love for everything that I suppose it was bound to rub off," replied Lady Margaret. "I had almost forgotten how much he meant to me. Somehow, your coming here brought it all suddenly back. He was the first one to call me *Maggie* when I was still a child, barely able to walk."

She paused, the memory clearly an emotional one. Her eyes filled with tears, then she laughed. Logan joined in with her.

"Oh, Logan, I can't think of him without wanting to weep! It makes me happy and sad at the same time. He was such a good man. He taught me about so much besides horses."

"How was that?"

"Mostly by his life. He was not a man of many words or great intellect. But he lived what he believed, and I think it shaped me as a child more than anything else in my life. My mother used to scold me, saying it was unseemly for me to spend so much time with a common groom, much less receive instruction from him. Though deep down, she liked Digory too. Everyone did, possibly with the exception of my father, though I think even he bore Digory a kind of respect. Digory couldn't help what he did. He was not trying to foist anything off on me. Just being around him was a learning experience. Sometimes he didn't have to say a word. You could see in the way he treated the animals, or in that glowing peace which was always in his eyes, that there was a difference in him not found in the average man. So many in our station of life look down on what they call the common man. But often real commonness lies in those the world counts greater. True nobility is a matter of the heart, Logan. And I can tell you, your uncle Digory was no common man.

He was a true aristocrat. When he spoke, every word possessed substance and came from a heart of love."

"Then he was an educated man?"

"Oh no, by no means," replied Margaret. "I doubt he ever read a book in his life, except for his Bible, of course. But then, that was the only book he ever needed. From it he gleaned the words of life, and those he imparted to others, especially to me, with more profound and simple wisdom than I've heard from many a clergyman."

"I wouldn't doubt that," Logan replied with more than a touch of cynicism.

"Are you a religious man, Logan? . . . I may call you Logan, may I not?"

"Of course. Please do!" Logan said, nodding. "I haven't been inside a church," he went on, "since the last time a pompous vicar told me I'd better mend my ways or go to hell. I was fourteen at the time and figured my ways didn't need mending."

"And are you still of that mind?" she asked simply. Her tone was benign, almost innocent, but he knew what she was driving at.

"I'm not saying I'm perfect," he countered defensively, "but I'm no less perfect than anyone else, especially that vicar. What would Digory have said to that?"

"Probably nothing," replied Lady Margaret.

Logan was noticeably astonished by the answer.

"In all the time I knew him," she went on, "I never heard him argue morals or theology with anyone. I suppose he understood that you couldn't get someone to believe or to see the holes in their own values by badgering them to death. Only God, not man, can change a person's heart."

"Then what's the use of sermons and preachers and churches and all that rigmarole?"

"Sometimes very little. But we never know the vehicle God may use in making His changes—it might occasionally even be something as outlandish as a sermon in church."

As she finished speaking, a small smile crept onto her face and it gradually broadened into a mischievous grin. Logan grinned, too. He hated to admit it, but he liked the old lady's style. Then she continued, "Tell me, Logan, do you believe in God?"

"Sure," he answered quickly. Too quickly, for it was in the manner of one who had never really given the question about what belief in God might entail, and still didn't care to think about it.

"I'm sure that would have pleased Digory," replied Margaret, not allowing her voice to reveal that she knew perfectly well what was behind Logan's answer.

They had begun to walk toward the farther end of the stable, and presently came to a steep stairway in the most distant corner. It was in a state of considerable disrepair, and from the dust and cobwebs covering it, Logan surmised that it had not been used in many years. He glanced toward the top, but saw only a closed door.

"That's where Digory lived," said Margaret, noting his interest.

"Really?" said Logan, his original scheme suddenly reemerging into prominence in his mind. He studied the stairway again, this time with heightened interest. The steps were narrow and steep, and there was no evidence they had ever had a railing. *For an old man,* he thought, *it looks rather unsafe.*

"Does that surprise you?"

"I suppose I would have thought that a servant held in such high regard would have warranted something . . . better."

"It was only I who had any special regard for Digory. Nonetheless, this was where he *chose* to live. He loved his horses, and no doubt he also loved the sounds and smells of the stable itself, as I did myself. Only I wasn't fortunate enough to live right here."

"How long did he work at Stonewycke?"

"All his life," replied Margaret. "His father was groom here before him. Digory sort of inherited the position."

"That was all he inherited," he said wryly, almost to himself, and when he realized what he had said, he immediately regretted it. "Forgive me," he added quickly. "I didn't mean—"

She smiled. "You're right, though. It doesn't seem like much for a man who gave his entire life in service to a family—a tiny, drafty room above a stable. No possessions to pass on except an old black Bible. Not much of a fortune, wouldn't you say?"

Logan's heart perked up immediately at the word. He glanced up and returned the look in Lady Margaret's eyes for a moment. *Is she baiting me? What could she possibly know?* he thought. "A Bible, you say. . . ?" he said at length.

"Yes. I won't easily forget that," she replied, glancing again up the stairs. Her voice contained no hint of hidden motive. Gradually Logan relaxed. *It must have been nothing*, he said to himself. "It was quite worn with use," she went on, "I remembered once when he became ill, he asked me to read to him from it. I wonder what ever became of it?"

"I believe I may have it," said Logan. He almost wondered at himself for being so free with the information. Yet what reason could he have to conceal it? And it would only go the worse for him if it was later discovered that he'd said nothing after the Bible had been mentioned.

"You...?" said Margaret.

"Yes. There was an old Bible among my mother's possessions. In a chest of family heirlooms, that sort of thing."

"Of course," mused Margaret. "I suppose when he died, someone must have packed up his few belongings and sent them to his relatives."

"Yes, I imagine so. It was the Bible, in fact, that put me on course to Port Strathy."

"Would it be possible for me to see it? It would mean a great deal to me."

"By all means. Alec was kind enough to retrieve my belongings from the inn, so I'll get it for you when I return to my room."

They continued walking about the stable, admiring the horses once again, and Logan was wondering how best to bring up the subject of the room again. Perhaps he was being overly cautious. It would be no more incongruous for him to want to take a peek at Digory's room than for Lady Margaret to request a look at his Bible. But before he had a chance to verbalize his request, she brought up the subject herself.

"You must want to see Digory's room as much as I want to see his Bible," she said. "To be perfectly truthful, I would very much like to see it again myself. I haven't been in there since that time he was ill."

"Never?"

"I left Scotland rather suddenly shortly afterward, and then I was gone some forty years. When I returned ... well, I hate to admit it, but I hadn't given it much thought until now. While Digory's presence remained with me, some other things grew rather dim. And of course, the general disrepair of the place, not to mention my age, has discouraged exploration."

"So no one has been up there in all that time...?" Logan tried to sound casual, but he feared a slight tremor in his voice might betray his eagerness.

"I'd see no reason for anyone to. We certainly didn't need the space for anything. Of course someone had to gather his things when he died."

"Yes, that's true ..."

"My mother, probably."

"Lady Atlanta?"

"My, but you are well versed in our family history already!"

"I just try to pay attention," laughed Logan.

Since the revelation of the room, Logan had harbored the hope that perhaps Digory had simply hidden the treasure in his own private little flat above the stable. Perhaps it was not too bright a move, but then Digory was a simple man whose whole world seemed to be his horses and that black Bible. He might not have been cunning enough to think of a more creative spot. Could it be possible that he had hidden it in a manner that anyone superficially gathering his belongings would have overlooked it? And overlooked any clues he might have left, hoping for young Maggie's return? If no one had disturbed anything since then ...

He had to get into that room!

Suddenly his mind reeled from the idea which would make him a rich man. As calmly as he was able, he turned his gaze from the broken stair and back again toward Lady Margaret.

"I was wondering," he began, "and it may be an entirely presumptuous thing for me to even ask, but Mrs. MacNeil mentioned that I was to receive room and board as part of my wages. Would you think it might be possible for me to stay in Digory's old room?"

Margaret smiled. Why the idea struck her as so perfect, she could not tell. Was it because this young man was of the same blood as her dear old friend? She could not deny that she felt a peculiar bond with him. She had almost from the very first. Thus, it was right for him to live where Digory had spent most of his simple existence. And who could tell, she reflected further, but that some of the old man's life, the life of the spirit, might yet haunt the place and turn the young man, still a boy in so many ways, toward Digory's God, who had become her own God as well?

"I think it would be very possible," she answered at length. "The steps will have to be repaired of course, and the room cleaned up no doubt."

"I can do the work myself," he offered, perhaps too eagerly.

"I'll send someone over to help you. You'll not want to do a great deal until your leg heals."

"Thank you, Lady Margaret," Logan replied sincerely. "This means a great deal to me."

She left him in high spirits over the prospects of seeing her old groom's room made habitable again.

Logan continued to stare up at the closed door at the top of the stairs, then leaning his cane against a wall, tried to pry loose a couple of the boards that seemed to be rotten. Most of the framing was still sound. It wouldn't take much to make the stairway fully navigable.

Again, he had to compliment himself on the perfect setup. Even if the treasure was not up there, the place might reveal any number of clues. According to Lady Margaret, the old fellow was nothing less than a saint. What would a man like that do with a treasure? But actually Logan did not believe in saints—everybody had an angle. What had been Digory MacNab's? It could not have been pure goodness of heart—Logan found such a notion difficult to swallow. But then, why hadn't he touched the treasure for his own use? More than likely the old duffer had died waiting for the loot to cool off enough for him to use it. But that wouldn't explain the cryptic letter to Maggie.

The whole puzzle was perplexing.

But was it really necessary to figure it all out? It hardly mattered what the man's motives were, except insofar as it might lead Logan to the location of the treasure. Yet in spite of himself, he could not help being profoundly struck by the ambiguous complexity of the man who was his ancestor. He had to keep telling himself that the man's personality had nothing to do with it. It didn't matter if he was a saint or sinner. No matter what he was, it would surely please him greatly to see his great-great-great nephew prosper for a change.

Engrossed in thought, Logan heard, barely in time, the squeak of the door between garage and stable. He grabbed his cane and spun around.

27 Heated Words

It would rain before the day was out, but Allison thought she would have a couple of hours for a ride.

Every heir to the Stonewycke legacy could ride, and Allison was no different. She didn't care that much for horses, but riding did prove some distraction from the nearly intolerable prison that home had become.

As she walked through the old wooden stable doors, still standing open, she thought of the days long past when her great-grandmother had been a girl, when Stonewycke's stable boasted the finest stock in several shires and a full staff to care for them—groom, stable boys, and blacksmith.

Today there were only six horses. All good ones, certainly. But there was no staff to speak of. Her father—she shuddered at the thought—cared for the horses, and Nat and a couple of the field hands cleaned out the stable when they could be spared. Mr. Dougall looked in from time to time, but when Allison thought of her father feeding and rubbing down horses, and her brother, who might one day bear the family title, mucking out the stalls, she wanted to scream.

None of the other families she knew lived like that. The Bramfords had a far smaller estate, but it was fully *and* properly equipped. Imagine Edward Bramford IV sweeping up horse droppings! The thing was inconceivable. Her mother preached about hard times and economy, but Allison knew her parents really, deep inside, *enjoyed* living this way. They would have carried on as commoners even if Stonewycke were as prosperous and mighty as it had been in its days of glory.

Someday, she thought, *I may, as Mother said, be the mistress of Stonewycke. And then things will be different!*

As she yanked the door open into the interior of the stable itself, she noticed a light on. Perhaps there'd be someone around, after all, to saddle up her mount.

"Hello," she called, "is anyone in here?"

"It's me, Miss MacNeil," said Logan, hobbling out from the corner. "Good afternoon."

She nodded curtly and walked to the saddle rack where she began to examine several before selecting one. She started to lift it off, then cast a quick glance at Logan.

"Do you mind, Mr. Macintyre?"

"Of course not," he replied, "that is, if you're in no hurry." He smiled slightly and held up his cane to remind her of his infirmity.

"Oh, I had forgotten. I'm sorry." Rather than remorse, her voice seemed to contain a note of annoyance.

Logan, however, was determined to be friendly. Although this girl was the most tedious person he had met in a long while, he was not going to let her sour disposition intimidate him.

"Please, Miss MacNeil," he said, "everyone around here seems to be calling me Logan. Why don't you do the same?"

"Mr. Macintyre," she replied haughtily, "I hope the congeniality of my family does not cause you to forget who you are, and who *we* are. And I especially hope you do not plan to take advantage of their kindness. You are an employee here, nothing more. And it would be wise for you not to forget your *place*."

For a brief moment he could only gape in astonishment at the rebuke.

The next moment he burst into a great laugh. She could not mean it! It was altogether too ridiculous!

"How dare you laugh at me!" she cried in a passion of anger.

"My . . . my place! Ha, ha, ha—don't you know that sort of thing went out with Victoria? Ha, ha!"

"Maybe it went out on the back streets you call home," Allison said, still enraged, "but persons of proper breeding still know to whom their respect is due."

If there was one thing Logan despised it was snobbery. He believed that he was as good as any man, pauper or king. He refused to take arrogance without countering it, especially when it was directed at him. This attitude had gotten him into trouble before, and no doubt would again.

His laugh subsided quickly and he glared back at Allison. His next words were controlled and cool. "And I suppose you think you are just the one to remind me of my *place*?"

"If I must."

"It's you, *my lady,* who needs to be put in her place. And I think *I'm* the one who's going to have to do that!" Though he, too, was angry by now, his tone was measured, and not without a touch of tongue-in-cheek. But Allison did not enjoy his humor, especially that it came at her expense.

"You dare!" she seethed. "I will have your job."

"It would be well worth it, *my lady,*" he replied. "To lose my job in order to see you put in *your* place, I would consider it a more than equitable trade."

Allison rankled at his sarcastic use of her title, and Logan, thoroughly enjoying her reaction, continued. "I must be honest with you, *my lady*; it's high time someone was. You are the worst snob I have ever known, Miss Allison MacNeil."

"How dare you!" she shrieked.

"Whatever you may think," he went on, "being a Duncan does not give you the right to walk around treating people like dirt. If you hadn't noticed, this is the twentieth century. We are not your feudal serfs."

"I don't have to listen to this!" she fumed. "Leave this stable at once!"

"And if I don't?" said Logan, leaning back against the saddle rail and cocking his head slightly to one side.

"Leave this place at once!" repeated Allison. "You have no rights here. I command you to leave!"

"*You* command me!" laughed Logan. "You are so insufferable I can hardly keep from laughing. You're living in the Dark Ages, Miss MacNeil."

In a white heat of passion, Allison grabbed a saddle off the rack and marched down the row of stalls, stopping at the black mare's. She heaved the saddle onto the horse, who stamped its foot, none too pleased at the brusque treatment. She began to untie her, thinking to lead her outside and saddle her there.

But Logan, not yet finished, hobbled after her. "Do you mean to tell me I'm the first person to inform you of this flaw in your character?"

Dropping her hand from the latch of the stall door, her only response was a furious but speechless expulsion of breath.

This conversation had not gone as Allison had intended. After impressing him with her superiority, she had planned to relent just a bit, grant him the privilege of calling her by her first name, and perhaps even invite him along on her ride. Now she was too enraged even to speak.

With fingers none the nimbler, trembling uncontrollably, Allison attempted to secure the saddle. She gave the girth such a taut yank that the mare jerked away. But with Logan's final words she spun around, looking as full of energy as the lively filly she was saddling.

"Flaw in my character!" she repeated indignantly. "Who do you think you are that you can talk to me like this!" Her voice had grown icy cold and full of the imagined pride of her superiority, as if she dared him to venture an answer.

With the change, Logan had suddenly seemed to have enough. He could never out-argue or out-yell someone so passionate and volatile as this. Maybe she would listen to reason.

His tone moderated and his voice softened. "Who do I think I am? I'm just someone who was trying to be friendly," he said. "I only suggested that you call me by my first name, not that we marry and spoil the precious Duncan bloodline."

She bristled, and he quickly added, "I suppose I was only hoping that your cool and formal behavior toward me did not spring out of something personal you might have against me. And I thought perhaps if you called me by name—"

"Personal?" she asked, cocking her eyebrow, confused but wary. "I have no reason to have anything personal against you—I hardly know you. It's you who has been making personal remarks, when *you* hardly know *me.*"

He nodded thoughtfully at her point, then said, "However, I gathered from what you said that I might not be good enough for you to become acquainted with."

She restrained a satisfied smile. He was attempting to concede, to back down. He *did* acknowledge her superiority after all.

"Well . . ." she answered, drawing the word out in a coquettish manner, "I might make an exception—with you."

"You would!" He clasped his free hand to his heart and beamed stupidly. "You really would do that—for me?" He was mocking her, but she did not catch it at first.

"Why, of course," she began, "I don't see why I shouldn't—"

Suddenly she stopped, seeing his face, which could contain itself no longer, at last break out into a smile.

Realizing she'd been the butt of his joke, she tried to stammer out something further. But taken so off her guard, nothing would come, and the next words were Logan's.

"Why? you ask." His laughing had given way to a brutal seriousness. "Because, my lady, it's you who's not good enough for *me!*"

His cruel words were meant to sting, and they hit Allison all the more severely when he spun hotly around and limped away. She wanted to scream something after him, the final insult which would put the low-life in his place. But she wouldn't give him the satisfaction. She let him think his words didn't bother her at all. Which they didn't, of course!

She stared silently after him, and when he reached out to open the rear door of the stable which led outside, she suddenly noticed his limp, favoring his right foot. Hadn't it been the left that was injured? She continued watching in silence until the door had closed behind him, then ran quickly toward it and peered out through a crack. There could be no mistake: he was favoring his right foot, putting his weight on the left. How curious! She'd have to observe him again, later in the day, to see if the limp of their new mechanic had changed.

Slowly she walked back to the stall and turned her attention to the mare, finished saddling her, then walked her outside and mounted.

What could the man's game be, anyway? Why fake an injury? To get the job? It hardly seemed reasonable. He hadn't appeared that desperate for work. Her parents almost had to beg him to take it. Why then? Was he trying to ingratiate himself to the family? He had certainly not tried to get into her good graces with his behavior today!

She'd have to watch him and say nothing to her family. Nor would she confront Macintyre. At least not yet. She would bide her time for now. With someone as arrogant and self-assured and plain-spoken as this man, she would want some distinct advantage over him. In the meantime, she would keep her eyes open and try to find out what he was up to. Perhaps she ought to get on friendly terms with him. That might not be so easy after the things they had said today. But if he confided in her, there could be no telling what she might discover. And if she went to her parents with something definite against him, it might teach them to respect her opinion a little more.

She dug her heels into the mare's flanks and galloped off, eagerly anticipating the days ahead. The challenge of a bit of mystery was always invigorating—especially when the prey was such a cocky beast. Yes, the next few days and weeks might prove most interesting. And if nothing else, her schemes would relieve her boredom.

28   The Hunt Begins

It took two days, with the demands of Logan's other new duties as Stonewycke's mechanic, to repair the stairs to Digory's room. He had done most of the work himself, since spring planting had required the attention of the other hands. Thus when he had hammered the final board into place, he was all alone.

He gingerly navigated the steps, not out of fear either for their weakness or that of his ankle, but out of anticipation of what lay beyond the closed door at the top. What might his uncle's room reveal to him? Would this prove the end of his quest? He had but to turn the latch to find the answer.

He reached out, placed his hand on the ancient iron bar, twisted it downward, and pushed open the rough-hewn door, creaking on its hinges, nearly decayed from disuse. The light inside was dim and shadowy. High on the adjacent wall was a single window, large enough only to admit a whisper of the morning's light that shone outside. Logan had come prepared for near-blackness, and now he held aloft the kerosene lantern he had been carrying in his other hand. Suddenly a rapid fluttering sound filled the room. Logan stepped aside and ducked as a bat flew directly toward him, missing his head by inches, escaping through the door into the stable.

The large room was covered with a thin dirt-film from neglect, with cobwebs hanging everywhere. Stepping fully inside, Logan saw that there were in actuality two rooms. The one in which he stood contained a small cast-iron stove and a bed with a rat-eaten straw mattress. The other, little more than an alcove where the roof of the stable sloped down to the floor, but in which a small gable added enough height to stand at the near end of the room, contained a rough pine table and a single chair. An empty shelf had probably contained books or eating utensils. Between the two rooms stood a wide-open doorway. Two people would have felt extremely cramped in these quarters, but for a single man, with simple tastes, it might be satisfactory.

At least, thought Logan dryly, he had holed up in worse places in London. He set the lamp on the table and walked about, coughing as his feet stirred up years of settled dust. Everything he touched was covered with a thin layer of gray. But of one thing he was certain—there were no personal items lying about that might have belonged to old Digory. Whoever had cleaned out this room had done a thorough job years ago. They appeared to have left nothing but dirt and dust. Still, he remained undaunted. He would clean away the dirt and see what might lie beneath.

Logan turned and bounded down the steps to fetch a broom. By now he had abandoned his cane and any pretense of a limp. When he saw Lord and Lady Duncan approach the stairway, he did not panic, only slowed to a gait which might be considered respectable for one so recently recovered from an injury such as his. He was pleased to see them, for he had feared his employment might slow up his interaction with Lady Margaret as he became more of a fixture around the place.

"We heard you were nearly done with the repairs to the stairs," Lady Margaret said.

"Just nailed on the last board a moment ago," replied Logan, grinning with enthusiasm.

"Lady Margaret has not rested since you began your work," said Lord Duncan. As he spoke he glanced merrily at his wife and gave her hand an affectionate squeeze.

"Well, sir," replied Logan, "the work on the stairs may be finished, and I believe the steps are sound enough for you to venture a trip on them. However, my lady, it is terribly dusty up there. I was, in fact, on my way to get a broom just now."

"You seem to be getting along on your ankle quite well. A remarkably quick recovery," said Dorey.

"Yes . . . I suppose it was," said Logan. "It's feeling almost back to normal now."

"A little dust won't hurt me," said Margaret, not to be deterred from her mission. "And once you have cleaned up the place and moved in yourself, I wouldn't dream of intruding upon your privacy."

"That would hardly be a problem," said Logan. "You may feel free to intrude upon me any time. But I can understand how you would want to see it as it is."

Standing aside, Logan allowed them to proceed up the stairs; then he followed. Lady Margaret walked first through the open door, and soon all three were standing in the midst of the small main room. Turning around, Lady Margaret surveyed her surroundings, and a vague look of disappointment gradually came over her face.

"What is it, my dear?" asked Lord Duncan, closely in tune with his wife's moods.

"I don't know exactly what I expected," she replied. "I should have realized that a room is nothing more than that—walls and a few sticks of furniture. Without even an article of his lying about, it's almost lost all connection to him. I suppose I had hoped for some sweet memories to be rekindled. But there is nothing of Digory left here—it's only a room."

Then she turned expectantly toward Logan. "More than in these four walls, his memory resides in you, Logan. And that's how it should be. The legacy a man or woman leaves is propagated through his descendants, not through his possessions; through the emotions and spiritual values he passes on, not through the things he owned. Digory had no children of his own. But somehow I think you are meant to be his progeny—the one to carry on his memory."

Logan swallowed hard.

She made it sound like a great honor had been bestowed upon him—to sustain the memory and legacy of a great man, who was, in fact, nothing more than a common groom, a poor man who lived a life of comparative insignificance. Yet she indeed did see him as nothing less than great, a man worthy of all admiration and respect and honor.

Despite his efforts to harden his heart against intrusion, Logan could not keep from squirming under the responsibility her statement placed upon him. He found he could not easily brush aside her words. Then he thought of something.

"Wait here a moment," he said, as he turned and hurried down again to the stable, where he had already deposited his carton of belongings.

When he returned a minute later he was carrying an ancient and worn black book—Digory's Bible. Except for his removal of the letter, it was exactly as he had found it in Glasgow.

"Oh dear," said Lady Margaret as she took it into her hands. Her lips trembled as she tried unsuccessfully to speak. At last, with effort, she said, "He would sit over there," she pointed a hand toward the alcove, "at the table, the lamp sitting almost exactly where it sits now, with this book open before him. Dear Lord . . ." she closed her eyes and smiled. "I can almost hear his soft voice with its thick brogue as he would read to me when I was a child. I could hardly understand him.—But Digory . . . the words remained within my heart, and they grew and flowered, as you knew they would. I hope you can see the fruits of your undaunted faith . . ."

"He does, my dear Maggie . . . he does," murmured Dorey.

There ensued a long silence among the three, each who had come for his own reasons to that bare room where had dwelt a simple man of faith. Even Logan was caught up in that moment of poignant reflection. He glimpsed old Digory for the man he was, the man he himself had tried so hard not to see. He could visualize him just as Lady Margaret had described, bent over his Bible, his wrinkled lips saying the words that were so precious to him, hoping that somehow he could touch others. But he probably would not have given himself credit to think that anything about his own life would have had a lasting impact on others so many years later. All at once it occurred to Logan that the old groom would hardly have relished the idea of one such as Logan being his only progeny. If Digory had been such a saint, the notion of a con man like him being his descendant hardly seemed right.

But Logan shook himself free from the spell. He could not let himself be influenced by the lady's tender memories. He forced his mind back onto his ignoble course, realizing even as he did so that such an action was becoming harder and harder. The more caught up he became in the personalities of Digory and Lady Margaret, and the more the whole aura of this stable and these people and the whole of Stonewycke itself settled around him, the less easily he could shake off faint hints of something speaking to him that he had ignored all his life—the voice of his conscience. Was this place getting to him? No! He would not admit that. He had his job to do, and this was just one more obstacle to be overcome. If the problem were his conscience, he could deal with it as he had with Chase Morgan.

Yet . . . these people were not easy to dismiss—the ghostly image of Digory MacNab, no less real and compelling at this eerie moment than the Lady Duncan who stood right before him. But he had to dispel these thoughts, these feelings of fidelity and honor and respect for the dead. There was too much at stake. And as he tried to convince himself to remain on course with his original purpose, he did not wonder that he could be so greedy, nor did he even attach to his attitude that heinous label. But despite his resistance, the low, soft, persistant voice of his conscience and the One who created the conscience were moving closer and closer to the heart of Logan Macintyre.

The next words he spoke came from his lips with great difficulty, as if he knew the deceit that was in them, spoken as from a man who was trying desperately to pull his mind out of a deep trance.

"I wish I had your memories to draw from," he said, his voice feeling thick and heavy in his mouth. But an opportunity like this might not come again, and he had to find out all he could before this window to the past closed up and was gone.

"And I wish there were a better way for me to share them with you," said the lady. "He so loved his horses, as well as his Bible," she went on in a dreamy tone. "I remember how he pampered our two horses, Raven and Maukin. Do you remember them, Ian?"

The old man nodded, tears standing in his eyes. "Remember? How could I forget what those two horses meant to the two of us?"

"I think that's why they were so special to Digory. I think he took pride in those two above all the others because of you and me, dear."

"No doubt you're right," said her husband.

"But in a way, the horses were his whole life in those later years," continued Margaret. "I hardly remember him leaving the stable."

"Never?" said Logan in surprise.

"At least not often. He was so old, even when I was a girl. He cared for the horses, but there were younger men to do the driving and riding. He was so arthritic. There was one time, however..."

Suddenly she retreated, as if an exposed nerve had been touched, a memory too painful to speak of casually.

But Logan felt instinctively that these were the very words he must hear. He might hate himself for it later, but he had to press on. "What happened?"

She glanced at her husband. Logan could not read the look that passed between them, but Lord Duncan's brow knit tightly together.

"We rode out to the granite pillars of Braenock Ridge," she answered, as if she were making herself answer because she did not want to be ruled by dark memories. "I should never have made him go, but... I needed his help... I couldn't do it alone. I... think that's why he became ill later. It was an awful night."

The old man reached out and touched her arm tenderly. The sense that she had caused his sickness had obviously been a pain she had borne a long time.

"Braenock Ridge?" queried Logan. "Is that around here?"

"A few miles to the south," answered Lady Margaret, composing herself.

"Not a nice place," put in Lord Duncan grimly. "It grows only gorse and wiry heather and that only on the bit of soil between the rocks. The rest is dreary peat moor intermingled with treacherous bogs."

Margaret smiled at her husband, seeming to have overcome her temporary melancholy. "Spoken like a true lover of flowers and forest," she said. "But the moor has its merits. It was Digory, in fact, who instilled an appreciation for Braenock in me. He thought it might hold a particularly tender place in God's heart because it was so tenacious. You could find an occasional primrose there, but there weren't many. If you did find one, it was hardier than the ones in the valley. It did not give up because of the ugliness of its surroundings, but became even more precious because of them."

"Oh, lass," laughed Lord Duncan playfully, "I shall have to take a walk and have another look at this veritable Garden of Eden of yours!"

"Yes, I should like to see it again also," replied Margaret. Then turning to Logan, she apologized. "Mr. Macintyre, I'm afraid we've taken up too much of your time with our old folks' meanderings."

"I've enjoyed every minute," replied Logan. "I should like to talk again sometime."

"By all means. And thank you for allowing us to visit your new quarters."

Logan saw them safely down the steps, then he hurried off in his own direction. He knew he had pressed the woman enough on the subject of Braenock Ridge for one day. But he had to discover more. There had been something in her tone, in the way her voice had faltered, that made him feel it imperative to explore this place which Digory had apparently thought so much of.

29   Braenock Ridge

For one inexperienced on horseback, the best way to reach Braenock was on foot. At least that was Fergie's opinion.

"What do ye want t' be goin' oot there fer, lad?" asked the factor. "Nothin' there but rocks an' shrubs an' bogs fer yer horse t' break his leg on."

"Just curious," replied Logan vaguely. "Sounds like an interesting place."

"The ruin's all growed o'er."

"Ruin?"

"Aye. 'Tis what all the foreigner's be wantin' t' see oot there. A thousand years ago, maybe more, there was some Pict village there, oot by the boulders."

"Really?" said Logan, trying to appear interested in what looked to be the prelude of a boring history lecture. All he wanted to know was how to get there.

"Aye. But the village was wiped oot by maraudin' Vikings. In a single bloody massacre, so 'tis said, every man, woman, an' bairn was killed. Jist because the Vikings thought the Picts had gold ..."

At the word Logan's interest suddenly came alive.

"Gold, you say?"

"Personally, I think the gold was jist added t' the story t' liven it up a bit. If ye ask me, 'twas all done fer a crust o' bread. That's what they did in them days."

"How would I get there?" asked Logan. "Is there a road?"

"Weel, there's a road o' sorts fer a ways. After that ye got no more'n an auld shepherd's trail, an' that's mostly growed o'er too. There be little traffic oot there these days. No one lives oot there anymore."

"You mean someone used to?"

"Jesse Cameron's daddy lived oot there when he were a lad, an' the Grants, an' the MacColls, but they moved clean oot o' the valley noo. That were years ago. No one's lived there in my time. Jist canna support life on a bog that's either too arid or too wet."

After further effort, Logan at length was able to extract sufficiently specific directions from the factor, continually interspersed with odd bits of local memorabilia. But it was late afternoon before Logan could get away from his duties to make his solitary trek to the moor.

A gray sky loomed overhead and a chilly south wind blew down from the mountains. A gust threatened his checkered cap and he reached quickly for it, planting it more firmly down upon his head. With the motion came a thought of Skittles. The pain of his death had seemed to grow distant, as had thoughts of Molly and old Billy. He wondered what they were doing. And for the first time in a long while a fleeting picture of Chase Morgan's face came into his mind. He shivered and gave a violent kick to a pebble at his feet. His revenge over the gangster had availed him absolutely nothing, after all. Even his anger had not been appeased. He knew that if he ever saw Morgan, he'd give him no better treatment than that pebble. So what good had it all done? Molly had some money to get her through a tough time. But as Billy had warned, it had not brought Skittles back. Instead, it had only separated Logan from those he cared for.

Funny, thought Logan as he walked along, how such an insignificant act as touching a hat could produce so many memories. He had been here less than two weeks. But his memories of London seemed as far removed as Lady Margaret's memories of Digory. Would he never see his friends again, as Lady Margaret had never seen Digory again after she left Scotland nearly sixty years ago? It seemed inconceivable that he would never return to London. But then, perhaps she had felt the same way.

Lady Margaret . . .

His thoughts always seemed to come back to her. Why had she left Scotland so suddenly, as she told him? What did it have to do with the treasure? Or was it completely unrelated? He remembered that Digory had stated in his letter that the treasure had wrought so much evil. Yes, Digory would have thought it evil indeed that his dear little Maggie would have been forced to leave Stonewycke. But people such as Digory—poor, and filled with religious fancies—always saw things in black and white, always considered money evil, and blamed the ills of the world on "filthy lucre" and "mammon," as they called it. But it did not have to be that way. If Logan found the treasure, he was certain it would be different. He would make it different.

Logan was relieved of his thoughts for a time as the road steepened and he had to focus his complete attention on his steps. He left the road as Fergie had described and struck off on the shepherd's trail. The rock-strewn path crept like a beaten cur through a gray blanket of dormant heather, most of it overtaken completely by the spindly shrubbery. It was hard to imagine that in summer this whole hillside would break out into a vivid purple, like a royal robe spread out over the neglected patch of isolated ground. Now it lay grim and dank, more like a shroud than a king's mantle, and the wind whistled a lonely tune over the silent earth. Logan had to agree with Lord Duncan—it was, indeed, a dreary and inhospitable place. Beyond the abundance of heather, he could see large patches of bracken, the inevitable result of hundreds of years of overgrazing. No wonder this place was now deserted of human life, for even the poor sustenance sheepherding had provided was removed—perhaps forever.

As Logan's gaze swept the horizon, it finally rested on a misshapen heap of granite boulders jutting up from the moor about a half mile off. He veered off the path and struck a line through the heather directly toward the rocks. The spot where a band of cutthroat Vikings had murdered an entire village was an ominous place to begin his own modern-day treasure hunt, but it was the most logical one, and Logan would not be cowed by some ancient legend.

In ten minutes he had come to the foot of the granite mounds that loomed a good twenty feet above him. He looked them up and down like a mountain climber studying a new challenge. But Logan was no mountain man, and he dearly hoped he'd not be called upon to climb these, for their sides had been worn smooth by the weather. Smooth, that is, on their exposed surfaces. But they were still jagged and treacherous at the points where the huge rocks leaned upon one another in apparently random fashion. Five or six major stones stood out from the rest, none looking more inviting than any of the others.

It took him twenty minutes to circle the entire area, exploring, poking, and prodding around the overgrown heather and bracken at the bases of the silent towers. He had no idea what he might be looking for, guided only by Lady Margaret's painful memory of a day she and her groom had come out to this very place. She had said she "made" him go. What could have been the mission that had drawn her out to this desolate corner of the estate?

At length Logan sat down on a small stone. Once more he glanced all about him. On both sides of him stood the granite pillars. In front of him was a sunken little hollow, seemingly which once might have been large enough to walk into but was now all overgrown with brush. He'd looked everywhere obvious, and now had no idea what to do next. Perhaps this seeming lead out to Braenock meant nothing, was no more than a red herring in his search. Yet somehow inside he sensed that this place had something to do with the treasure, or at least had at one time. Had the Picts truly buried their gold somewhere here, only to have it discovered centuries later? And where was it now? *What were you trying to tell Maggie, Uncle Digory?* thought Logan. *She said you loved horses. And in your letter you even mentioned riding. And a cliff ... and some path. If you moved it, then it must not be here. It must have something to do with the horses,* thought Logan; *somewhere Maggie rode, or you and she rode together. But if not here, then where?*

Finally Logan rose with a sigh.

There was nothing more he could do here. He just didn't know enough yet.

Striking out in a different direction than the way he had come, Logan walked south from the pillars several hundred yards farther, then began to descend the ridge westward, hoping to pick up the road by which he had come at a more southerly point than where he had left it. As he tramped along with no path now to guide him, he spied in the distance what looked like a broken-down house. He continued on toward it, and coming closer saw that at one time indeed it must have been one of the crofters' cottages Fergie had told him about. Fences had at one time enclosed a small garden and no doubt a modest stockade of household animals. A couple of dry stone dikes ran away from the house, standing, despite their antiquity, nearly to their original height. The house itself, like all those abandoned hovels throughout the highlands and lowlands of Scotland, was roofless but still displayed four stout, stone walls, impervious to wind, weather, and time. It was a sad and melancholy reminder of a time gone by when the land, however poor, had been able to sustain the life of those poor tenant crofters who worked it with the sweat of their brow and the love of their hands.

Could this place be where Jesse Cameron's father was born and raised? wondered Logan. *She said it was out here. And if it was, Lady Margaret had been here, too.* "She must have been well acquainted with the whole valley and the hills that surrounded it," murmured Logan. "No wonder she is so fond of horses; she must have ridden here, and all about, by the hours." *Raven and Maukin,* he remembered, *the horses she mentioned. And Digory spoke of a horse named Cinder. If the treasure has something to do with where she rode, it could be anywhere!*

Arriving no closer to a conclusion than when he had begun his afternoon's outing, Logan left the abandoned cottage, made for the valley road, and thence back toward Port Strathy.

30   Telegram from the Fox

So, Macintyre had entrenched himself in the old castle!

Ross Sprague made a hasty departure from the Bluster 'N Blow where he had gleaned this nugget of information from the talkative innkeeper. *Well, the kid is a smooth operator, indeed,* thought Sprague as he ambled down the cobbled sidewalk of Strathy's main street. He would never have thought that Macintyre could have managed to get that close to the town's resident nobility. He wondered how he had done it, and if it meant he was any closer to the treasure.

It had been only a few days since Sprague's arrival in Port Strathy, and nothing of great import had occurred. He had managed to keep tabs on his young quarry mostly by listening in on the village gossip and occasionally asking a few innocuous-sounding questions. It seemed Macintyre had been making quite a name for himself around the card tables, and despite the fact that he had recently fleeced several of the locals, he appeared to be held in rather high regard. He had become a regular mascot on one of the fishing boats and now was setting up housekeeping with the town highbrows.

Well, Logan Macintyre, thought Sprague as he turned into the mercantile, *enjoy it while you can—it won't last.*

Sprague got no particular thrill out of hurting people. When it came time for him to walk in and ruin all of Logan's hard-wrought labors and plans, he would feel no sense of elation or particular pleasure. In fact, he would probably not feel a thing. He never became emotionally caught up in his work, and was thus considered by some as downright cold-blooded. But a man didn't get ahead by allowing his emotions to rule him, he reasoned. And that's exactly what Sprague's goal was—to get ahead. He would do whatever was necessary to achieve that end. Tailing a kid from London was nothing compared to what one of his particular calling was usually asked to do. He expected his boss would have him let Macintyre find the treasure, and then Sprague would jump in at that moment and take possession. It was a pretty standard plan that should work, especially with a man like Sprague in command. He was neither greedy, nor angry, nor vengeful—emotions that usually fouled up even the best-planned scheme.

Sprague suspected his boss's interest in this whole affair had roots in the nonreasonable—revenge was the most likely candidate. Probably something had happened years ago and he felt he had some score to settle. But that was hardly Sprague's concern. He was a man who could do his job. He'd walk in, cool as you please, and take what he came for. He'd do whatever he had to. If it meant not only retrieving the treasure but also getting rid of Macintyre, well, so be it. It wouldn't be the first time. Sprague was not squeamish. This Macintyre kid was not a bad sort. Sprague had known a lot worse in his business. But that would not prevent Sprague from successfully completing his assignment.

And he was ready to find out exactly what that assignment was going to be. He didn't like working in the dark, as his boss was forcing him to do on this case. With this sudden change in Macintyre's living situation, things could start happening pretty fast, and Sprague wanted to be prepared.

He walked up to the cluttered counter. The woman behind it was about his own age, although her rough appearance made her appear older. She was seated in an old captain's chair thumbing through a catalog of boats and fishing equipment.

"Mornin' t' ye," said Jesse Cameron, filling in while Olive Sinclair stepped out for a moment.

"Hello," said Sprague in a tone not unpleasant, but nonetheless laced with a certain arrogance. "I was told you have a telegraph here."

"Aye we do." She laid aside her catalog and rose, motioning him to follow. "Olive put it back here," she added as they entered a small back room crowded with a roll-top desk, stacks of cartons, and a narrow table which held the telegraph equipment. "It doesna get too much use in these parts, but the auld laird had t' hae one." Jesse blew away a layer of dust to punctuate her point. "Jist fix yer message doon on this," she went on, handing him a small piece of paper.

Sprague cleared a space on the corner of the desk in order to find room to write, then he chewed at the end of his pencil for a moment while he clarified in his mind the code he and his boss had settled upon. Finally he scribbled several lines on the paper and handed it back to Jesse.

"Noo, let me read it back t' ye, so's I know I hae e'ery word aright." She cleared her throat and began in an oratorical tone: " *'To Hawk: The pigeon is in nest. The robins are blind. The worm remains hidden. When and how will fox strike? Signed T.H.E. Fox.'* "

Jesse paused and cast a puzzled glance at her customer. "That's what ye're wantin' sent, Mr. Fox?" she asked, trying with little success to subdue the incredulity of her voice.

"Birdwatchers," Sprague offered by way of explanation. "My employer is one of those—what's the fancy name?—ornithologist, that's it! And a bit eccentric, too."

"Oh . . . I see." But the way Jesse drew out the words seemed to indicate that she did not see at all, but was willing to let the matter drop. "Noo," she went on more briskly, "Olive will send it soon's she gets back."

"But this is urgent."

"Weel, I canna run the machine, but Olive'll be back directly."

"I expect it to go out today."

"Dinna ye worry aboot that." Jesse impaled the telegram decorously on the outgoing spindle. "I'll make sure Olive checks this first thing."

"And I'll be expecting an answer. Deliver it to Roy Hamilton's place."

Sprague turned smartly and strode from the store, leaving Jesse shaking her baffled head and wondering just what the world was coming to.

Sprague glanced at his watch. Well, if the telegraph was par with the rest of the service in this little village, he'd better not expect an answer until tomorrow. That would mean another whole day of sitting around this hick town. He'd end up going crazy before he had any real work to do. That wire might spur his boss to some action. But what could he do before Macintyre located the treasure?

Actually, Sprague hoped the telegram from London would tell him to abort the whole crazy mission. There couldn't be any treasure. And even if there was, there were certainly easier ways of earning that kind of money.

Whatever the reply to his wire, he'd have to figure out a more foolproof way to keep track of Macintyre now that he was situated at Stonewycke. He couldn't very well hang about the place without attracting attention.

Sprague decided to spend the rest of the day assessing the castle's staff. There must be at least one person out there whom he could buy, someone who could deliver regular communiques about Macintyre's activities, and especially someone who wasn't apt to run off at the mouth.

Glad for the prospect of some activity, Sprague turned into Hamilton's pub in much better spirits than when he had left an hour ago.

31   An Unexpected Invitation

Allison saw him in the kitchen.

But standing as he was in the dim glow of the banked fire in the hearth, with eerie shadows reflecting off his face, he looked so much like a thief in the night that she was at first timid to approach.

In the two days since their fiery conversation, she had given Logan Macintyre a great deal of thought. She had not been able to help herself. How could a man make her so angry, and yet so fascinate her all at the same time? Perhaps that accounted for some of her present timidity.

But she couldn't let this opportunity pass. She couldn't tolerate a situation in which she had no leverage, no control. Thus, something had to be done to reestablish her supremacy over him. She had been looking for him for the last twenty-four hours, always just missing him. Or at times, as now, she would come upon him unobserved, but, losing her resolve, would quickly depart.

Shyness could never be accounted to Allison MacNeil as one of her faults. Had there been a morsel of it in her personality, it would have been considered, in her case, a virtue. But shyness was not what had held Allison back, it was more a case of stubbornness and pride. It galled her to make up to him—he was such an incorrigible cad. He should be crawling to her, not the other way around. And yet the very fact that she knew he would never do such a thing almost compelled her to make the first move. She had never met anyone quite so ... so impossibly aloof from what she considered the strength of her own personality. He could not have cared less what she thought of him. She hated him for it, of course! And yet, at the same time, she couldn't help feeling...

Well, she didn't know what she felt!

She just had to remind herself that there was a purpose behind her decision. She would turn the tables on him, put her feminine wiles to work, and in the end—well, whether she made sure the arrogant Mr. Logan Macintyre received his just desserts, or whether she granted him mercy ... that would remain to be seen.

Amid such a jumble of emotions, Allison cleared her throat to announce her presence, and stepped boldly into the room as if, indeed, he were a thief and she were about to apprehend him. But when he turned to face her, she instantly softened her expression, remembering that she planned to try out a new tack on him this time.

"Good evening, Mr. Macintyre," she said sweetly. "May I be of assistance?"

"Hello, Miss MacNeil," he replied, not showing that he had been disturbed by the sudden intrusion, nor displaying his surprise at her congenial tone. "I hope my fumbling about hasn't dragged you all the way down here?"

"Not at all," she answered in her most pleasant manner. "The sounds of the kitchen hardly penetrate to the next room, much less into the rest of the house. I was simply in the mood for a cup of tea."

"I can't seem to locate the light switch," he went on, asking himself even as he said the words what she could possibly be up to by being so friendly. "The cook said I might avail myself of the kitchen if I should ever miss a meal. I'm afraid I worked up a healthy appetite today."

"It's quite a walk out to Braenock Ridge." As Allison spoke she laid her hand on the elusive light switch. The bulb flashed on as the last word escaped her lips, and the illumination revealed her dismay at having said something she would have just as well kept quiet.

"I didn't know you kept such careful track of the activities of your hired *help*."

"Well, I . . ."—the last thing she wanted him to know was that she had been asking after him—"I had need of the car and wasn't sure it was in working order." The lie was too obvious but she couldn't help that now. She probably should have come right out and told the truth at that point, but she was so unused to such honesty that it simply did not occur to her. "We had kidney pie tonight," she changed the subject adroitly. "The cook's is every bit as good cold as it is hot."

"Thank you for the advice."

Logan crossed the room to the stove, where he found a covered crock. He decided to let the slip about Braenock pass, for she was obviously flustered enough without his adding to it. What was on her mind, anyway? And why was she so nervous . . . and so friendly all at once? It was rather interesting to think that the grand Lady Allison had been asking about him. The whole thing intrigued him, and since he could find no threat in her actions, he decided to play along.

"Kidney pie!" he announced, lifting the lid of the bowl. "Shall I also put on a kettle for tea?"

"That's woman's work," she replied, bustling up to the stove as if she were actually accustomed to standing there. She checked the waterline of the kettle, then turned on the burner.

Resisting a strange urge to comment sarcastically on her uncharacteristic words, he, instead, suddenly reached out and took her hands in his.

"Funny," he said, "I would never have associated these hands with work—of *any* kind." She tensed, but did not pull away. "I'm sorry," he said, almost embarrassed now himself. "I didn't mean to startle you. But they are lovely hands. I doubt they were meant for menial tasks." Slowly, almost reluctantly, he loosened his grasp and she let her hands drop to her sides.

She then flitted, with almost too much affectation, to a cupboard where she took out cups and saucers and plates.

"And what of *your* hands, Mr. Macintyre?" she asked airily.

"They do not feel like rough, workingman's hands, either."

"No. As I mentioned earlier, I have lately been busying myself in investments and finance, an occupation which develops calluses only where they cannot be observed."

"I had forgotten."

Allison set the crockery on the table, and by the time she had cut off two slabs of the kidney pie, the kettle was whistling.

"I'm glad to see that you are joining me," Logan said casually.

Allison poured the tea and they seated themselves at the old round table nestled in a warm corner of the vast kitchen. Had there been an intelligent mouse perched in the rafters above, a creature who knew the inner motives and designs of the two seated at that table, he might have thought the scene a very incongruous one indeed. Neither fit very well into the environs of a homey country kitchen, despite the fact that it was the kitchen of an ancient castle. Something about that setting, for the moment at least, seemed to soften all the rough and selfish edges both had accumulated in their short lives.

They chatted easily for a time about various inoffensive topics— the quality of the food, the castle, the weather, the horses, the countryside. Forgetting herself, Allison even laughed a time or two—a free, easy laugh. In those moments, the contours of her eyes and face seemed to change. A freshness and innocence flashed upon her. She looked as though she could be kind and warm, if only she would let herself be. And the way she tightened up immediately afterward, as if even the sound of laughter coming from her own mouth was too revealing, too threatening, caused Logan to wonder what she was hiding with the veneer of haughty distance she seemed bent on wearing.

"From the way you talk," Logan observed, "I detect that you have a deep attachment for this country."

"Does that surprise you?"

"Well . . ." he hesitated, not wanting to renew the previous tension between them.

"Speak freely, Mr. Macintyre."

"Until now I've sensed you're not particularly happy with your life here at Stonewycke."

"You're very observant." She sipped her tea as if she expected to be prodded to reveal her inner feelings.

"I see a girl who has everything, and I ask myself, what could possibly be missing that makes you so unhappy?"

"You're not going to start preaching to me, are you, Mr. Macintyre?"

"Heavens no!" He threw his hands up in mock surprise at such an idea.

"Good," she said crisply, suddenly reverting to her old self. "I get enough of that already. As if I were some kind of heathen or something."

"I think I see now," he said, drawing out the words thoughtfully. "It is the family that is the source of contention."

Allison said nothing, and there followed a moment of silence during which Logan wondered if he'd overstepped his bounds. Then suddenly she jumped up. "It's getting late," she said in a voice higher pitched than usual, apparently ignoring what he had said.

"Forgive me," he said quickly, laying his hand on her arm so she would not leave. "I spoke out of line."

"Not at all." She seemed to be struggling with whether to admit the truth in what he had said and thus allow him to see further into her real self than she had planned, or to lash out against his words in angry denial and self-defense. The mask of her outer self was momentarily stretched so thin that Logan might have seen something akin to desperation in her eyes as she wrestled with how to reply. Then just as suddenly the look vanished, and she said in a cool, controlled tone that kept her from either of the two emotion-charged extremes: "You simply made an observation, however far from the mark. Do not worry about offending me, Mr. Macintyre. My family is *wonderful.*" The final word was spoken with such an emphasis as to drain it of the sincerity inherent in the statement.

Allison wanted to flee. She didn't care for observations like his and wasn't used to such honesty. None of her friends were this open with her. She intimidated them into a sort of subservience which kept everything on a superficial level. But this man refused to be intimidated by her. And yet even as he probed in his most discomforting way, he was not without a certain sympathetic, even tender side which seemed concerned lest his—

But what was she thinking! Hadn't he been downright cruel in his outbursts in the stable earlier? *Tender? Logan Macintyre! Pshaw! The man ... why, he is insufferable!*

She was about to frame some caustic word which would again put him in his place when the thought of her friends came again to her and made her recall her original purpose in seeking Logan out. She became calm inside, reminding herself that she could be more successful by keeping up the front. Concentrating her attention on her previous intent, she let herself forget her awkwardness under his questioning and whatever else she might feel toward him.

She sat down once more, but Logan could sense that the previous pleasant mood had retreated, and the pretense was back again in full force. The words, however, when they came from the mouth, were agreeable enough.

"I've enjoyed our conversation, Mr. Macintyre," she said, pouring out some fresh tea.

"So have I."

"I'm afraid you might have misunderstood me on our last meeting."

"I feel certain I must have," he replied.

He thought, even as he spoke, that he had understood her quite well *then*. It was *now* that confused him—this changeableness, the flip-flops of her moods, the brief glimpses of a character she seemed desperate to hide, the congeniality followed by unspoken flashes of anger. What was going on inside the hidden inner self of this attractive young girl who seemed so in need of friendship, even love, but who so violently resisted any attempt by another to draw near on a human level? She was intriguing, despite his confusion; Logan would no doubt have been highly amused to learn that her own feelings for him were very similar.

"I'd like to make that up to you in some small way," said the congenial Allison.

"If there was any need for restitution," he replied in cavalier manner, "you have already done that tonight."

"I was thinking of some other way," went on the designing and contrived Allison.

"It isn't necessary," replied the wary Logan.

"I know," she said, touching her chin as if she were uncertain how to proceed; in reality the scheming side of her nature was now fully into place. "You may even think me forward in suggesting this, but ... I feel justified in that I'm certain you must long for the company of people your own age—everyone around here is so ancient. Well—there is to be a gathering of some of my school friends this Saturday at Lord Bramford's estate. And I thought you might like to accompany me."

Logan could not help wondering what he could possibly want with the company of a roomful of teenagers like Allison. And the way in which the invitation was phrased sounded as if she thought she were doing him a great favor in asking him. It hinted at the condescension so evident in their earlier encounters. Yet, could it be possible that she was sincere? He doubted it! Something in her tone . . .

But on the other hand, he could hardly resist such an opportunity to find out more of what made the complex Allison MacNeil tick. He could ignore the irritation stirred by her tone; after all, old habits die hard. And he was inclined to accept the invitation regardless. The enigma of this young lady was positively too fascinating, even though at the same time he was fully aware he could get burned by getting too close. Hers was not an emotional nature to be toyed with.

"That's a very kind invitation," he replied slowly, after a pause. "But I really doubt that I'd fit in."

"You deport yourself quite well—that is, you'd hardly know—"

"Hardly know I wasn't *really* of the same stock?" He shouldn't have said it, but he couldn't resist. He waited for her fiery response.

But instead, "No ... that's not what I meant to say—I mean ..." she said, then broke off, flustered.

He responded with a good-natured grin. Realizing that he was not disposed to making an argument out of it, she returned his smile.

"That is to say," she went on, the mask dropping again for a moment, "you would have no problem fitting in. I'm sure of it."

Logan was sure of it, too. He had mixed with such crowds before, and knew all the proper moves. How else could he be invited into the richest gambling salons or into the action around the wealthiest card tables? Still, he was hesitant. He reminded himself that he had to remain cognizant of his purpose in coming to Stonewycke, that he could not jeopardize his plan in any way, especially by becoming too involved with any of these people.

"I don't know," he said, looking her full in the eyes, seeing if he could find the real Allison somewhere.

"I'd . . I'd really like you to go with me," she said, returning the gaze.

He stared back, still wondering. *She was something!* he thought.

"I doubt your parents would approve of your being escorted by one of their employees," he said.

At this Allison laughed, and the bitterness of her tone only added to the paradox.

"Believe me," she said, "my parents like nothing better than the mixing of the classes. You needn't worry about them!"

"Well, then, if they approve, I'd be happy to escort you."

She rose.

"Now it really is getting late. Thank you."

He stood and bowed grandly. "My pleasure."

She seemed to float to the door, then stopped, turned, and added casually, as if she had just thought of the trifling matter. "The affair is black tie. I hope that won't present a problem for you."

"Not at all," replied Logan.

The young lady fairly waltzed through the corridors back to her room. She was quite pleased with herself. She had managed Mr. Macintyre quite well. But more than that—though the haughty Allison would never admit such a thing—she was extremely pleased at the prospect of being with this man. The sensitive Allison had enjoyed him immensely this evening and could almost forget that he was of low birth.

The haughty Allison hoped he'd see fit to keep that fact quiet on Saturday. She also found herself wondering what her friends would think of her dating such a person. It might even be considered rather chic, she told herself. It had always amused her friends to go "slumming," as they called it, while on holiday.

Whatever happened on Saturday, it was sure to be a memorable evening. The three days until then were positively going to drag by. At least she had gotten her new gown—not the exact one she had wanted, but close enough.

It would dazzle everyone. Including Logan Macintyre.

32   Glasgow Red Dog

There is a pride often associated with those who have known poverty, a pride that can be the result of stubborn pigheadedness rather than stemming from anything noble.

Logan Macintyre possessed just such a pride, however mixed it was with a colored sense of morality. He would make his own way in the world whatever it took. No handouts for him. He would rather "earn" his money in a poker game, employing questionable methods of skill, than to take a few shillings from a sympathetic friend. Even with Molly and Skittles, he had adroitly turned their acts of charity toward him into situations of mutual benefit. If they fed him when he was penniless, he reasoned that they needed his youth and energy in order to make their various schemes successful.

Thus, when Logan assessed his meager finances immediately following Allison's invitation, he found them sorely wanting for the necessities he supposed such an occasion would require. To ask Alec, the only likely candidate, for the loan of a tuxedo was out of the question. Not only was Alec several sizes larger than Logan, but it would have been too degrading to attend such an affair in a borrowed suit. Logan was extremely conscious of appearances. What money he had possessed had always gone toward the very best in attire. His tailor in London was reputed to have outfitted the Duke of Marlborough at one time. These things were important to Logan.

Unfortunately, he did not just now have the funds to meet these standards. But he did know where he might quickly acquire them. So the next evening found him at Hamilton's place, around a coarse table with several of his recent acquaintances, among them Buckie, a few other fishers, and a farmer or two. The stakes were not high, but he needed to raise only ten or fifteen pounds, and that should be possible. So confident was Logan of his success that he had already made arrangements with a tailor in Aberdeen for a fitting, and had requested the following day off from his employment at Stonewycke.

Buckie dealt the first hand, and bets were laid on the table.

Ale and pleasant conversation, however trivial, mingled with the business of poker. It was a congenial, easygoing group; none were apt to flare up angrily at their companions. Logan played a straight game, not caring whether he won or lost, just making sure he kept his stake in readiness for the real game, which would come later. He was simply lubricating the pursestrings for the time being.

Tonight Logan had a difficult time making himself forget how much he liked these simple country folks. It was especially hard to forget that Buckie had helped save his life. He would make it up to them all, he reminded himself. Now, he had to have the money, and this was the only way he knew to get it. He'd give them all a more than fair chance to win every shilling back later. But his once-be-numbed conscience had been raising it's head more often of late, and it took more than a concerted effort to squelch its insistent remind-ers that what he was about to do was wrong.

"I'm rather tired of poker," he said at length, leaning back in his chair with a yawn. "What about something else?"

"What did ye have in mind, mate?" asked one of the men.

"You ever hear of Glasgow Red Dog?"

"Canna say I have."

"Any of the rest of you?" asked Logan, looking around the table. They all shook their heads.

"It's simple enough really. And everyone makes just as much money as he wants. You're not even playing against each other, in a manner of speaking."

"Sounds too easy," said Buckie, with a skeptical expression.

"It is! But it's a good way to make a lot of money. That is, if you're sharp. But everyone's playing with the same chances. Shall I explain it?"

Shrugs and nods followed. Logan pulled out the cards Jesse had given him.

"Here, Buckie," said Logan, "try it. I'll deal you five cards, just like in poker." He did so. "Now, you look at your hand, and if you think you can beat the card I'm about to turn up, in the same suit, then you place a big bet, anywhere from a shilling up to the size of the pot. If you win, you collect the amount of your bet from the pot on the table. If you lose, your bet stays on the table."

Buckie surveyed his cards. He had a queen, a jack, two nines, and a six.

"What do you have?" asked Logan. Buckie laid his cards down on the table. "Well, that's a fair hand, Buckie, but not great. What do you think your chances are of beating this top card in the same suit?"

"I dinna ken," said Buckie slowly. "I'd say, maybe fifty-fifty."

"And how much would you bet?" asked Logan.

"I'd say a shillin'."

"Well, then, let's see how you'd have fared." Logan turned over the top card of the deck. "An eight of clubs. Your nine of clubs wins. You would then take a shilling out of the pot . . . or however much you had bet."

Nods of approval and general laughter spread around the table.

"What do you all say?"

"Let's gi' yer game a try," said Buckie.

"Okay," said Logan. "Everyone put in a shilling to start. Then from now on you can bet from a shilling to whatever's on the table."

Each tossed a shilling into the middle of the table and Logan dealt each man five cards. Each then took their turn betting, all starting with shilling bets, followed by Logan's displaying the top card off the deck against each hand. Two of the men won, four lost, including Logan; as the second round began, the pot stood at eight shillings, and Logan passed the deck to Buckie.

"Your deal," he said, and the game continued.

With every successive hand the pot grew larger, occasionally dwindling temporarily when a five or ten shilling bet was won, but steadily rising. With every hand, Logan's bet remained the same— one shilling—never varying.

At the end of an hour, the table contained some four pounds.

It was now the turn of a farmer by the name of Andy McClennon. He surveyed his hand for some time, obviously in doubt, then looked at his own money in front of him, an amount of about four and a half pounds. The cards in his hands were good ones, and at length he said, "I bet the size o' the pot!"

Exclamations followed and raised eyebrows. It was the first such bet that had been made.

"The size o' the pot, man. Ye're loony!" said Buckie.

"I got nothin' smaller than a ten, Buckie, an' three faces!" said Andy excitedly. "Hoo can I lose?"

The dealer turned over the jack of hearts. Andy's face fell.

"Blimey!" he shouted in a disgusted voice, throwing down his ten of hearts onto the table. "The one low suit I had!"

"Sorry, Andy," said Logan, and general condolences were mumbled around the table.

By this time, with the judicious use of his stake money and his slight winnings from the preliminary poker game, Logan had slowly boosted his cash to approximately five pounds. For the next several rounds the mood at the table was subdued, each man greedily eyeing the money on the table, but at the same time somewhat sobered by Andy's plight. Three hands later, the first of the moments Logan had been waiting for had come. Having carefully scrutinized every card on the table before him, and holding an ace, two kings, a jack and a nine, he knew there was only one card still out—the queen of diamonds—which could beat his hand—his own nine of diamonds. Deciding the risk to be worth it, he took the chance.

"I bet four pounds," Logan announced.

"That's nearly all ye got in front o' ye, Logan," reminded Buckie.

"Ye done nothin' but one shillin' bets all the game," said Jimmy, hardly hiding his perplexity.

"Just a difference in styles, I guess," said Logan.

"An' yet noo ye're layin' doon four pounds!"

"This is just my time to live dangerously," said Logan with a laugh. "Come on, Andy, turn up the card."

Andy flipped over the top card—a king of spades. Logan's black ace was higher.

"If that don't beat all!" exclaimed Jimmy. "It's like he knew what was comin' all along."

"You all saw that Andy was dealing me straight," said Logan, gathering in his winnings, leaving eight pounds in front of him, and only four in the center of the table.

Disbelieving shakes of the head followed. However, concurrent with Andy's dejection were several eyes twinkling with renewed enthusiasm. If Logan could do it—and they all saw that the game was fair—so could any one of them. And there was still plenty of money to win. Logan had been right. You could win just as much as you wanted.

Once again bets of five or ten shillings began to flow, with now and then a one-pounder thrown in. The size of the pot ebbed and flowed, steadily rising over the course of time. And once again, hand after hand Logan's bet remained the same—a single shilling.

Still he bided his time, waiting for another opportunity, watching the cards being played like a hawk, memorizing each as it was displayed, then carefully eyeing his own hand. He now had enough in front of him to go for broke—*when* the right moment came. He could not be over-anxious. He couldn't even risk it if a single card was out. He'd have to wait for what Skittles always called a lead-pipe cinch.

After another hour, the moment came. His own stash stood at about eight and a half pounds. The pot was now something slightly over seven.

The hand he'd been dealt was not all that strong on the surface of it—a king, two jacks, a ten, and a seven. It happened, however, that as Jimmy, immediately to his right, was dealing, he was the last man to play. Therefore, when time for his bet came, twenty-four cards were displayed on the table. With his own five, more than half the deck was known to him. Every heart above his seven of hearts was out, as were all the spades over his ten, and so on.

When his turn came, therefore, Logan was confident.

"I bet the size of the pot!"

"Ow!" whistled Jimmy. "Not again! Logan, ye'll put us oot o' the game!"

"Or maybe myself!" suggested Logan with a wry grin.

"Somehow I doobt that," said Andy sarcastically. He didn't exactly think this clever fellow from London was cheating. But he didn't like the idea of his betting nothing but one shilling until . . . wham!—the pot was suddenly empty.

"Weel . . . what'll it be, Jimmy?" said Buckie, anxious to get on with it.

Slowly and dramatically Jimmy lifted the card and threw it down in front of Logan.

"Ten o' diamonds!" exclaimed Buckie. "Tough t' beat, Logan!"

"Not for a king of diamonds," returned Logan, laying down his entire hand on the table beside the ten.

"Somehow I knowed it!" said Andy. "I jist knowed it!"

"Weel, lad," said Buckie, with a sigh, "I guess that's the end o' this game, seein' as hoo Logan has all oor hard-earned cash." They all began to rise, and Buckie gave Logan a friendly slap on the back. "Ye're the luckiest bloke I e'er seen!"

"I'd be happy to give you fellows a chance to get even," offered Logan, stuffing the sixteen or so pounds—mostly in coin—into the pockets of his coat.

Buckie laughed. "Na doobt . . . na doobt! But ye always seem t' come oot on top!"

"Like you said," replied Logan, "I guess I'm just lucky."

"An' I already dipped sorely int' this week's grocery cash," Buckie went on. "I'll hae the de'vil t' pay wi' me wife as't is."

Logan could not keep a pang of guilt from rising, but he quickly dismissed it with the thought, *I'll make it up to you fellows. Just you wait and see. I'll find that treasure, and I'll do right by you all.*

Andy McClennon, dour of disposition and in much less friendly tones than the others, added, "Seems t' me ye made fairly certain we'd no hae the means t' get e'en wi' ye."

"I can assure you—" Logan began, but Buckie did not give him the opportunity to finish.

"Come on, Andy," he said, laying a hand on the poor crofter's shoulder. "Dinna be a sore loser. 'Twas a fair game. We all knew what we was gettin' int'. Logan's as guid a man as one o' oor own, an' I'll be hearin' nae different. Noo, what aboot those drinks ye mentioned, Logan?"

"What! I mentioned no drinks."

"Dinna they do that in London?" said Buckie, winking knowingly at Jimmy. "Why, here in Strathy, man, the winner buys fer e'eryone!"

Logan laughed heartily. "Well, you've got me there, my friend," he said, glad to be able to buy his way graciously out of the potentially awkward situation with only a few pints.

The laughter and Buckie's good sportsmanship seemed to appease any further unrest, except perhaps in Logan's inexperienced conscience. Rising and shoving their chairs back, the rest of the group ambled over to refill their glasses, for Roy was not in the habit of serving his guests at their tables unless absolutely necessary.

Bringing up the rear, Logan passed the small table where a lone customer sat, quietly sipping a brandy. Catching Logan's eye, he gave him a sly half grin.

"Those yokels don't even know what hit them," said Ross Sprague in a soft, almost conspiratorial tone.

"What do you mean by that?" asked Logan in a tone made more defensive by the guilt he was trying to repress. "There was nothing crooked about that game. We all had the same chance."

"Except that you knew the game. I can spot a sharp a mile off." But as Logan opened his mouth to speak, Sprague held up his hand. "Oh, don't worry. Your secret's safe with me."

"To what do I owe that honor?"

"You and me live by the same motto, young fellow," Sprague replied. "It was stated very succintly by an American actor, W. C. Fields: 'Never give a sucker an even break.' Why, you had that game in the palm of your hand. That last hand—you couldn't lose! Well done, I must say."

Logan shrugged noncommitally. "Leave it to an American to sum it up so well." He started forward once more.

"Have a drink on me, kid," Sprague called after him.

Logan nodded his thanks, but after the encounter, his ale did not taste very good. He didn't like to think of friends like Buckie as "suckers." He didn't like to think that he might live by such a motto, even if he had never quite put it in those words. And since he didn't like to think of such things, he didn't.

Instead, he poured more than his usual measure of Hamilton's foul-tasting brew down his throat, and for the time at least, it dimmed the pangs of his conscience.

He didn't return home that night.

Somehow the thought of that unaffected loft where his simple, honest ancestor had dwelt was not appealing to Logan just then. Instead, he staggered up the street, where Sandy Cobden, against his better judgment, rented him a bed for the night. Logan made his way up the stairs weak-kneed, fell upon the bed, and drifted into a restless sleep, filled with the kind of dreams dragons might have while perched upon their ill-gotten treasures. In fact, at one point a dragon came into his dream, dressed in a grand tuxedo, with a plain fisher wife on his arm, carrying in her other hand an empty basket, which he knew had been intended for groceries.

But even in his sleep, when the dragon turned his direction, Logan shut the eyes of his mind even tighter, refusing to look at its face.

33   The Party

Logan called for Allison at five o'clock sharp.

He was invited by Joanna into the formal parlor where they engaged in a very awkward conversation for several minutes before Allison finally made her entrance.

He hadn't realized until that moment what a lovely *woman* she was. He had always known she was pretty, but tonight she seemed to have matured far beyond her seventeen years. Before, she had been an attractive *girl*, but now her budding womanhood was given full reign. Some of it, to be sure, was affected by Allison. But what struck Logan was the natural beauty and grace which could not be feigned, a hint of the loveliness and poise of her handsome mother. Logan could only think that what she tried to put on with grown-up airs only detracted from what naturally dwelt within.

Her golden, silky hair was piled in curls atop her head, some of them falling daintily about her face. Tufts of baby's breath were tucked about the curls like a crown. Her gown of periwinkle blue strongly resembled the one she had discovered in the catalog, only its stark severity had been softened by demurely flowing butterfly sleeves that fell to her mid-arm, and a satin belt around the waist, clasped with satin rosebuds. The overall effect had been to Allison's satisfaction, the price to Joanna's, and thus a very stunning compromise had been negotiated. An ancient strand of pearls that had been her great-grandmother's graced her lovely, porcelain-smooth neck.

At that moment, Logan did not feel so bad about his winnings of the other night. He had been to Aberdeen and had purchased a tuxedo, if not the finest evening attire to be had in that provincial city, certainly more than adequate for whatever he would encounter north of London.

There was little call for a florist in Port Strathy, but Logan had engaged Dorey's willing assistance to fashion a corsage of creamy white orchids, nurtured with love in the laird's own greenhouse. He fastened the blossoms about Allison's tiny wrist.

When he helped Allison into her rabbit-fur stole, he noted a tear glistening in Joanna's eye. He wondered if it was simply the sentimentality of a mother seeing her daughter looking so grown-up, or if it had other more remote origins. Was she having last-minute misgivings about letting her precious daughter go off with a man they barely knew? She had given her approval, but perhaps was now having second thoughts.

Well, it was too late for that now, and perhaps Joanna sensed that fact as well. For she bid them goodbye and did not even remain in the doorway while Logan maneuvered the Austin down the long drive and out through the iron gates.

The Bramford estate, located a few miles southwest of Culden, was one of those early Victorian country homes which, from the passage of years, could have either taken on a quaint historical charm, or have become a run-down white elephant. In the Bramfords' case, due to yearly maintenance and an ongoing familial interest in the estate, the former was happily true, and the home was one of the more elegant in the entire region.

The continued foul weather had prevented much in the way of outdoor festivities, and even as Logan and Allison stepped out of the Austin, leaving it to be parked by an attendant, dark clouds could be seen massing overhead. But that hardly dampened the party spirits of the young people gathered inside. Music, heavy with brass and drums, blared from the ballroom, creating a scene quite alien to the affairs the same room had seen in the days of Queen Victoria. The youths danced in a fashion that left Lady Edwina Bramford, who was positioned by the door greeting guests as they arrived, with a bewildered look on her highly refined face. She smiled thin smiles at the constant stream of arrivals, most of whom she did not even know, wondering how long her motherly duties would force her to remain in such close proximity to this unseemly display of modern merrymaking. She was from the old school, where young ladies *did not* wriggle around thus on the dance floor, and where *gentlemen* politely asked the favor of a young lady before a dance, not with a slick, "Come on, baby, let's dance." There had hardly been a polite word spoken, in her estimation, all evening. And these were the flower of the nation's populus, the offspring of the very best—lords and ladies, financial magnates, military leaders. What was the world coming to if the children of the land's elite had completely forgotten how to behave?

Thus, when Logan and Allison walked toward the ballroom door, it was little wonder that she was pleasantly surprised. Allison would have strode into the room without giving the woman a passing glance, but Logan took Lady Bramford's hand, kissed it respectfully, and bowed with what she could only consider very gallant taste.

"I am honored, my lady," he said when introductions had been made.

"We are pleased you could come, Mr. Macintyre," replied Lady Bramford. "I haven't heard your name mentioned, but you must know my son from Oxford."

"I'm afraid I haven't had the pleasure of his acquaintance, nor that of the remainder of your esteemed family."

"Mr. Macintyre is a friend ... of my family," broke in Allison, feeling an explanation was due before Logan was accused of party-crashing. "I hope it was all right for me to invite him."

"Of course, Allison, my dear," replied Lady Bramford. "I'm certain any friend of your family must be of the most sterling character."

At length Allison steered Logan onto the dance floor. A five-piece band was beating out Fred Waring's version of the 1927 hit *My Blue Heaven,* and the glossy parquet floor was alive with other dancers shimmering in brilliant color and displaying the wealth they represented. There were many friendly calls of greeting to Allison who, in return, waved and generally behaved as if the Bramfords' ball had been given exclusively for her benefit. And, whereas the greetings had been largely lodged at Allison, the curious glances and muttered comments of *Who is that she's with? ... quite a handsome chap, don't you think?* were reserved for Logan. The looks sent his way by a number of the young men, while not exactly hostile, were nevertheless guarded, as if to imply, *He's too suave . . . he must be up to no good.* The girls, on the other hand, all wondered where Allison had found such a gorgeous man outside their circle, some asking themselves whether he might be fair game or whether Allison had him already sewed up.

Saundra Bramford, as hostess, took the opening initiative with the new arrivals.

"Allison, dear," she said, approaching them graciously, as if she were a model for one of the new fashion magazines. All the years of training and dental work had paid off, for her natural homeliness was hardly evident beneath the exterior gloss. When she turned her head toward Logan and smiled, showing perfect caps, he might not have noticed her striking resemblance to her lumbering football-playing brother. But unfortunately, Eddie Bramford turned up almost at the same instant, accentuating the similarities in comic paradox—where he was thick and imposing like a mountain, she was thin and imposing like a tree. Yet despite their handicaps, they remained a good-natured pair.

"I'm so glad you could make it," Saundra went on. "It's such a long ride, and in this abominable weather. And you even managed to bring a guest." Here she smiled at Logan.

"I hope you don't mind," Allison replied as if it really didn't matter anyway. "This is Logan Macintyre. Logan, these are our hosts, Saundra and Eddie—I should say *Edward*—Bramford."

"Macintyre . . ." mused Eddie. "Didn't you play for King's College."

"I'm afraid not," Logan answered politely, not elaborating on the fact that he had played nothing for any college, had never so much as set foot on the campus of an institution of higher learning.

"Now don't you go talking rugby, Eddie," Saundra scolded. "You said you were cousins. . . ?" she prompted, wanting to know immediately where Allison and this good-looking Logan Macintyre stood.

"No relation whatsoever," said Allison.

"I'm in the employ of the MacNeils," Logan offered, part of him warming up to the challenge of keeping up the charade, another part curious to see how Allison might handle herself if he revealed just what a low fellow he was. He had agreed to come with her, but he didn't want to give her *too* much control over him.

"What line are you in, Macintyre?" asked Eddie.

Logan opened his mouth to answer, but it was Allison's voice that rushed in ahead of his.

"He's in investments," she said.

Logan snapped his mouth shut, wondering just what he would have said given the chance. As it was, he could not call Allison a liar, so he was forced to play the game.

"Investments," parroted Bramford. "A sticky business these days."

"We've weathered the crisis quite well."

"And what firm would that be?"

"Oh, look!" broke in Allison conveniently, "Punch—I'm simply dying of thirst!" She grabbed Logan's arm and dragged him toward the refreshment table.

Logan handed her a glass of the sweet red liquid but Allison stared into it as if it were the furthest thing from her mind. As Logan set the glass back on the table, his lips bent into a smile. *Why not?* he said to himself. He took her hand and tugged her toward the dance floor.

"Shall we dance?" he said. It was more of a command than a question.

She started at the initial gesture and glanced toward him, not a little bemused. In picturing this evening beforehand in her mind, somehow she had never envisioned what it would actually be like to have Logan Macintyre take her in his arms and dance with her. She had thought about what she would wear, about which perfume to choose, about what her friends would say, and about how she might flirt with Logan just enough to raise the attention of, say, Charles Fairgate. But of the moment when they would inevitably move around the dance floor, holding one another close, keeping time to the strains of the music, her face but inches from his shoulder—that was a moment she had not fully considered. Perhaps she was afraid of the effect such a moment might have on her.

The band had just begun playing *Girl of My Dreams*, and Logan gripped her waist for the waltz with rather more strength than she was accustomed to. She wondered if he was angry, but when he spoke his voice was smooth and pleasant.

"I think, Ali, my dear," he said, "that you should have gone for broke. Why stop at a mere investment broker? You could at least have given me an earldom."

"I thought you'd *thank* me," she replied.

"Thank you?"

"I only thought to save you undue embarrassment."

He chuckled softly in her ear, which was resting very near his lips. *Embarrassment for whom,* he wondered—*herself or me?* But he said nothing further. He had invested too much in this suit to see the evening degenerate into an argument. Besides, he wanted to enjoy himself. This young vixen was not altogether without her charm. Whatever her motives had been, he decided, she had apparently resolved to make the best of the situation, for she snuggled closer to him as the tune progressed. For all their discord of a few days earlier, they seemed to move like a single dancer, in almost perfect unison. Wary as they had been of one another, neither had to be forced to enjoy floating over the dance floor. Nor did they say a word for some time. On they danced, and Allison had just rested her head softly against Logan's chest and shoulder when Logan felt a firm tap on his shoulder, intruding into his contented thoughts.

He loosened his hold on Allison and spun around to behold an uncomfortably familiar face out of his past. Suddenly the years fell away in his mind, and he was fifteen, sitting in a card game, trying out his skill against the wealthy son of a lord. And after seven years, his adversary—though older and wiser, and now a man—had not changed. If anything, his dark and arrogant good looks had become even more pronounced.

Charles Reynolds Fairgate III! thought Logan, managing to keep his expression as cool as ever. *If he recognizes me, the jig's up! He would love nothing better than to expose me now after he couldn't make the charges stick the last time!*

"I hope you don't mind, old chap," said the man who had caused Logan several anxious days in jail. He nodded toward Allison, and Logan was momentarily relieved. *Perhaps, this far away, in this setting, after seven years, he won't recognize me,* thought Logan. But then almost as if reading his mind, Fairgate's brow wrinkled in puzzlement. "Have we met before?" he asked.

"I don't think so," Logan replied, thrusting out his hand.

"Macintyre's the name." He cringed inwardly even as the name left his lips, but he could see no way to avoid it. He only hoped Fairgate's memory for names was as fuzzy as it apparently was for faces. Besides, back in those days, Logan went by so many aliases that perhaps he could sneak his real name by with minimal risk.

"Hmm . . ." muttered the young lord thoughtfully. Then in a different vein, "Allison," he said, "I've been waiting for a dance with you."

"By all means, Charles." She stepped away from Logan, betraying a twinge of disappointment, which surprised her more than anyone, and into Fairgate's arms.

Logan stepped back, folding his arms, and watched the couple swing away from him. He tried to keep a nonchalant smile in place, but it was not as easy as it once might have been. He had rather enjoyed that last dance, or more accurately, had enjoyed holding Allison in his arms.

No doubt most observers would have felt the two made a fine couple, he thought. She probably had brought him here as part of a scheme to work her wiles on Fairgate. It would be just like her, he thought. But as he watched them, Logan could not help but think there was something sharp and dissonant about Fairgate's harsh, angular features next to Allison's soft loveliness. It grated against Logan's sensitivities, even as he tried to convince himself that he should not care whom Allison danced with. He would not be here that much longer. He would be gone and that would be that.

With the thought of his business in Port Strathy came the jarring reminder that Fairgate's sudden appearance could prove a major dilemma. If he should chance to remember their previous association, and revealed what he knew, it might be difficult for Logan to talk his way out of it. But Logan was not left to his thoughts, or his aloneness, for long. The moment Allison melted away with Fairgate, several girls swarmed toward him. The first to lay claim was Saundra Bramford.

"We are very progressive around here, Mr. Macintyre," she said. "The girls are not expected to have to wait to be asked. And I especially, as hostess, must see that my guests are properly cared for."

All for progress, Logan took Saundra's slim arm just as the slow beat reverted to a swing. For that Logan should have been thankful, for the Bramford girl, in many years of trying to teach her cloddish brother to dance, had nearly forgotten how to do anything but lead. But Logan soon found himself being handed off from girl to girl to girl, and it was not until the call for dinner sounded that he saw Allison again.

Following dinner, Logan and Allison found themselves together for several more dances. Whenever the music turned to a slow tune, each unconsciously sought the other out, trying, however, to make their encounters seem accidental. But whenever Allison was in the company of another man, Logan found himself with no scarcity of society girls, for they seemed ever available. He was frequently the object of scowls from the young men whose dates seemed far too intrigued with Allison's mysterious friend.

He managed to avoid any further contact with Fairgate, though Angela Cunningham, who had accompanied the young lord of Dalmount, always seemed to migrate toward Logan whenever Charles was with Allison. The last thing Logan wanted to do was attract Fairgate's attention. But Miss Cunningham, in addition to being rather pretty herself, was precocious and difficult to refuse.

When the huge grandfather clock in the entryway chimed ten o'clock, Logan began to give thought to the trip home. It had taken a good hour to drive to the Bramford estate, but since their arrival a fresh rainstorm had descended and the roads, already poor, might add still another hour to the return. The MacNeils had said nothing to him about when they expected their daughter home, but he did not want to take any chances with their good graces.

He determined to seek out Allison at the first opportunity. However, when next the music stopped, it was to the sharp ringing of a spoon against a crystal glass. A gradual hush fell over the crowd, the band stopped playing, and all eyes turned toward where Lady Bramford stood on the platform beside the band.

"Children," she said, "I have an announcement." She paused, as if for effect, then continued. "I've just had word that our road is washed out. I'm afraid you are all quite stranded—"

Before she could finish, a great cheer rose from the young people, for in their youthful estimation, the most perfect end to an evening such as this would be not to have it end at all.

Lady Bramford, none too pleased at the prospects, but attempting to make the best of it, cleared her throat daintily. When that had no effect on the reveling group, the cornet player blasted a shrill note, bringing silence. "As I was saying," she continued, "you will be our guests until morning, at which time we will be able to send a crew out to repair the road. Accommodations will be prepared for you all—I hope you won't mind being a bit crowded."

Far from minding, the guests doubted that anything could be more exciting! Logan, however, was hardly looking forward to another twelve hours of such highbrow company. He would have given anything to be able to spend the night with the fishermen at Hamilton's.

The next hour was spent telephoning families with the news, made all the more frantic by the fear that the phone line would go out any minute.

"I know, Mum, it's a rotten go, but what can I do?"...

"Yes, Father, you'll have to mention the conditions of the roads in the next House session. Until then ... we'll just *have* to make do."...

"It's terrible—but somehow, Mother, I'll survive it."

And so went the calls until scores of parents were feeling sorry for their hapless children. And the children themselves did little to dissuade such feelings, knowing that no parent would feel very comfortable with the thought that their children were having a *good* time.

By midnight the sleeping accommodations had been arranged—the young ladies in the east wing, the men in the west.

It would be hours before slumber would descend in either wing, however. To the east, sleep was forestalled by the endless gossip concerning the evening. Who had danced with whom, and how often. Wasn't Saundra Bramford's engagement to be announced tonight? What had happened? And why was her beau so conspicuously absent?

Logan's name came up frequently in the various rooms of the east wing. Who was the dashing stranger? Why hadn't anyone heard of his family before this? Could he be from the Continent? No, he had an unmistakable Scottish accent. But hadn't someone said he was from London? Too bad of Allison to keep him all to herself.

On her part, Allison wasn't quite sure how to react to all the attention Logan had generated among her friends. She had brought him for this very purpose, but now that it had worked so well, she had mixed feelings about the whole thing. He *was* her discovery, and the raves of the other young ladies naturally reflected on her. But they detracted from her in a sense, as well. She wouldn't have minded so much if during her sallies among the other young men, he had been idle and disconsolate at her absence. But he hadn't appeared to miss her company in the least.

She joined halfheartedly into the girlish banter around her, and was downright sullen as she finally snuggled down under the blankets to try to find some solace in sleep. What she had expected from the evening, she couldn't quite specify. Had she brought Logan Macintyre here hoping to make him fall in love with her? Was she irritated because she was unexpectedly beginning to fall in love with him? No—of course not! That was ridiculous! He was nothing! A commoner! And a brash egotist as well! She refused to think about it anymore.

And with such a turmoil of confusions and questions rattling around in her brain, Allison drifted into an uneasy but dreamless sleep.

Logan had other matters occupying his mind at that moment. The young men, not given to gossip, had found more practical means of passing their time. By some ill stroke of the draw, Logan had been housed with the boorish Clifford Arylin-Michaels and Charles Fairgate. His first thought was that the young lord had purposefully machinated the seemingly coincidental accommodations in order to get him alone to question him, or perhaps for some other purpose yet to be named. Somehow he did not perceive Fairgate as a man who ever fell victim to mere chance. But as the young lord said nothing, there was no way for Logan to find out what he knew without dangerously jogging his memory. His only choice for the present was to continue playing the innocent, and hope that what Fairgate knew about his Glasgow background would not come to light.

A few minutes after they were settled, Eddie Bramford and two others whom Logan did not know came into the room.

"It's too early for sleep," said Bramford, brandishing a deck of cards. "Anyone game?"

Fairgate nodded his assent, but Arylin-Michaels abstained on the grounds that he was too intelligent to participate in low games of "chance." Then several eyes turned to Logan. What he most feared was to get involved in a game which would simulate that situation so many years ago and which might therefore refresh Fairgate's memory all too keenly. He had changed a lot from the coarse and grubby fifteen-year-old he was then. But not enough to stand up to a test this severe.

"I think I'll pass," he said, punctuating his words with a convincing yawn and stretch. "I'm awfully tired."

"Aw, come on," prodded Bramford. "You stole all our girls tonight. The least you can do is give us a chance to get even." His voice revealed his cheerful nature.

"I hope you don't think I was trying to—"

"No," interrupted Bramford. "We'd never hold a little thing like that against you. It's hardly your fault if those crazy girls—you know they're all younger than us *men!*"—he looked around at his two friends knowingly and with a sly grin—"all go a bit featherheaded the minute they lay eyes on someone new."

Logan laughed, looking quickly from face to face. They all seemed in accord except for Fairgate. His look, fairly well concealed but evident to one like Logan whose business required a knowledge of faces and their masks, revealed that he had indeed not forgotten Logan's advances in the directions of his Angela Cunningham. His silence was all the more foreboding, knowing what Logan knew he knew, and he wondered what revenge the young lord might even now be planning.

"I'm not really much of a card player," said Logan.

"We'll be more than happy to teach you," replied Fairgate, speaking now for the first time and looking him evenly in the eyes.

"I . . . I really—"

"We won't take no for an answer," insisted Bramford, "except from Clifford, because he's a wet blanket, anyway."

Seeing that to continue with his resistance would only raise more questions than to give in, Logan resigned himself to his fate.

The five, including Bramford's Oxford cronies Raymond Crawford and Mitchell Robertson, sat in a circle on the floor since there was no table in the room large enough for the gamesters. Ray produced a box of chips and began placing stacks in front of each player.

"I'm afraid," said Logan, making one final attempt to retreat, "that I haven't come prepared with much ready cash—"

"Not to worry," said Bramford. "We know you're good for it."

Logan didn't even want to think about what the progression of chips were worth, and he certainly wasn't about to ask. Perhaps, being but the *sons* of wealth, these fellows might have little *real* wealth at their fingertips. The stakes might not be that high. But who could tell? He'd just have to put it out of his mind, and concentrate on playing like an amateur, making sure he neither won nor lost too much, and making sure the attention stayed on someone else when the pot grew large.

Bramford dealt out the first hand, identifying the game as five-card draw. Each player threw a white chip into the pot. Logan had no idea if it represented a shilling, a quid, or a hundred pounds, but he tossed it in as if it were worth only the wood from which it had been made.

The game progressed without incident. The pots remained small, the hands nothing much more than an occasional full house or straight, and Logan managed to lose an occasional big one for the sake of appearances, always gradually winning back his losses over the following several hands in small enough chunks that his profile in the game remained obscure.

Whether Fairgate was watching him he could not tell, but the longer the game went the more he remembered why Fairgate had been such a perfect setup seven years earlier. Not only was his manner irritating and conceited—a fact which had only grown worse with the passage of time—his poker playing was of the worst sort. It was all Logan could do not to forget that he was supposed to be an inexperienced gambler. He simply could not pass up such an opportunity to outplay these "golden boys." Especially Fairgate.

At length the hand Logan had been waiting for came. With deuces wild—a typical university trick, Logan told himself, which had no part in men's poker, but which he would take full advantage of since it was the house rule—he had drawn two cards to a jack-high full house. Bramford and Crawford were out. Robertson had raised twice, and he and Fairgate had both remained in. After

Robertson's second raise, Fairgate had raised again. Robertson folded. His eyes gleaming with the old magic, Logan threw in the calling chip, hesitated a moment, then threw in another blue.

"Let's see how good your hand really is, Fairgate. I'll raise you again."

"You're a cocky one, aren't you, Macintyre," replied Fairgate. "On the poker table as well as the dance floor. But this time I don't think you can beat me. In fact, Macintyre," he added with a slight curl to his already scornful lip, "I think you're bluffing. I don't think you're quite man enough for our game. I don't know where you come from, though I could swear I've seen you before. But one thing you'll soon learn is not to mix where you don't fit. So I'm going to call your bluff, Macintyre."

With the words he brazenly tossed a final blue chip into the middle of the floor, and with a flourish abandoned protocol and displayed his cards for all to see—a queen-high straight.

"Beat that, Macintyre!" he said with a sneer, looking Logan deeply in the eyes, as if still trying in vain to recall the connection his mind seemed intent on making.

Logan returned his gaze, debating within himself. After a pause of several moments, he laughed, almost nervously, and said, "You're right, Fairgate; you're a better man than I!" With that he threw his winning cards face-down onto the rest of the discarded deck. "You win!"

34 The Drive Home

Allison was glad when the final goodbyes had been said and they could finally get away. She wasn't quite sure what to make of the events of the previous evening, or where exactly she now stood with Logan. By inviting him, she had hoped to gain ground both in the estimation of her friends and in Logan's eyes. But it seemed he had in fact been the one to become the talk of the ball, not her. She had hoped to play the new appreciation Logan would surely have for her to an advantage; now she realized she was in no position to do any such thing. If anything, he now held the upper hand.

The rain had let up for a short while that morning, allowing workmen to repair the damaged section of road. But by the time Allison and Logan reached the Lindow Bridge, the clouds had amassed again. Below, as the Austin plodded across the ancient wooden structure, they could see the waters of the river lapping nearly at a level with the road. Allison had never seen the river this high before, but she had heard of other floods in the valley that had ripped away bridge, road, and anything else within several hundred feet of the river's shores. Already the mighty rush of water was making the pilings of the bridge creak and sway dangerously. Allison held her breath as they crossed, wondering what the road ahead would be like.

Logan slowed the car through a muddy bog shortly beyond the bridge, then suggested they turn back. But Allison made light of the weather.

"Oh, this is nothing. It gets this way every spring." She could hardly disguise the fact that she was more than a little frightened to be slipping and sliding around the road as they were. But she wanted to get home, and she could not betray her inner anxieties to a man of the world like Logan.

Logan proceeded forward. The road was muddy, in some places covered completely with water, but still navigable. The Austin crept along like some strange amphibious creature. All at once a deafening crack of thunder shook the landscape, and the sky belched forth an almost instantaneous deluge of fresh rain. It fell so hard and thick that the automobile's small windshield wipers were hopeless to fulfill their intended task. Logan could see nothing ahead of him.

"Ali," he said, "put your head out the window and let me know when I have to turn."

"What?"

"I said stick your head out—"

"I *heard* what you said. You must be joking. I'll be drowned!"

"Would you rather end up in a ditch alongside the road?"

"It's miles till the road turns."

"I saw a bend in the road just ahead."

"Impossible!"

Logan blew out a sharp breath. "Ali, *you* are impossible!"

"Don't call me Ali!"

"I'll call you anything I please," he retorted, the tension of trying to drive in the storm undermining his usual patience. "And unless you want me to think of something even more unpleasant, you had better—"

He broke off as the steering wheel suddenly jerked out of control and the wheels of the car lurched over the edge of the muddy road. Logan pumped furiously on the water-soaked brakes. But he hardly needed to. The car bumped to a jerky stop, its two front tires off the road in a ditch full of water, its engine dead. Logan turned the key, but it only coughed and sputtered in response.

"Now look what you've done," said Allison smugly.

Logan turned his head and stared at her, his burning eyes saying more than could any words.

She turned away, perhaps humbled by the sound of her own outburst. "Now what?" she asked in a more contrite tone.

"I suggest we sit here until the storm passes."

"That could take forever!"

"Well, what do you expect me to do? Stop the rain? Would you prefer to walk for help in this downpour?"

Pouting, Allison folded her arms and stared out the window as if she could see something. Finally, keeping her eyes focused ahead, she said, "I suppose I should have helped when you asked. I'm . . . I'm sorry I blamed you."

"Don't worry about it," he replied. "It'll be alright."

Trying the key in the ignition again, Logan jammed his foot on the accelerator and pushed to the floor. Much to his surprise, the engine revved right up. He threw the gearshift into reverse and let out the clutch, but nothing followed except the sickening sound of helplessly spinning wheels in the mud of the road.

"Don't say a thing!" he growled in frustration.

"I wasn't going to," she replied, sounding truly hurt. When he turned to look, he saw her lip quivering. "What are we going to do, Logan?" she said after a moment.

"We'll get out," he said confidently. "I'll flag someone down. At best we can walk."

"Logan, it's Sunday morning. No one will be out, especially in this weather. We should have driven down to the Inland Highway, even if it was longer."

"Don't worry. Remember, I'm a lucky fellow."

She glanced at him and managed a laugh.

"You see," he said, sounding as cheerful as if the sun had been shining, "it won't be so bad if we keep our spirits up. Trust me. I've been in tighter spots than this!"

"Yes, I imagine you have!" she said, with a tease in her voice.

Now it was his turn to laugh. "Ah, you are finding out my secrets."

"Logan, do you think the river will flood?" she asked, serious again. "If it does, the water will head right down this road and turn it into a new river."

He didn't want to think of that. Instead, he reached out and gently touched her hand. Something in her vulnerability had touched him. It was a side of Allison MacNeil he had not seen before this moment. Suddenly he saw her without all the pretense and affectation. Again he wondered what made her surround herself with such a hard wall. He wondered, too, what more there might be to the *real* Allison MacNeil that he was still unable to see.

She did not pull her hand away. But neither did she look over at him. The moment passed in silence. Awkwardly Logan lifted his hand from hers and, hugging his overcoat about him, opened the door of the car and stepped out into the fury of the storm.

Wind lashed rain into his face like sharp needles. The sky was so dark that it could have been evening instead of morning. Where he stood, water lapped at his ankles. His shoes and new tuxedo trousers were ruined. He plodded back onto the surface of the road, though it was hardly visible through the water running over the top of it. It seemed to have risen in just the few minutes since they had come along. He looked around, trying to survey their options. Then he spied an object floating down the ditch stream on the other side of the road, that appeared to be a piece of wood. Hastening toward it, he stooped down and pulled it out. It was no tree branch, but an old piece of milled lumber, ragged at one end. Of course it could have broken free from anything, but Logan immediately thought of the bridge. If the bridge was about to give way, there would certainly be no more travelers along the road. And if the Lindow was rising as quickly as he feared, he and Allison could never outrun, or more likely, *outwalk* the flood. They *had* to get that car moving before the river broke its boundaries and spread out over the entire Strathy Valley. It was their only hope, even if it was a slim one. And they had to do so before the water level on the road became too deep to drive.

Clutching the board, Logan turned back toward the car. It seemed to be settling even deeper into the muddy ditch already, water up to its fender. It would take a miracle to get it out, but Logan knew he had to try.

Allison was anxiously looking out the window for him when he approached. Anxiety was etched all over her face. Logan ducked his head through the window and smiled as if to allay her fears, suddenly realizing the responsibility that faced him. He knew she was depending on him, and that awareness both humbled and intimidated him. He tried to infuse his voice with its usual confidence.

"Get behind the steering wheel," he instructed Allison. "I'm going to use this board as leverage. I'll shove when you try to back it out. But hit it easy . . . not too much throttle."

He walked around to the front of the Austin and knelt down in the water, jammed the end of the board into the ground and tested it by lifting until it hit the bumper. "Start the engine," he yelled to Allison, "and push down on the accelerator as easy as you can."

She did so. As the wheels began to spin, Logan bent his full weight on the board against the Austin bumper, trying to rock it backward enough for the rear tires to grab. But it was no use. Other than rocking the car back and forth, he accomplished nothing. The slick rubber tires simply spun through the tracks they had made for themselves in the mud.

"Once more!" he called out in desperation, giving the board every ounce of strength he possessed. The car did not budge. However the board, lodged none too securely in the loose soil, slipped, and the thrust of the motion threw Logan off his balance. The next instant he was on his back in the little stream.

Within seconds Allison had shut off the ignition and, without

253

thinking, jumped out of the car to his aid.

"Oh, Logan . . . Logan!" she cried. "Are you hurt?" Struggling through the water and rough surface of the ground to reach him, she never noticed that the rain quickly soaked her pretty curls, or that the muddy water was splattering her expensive new dress.

Logan looked up at her from his position with a grin. It was difficult to distinguish his body from the mud and debris covering him.

"So much for this lucky fellow," he said with a laugh.

"You're not hurt?" she said, holding out her hand.

"Nothing but my pride," he replied.

At last a smile broke from Allison's lips, which soon became a giggle, and finally erupted into a great laugh. "This is hardly the time for a swim, Mr. Macintyre," she said as he took her hand.

He laughed with her. Their predicament was made all the more ridiculous in that she was unable to pull him out on the first attempt. Her thin shoes and inexperience were no match for the mud, and on the second effort, with a great flying slip of her foot where she had tried to anchor it, she lost hold and flew into the water next to him.

He burst into a great roar of laughter.

"You did that intentionally!" she cried in her old petulant tone.

"Even if I had thought of it," he replied, still laughing, "I would never have dared!"

"And why is that?"

"You should know! You've been watching me like a hawk, ready to pounce on me if I step out of line," Logan replied playfully.

"I guess I have been rather cross with you," she said, smiling. "I'm sorry."

"Fine time to apologize, now that you have me at such a disadvantage!"

She laughed again. "You should see yourself! Lying in the mud in a brand new tuxedo, with—"

"How do you know it's new?"

"What do you take me for, a complete fool? I know new clothes when I see them. You're not so very clever, you know."

"So—I've been found out!"

"Logan Macintyre unmasked!"

"And what else do you know about me?" he asked.

"Just that I'm glad you stopped by to help us fix our car in town."

"I'm glad too," he returned. "And I'm glad you wanted me to go to the Bramfords' with you."

"Even though it ended like this?"

Logan laughed again. "I wouldn't miss this for anything! How many people around here have had the chance to see the uppity Miss Allison MacNeil—"

"Watch yourself, Logan," Allison warned.

"Sorry. How many people have the chance to see the charming and beautiful Miss Allison MacNeil—"

"That's better!"

"—have a chance to see her in an expensive new evening dress, lying in a mud puddle in the pouring rain? Now I ask you . . . would *you* miss this?"

"Careful!" she said, with a teasing gleam in her eye, then splashed a handful of water in his direction.

He turned away, but not before she had splashed him again.

Then a pause came. Logan was the first to speak. "You know, Ali—I mean, Allison—"

"It's all right. You can call me Ali," she replied. "It sounds good in your mouth too, just like in Grandpa Doréy's."

"Thank you. What I was going to say was that I like you best like this."

"What! All covered with mud and soaked to the skin?" She tried to sound affronted, but it was a difficult facade to maintain with fresh laughter attempting to escape from her lips.

"You know what I mean," he went on, trying to be serious. "I like how you laugh—really laughing, like you mean it."

"I suppose it's pointless to remain angry at this point."

"Were you truly angry with me all this time?"

"Not *all* the time. But you can be infuriating."

"I thought perhaps you were just angry at the world in general." His words were sincere, completely without any mocking tone which might have characterized them a couple of weeks earlier.

She sensed the sincerity of his remark, but found she was unable to easily frame a reply. It was not easy to open up that part of her life which had been shut tight for so long.

"We're going to catch pneumonia if we stay here much longer," she said, repressing everything her heart wanted to cry out.

Logan struggled to his feet, then leaned over, took her offered hand, and pulled her up. However, he did not quickly release her hand, but instead kept it cupped in his.

"Ali," he said, "let's not let things go back to the way they were."

"I'm ... I'm afraid that when we get back, that somehow, all this will seem like a dream ... and we'll—"

"But it can be different now. We don't have to fight anymore."

"Has it really changed? I mean, is it really different?"

"It could be. Sometimes mud and grime have an odd way of cleansing. When we do get cleaned up and back into our old clothes, who knows what might happen?"

Suddenly an urge came over Logan to tell her everything. He hesitated, not for fear of the failure of his scheme, but because he desperately didn't want her angry at him all over again. Instead, saying nothing, he leaned forward and kissed her lightly on her rain-streaked lips.

It was over so quickly, Allison was not even sure that it had happened. But she knew that it had, and that it had been nice. She had enjoyed it so much, in fact, that she let herself forget the deception of his injured foot. There had to be an explanation, she told herself. Better that she wait for him to tell her when he was ready. She was feeling so wonderful, none of that seemed to matter anymore. Oh, she didn't want to go back and then find it impossible to recapture this special moment. Why couldn't it last? Could things be different, like he had said?

Logan released her hand and they made their way back toward the car, still not knowing what they'd do.

"Can I ask you something?" Logan said after a moment.

"Yes, of course," she answered softly.

"Why do you hate to be called Ali?"

"I don't hate it. But only my great-grandfather calls me that. Why have you wanted to call me that?"

"At first, partly because it made you angry, I suppose. But mostly now because it seems to fit you better."

"That's funny," she answered thoughtfully. "Grandpa Dorey always says that too. Why?"

"Allison sounds like some frail little girl. You know the kind, with pale skin and a dainty voice to match." He saw her bristle slightly, then added quickly, "I'm not saying that about you. Why does everyone think that kind of young lady is more to be desired than one with spirit—as a friend of mine used to say, 'with a little spunk.' That's an *Ali*—a girl with spunk. Like you."

"I suppose people like the dainty, quiet sort," sighed Allison, "because they are the ones who are good and saintly and kind."

"You can't really believe that. Why, look at your mother and great-grandmother."

"Exactly! That's just what they are like!" she retorted as if she were lodging an accusation.

"Lady Margaret seems pretty spirited, even shrewd, for a woman over eighty! I bet she was something when she was your age!"

"I suppose," said Allison in a dejected voice. "But don't you see? That's just it. I can't measure up to what she was, and that's what they're all expecting of me. I can't even measure up to my own name, just like you said. I've tried so hard, but it's impossible. Spunky, spirited girls, as you call them, just can't be very good Christians."

"Well, I wouldn't know anything about that. My mother was pretty religious, though I've never had any use for it. But I think what you said is wrong. Look at Jesse Cameron. The way she talks, I'd imagine *she's* a Christian. At least she sounds religious enough. But you should hear her bellow and whoop aboard her boat—and she's the furthest thing from frail I can think of. Yet I've seldom been treated with more kindness. No, Ali, I think you're wrong about what you said."

"Well, one thing I'm not wrong about," she said, changing the uncomfortable subject, "is that we're going to drown if we stand here and philosophize much longer."

"How far is it back to Stonewycke?" asked Logan.

"Probably seven or eight miles."

"Well, we've got to get moving. That water's rising fast, and Noah had a better chance of finding a fellow traveler than we have."

"I wish I could pray," said Allison.

"I only wish I believed there was someone up there who could hear."

She stared at him with mild surprise. "You don't believe in God?"

She had never actually known anyone honest or impertinent enough to admit such a thing.

"I don't know. I suppose neither of us has had much use for the other in the past," replied Logan.

As Allison passed the car door, she turned aside and reached for the handle.

"What are you doing?" asked Logan.

"Getting an umbrella. If we are going to walk all the way home, we could use it," she replied innocently.

Logan laughed. "In this downpour! I doubt it'll do us much good," he said, then reached for her again and pulled her toward him.

He studied her face intently for a moment, then said, "Let's stay . . . friends." He wanted to kiss her again. But, of all things for Logan Macintyre, he felt strangely bashful. The kiss before had been on impulse, done before he even realized what he was doing. Now there seemed to be more between them. And a kiss now meant more also. More than he was certain he could give.

But she was already replying to his words; perhaps she had not even noticed the awkward moment that had just passed.

"I'd like that, Logan," she had said. "I truly would."

In fact, she *had* noticed. But like Logan, Allison was confused and timid. Too many new emotions were assailing her all at once.

Actually the emotions weren't new at all. But for so long she had tried to repress things like honesty and sincerity and tenderness that she felt more comfortable pretending they didn't even exist.

Yet she couldn't deny that these past fifteen minutes with Logan had been wonderful; she had felt a freedom to be herself, unlike any other time she could remember. Still, to give up her protective shield, even for the sake of Logan, would mean facing some difficult things.

Logan had come close to hitting the core of her inner conflict, without his even knowing it. How miserably she had always failed to measure up to what her family expected of her! Didn't they know she could not be like them? She couldn't be perfect—a saint. How could Logan know how much deeper it all went? To him it looked merely like a twist in her personality.

They walked along, each deep in thought. The falling away of their fear and reserve toward each other had opened them unexpectedly toward their inner selves as well. And now Logan found his thoughts turning to the man who had sent him here in the first place—his uncle Digory. According to Lady Margaret, he was surely a man who could pray when things got tight. He found himself almost wishing he were here now to send up a few words heavenward on behalf of the stranded party-goers. *Why, if we get out of this mess,* Logan thought, *I might even read some of that old Bible of yours.*

All at once Allison grasped his arm. "Logan . . . listen!"

"What is it?" Logan listened hard, and faintly in the distance could make out a sound he could not place. It wasn't the noise he had been hoping for—an engine. Rather, there was a creaking sound, as of wood, mingled with an intermittent *clop-splash . . . clop-splash.* He could not recognize it.

He did not have to ponder long, however, for in a few moments, from the mist of the thick downpour emerged the last thing he would have expected to see—a rickety old haywagon, pulled by two great, gray, tired-looking, wet draught horses.

Both he and Allison broke into simultaneous yells, accentuated with a jump of joy on Allison's part and a fist-pounding of relief on Logan's. But even in his ecstasy, the first thing that returned to Logan's mind was the thought of what he had vowed to himself in connection with Digory's Bible.

Was it possible that someone could actually have *heard* those thoughts? Could there really be a God ready to intercede, even for unbelievers and doubters?

He'd have to think about this a little more. He wasn't ready to call this a miracle. But it certainly did cast a cloud—even heavier than the one in the sky—over his previously comfortable unreligious notions.

35 Back to Stonewycke

Into view came Fergusson Dougall, perched atop the hardwood seat, looking like anything but a guardian angel. Allison clambered aboard, threw her arms around him, and kissed him unabashedly on the cheek.

"God be praised!" said the factor, when they had briefly related the story of their car trouble. "Weel, the folks sent me oot t' look fer ye, seein' as ye were overdue an' the river was risin' fast. Actually, I was the only one available. Yer father left early this mornin' t' help some o' the farmers clear oot. Most o' the lowlan' crofts are already under water. Ye're lucky the road's mostly on high land or ye wouldna hae made it this far."

"And how's everything at home?" asked Allison.

"All's fine, but wet, at the hoose, but we've already lost two or three hunnert acres o' the new plantin'. 'Twas poor timin' fer a flood." As he spoke, Fergie had been driving at a healthy clip, but as he finished, he slowed to nearly a stop. He stood, gazed off ahead of him and to his left, and then continued. "I didna think I'd get back on the Culden road. Look oot there." He pointed down the valley toward the sea; where yesterday had been green farmland, now stood a huge, brown lake. Any traces of the road were completely obscured.

"We'll go as far as we can, then skirt aroun' t' Braenock. I ken a few sheep trails an' sich like. It'll take hours, but we'll eventually strike the Fenwick Harbor road. We can be thankful I brought a wagon, not an automobile."

"Sheep trails, Fergie!" said Allison dismally. "Can even a wagon travel on them?"

"If worse comes t' worst, I tossed a couple saddles in back an' we can unhitch the horses an' ride. Leastways we willna drown."

"Did you happen also to toss in some dry clothes and rain gear back there?" asked Logan, almost facetiously, hardly relishing the misery of spending several more hours in their soaking party clothes.

"Aye," answered Fergie, quite pleased with himself, "Lady Joanna fixed us up right weel. There'll be a deserted cottage or twa where ye can change."

They traveled along a somewhat decent surface of road for about half an hour, the rain still pouring relentlessly. But even in that short time they gained considerable elevation and seemed to have left the flood far behind. But then the road veered left again, beginning a gradual descent toward the valley, now a lake, then disappeared. Fergie led the horses eastward, off the road. Now their way became so rough with potholes, mud, rocks, and shrubbery that it took nearly an hour to traverse a mile; the three passengers bounced mercilessly against the hard board seat of the wagon, but Fergie doggedly encouraged the two horses forward.

At last they ascended a small rise and there in a shallow hollow before them, on the edge of Braenock Ridge, stood a small stone cottage, meshing perfectly with the barrenness of the moor and the bleakness of the weather. Even inhabited, it could not have been much to look on, but now it was like recalling a sad memory. In places the mortar between the stones had long since crumbled away, leaving gaps in the walls which made the boarded-up windows appear even more pathetic and hopeless. Adjacent to the cottage stood the remains of what had no doubt once been a cattle byre. Only three stone walls still stood, and any thought of a roof was long since gone. Over the cottage, however, a roof still remained. But even it was sagging, and would collapse before many more years, leaving this poor home but an abandoned shell like so many thousands of others scattered throughout the poorer regions of that northern country.

The moment they walked inside, it was clear that, even though the structure of a roof was still present, the thatch upon it was in such poor repair that it could not hope to keep out such a rain. Numerous muddy puddles on the floor marked the presence of each hole above. The dirt floor was in hardly better condition than the ground outside, except that there was no wind, and one small corner did remain which had somehow escaped time's destruction. Allison entered first, made her way through the maze of puddles to the only dry spot to be found, and changed into the corduroys, plaid flannel shirt, fresh socks, and heavy boots her mother had packed for her. Then, throwing a mackintosh over her shoulders, she stepped outside while Logan went in and changed into similar attire, provided from Alec's oversized wardrobe. Greatly to their relief, Fergie suggested that they take a few extra moments to enjoy the cold meals Lady Joanna had included.

The dry corner of the hut, while not cozy by most standards, seemed to welcome the three travelers, who unwrapped sliced cheese, fresh baked bread, oatcakes, and crisp red apples, accompanied by a flask of hot tea to wash it all down. When the humble but delicious fare had been consumed, no one seemed particularly anxious to brave the elements quite so soon again. Fergie leaned against a wall and lit his pipe, but had barely taken three puffs before he was sound asleep. Logan reached over, removed the still smoking pipe from his hand, and set it on the dirt floor beside him.

Allison hugged her knees to her body to ward off the chill.

"Perhaps I should try to build a fire," Logan suggested.

"You'd never find any wood dry enough," said Allison, taking up the flask of tea and refilling their cups. "Perhaps this will help."

"Thank you." Logan stared at the dirt floor a moment, then said, "Is this Stevie Mackinaw's cottage?"

"How do you know about him?"

"Jesse Cameron told me a few things."

"Oh. I had forgotten you were friends." Her tone contained a hint of its old hauteur, but she must have been aware of it too, for her next words were more mellow. "Lady Margaret was quite close to the Mackinaws when she was a girl. They lived a little ways from here, farther up onto Braenock. This was the old Krueger place, I think. She used to come out to both places a lot, from what she's said."

"Yes. Jesse mentioned that. She also said she thought Stevie Mackinaw was in love with your great-grandmother. But the feelings must have been only one-sided."

"That doesn't surprise me," sighed Allison. "Everyone—especially the crofters—loves her. It was probably even more so when she was young and beautiful. Did you know it was love that forced her from Scotland?"

"No. I haven't heard much about your family's history."

"Lady Margaret married Grandpa Dorey against her father's wishes; he was furious, vowed to get back at them, even once tried to kill Grandpa."

"And that's what forced them away?"

"My great-grandmother sailed for America, but Grandpa Dorey stayed behind to clear his name of a murder in which James Duncan had implicated him. He was to follow later, but his father-in-law schemed against their plans until in the end, each thought the other was dead. This is how my mother explained it all to me. Neither my great-grandmother nor Grandpa Dorey talk much about it, but my mother has spent hours getting the facts from them, writing it down so the story of their love for each other and the legacy of their sacrifice for the land and for Stonewycke won't ever be lost. In fact, all my life I have memories of my mother quizzing my great-grandmother and great-grandfather for details. Pictures of them sitting side by side in front of a fire, talking, as it seemed to a little girl, for hours on end. It's been something that has been really important to my mother. I think she almost looks upon it as her mission in life to preserve the legacy. As if it were Lady Margaret and Grandpa Dorey—or Maggie and Ian, as they were known when they were young—who were the central characters of the story, and her role was more to make certain their story was preserved and passed on to future generations."

She stopped and was silent for a few moments.

"So what happened?" asked Logan. "Lady Margaret was in America, and. . . ?"

"It drove Grandpa Dorey mad. Lady Margaret remained in exile for forty years, thinking there was nothing left for her here."

"What made her finally come back?"

"Actually my mother came first, while my great-grandmother was in a coma in America. My mother knew nothing about the family in Scotland. She came here blindly, merely hoping to fulfill her grandmother's last wish before she lapsed into unconsciousness."

"She knew nothing about the family or the inheritance which would have been hers?"

"That's why she says she got more than she bargained for."

"I guess so—quite a bit more!" Logan took a swallow of his tea as he considered Lady Joanna's stroke of fortune.

"But none of that means anything to *them*." Allison's words were mixed with reproach, with the old tone returning once more. But to the more sensitive observer, there was also an unmistakable touch of envy, of which even Allison was unaware. "Why, the prestige of Stonewycke means nothing to them. They gave away half the estate to the tenants. There was even a treasure—"

"A treasure?" Logan's voice was so calm that Allison could not have guessed that he had nearly dropped his cup at her words.

"When she returned home, Lady Margaret looked where she had hidden it before she left Scotland, but it was gone. And no one ever made any other attempts to locate it—not to say that it even exists! But it just proves all the more how little they all care for our family position. They'd all be just as content in some fisher's hut! My own parents lived in nothing more than a little cottage for years. I was born there, can you imagine? I've lived at Stonewycke only half my life."

"Are you saying your great-grandmother may have *imagined* the treasure?" Logan could not help it if the question was ill-timed. He *had* to ask!

"You know how old people's memories are," Allison replied. "What does it matter?"

"Nothing ... certainly—nothing at all!" replied Logan hastily, perhaps a bit too hastily. "Simply a curiosity." He tried to interest himself in his tea for the next few moments, his racing thoughts circling once again about the person of Lady Margaret.

No, the old lady's memory is just fine, he told himself. There *must* have been a treasure—must *still* be a treasure. She had seen it. She had placed it somewhere. And now it was gone.

That was no surprise to Digory MacNab's great-great-great nephew, who had read the old groom's letter and confession. But this was a new bit of news, to learn that Lady Margaret had hidden the treasure before she had been forced out of the country. Could it be possible that only she and Digory had known of its existence originally? Why wouldn't she tell her husband on their parting, for surely such a valuable find could have helped save him from the clutches of James Duncan?

Logan wondered if he'd ever have the chance to find out the entire story. He couldn't go about asking too many questions. He would have to content himself to pick up bits and pieces however he could. He hoped that one of those pieces would lead him to the treasure. Nothing else mattered.

Or did it?

Suddenly the thought of Allison came back into his mind. Had the events of this day changed anything? With the mere mention of the treasure, all at once his thoughts had flown off wildly, completely forgetting the brief moments of intimacy they had shared. It was as if he had become two separate persons—the old Logan, still intent on nothing but the treasure, and the part of him which could hardly ignore a growing attachment to this place and its people, Allison in particular. And even Allison, he recalled, had suddenly reverted to tones reminiscent of her old self the moment she began talking about her family. *Was this part of the curse of the treasure to which Uncle Digory had alluded,* Logan wondered? While everyone sought the treasure for the wealth it would bring, was it, in fact, a messenger of evil? What was the treasure, anyway? Was it something which could bring fulfillment and peace and lasting meaning to life? Or was it instead something which, as Digory had said, would best serve the family legacy by being thrown into the sea or destroyed? *What could be the real treasure?*

Again Logan dragged his thoughts back to the present. Once again thoughts of the treasure had pulled him away from Allison, in just a few seconds of time. What a strange lure it had on him!

What did matter now? Only the treasure? Or were there new factors to consider? He tried to dismiss the matter from his mind. He didn't want to have to think about how these new relationships might figure into his scheme. He hadn't planned on them—nor had he planned on Allison. A few weeks ago in Glasgow when he had concocted all this, he saw himself simply walking into Port Strathy, finding the long, lost treasure, and waltzing out again with no one being the wiser and himself being a good deal richer. But now for the first time he began to wonder just how easy it was going to be to walk away from here.

Logan's thoughts were interrupted as Fergie suddenly started awake. "Hae I been sleepin'?" he exclaimed. "Ye shouldna hae let me drop off like a fool bairn," he continued in a fluster. "We must be goin'."

They all rose, packed up everything, clutched their raingear as close to their bodies as possible, and shouldered their way back out into the storm.

The rain had abated somewhat, but their way—now a sheep path, now simply open moor with treacherous peat bogs to beware of—became increasingly difficult to navigate the farther across Braenock Ridge they went, making for the higher ground of the road across Strathy Summit to their northeast. They had been on their way from the cottage no more than an hour when Fergie finally stopped the animals.

"Can't go no farther wi' this wagon," he announced. "We'll hae t' come back fer it when the weather clears."

Fergie stepped down and proceeded to unhitch the wagon and saddle the two horses, while Allison and Logan gathered supplies and strapped them on behind one of the mounts. The young couple rode together, while Fergusson, weighing nearly as much as the two others combined, rode the other horse. The portly factor took the lead, a sight to see astride his animal, his ponderous bulk bouncing and swaying with every step, while Allison, with Logan behind her, followed.

Once they left the wagon behind, the going became easier, for the narrow paths and steep inclines of the high moor were far more suitable for horseback than for the awkward vehicle. The flooded valley was by now far behind them, but even the high country had not been left untouched by the storm. Great portions were covered with water, little streams were going every which way, and Logan occasionally found himself being splashed by water and mud from the horse's heavy hooves.

Once they abandoned the wagon, they no longer had to go all the way to the Summit road, and they struck due north instead, directly through toward Stonewycke from the back side. At one time there had been a rather worn trail, though steep in parts, which they were now following. As they went, gradually Allison and Logan began talking again, and it seemed they were about to fall back into the free and easy manner of the earlier part of the day. However, Allison was cold and tired and growing extremely weary of this journey, which it seemed would never end. She had begun to wish she had never been invited to Saundra and Eddie's ball in the first place.

A pause had come in their conversation and Allison had drifted into a somewhat irritable mood from the cumulative effects of the weather and her exhaustion. Oblivious to the flying mud and inexperienced rider behind her, she began unconsciously to pick up the pace whenever their way allowed.

"Ali, must you splash through *every* puddle!" said Logan at length, his tone cheerful, while he reached up to brush a fresh splat of mud from his cheek.

"What right have *you* to complain?" she snapped in reply.

"I was only joking," he laughed, not aware of his peril at the mercy of her changing mood. "I haven't a single complaint about this day." As he said the words he loosened his grip from the edge of the saddle and placed his arm around her waist, hugging her close.

"What do you think you're doing?" she barked in an outraged tone.

"I don't know ... I just—" he faltered, bewildered by her outburst.

"Just because you stole an unguarded kiss from me, Logan, at a time when my defenses were down," she said snappily, "does not mean that you now have total license with me."

"I had no intention—" he began, but broke off, stubbornly refusing to swing pliantly with her moods. He didn't need to defend himself, he decided. "What's gotten into you?" he asked instead.

"Things may have gotten out of hand today, but—"

"Is that what you call it?"

"Well, it's easy to forget yourself in that kind of situation," she answered matter-of-factly, as if *now* she had come to her senses. "But I'm not some empty-headed trollop like that Angela Cunningham, who would positively swoon at the merest nod from a man."

"You can't be stewing over the party? I thought those games were behind us. We had decided to be friends."

"Friends," she smugly informed him, "don't go pawing at one another."

"I suppose you're right," he said with an air of defeat. He wasn't sure if she was right or not, but he saw no sense in arguing further. He had learned from past experience that the haughty Allison was not open to reason. And he didn't want to get into any more shouting matches with her. Even if she reverted back to her old self, it didn't mean he had to.

For the next ten minutes the only sounds either could hear was the *clop-splash . . . clop-splash* of the horses' hooves, and the steady raindrops falling on the ground and puddles all about them. Neither said a word.

At length Allison sighed. "Logan," she said, realizing she had perhaps been a little unfair, "I . . . I—" she wanted to apologize, but it was new territory for her. "Well . . . we'll be getting home soon, and . . . I have to maintain . . . you know, there's a certain dignity expected with my . . . the position I'm in. And I'm just not certain . . . that is—"

"Say no more, my lady," Logan broke in, with no rancor in his voice. "We are entering the real world, as we feared. And in that world, you are an heiress and I the offspring of a mere groom. You know, of course, that I don't give a fig for such distinctions of class. But I understand that they have been with you all your life."

"Life . . ." she murmured, repeating him, but with a pensive tone. Then after a moment, she added more emphatically, "I hate it!"

"What, Ali?" he asked as the wind had carried off her words.

"Nothing," she answered glumly. "How can you be so understanding?"

"I've seen something special in you today, Allison MacNeil," he answered earnestly, "but I have also seen a very confused and mixed-up young lady. I'm willing to be patient until you sort out the two."

"How kind of you!" she snapped sarcastically. Then she dropped her head, confused and possibly a little ashamed, and added, "Oh, forget it!"

They fell silent again, and remained so until the gray walls of Stonewycke broke through the gray mist of the storm.

The castle was not exactly a welcoming sight. It had been built four hundred years before, not to welcome but to strike fear into the spirits of any who dared approach it. But Allison was glad, nonetheless, to see it.

She needed the protection of its thick granite walls just now, for her own personal walls were growing far too weak for her liking.

36 Grandpa Dorey

But even Stonewycke's thick walls did not prove fortress enough for Allison. However much she tried to shut out every outside element that attempted to intrude upon her inner being, she could never fully shut out herself. And her own thoughts, and nothing else, caused her unrest.

For years she had allowed the flow of her existence to be determined by her confused and often conflicting emotions. Even after she had reached an age where serious thought began to be possible, she continued to steadfastly avoid analyzing why she acted as she did, why she felt as she did, and what her responses to life should possibly entail. In short, she avoided looking honestly in the quiet of her own soul at the most basic of life's questions: *Who am I, and what should I be about?*

Since her earliest childhood years, she had known two things: that her family believed in God's active participation in their lives, and that her family held a position of importance and esteem. As a child she adopted the external appearance of pursuing her parents' spiritual values. Yet as she grew into her teen years, without revealing it to any observers, more and more she began to sense a divergence between what she came to term her "religious" parents and her own inner spiritual void. How could she know of the turmoil and struggles and periods of doubt that her parents and great-grandparents had experienced on the way to their present lives of faith? All she knew was that they spoke and acted as if God were an intimate friend, while to her "religion," as she called it, was dry and impersonal. The end result of this divergence was the feeling that somehow there was something wrong with her intrinsic being. She was out of step. Something about her was incomplete and inadequate. She was supposed to be like them, but wasn't. Yet she couldn't help it. And, of course, the more this feeling grew upon her, the more she tried to hide it from view, both from her parents and great-grandparents, and even from herself.

Added to this was the knowledge that everyone looked up to her mother and father, and the matriarch and patriarch of the community, Lady Margaret and Grandpa Dorey, with a love and veneration akin to that given to royalty. The fact could hardly escape her that the family line had come down from the Lady Atlanta through the women of the family—all solid, virtuous, strong, capable, and—in Allison's mind—far more religious and compassionate toward Strathy's common folk than she. And now here she stood, next in line to wear that mantle, and yet totally lacking the attitudes and qualities which set her mother and great-grandmother apart in people's minds. They would all expect her to be like them, to be just as good and selfless and wise and strong and godly. Yet down inside, Allison knew all too well that she was none of those things. And maybe never could be.

The result was a growing feeling of pressure, from about her tenth year on, to be something she was not. In the bewildered, hurting inner self of a girl struggling to enter into her own womanhood, young Allison through the next several years came to resent the very things she wanted most to be. What she considered to be her inability to measure up to standards set before her in both matters of spirituality and her place in society, caused her to begin tearing away at those very foundations of virtue and holiness.

Thus her own spiritual and personal insecurity, by the time she was fifteen, had taken the form of an independence that seemed bent on carving out a life for herself which was at odds with everything previous generations stood for. In her innermost being—a part of herself by now so hidden that even she did not know of its existence—she still hungered desperately for the reality of a friendship with God such as she witnessed daily in her mother and father, and even more so in the older people. But on the surface level of her daily life, she resisted their attempts to say that God was a "personal" God. *He's not personal to me,* she thought, *and I don't need Him! I can make it just fine on my own; I don't need them OR Him.*

And in the same way she seemed determined to rebel against

the very attributes within her mother and great-grandmother that others so admired, even resenting their goodness and qualities of strong character. To defend her own insecurity, she tore at the very roots of her being, seeking to find refuge in being someone of importance. She scoffed at her father's common origins and her mother's identification with the poor of the community. Because she was not secure in who she was, she attempted to elevate her stature in the eyes of the world, clinging to an elusive sense of superiority. But even her seemingly egotistical pride could not conceal to perceptive eyes that deep inside remained a pain which nothing but a personal encounter with the God of her fathers and mothers could heal.

And now, at seventeen, she still had not allowed herself to reflect on these matters. When thoughts of conscience came, she quickly dismissed them as childish carryovers from the outmoded values of her elders. She did not need them, she tried to convince herself. This was a new age, and she would be her own person. She did not recognize the steady tapping on the door of her heart. Her hour had not yet come, but it was nigh at hand. The prayers of the generations before her were on the verge of being fulfilled in her. For no word from the mouth of the Lord returns void, but always accomplishes that which He pleases. The prayers of the righteous avail much in the lives of their descendants, for the Lord pours out His love and mercy to the third and fourth generation of those who love Him and keep His commandments. The prayers young Maggie prayed in her exile—fulfilled in part in the life of her granddaughter, whose more recent prayers for her own daughter combined with them in the mysterious stream of God's mighty purpose—now came to bear on the heart of young Allison MacNeil, resistant to God, yet chosen by Him to share in the inheritance of the saints.

And the instrument in God's hand to begin this process of healing was one in whom the treasured generational flow of righteousness was also silently at work. How could the nearly crippled old Digory MacNab have foreseen that his quiet prayers in his lonely loft would stretch across the years, down through time, to unlock the hearts of both his own posterity and that of his beloved Maggie, for whom the humble witness of his life had accomplished so much? But no man can ever know how far his prayers and the impact of his life will reach. In the infinite provision of God's wisdom, the prayers of the righteous always come full circle, though none but the God who inspires them will ever know the full stories of their impact.

For now, in the somber solitude of a cheerless upstairs room in the austere castle known as Stonewycke, and in the darkened stable loft where the spirit of a godly man's prayers still dwelt, the loving heavenward cries of former generations were at last coming to bear upon the hearts of two young people. The Hound of Heaven, who had been stalking them all their lives long, was closing in.

Allison stood quietly staring out her window into the dreary wet below. What she was thinking she hardly knew herself. Her mind was more confused now than it had been two days ago. She had been so looking forward to that party. Now the mere memory of it left a bitter taste in her mouth. Everything was all wrong now! Life had been smooth enough—a little boring, perhaps, but at least predictable—before. But now that he had come, it was all mixed up! Why couldn't he have left well enough alone, left them to get home by themselves without having to meddle with their car? He had no right to interfere! And who was he, anyway? Supposedly the nephew of some stupid old groom. She doubted it! He was a fake. Limping with the wrong foot! But of course everyone thought he was wonderful, thanking him for getting her home safely. Why, you'd have thought he was the son of the Prime Minister, the way her father treated him. But that was just like him, just like them all! Always making over the peasants and ignoring her. Didn't anybody care that she had almost been swept away by the flood? What if that bridge had given way? Then what would they think of their precious Logan Macintyre? What a fool she had been to let him kiss her! Now he would think she felt something for him. He'd begin to take liberties. And, of course, she hadn't felt anything for him. She couldn't have! He was a nobody. He had no family. No position. What she had felt was nothing more than—well, it was nothing at all! She had been cold and afraid. Everything was just an accident! It meant nothing! She couldn't trust her feelings for him. She'd been emotionally caught up in the party and the storm, it just all—

Allison turned away from the window, hesitated a moment, then fled her room. She could take no more of this inner mental wrestling with herself. Everything was all a jumble!

She couldn't go outside. It was wet and cold. Even worse, she might run into *him*. And that would never do. She wanted no more chance meetings. Who could tell what he might do?

Perhaps a good book would liberate her overactive mind and help her to concentrate on other things. She turned and walked toward the library.

As she opened the great oaken door of the austere, book-lined room, Allison stopped short. There stood her great-grandfather in front of a shelf of first editions of Scott. He had been reaching up for one of the volumes when he heard the door open, and turned. Escape was impossible for Allison, who did not think she wanted to see anyone. But when he smiled, she realized that a small part of her at least was glad to see him.

"Ali, how nice to see you," he said in that soft and sincere tone he used most often these days.

"Hello, Grandpa Dorey," she answered, trying to be friendly but her voice betraying a touch of formality. "I didn't mean to interrupt you," she added, as she made to retreat.

"You haven't at all," he said hastily. "Do come in and sit down." He let his hand fall from the shelf and moved to one of the comfortable brocaded chairs positioned for the use of readers. He sat down, indicating an adjacent one to her. "I've been hoping I'd see you," he went on, his whole demeanor indicating that this encounter was much more to his liking than a leather-bound Sir Walter Scott.

"Oh?"

"I wanted to see how you were after your ordeal."

"What ordeal, Grandpa?"

"Your mother told me about the unfortunate events of two days ago. I'm sorry the party and all that followed turned out such a disappointment for you."

"Disappointment?" She may have placed many labels on that day, but somehow "disappointing" would not have been one of them. "I suppose it was rather disastrous," she went on after a brief pause, "but—well, it wasn't so bad."

Dorey chuckled softly. "I had nearly forgotten the capacity you young people have for making the most out of everything. A rather godly attribute, too, when you think about it. For after all, He originated the truth that it is possible for all things to work for good—

though of course on a much higher plane." In truth, he had forgotten no such thing. He knew perhaps better than anyone that the older one becomes the more clear that truth becomes, and that often the young are utterly blind to it—as he had once been. But he had been feeling a gentle prodding to speak to her for some time, and thus made the most of the opportunity when it at length presented itself.

In her present rather befuddled state, it rankled Allison that her great-grandfather had chosen to turn what might have been a pleasant conversation into another religious dissertation. He was usually less irritating in that regard than any of them. Thus she took a more biting tone than she ordinarily would have with him.

"I don't see how you, of all people, can say that, Grandpa."

"I'm not sure I understand you."

"After all you've been through," said Allison, "how can you claim that God works everything for good?"

"I didn't exactly say He *does* work everything for good," Dorey replied. "I said *it is possible* for all things to work for good."

"Don't split hairs, Grandpa. What's the difference?"

"A great deal, my dear. God works things for good only when we allow Him to. The Bible says He works all things for the good of those who love Him if they are living according to His purpose. That's a rather big if."

Allison smiled oddly. She could tell what he was driving at. But she was not going to be sidetracked.

"That may very well be," she said. "It's all too pious sounding for me. But I still want to know how you can say that all things have worked for your good after the rotten deal you had?"

He smiled and nodded, not at all affronted by the turn of the conversation.

"The fact is, my dear, that of all people, I may know it best. When I was young I was determined to make my life go the way *I* thought was best. I ignored the Lord, and—you're right—things did not turn out very well. But as I gradually and painfully realized the futility of what I was trying to do, more and more I saw the necessity of giving the Lord my life—all of it, not just bits and pieces here and there. Then *He* was able to take the reins, so to speak, and begin working everything that happened for my good. And now here I am, content and happy, surrounded by my dear family, at peace and rest, more ready than I ever could have been in the past to be with my Lord. My life is a perfect example of that truth. So perhaps I was amiss before when I said that young people have the capacity to do the same thing. It may be that it is the passage of years that allows one's eyes to be opened."

"But, Grandpa," insisted Allison, "your life has been anything but happy!"

"Oh, my dear," sighed Dorey, "happiness is not what we were put on this earth to strive for, or to achieve. It may come our way; it may not. But we are called to something so much greater."

"Like what?"

"To know Him! If it takes heartache and loss for us to know Him, the price is a small one to pay for the timeless and eternal treasure of that relationship. Ali, do you know that I would not trade one hour, not one minute of my past for years and years and years of earthly happiness! I was such a stubborn young man. It took those years of grief to break the shell of my stubborn pride. And I am so thankful He loved me enough to see the job through."

He stopped momentarily, and Allison could almost detect a glow on his face. Though she could hardly grasp the depth of his words, she could sense how truly he meant what he said. He really was, as he said, *thankful* for the ups and downs of his life. The look on his face sobered her, and took from her the desire to pick his words apart. She could feel the reality in what he was telling her, although her conscious mind was unable to apprehend it fully.

"So you see, Ali," he went on, "it is God who turns evil or unhappiness or confusion or heartache into good, even when the recipient is unaware of His hand."

Allison knew his statement was directed at her, but she had to ask regardless. "Do you really think God's hand is on me?"

"In everything you do, my dear."

"But I don't always try to live by His purpose, like you said. So how can His hand be on me? How can He be working good in my life?"

"Because He has a purpose for you, Ali. The day will come when you will see His hand guiding you."

"If only I could believe that, Grandpa," sighed Allison, in a rare relaxing of the stoic pretense which she showed the world. "But—"

"He loves you, Ali!" said Dorey tenderly, taking his great-grand-daughter's hand in his. "And so do I, and the rest of the family."

"I just don't know, Grandpa ..." she said, her voice unsteady. "It's so hard to believe that when I've been so ... you know."

He gently patted her hand with his, old and gnarled as it was. "There are many who are praying on your behalf, Ali. I am praying that you will know His love ... and mine, toward you. You are not alone. You can take strength from that."

Allison's eyes were moist now, but she fought the compelling urge to break down. She had to maintain her composure! "I ... I know I must be a terrible disappointment to you," she blurted out.

"Oh, Ali," replied Dorey in a voice full of both anguish and compassion, tears standing in his ancient eyes, "you have never been that! God forgive us if we have somehow led you to think so!"

"Maybe not to you, Grandpa," she said, "but I know Mother and Father don't think I measure up to the grand family traditions." There was not a trace of accusation in her voice, only broken, self-inflicted hurt.

"I think you misunderstand them, Ali. I know your father thinks the world of you. He—"

Suddenly the door burst open, and Allison was rescued from having to show the tears which seemed determined not to stay where they belonged. The door she had opened toward the heart of her great-grandfather quickly shut, and she returned to normal.

Nat's red head popped into the library and, breathless, he said: "Oh, there you are, Allison! You've got a visitor."

37 Unexpected Guest

As she descended the stairs, Allison quickly scanned her appearance. She probably should have taken a few minutes to change her clothes, but maybe it would be no one important.

She had donned her kilt of the green Duncan plaid and a navy cashmere sweater that morning, mostly for warmth. The navy blue knee stockings and oxfords only added to the schoolgirl look. As she thought about her clothing, it momentarily dawned on Allison how quickly her mind had shifted from the deep, emotional concerns of the morning to the trivial. Actually, she was relieved to be able to think of something of no more lasting significance than her clothes. The conversation with her great-grandfather had further stirred up thoughts she preferred to keep in place. She didn't like all this meditation! The yearnings which had always been buried deep inside her were now stirring into activity. But like all awakenings, the birth of spiritual consciousness would not occur without the pain of the breaking of the shell which enclosed it. And before the process was complete, the being in whose heart that embryo lay would more than once seek refuge in the comfortable womb of the past, resisting the painful process of being born again.

Allison walked into the family sitting room. There by the great hearth, thumbing through a recent copy of *The Strand*, stood Charles Fairgate. Inwardly Allison cringed with mortification. This schoolgirl look was the last image she wanted to portray to him!

"I hope you don't mind my coming without an invitation," he said, laying aside the magazine and approaching her.

"Of course not," replied Allison, trying to sound cheerful. "But if I'd known you were coming, I would have dressed more suitably. As you can see, I just threw something on to keep warm—this dreadful old castle, you know. So drafty!"

"You look exquisite," said Fairgate.

"Don't fib, Charles," replied Allison, trying to hide her embarrassment, not over his comment but from how she looked. "But I am surprised to see you out in this awful weather."

"It's settled down quite a bit since yesterday," he replied. "Even the sea is calming rather nicely. And besides, what's a bit of weather where friendships are concerned?"

He moved to a sofa where he reclined easily. She sat in an adjacent chair, strangely uncomfortable with his visit thus far, though she couldn't say why.

"I went directly to Aberdeen after the Bramfords' ball," he went on after they were settled. "My family has some interests in the shipyards. Waiting for me there was a telegram requesting my presence in London next week. A friend of mine was about to take his new yacht out on a shakedown cruise the moment the storm let up. I convinced him to take it north. I said to myself that I couldn't go to London, which would surely detain me for weeks, without seeing Allison once more. So when the winds died down yesterday morning, we sailed stopping off at Peterhead, and here we are. He's moored down at the harbor right now."

"That's very flattering of you, Charles," said Allison, still uncomfortable, but warming to Fairgate's charm. He had never been this attentive to her before.

"I didn't mean it entirely to flatter you."

"Oh?"

"I must admit I do have an ulterior motive."

"Sounds suspicious," she replied, her old coyness gaining the upper hand.

"I hoped I might be able to pry you out of this grim nest. What would you say to an exhilarating sail to Inverness, then a train to London?"

"My, that *is* a daring proposal! I hardly know what to think."

"You'll have a grand time."

"I'm sure I would." Allison laughed just at the thought of it. Just to imagine what it might be like sent a tingle through her—the exciting thrill of high society life which Charles was sure to be a part of. "But alas," she added, inexplicably feeling less regret than her tone indicated, "you know my parents. They are extremely old-fashioned—they hardly let me out of the house without a proper chaperone."

"The party at the Bramfords' must have been quite an exception, then," he said tightly. "I don't believe I saw a chaperone with you and Mr. Macintyre."

"Oh, that . . ." she said with a nervousness she couldn't hide and which Fairgate duly noted, to his further annoyance. "Mr. Macintyre is . . . a trusted family employee."

"Rather remarkable, isn't it, for one so young to acquire such trust?" His eyebrow cocked slightly, revealing that he saw only too well through this amplification of the truth. What he tried not to reveal was that the mere mention of Logan Macintyre was an irritation to him. "And it's funny," he went on, "I cannot seem to recall

ever hearing his name mentioned before in connection with Stonewycke."

"He hasn't personally been here long, of course," said Allison,
"but his family has been in the ... uh, service of our family for ...
er, years. Several generations, in fact."

"Well, it is remarkable nevertheless," repeated Fairgate.

"You might say he is a bit remarkable, that is ... in the area of
maturity. He's rather like ... a big brother to me. That's all."

Fairgate didn't much care for the look in her eye or the tone of
her voice. He had labored under the same reaction with Angela Cunningham two days ago when Macintyre's name had been mentioned.
Angela, however, had been less subtle. She had rambled on inces-
santly about the dashing newcomer on the drive home, hardly trying
to hide the fact that she was attempting to make her beau jealous—
and succeeding rather admirably in one so cocky as Charles Reynolds Fairgate III.

Until now Charles had had things pretty much his own way.
Though he had been working his way toward the heartstrings of
Stonewycke slowly, the future earl of Dalmount was anything but
subtle when it came to his ultimate design. He already dared to en-
vision himself as the future laird of Stonewycke, and looked forward
to the time when he might once again extend its boundaries and
reestablish its preeminence in northern Scotland. If neither Alec nor
Joanna dreamed what was in the mind of the young man who came
calling upon occasion, neither did Allison, despite all her seemingly
worldly wisdom. She enjoyed his company, and flattered herself that
he seemed moderately interested in her. But she had no true sense
of his eventual aspirations.

Fairgate, on his part, had enjoyed himself juggling the attentions
of the two very lovely and high-bred young women. Angela was
pretty enough, but her family was no match for Allison's in prestige
and status. She was a pleasant distraction while Fairgate was biding
his time. He could afford to wait a year or two until Allison matured.
He would gradually work himself into a more intimate friendship
with her simpleton vet of a father, until the appropriate moment
came. He knew he was the most eligible and sought-after bachelor
in his social circle—though he wondered why the people at Stonewycke did not seem aware of that fact—and had the pick of the

available debutants. He could thus afford the impropriety of being seen with two women at once.

Such had been his plan, at least. But he hadn't planned on this Macintyre fellow suddenly coming in and brazenly rocking his comfortable little boat. Most provoking of all was that in a single evening, Logan had threatened him on both feminine fronts and came dangerously close to cleaning him out at cards. It was just lucky for him he'd drawn that straight on the last hand.

He didn't like being put in this position by anybody, even a nobody who would never get far in his pursuits. The fact was, no matter how far Logan might reasonably get, he had already cast a shadow on Fairgate's parade. And Charles Reynolds Fairgate was not the sort to share anything, especially the limelight. Thus he arrived at this madcap idea of attempting to spirit Allison away for a visit to London. He knew it could not hope to succeed. But perhaps the mere thought of a romantic flight south with him would implant sufficient thoughts of him in Allison's mind to waylay the wiles of Macintyre. If only he could recall why he was so certain he knew him!

"We shall miss you," Fairgate said coolly. "Perhaps when you are a little *older* . . ."

The jab struck its mark, and Allison pulled herself up with all the self-importance a seventeen-year-old could muster. "I can jolly well go to London whenever I please," she asserted with emphasis, "chaperone or not. It's high time my parents got out of the Dark Ages, anyhow. But as it happens, I don't fancy a sail anywhere in this weather, or a long train ride either. And I was already considering traveling to London later in the year."

"Then perhaps I shall meet you there," said Charles, a bit more warmly.

"Perhaps . . ." Now it was Allison's turn for a calculated cooling of her tone.

The conversation drifted to more benign topics while they had tea. Then Allison invited Fairgate to accompany her on a walk about the place. As they walked through the gallery, he could not help but be impressed at the originals by Raeburn, Reynolds, and Gainsborough. On the wall hung the sword reputed to have been a gift from

Bonnie Prince Charlie to Colin Ramsey, who gave his life in the would-be king's futile cause.

But Fairgate's mind was only half on the valuable antiquities, though he had to admit he wouldn't mind possessing them. He could not keep himself from sulking vengefully over the impertinent so-called trusted servant Logan Macintyre. Not only was Logan's position right on the estate and so close to Allison dangerous, but as Angela Cunningham had left him she had slipped in a final crafty thrust with her incisive tongue. "I really must renew my acquaintance with Allison MacNeil," she had said with a more than knowing glint in her cunning eye. "I think I'll run up there next week while you are gone, Charles dear, and pay a little visit." She well knew that Charles had not missed the underlying message that it wasn't Allison she was particularly interested in seeing.

So, Macintyre would have both young things within his clutches, would he? And Charles himself did indeed have to go to London— it could not be avoided. *Lucky in cards, lucky in love.* Charles mused as he pretended to keep up a passing interest in what Allison was showing him.

That card game the other night at Bramfords' still stuck in his craw. Even if he had won, something in Macintyre's supercilious manner had annoyed him, and it only added to Fairgate's account against him. He did not like losing, at cards any more than with women, and he was the type who did not easily forget his losses at either. But to win, and yet to walk away with the distinct impression that the other had nevertheless maintained some unspoken and invisible advantage over him—that was worse than an outright defeat.

Lucky at cards . . .

Subconsciously Fairgate began to tick off his past losses at the gaming tables. Something about Macintyre had unsettled him since the moment he had laid eyes on him. Why could he not shake that nagging feeling that they had met?

Of course—they *had* met! All at once the scene flashed through his mind's eye as if it were yesterday.

How could he have possibly forgotten?

The recollection struck him with such impact that he gasped audibly.

"What is it, Charles?" asked Allison in the midst of an explanation of the history of the fine Raeburn clan chieftan hanging in the formal parlor.

"What?" replied Charles in a detached tone, then suddenly recalling himself, "Oh . . . nothing . . . I—I just banged my shin on this chair." He laughed lightly, trying to cover himself.

"My great-grandmother always makes over this portrait," Allison went on. "It's of her great—let's see, it would be her great-great-grandfather Robert Ramsey. Tradition has it that he and his mother helped hide Prince Charlie for a few days after the '45, on his way from Skye to France."

"Very interesting," commented Fairgate politely. Then, as if his mind had not been intent on the very subject for the last hour but it had just occurred to him, he added casually, "I say, it just crossed my mind that it would be terribly impolite of me to come all this way and not give my regards to your Mr. Macintyre."

An hour earlier Allison would have gone to whatever lengths she could manage to avoid such a meeting, and to avoid having to lay eyes on Logan herself. But her brief foray into the regions of healthy self-reflection had already faltered as a result of Fairgate's presence. The threat to her emotions was not nearly so great now. It might even be enjoyable to watch the two men spar because of her.

After a brief pause as Allison considered the implications of Fairgate's statement, she smiled, and led him toward the corridor which would take them to the ground floor and outside to the stable.

"How well do you know Macintyre?" asked Fairgate, diligently trying to keep his voice sounding indifferent.

"Well . . . he is, as I said, of a family which has been—"

"But *he* hasn't been here long?"

"No . . . not long, really."

"So you personally haven't been acquainted with him for many years?"

"Not really . . . No, not exactly. Why all the sudden interest in a mere hired hand?"

"Oh, just curious. His face struck me the other night somehow, that's all. Just curious."

Without another mention of him they made their way outside, Fairgate anticipating the encounter with relish.

38   Confrontation

Logan had noted Fairgate's arrival. Whether it irritated him because of Allison, or whether it worried him because of himself, he didn't exactly know. But he did know that the heir's appearance at Stonewycke was not a welcome sight.

Allison was growing to mean something to him.

He could scarcely admit it to himself, but he had hardly stopped thinking of her since yesterday. Her abandoned laughter in the rain and mud beside the broken-down Austin still lingered in his ears. To find himself stymied with his work because his mind was filled with the pretty face of a young lady was an altogether new sensation to Logan Macintyre. Even her petulence reminded him of a jewel that, with the rough edges smoothed out, would be precious beyond price. He had enough of his own rough edges to worry about, so he could hardly be too critical. What was it old Skittles used to say? "Molly and me are like two rocks in a tumbler sometimes. But if we stick together we'll soon end up smooth and shiny."

Like rocks in a tumbler . . . yes, that could describe his relationship with Allison—if he wanted to presume so far as to call it a relationship at all. Up and down, now arguing, now laughing, now self-protective, now opening up. The process was as new to Logan as it was to Allison.

Logan was still valiantly trying to maintain his single-mindedness toward his goal. But it was becoming more difficult with each passing moment.

Fairgate had added a whole new dimension to the scenario—jealousy, although Logan would have disdained giving it that name. He tried to look at it more pragmatically, like a card game. Did he want to fold or raise? The stakes were clear. It was a simple decision, not some emotional ordeal, he desperately tried to convince himself. Could his three jacks beat whatever Fairgate held? It would cost him to find out. It could well cost him Allison. But even so, he could retreat and nothing would be changed. Logan could still get his treasure, and leave Fairgate with Allison.

Thus he tried to reason with himself. But the fact of the matter was that it *was* an emotional response. He could not be entirely pragmatic about it. The price of losing Allison to a contemptible fellow like Fairgate was enough to raise the hair on the back of his neck. Therefore, when he saw the two approach, looking every inch the ideal aristocratic couple, foolhardy though it would be and little chance as he had, he knew he would call Fairgate's bluff. He pretended not to see them coming and went on with what he was doing.

Logan glanced up from his work on Jesse Cameron's power winch as they pushed open the stable doors. He didn't like the fact that they had apparently sought him out. Fairgate did not strike him as the type to make friendly calls, and the look on Allison's face displayed not a hint of any previous familiarity with him; the glassed-over look of her former shell was firmly back in place. Regardless, Logan attempted the gesture of a friendly welcome, not unlike he supposed his uncle might have welcomed visitors to *his* stables.

"Hello," he said, wiping his hands on a cloth. "What brings you all the way out here?" He extended his hand to Charles, who took it in a gentlemanly fashion. The handshake was firm and sincere, if one judged merely by the feel of its grasp. But over the years Logan had developed the habit of assessing a man more by the look in his eye, and Fairgate's glance was cold and hard, with a hint of cunning, which Logan did not like.

"Charles dropped by on his way to Inverness," said Allison lightly, "and he wouldn't have forgiven himself if he had not at least given you his greetings." Her voice was too pleasant, too easygoing. She and Fairgate did indeed seem most suitably matched.

"Very considerate of you, Fairgate," Logan replied, on his guard.

"Well, I've always thought a night of gambling instills a certain bond between men," said Charles. "Don't you agree?"

"I suppose so," replied Logan warily.

"Charles sailed here from Aberdeen," put in Allison. "Isn't that daring?" She was playing her own little game, pitting the sensitivities of the two against one another, unaware of the more perilous war of nerves going on between the men.

"It must have been—for you, Fairgate," said Logan, "especially in this weather."

"It heightens the challenge, but then you'd know all about that sort of thing, wouldn't you, Macintyre?"

"I'm afraid I know nothing about sailing."

"I was talking about challenges."

The real intent of Fairgate's words was becoming clear, assisted by the sly glow of anticipated victory in his eye. So, he had at last remembered their former acquaintance and was now going to make his adversary pay! That had to be the purpose of this contrived little meeting. Well, there was no way out of it. There was nothing for Logan to do except remain cool. "Whatever 'appens," Skittles always said, "don't bolt. Always play the dodge to the end—unless the Bobbies are breathin' down your neck."

"Ah yes . . . the challenge of the sea," said Logan. "I was on a fishing vessel recently and almost lost my neck from the challenge." He laughed, trying to divert the attention from Fairgate's probing remarks.

"A fascinating life—the sea," replied Fairgate. "But then it runs in my family. It has since the days we built frigates for Queen Elizabeth. Drake sailed one of our vessels."

"How positively intriguing."

"In fact, I'm off now for Glasgow to oversee the launching of our new liner."

"You didn't say anything about Glasgow," intruded Allison, a bit confused at the direction and stilted quality of the conversation. Around her eyes could be seen a slight cracking of the shell. She wasn't sure she liked what Fairgate was doing to Logan.

"I don't look forward to it, though," continued Charles, heedless of Allison's remark. "It's a rum city, that. Have you ever been there, Macintyre?"

"Once or twice."

"Then you know. A worse city there never was—for civilized folks, that is."

"I'm sure you're right."

"Gentlemen have to watch what they're about in that city."

Logan said nothing, only returned Fairgate's gaze. The cards had been laid face down on the table, and now only the eyes betrayed the steely determination of the bluff.

"No telling when you're going to be fleeced," went on Fairgate, probing Logan's eyes.

Still Logan did not reply, but his blood was starting to run hot.

"Why, I remember one time—"

"I don't mean to sound rude," Logan broke in, glancing over at Allison with an easy laugh intended to convey warmth and hopefully enlist her support in halting Fairgate's runaway reminiscing about the past. "But I promised Jesse I'd get this winch to her this afternoon."

"Don't let us keep you from your work, by all means," said Fairgate. But he had no intention of releasing this grip he had by now so forcibly seized. "You know, Macintyre," he went on, as if the thought had just occurred to him, "since the other evening at Bramfords', I've had the strangest sensation that I've met you before."

"I've never been in this area before in my life."

"Could it have been in Glasgow?"

"I suppose anything's possible," returned Logan bravely, deciding to face it squarely.

"Something about your face reminds me of that city."

"I have a terrible memory for such things myself."

"There was one fellow," Charles pressed relentlessly, clearly enjoying every moment. "You resemble him somewhat." Here he paused and laughed. "But of course, it couldn't have been you." He laughed again. "He was a grubby little street waif ... and it was some years ago. Fancied himself a card sharp." As the words flowed from Fairgate's mouth, his good humor gradually turned into an icy stare of hatred, even while his mouth kept up its smile for Allison's benefit. "And he proved it by cheating me out of a tidy sum. Spent a few days in jail for it as I remember."

He turned to Allison, who was now more bewildered as she found herself torn between the two men. The old Allison stood beside her companion while he grilled a low employee; the new, squirmed with compassion and genuine sympathy for Logan. "Quite something, wouldn't you say, my dear?" laughed Fairgate merrily. "Can you imagine, a runny-nosed little kid trying to slick me and get away with it?"

He threw his head back and roared with laughter.

"Of course getting thrown in the clink wasn't anything new to *him*, for it came out in court that his father was a dirty jailbird too—"

"That's enough, Fairgate!" Logan exploded. Had Fairgate chosen any subject other than his father, Logan might have been able to let it pass. But he had spent too much time trying to dissociate himself from that man, too much time trying to forget his past, to hear Fairgate's accusation calmly.

Even then, Logan might have been able to restrain further outbursts had it not been for the silky, smug grin of satisfaction that spread across Fairgate's patrician face. That look caused Logan to lose his cherished control.

"Enough?" sneered Fairgate. "Enough! After what you did to me, infinitely your superior in every way, and you say *enough*!"

"Yes!" snapped Logan, "and I say it again—enough, or you'll be sorry you ever opened your mouth."

Fairgate roared with laughter again. "*I'll* be sorry! This is really too much, Macintyre! And what are you going to do if I persist?"

"To find that out," replied Logan, "you'll have to call my hand. But in the meantime, you leave my father out of it."

"Oh, so that's it! Your father! Sensitive whelp you are, I must say. But I hardly see what's to defend. The man was nothing but a low-down—"

Logan lunged forward, his hand knotted into a fist and his eyes full of rage. The blow nearly felled the fine lord, but as it reached its mark and he staggered back, he caught himself against the work table and remained on his feet. Fairgate made no counterattack, only stood his ground and grinned back toward his assailant. Then he turned, almost casually toward Allison, who was looking on with horror. "So, Allison," he said, bringing his hand to his chin to stop a small trickle of blood, "at last we see the true colors of your houseguest. Or should I say your *trusted* family employee?"

White with mingled rage and chagrin for what he had done, Logan shot a glance at Allison. He had nearly forgotten her presence. And suddenly he knew why Fairgate still wore his proud grin. Logan had played right into his hand. He had proved with his angry outburst that every word Fairgate had said about him was true. Fairgate had raised the bet to the limit, had called Logan's hand,

and had won it all. In that single act of violence, Logan had undone everything. And Fairgate's unmistakable victory was only punctuated by his refusal to reciprocate in kind. He was the gentleman, Logan the cad.

Allison had been so shocked by the turn of the confrontation that she merely stood gaping, hardly noticing Fairgate's words. When she did speak, all pretense and command was gone. The sensitive side of her nature was struggling desperately to absorb what had happened. She tried to answer, but her voice had not yet caught up with events.

"People of our station must take care for such riffraff," Charles advised, pressing his advantage to the full.

"He's ... he's not a houseguest ..." said Allison at length, still lagging behind Fairgate's half of the exchange. But her sentence ended unfinished as Logan swung around and strode from the stable.

Seeing her gaze following him, yet more sure of himself than ever, Fairgate chuckled cockily. "Let him go, Allison," he said. "*He* can mean nothing to *us* now."

But the words were unwisely spoken. He had pressed Allison too soon to make a choice between the victor and the vanquished, and like most sensitive women, Allison allowed her heart to follow Logan in the pain of his defeat.

Coming awake suddenly, without realizing what she did or why, Allison turned and ran after him. "Logan!" she called. "Logan!"

Whether her voice was not loud enough or whether he chose to ignore it, Logan kept walking, and was soon out of sight behind the stable.

She stopped and watched him silently, while Fairgate walked slowly up behind her from the open stable door.

"Let him go," he repeated in the same self-important tone. "He has deceived you, Allison. If I were you, I'd go and check the family silver."

She spun around, her face flushed with anger.

"What could you possibly know about him? He has behaved nothing but honorably since he came to us!" she lashed out.

"So, you're going to take up the cause for a common street swindler! Come now, Allison, it doesn't become you."

"You think I am somehow obligated to take your side against him?" she snapped. "Because you are more of a man ... of better blood. Is that it?"

"Allison, Allison," he tried to soothe. "Men from his, shall we say, 'origins,' never do amount to anything. He's a deceiver ... a swindler. I shouldn't be surprised to learn he's a thief. I ask you again, just what do you really know about him? And why is he here? That's another question one might reasonably ask." He gently placed a calming hand on Allison's shoulder.

She stood a moment longer, staring at the last place she had seen Logan, then, her anger at Fairgate subsiding, she shrugged off his touch, turned, and sat down on the bench next to the stable wall. What he said did make sense after all.

"He didn't exactly *lie* to us, Charles," she said finally. "That is, no one really *asked* about his background. And some uncle of his, or great uncle, used to work here."

"How convenient," said Fairgate sarcastically.

Allison shot him a questioning glance as another defense of Logan rose to her lips. She apparently thought better of it, however, sighed, and finally threw up her hands and said, "Oh, I don't know what to think."

"Any man who withholds information about a prison record—" Charles knew very well that Logan's few days in the custody of the court could not even broadly be termed a *prison record*, but he saw no reason to take particular pains to clarify this point—"well ... such a man is practicing deception. There's just nothing else you can call it. You ought to inform your parents immediately."

"You don't know my parents," said Allison. And even as she spoke a picture leaped into her mind of how her family would receive such information. She especially saw her grandmother in her mind. Lady Margaret had always taken such pains with the poor and downtrodden, the "grubby street waifs" of the world. When they heard that he was an ex-convict, what would that matter to her elders? Hadn't Lord Duncan, the most revered man in all of Strathy, spent months in prison? No one here would turn Logan out, no matter what he had done.

For the last seven or eight years of her life, Allison had taken great pains to do just the opposite of what the rest of her family might. She had resented their compassion and had tried to rise above what she considered their family weakness. Yet doing so had never brought Allison peace. It had, in fact, produced just the opposite reaction. With a dual personality, she looked with disdain on her mother and great-grandmother and their charitable attitudes, but at the same time, the deepest part of her nature felt guilty for not being more like them.

Suddenly she had a chance to reach out to someone just like they would. And if she didn't, she had no doubt that Logan would walk right out of Port Strathy. But she was not ready to lose him. She could admit that now. She didn't want to lose the happiness she had felt with him for those brief moments on the road back from Culden. She had tried to hide from it, pretend it hadn't happened. She had been horrible to him afterward. But with Charles standing here now, suddenly everything was coming clear. She had never felt that way around him—all the titles and numbers after his name meant nothing. Maybe Logan was just the nephew of a groom. But she had *felt* something! And she couldn't just let it go. She had to find out what the feelings he had stirred in her meant.

She jumped up and started back toward the stable door.

"Where are you going?" asked Charles.

"I'm going after him."

"To make him face the music?"

"No. To apologize. You . . . you were very unkind to him, Charles." The words had been difficult to say to someone so imposing as Charles Fairgate. She knew her change of heart would "get around." But oddly, it felt rather liberating to stand up for something important.

"You'll never find him now," said Charles, coming up next to her.

"Just you watch me!"

"Don't be a fool, Allison."

They were inside the stable now and Allison was hurrying toward the stalls in back. The heavy clouds had returned overhead, and all at once a crack of thunder echoed outside.

"You'll not catch him," said Fairgate, hastening after her. "He's made a run for it. He probably has other warrants out for him."

"That's cruel, Charles."

"Where are you going, Allison?" he asked as she rushed through the rear door of the workshop. Something had gone wrong with his plan and he was not liking it.

"I'm going to saddle a horse and ride after him. He can't have gone far."

"It's starting to rain!"

Allison had already grabbed a saddle and thrown it atop her favorite—the bay mare. Rain was certainly the least deterrent for her at this moment; she had, in fact, very pleasant memories of rain. She only hoped it was not too late to recapture some of them.

She quickly tightened the saddle, opened the stall door, and led the horse out. She paused to throw a macintosh over her shoulders and jam a hat on her head. When she finally mounted, small droplets had begun to fall in earnest. But she welcomed the rain. The look in her face showed it clearly as she turned in the saddle toward Charles, who still stood inside, utterly baffled at the inexplicable change that had come over her.

"Have a nice sail, Charles," she called out, "and give my regrets to everyone in London!"

Without awaiting an answer, she dug her heels into the horse's flanks, galloped off, and was soon out of sight.

39   The Healing Rain

Allison found Logan tramping across a wet stretch of moorland about a quarter of a mile behind Stonewycke.

He turned when he heard the horse making its way through the shrubbery. She pulled up beside him and slid gracefully off the bay. He continued to walk. Allison grabbed the reins and jogged to catch up. "Logan . . . please!" she called after him.

"You still don't know enough to get in out of the rain," he said, still walking, staring straight ahead.

"I don't care about the rain!" she answered passionately. "I wanted to apologize. It was just awful what Charles said to you."

Logan stopped. That was the last thing he had expected her to say. Of course, how could he have any idea what to expect from her? He had all but concluded that everything which had happened two days ago was a mirage, when suddenly it seemed possible their blossoming friendship had meant something to her after all.

But until this very moment it had not occurred to him how Allison would conflict with his designs. Logan had always maintained a hard and fast rule—one he had learned from Skittles: *Never hustle a friend.* He might lie, cheat, and steal from anyone else. But with his friends—of which, to be sure, there were few—he had always been open and honest.

Were these people his friends? Was Allison his friend?

The latter question hardly needed an answer. The sincere expression on her face was more convicting in his soul than any reasonings he could have made with himself. She had never been honest with anyone, not even herself. And yet her face said that she wanted to change that—with him. She was trying to be forthright. How could he lie to her anymore?

His thoughts had taken the merest seconds. Now he turned abruptly and faced her.

"Allison, everything he said about me was true."

"I'm sure you would have told us if we had asked."

"How do you know that?"

"It doesn't matter. I don't want to know what you would have done. And no one in my family will care, either. That's all in the past, anyway. I know just what my great-grandmother would say— that none of us are perfect, least of all me. And besides, none of them need know what Fairgate accused you of. I'll not tell."

"Why?"

"There's no reason. And besides, who's Charles Fairgate that I should believe him over you?"

"He's someone who knew me many years ago."

"I don't care. That was then, now is now."

"I'm not sure I understand," said Logan, still reeling from this sudden turnaround.

Allison paused a moment, and when she spoke again there was a quiet seriousness in her tone. "I haven't behaved in a way I'm proud of these last couple of days."

"Don't worry about it."

"I do worry about it. Sometimes the person I am isn't very nice. And ... I'm sorry. Logan, I *do* want to be your friend."

"Thank you. You don't know how much that means to me. But there's still so much you don't understand."

"What does it matter? Don't spoil it, Logan Macintyre, or I might run out of sweetness for you yet. A girl can be only so nice in one day." She laughed, and he joined her.

Then Allison swung back up upon the bay. "Now!" she called down to him. "Get up here with me, and let's go for a ride!"

"But it's raining," he protested with another laugh.

"That never stopped us before."

He laughed, reached up and took her offered hand, and swung up behind her. He hadn't forgotten his earlier decision to be honest with her. But why spoil the moment with confessions and revelations? They could wait for a more opportune time.

Allison led the mare eastward, away from the flooded low country. The rocky ground rose steadily until they reached the Fenwick Harbor road which, had they followed it, would have led them to Aberdeen. They rode north instead, toward the sea. As they trotted along, the wind increased in force and the droplets of rain became larger and larger. A ragged flash of lightning lit the afternoon sky, followed almost the same instant by a crack of thunder.

"That was close by!" shouted Allison. "Right over on the coast, I'd say."

It was not much longer until they reached the Port Strathy road, with Ramsey Head directly to their right off the shoreline, shrouded in mist and clouds. Allison could not hold back a shudder at the granite promontory that would always be associated with evil doings.

"It might not be a bad idea to think of turning toward Stonewycke," said Logan. "If we wait much longer we'll get soaked again."

"I don't mind if you don't," said Allison cheerily. "But you're probably right."

They rode on past the Head. There had been a time, even during Lady Margaret's childhood, when the place had been used for pleasant afternoon walks and picnics, despite its ancient history as a hideout for smugglers and shipwreckers. But since then, it had re-verted to its former ways in the minds of the local inhabitants. The caves surrounding it were well known to house occasional drunks and derelicts who were unconcerned about the dark legends of the place. And every Halloween, a report would begin to circulate of a body popping up among the jagged and treacherous sea rocks.

"Cold?" asked Logan, concerned over Allison's sudden silence.

"No, it's just this place, I suppose."

"What about it?"

Allison tried to relieve her nervousness by relating a portion of the history of the place. For the first time he discovered that the murderer who had killed himself had been involved in the events of Lord and Lady Duncan's early history, news that on first hearing struck him as incredulous.

All at once, as if to emphasize the heavy, ominous feeling that had descended upon them, a figure darted out onto the road from the very point in which they had been staring, coming it seemed directly from the trail down to the shore at Ramsey Head.

Allison reined in the mare, and there beside them stood Jesse Cameron. She had been running and now stopped with her hand to her chest, trying to catch her breath again before she could speak.

40   Tragedy

"Jesse!" exclaimed Logan. "What's all the hurry?"

"There's been an accident," she replied between gasps. "Some children were a playin' in one o' them sea caves on the Head. I don't know what the parents was thinkin' t' let them oot on a day such as this. But one o' them—young Harry Stewart—got himsel' hurt an' couldna climb oot. Alec happened t' be at my place seein' t' one o' my goats when the other young'un came fer help.Weel, he went doon t' lend a hand. He was gone sae lang I went doon. An' the cave they were in was all blocked up wi' rocks!"

"How—" asked Allison anxiously, "what do you mean?"

"Looks like one o' them tall pinnacles up above't may hae been struck by that blast o' lightnin', an' when it fell, it must hae dislodged the boulders that formed the walls o' the cave. 'Tis all I can think o'. But Logan, man, they're trapped inside. I'm goin' t' toon t' get the others."

"How can you be certain it was the right cave?" Allison's voice was shaky. Many new emotions were assailing her all at once.

"The boy—oh, here he is noo—" A boy of about eleven came trotting out onto the road. He was smudged and wet and trembling with fear, exhaustion, and cold. Jesse put her thick arm around the child. "Tommy's certain. An' we'd hae seen them by noo. I'm sorry, Lady Allison. I canna believe otherwise."

"You think they might be . . ." Allison managed to say in a weak whisper, then stopped, swaying unsteadily in the saddle.

Logan caught her and held her tightly with one arm. Then with his free hand he took charge of the reins.

"Could you hear them?" he asked.

"No," Jesse answered, "but wi' the wind an' the noise o' the sea, not t' mention the solid rock blockin' up the mouth o' the cave, 'tis not surprisin'. There's still reason t' hope fer the best."

"You look spent already, Jesse," said the practical Logan. "You best take the boy back to your place and we'll ride for help."

"I'm going to my father," said Allison firmly, and, springing back to life, she wrenched the reins from Logan and dug her heels into the bay.

"Lass, ye canna do that," Jesse called. "Yer mother'll hae worry enough!"

But it was too late. The riders were already well out of earshot, even if Allison had been listening. Jesse wasted no more time trying to yell after them. Perhaps the two young folks could do something while she went for help. In the meantime she hurried back down the hill to her house, deposited the boy, hastily saddled her own horse, and rode for town.

Allison's bay found the going slow down the trail to the neck connecting the Head to the mainland. From there the animal had to thread her way cautiously up the muddy incline of Ramsey Head. In summer, the terrain on this, the leeward side of the promontory, was green with heather and bracken, dotted here and there with a handful of trees, bent and contorted by the constant sea winds. But at this time of year the foliage was brown and wet, beaten down by the steady barrage of rain. From the bleak face of nature, it would have been difficult to surmise that spring had already come to this region—come, and then seemingly given way again to winter without a hint of anything in between.

The horse was surefooted enough on this turf, but when they had climbed the path toward the seaward side, the hard and rocky surface, stripped of nearly all vegetation and slick with rain, became impossible to traverse. Several caves crowded this part of the promontory, some merely large crevices formed by the haphazard placement of boulders and cliffs, others extending well into the depths of the Head, bored through the rock over thousands of years by the constant contact with the sea. The floors of most were under water either part or all of the time, but there were a few high enough to remain snug and dry even at high tide. Those most challenging to Strathy's children were the ones accessible during low tide, but whose floors sunk below the ocean's surface as the tide came in.

"We'll have to leave the horse here," she called back to Logan over her shoulder. Though he was only inches from her, the wind velocity forced her to yell in order to be heard.

They dismounted and made their way along a narrow footpath skirting the circumference of the bluff some fifty feet above the water's edge. In a few minutes they rounded a curve, reaching the outermost point of the promontory, and were suddenly met with the full force of the wind and the open expanse of the sea. The gray waters frothed white around the edges like the mouth of a mad dog. The rain-filled blasts lashed at Allison's face, whipping her hair into a tangled mass about her head.

"There it is!" shouted Allison, pointing to a spot some distance down the path below a steep grade. They could make out the scattered rubble on the ledge, broken shards from the larger rocks that had been dislodged. A spike of stone, larger than a tree, lay against the wall of the mountain as if some giant had leaned his walking stick against a garden wall. On closer inspection, Allison saw that the cave was indeed one of the rock crevices. When the spike had fallen, its movement had displaced the boulders forming the walls of the cave, as Jesse had described.

Before they reached their destination, they had to traverse a steep descent which dropped about ten feet, where the trail had once been. Allison scrambled down with little difficulty, too intent on her father's peril to pay the least attention to her own. But Logan, afraid for her safety, was paying closer attention to the dropoff to the sea fifty feet below, just beyond the ledge. Into his imagination came a vision of the legendary murderer flying off a spot just like this to his death on the sharp rocks below. Even as he shook his head to rid his mind of the ominous picture, his foot slipped, and he had to struggle and claw at the precarious surface to keep himself from falling. He let out an involuntary cry which, muffled by the gale, went unheard by Allison several feet ahead. With trembling knees he followed slowly, none too confident they could accomplish anything even if they could reach the cave alive, resisting the great urge to turn around and run.

Slipping and sliding, and walking where possible, they made their way farther, till at last they neared the place where the cave-in had occurred. Still racing ahead, Allison began to yell for her father. But the wind carried her voice off as a vanishing puff of smoke.

She came to the heap of rock and immediately began to tear at the jagged slab of stone with her bare hands. Seeing her pathetic gesture, Logan set his hands also to the task, but nothing budged, save a few inconsequential stones. Her bravado tempered somewhat, she looked helplessly at Logan. She didn't have to speak for him to know what she was thinking. Even if the whole town turned out, they'd have difficulty moving these stones. And what good would the entire town do anyway? Only a handful of people could move about safely on the ledge that faced the cave.

In an agony of despair Allison stood back and began pacing around the area. Where was everyone? Why was it taking them so long to get here? All at once her eyes filled with tears.

"Daddy . . ." she murmured.

It had been so long since she thought about him as she once had when a child, how much he meant to her, how she needed him. She had been so cold to him in recent times, so independent, so unfeeling. What would happen now if she never had the chance to make it up to him?

"Oh, please ... please," she whispered, hardly realizing her distraught mind was forming a prayer for the first time in years, "please don't let anything happen to him."

Logan went to her side.

"You have to believe he's safe," he said gently. "We'll get him out."

"Oh, Logan," she wailed, "I'm so afraid I won't ever get a chance to tell him—"

She could not go on. A sob choked out her words. She turned away, embarrassed at the show of emotion.

Logan laid a hand on her shoulder to comfort her, but said nothing.

"I've never been much of a daughter to him," she blurted out, crying now. "I don't think I've ever told him how proud I am to have him for my father."

"He must know."

"Oh, how could he know?" she wailed despondently. "I've let him think I'm ashamed of him because of his common birth. I've just been all mixed up, Logan," she confessed. "Why, he's better than a hundred highbred men together. It's just that—" she sniffed and brushed a sleeve across her nose, all pretense at playing the sophisticated role now gone. "Oh, I was so blind ... I've been so confused. Why did I treat him like that?"

"Don't think of it now," said Logan lamely. He did not know any words of real comfort to give, so he settled for hollow phrases he had heard others give. Yet even as he spoke, he knew his words were empty, and wished he could offer more to soothe her aching heart. "It won't be long until he'll be right here next to you, and then you can make everything right."

"Oh, Logan," she cried, "if only I could do something *now*!" She turned her face back toward the rock wall and shouted with all her might, "Daddy, can you hear me!"

41   Rescue

Alec lay sprawled on the bare rock in pitch darkness. A trickle of blood ran out of a deep gash on his head.

At last he tried to move, slowly and painfully. His head may have been the most seriously injured, but his shoulder and foot had also been grazed by the falling rock. Feeling a sharp throb in his head, he brought his hand to the wound and felt the sticky moistness of blood. He could see nothing around him and might reasonably have feared blindness until his eyes adjusted and he began to distinguish dim shadows.

"Harry!" he called, thinking of the boy the moment his head began to clear.

"I'm here, Mr. MacNeil."

"Are ye safe, boy?"

"Aye, sir. 'Tis jist my leg hurts sorely."

"Stay where ye are, Harry, an' I'll get t' ye."

Alec rolled over and attempted to pull himself up. He barely reached his knees when everything solid seemed to melt from under him and he crumbled back to the ground. " 'Tis goin' t' take me a minute or twa, lad. Can ye wait?"

"Aye, sir," said the boy, but his voice trembled with each word. "Mr. MacNeil, do ye think we're stuck in here fore'er?"

"Not a bit o' it, lad," Alec replied as buoyantly as he could make his voice sound. "We'll be oot o' here afore supper. Jesse will get help an' they'll clear away the rock before we know it." He paused, then added, trying to conceal his concern, especially with the rising tide in the back of his mind, "Hoo lang hae I been lyin' here, lad?"

"A powerful lang time, sir. I thought ye was—" Harry's voice broke, and the remainder of his thought hardly needed to be spoken. Then he added in a tearful rush, "Oh, I'm glad I'm na here alane!"

"Noo, lad," said Alec, "ye wouldna hae been alane whate'er had happened. Our Lord's here wi' ye—wi' us both, lad. He'll ne'er leave us alane—ye ken that, dinna ye, lad?"

"Aye, sir, but I'm guessin' I forgot for a bit."

Alec's smile was unseen in the darkness, but it could be heard in his gentle words. "I'm thinkin' the Lord understan's that. But let's remember t' remin' one another o' it."

"Aye, sir," said Harry.

"I'm comin' t' ye noo," said Alec, praying silently for strength.

He crawled along the floor of the cave for a foot or two until he came to an upright wall. He could not tell if it was the wall of the cave or merely a section of the rubble that had shut them in. At least it was solid enough to hold his weight. Groping at one protruding rock after another, he pulled himself to a standing position. Everything spun before him, and he felt fresh blood flow into his eyes, obscuring what little vision he had. He wiped a hand across his eyes, then steadied himself for a moment before beginning to inch his way along the wall toward the boy's voice. His foot throbbed, seemingly in rhythm with the ache in his head. He must have twisted it during the fall.

It took him five long, torturous minutes to reach Harry. When he finally did so, he nearly collapsed on the ground beside him. He rested a moment, then tried to examine the boy's leg.

It was a definite break, but there was little he could do. It was a wonder the poor boy had not yet fainted from shock. His medical instinct forced him to make some attempt to help, no matter how feeble it turned out to be. But he had not even come across a piece of driftwood he could use as a splint. He lurched to his feet, and, after instructing Harry to keep perfectly still, began groping about the cave. Vagrants and wanderers often camped out around here. Perhaps some sticks from an old campfire might be lying around.

After some searching, his hands lit upon several pieces of charred wood. They were irregular, and it took some skill to suit them to his purpose. But with the aid of his shirt, torn into strips, he made them work. He had made better splints for injured kittens, but at least the boy's every movement would not incapacitate him.

When he had done all he could do medically, he turned his attention to their plight. After loosening a few of the smaller stones and forcing his shoulder several times against the large ones, he realized there was no way a single man, especially an injured one, was going to be able to begin to budge the debris. Not a man given to fits of hopelessness, he limped back and forth across their narrow prison for several minutes, thinking and praying, wishing there were something he could *do*. Strong as his faith was, it was agony to Alec MacNeil simply to sit and wait for the hand of the Lord to act, without being able to participate in the process himself.

At length, so that his agitation would not further upset the boy, he sat down once more next to Harry, reaching his arm around him to give the child both warmth and comfort. There was nothing else to do but to wait and pray, and give what strength he could to the frightened child.

When he started awake after some time, he wasn't certain if the sounds he heard were from his dreams or from somewhere beyond the blackness. He cocked his head and listened intently.

There it was again! A high-pitched sound, almost like the wail of the wind, yet there was a desperate human quality about it. He jumped up, forgetting his injured foot, and nearly fell again to the ground. Supporting himself as best he could, he hobbled as quickly as his head and foot would allow to the mouth of the cave.

The sound came again, more distinct now, yet seemingly still as part of his dream. Yet he was almost certain he could make out the single unlikely word:

Daddy!

He shouted out a reply, and Harry's small voice joined his own. "We're here! We're all right!"

————

The sound of her father's voice filled Allison with an unabashed and childlike joy such as she had not recently allowed herself to feel.

"He's safe!" she exclaimed, throwing her arms around Logan and squeezing him as if he had been the object of her anxieties. The tears were flowing freely now, but she seemed unconcerned and did not try to hide them. She stood back, looked into his eyes, laughed with relief, then embraced him again.

All at once a loud clamor reached them from above the wail of the wind. It was the approach of the rescue party. Logan and Allison fell apart awkwardly, trying quickly to regain their composure. But Allison hardly cared what the others might think. In a single bound, she had, for the moment at least, moved beyond that. Her embarrassed reaction was merely a response of habit, and now as the men came, she ran toward them with an uncharacteristic exuberance. For the first time in her life she realized how glad she was to see men of this sort, men like her father, men of brawn, men of loyalty to their kind, the kind of men her arrogant eyes had always been blind to. Suddenly, the inner door of her spirit was flung open to the truth that her parents and great-grandparents had always stressed, that the simple and common people of the valley of Strathy embodied the true and lasting Stonewycke heritage. How glad she was that these men came to rescue her father, not the smooth-of-speech, silky-of-dress, dainty-of-hand Charles Fairgates she had known.

Seven men appeared around the bend in the path, each a shining specimen of Port Strathy's manhood. Burly and muscular, they represented the fishing and farming communities. They carried rope, picks, crowbars, long lengths of metal pipes, and anything else they thought might aid in the excavation.

"Oh, thank you! thank you!" cried Allison. "Do hurry. They're all right . . . I heard them!"

Dislodging the great stone spar that had caused the mishap in the first place proved rather a simple matter when eight strong backs, including Logan's, were thrust against it. With a booming crash which rose even above the din of wind and waves, the spar tumbled to the sea.

But the boulders blocking the entrance were another matter. Six of the men climbed to a point above the cave, and, using pipes and crowbars as levers, attempted to separate the largest of the rocks. They inched it slowly apart, but before an opening even six inches had been made, the strength of the laborers gave out and the rocks snapped back together.

"We'll ne'er be able t' keep the rocks open lang enough fer them t' crawl through!" yelled Jimmy MacMillan from his perch overhead.

Logan, waiting below, shook his head in despair. The thing looked so hopeless! Glancing around, his eyes focused on a foot-long length of pipe lying on the ground where one of the men had abandoned it. He ran to it, caught it up, and hurried back to the site.

"I have an idea," he shouted. "Spread the rocks apart again. I'll try to wedge this pipe between them!"

Again the men set their shoulders to the bars, this time with yet greater determination, and again the rocks were pried apart—five, six, seven inches. Logan could hear Alec and Harry shouting encouragement from deep within the cavity. He scrambled toward the small opening, placing himself in the middle of the temporary breach they had made, and gripped the pipe firmly in his fingers, waiting for the exact moment when the pipe could be wedged in perpendicularly so that it would hold the rocks apart. No one needed to tell him that if the men above lost their traction, or if the pipe proved inadequate, his arm, and perhaps half his body, would be crushed in an instant.

... Nine inches ... eleven ...

Logan set the pipe into place. It was still a little crooked.

"Another inch or two!" he shouted, hiding his fear.

Carefully the men continued to increase the pressure. At last the opening was wide enough and Logan jammed the pipe securely in place.

"Back off slightly!" called Logan. He removed himself from the hole as the men eased the tension on their bars, everyone holding his breath during the tense moments, waiting to see if the bar would hold. At that moment Logan found himself worried more about saving himself than about saving Alec and the boy.

"It's holding!" cried Jimmy.

Alec needed to hear no more. Now it was his turn to spring into action.

"Help me wi' the boy!" he called out.

Still closest to the opening, Logan peered into the blackness below. Gently, but with great haste, Alec lifted Harry into the breach where Logan took his outstretched arms and pulled him up to safety.

"A rope!" called Logan out behind him, and in moments felt Alec tugging on the bottom of the line he had fed through. Several men joined him, holding the upper end of the line secure, while Alec pulled his bulky frame, not without some difficulty, through the narrow opening. Within three minutes more, he was standing safely on the ledge with the others. A great cheer went up. Alec greeted them with a smile and a wave of the hand, then turned back, picked up a length of wood, and with a great blow knocked the pipe loose. The rocks crashed firmly and permanently together.

"We canna be havin' anyone else gettin' trapped in there!" he said.

He turned back to face the small and happy crowd, but then swayed unsteadily. Abandoning the reluctance that had come upon her at the sight of him, Allison ran forward and threw her arms around him. "Daddy," she said, "you're hurt!"

"Allison, lass," Alec answered stroking his daughter's hair. "I thought I was jist dreamin' when I heard yer voice."

"No, Daddy. I was here, and I'm so happy you're safe. Here, let me help you."

Logan stepped forward to lend some support to the brawny veterinarian, but he almost wished he had remained in the background when Alec turned his attention toward him.

"Thank ye, Logan, fer what ye did there. It took a good bit o' courage, an' jist may ha' saved my life!"

The temporary glow and sense of satisfaction with having done a brave deed suddenly vanished. The words *a good bit o' courage* resounded in his brain like a painful gong intended to humiliate him before the whole world. He had almost forgotten who he really was, and why he had come. So caught up in his happy ride with Allison and the struggle to free Alec and young Harry, he had temporarily blanked his true self out of his mind. But now, reminded so graphically of his deception by Alec's thanks, he felt like throwing his hands over his ears. Those were the last words he wanted to hear, for he knew he deserved none of them.

"There were others who did as much," he answered.

"Aye, an' I'll be thankin' them, too. But ye're a stranger an' so it means even more comin' from yersel', riskin' yer life fer a man ye hardly know. I'll na be forgettin'.'"

The clamorous approach of the men who had been scrambling down from their perch on the rocks above relieved Logan of the necessity to make any further response.

But his conscience was not relieved of the fact that Alec's praise was both unmerited and unfounded. He was a liar and a con man, and, if his plan to make off with the family's lost treasure succeeded, he would also be a thief. He deserved no praise.

He was far from brave. And he knew it. Because he lacked the most fundamental courage of all—the courage simply to tell the truth.

42   New Dawn

Sunshine spilled in through Allison's window. At first she noticed nothing unusual about it. She rolled over in her bed, yawned and gave a great stretch, and then realized it was the first ray of sun she had seen in days.

She sprang out of bed, ran to the window, and flung open the drapes. Yes! Spots of blue were piercing the gray covering overhead. Allison did not mind the rain. Indeed, in the last few days it had been friendly to her. But it had also wrought havoc in the valley and along the coast. And it was because of the storm that her father had been trapped in the cave.

But it was just like Grandpa Dorey had said—God had turned a seeming tragedy to good. Her father would be in bed a day or two with his injuries, but he would be fine. And out of his accident a profound wonder had occurred. When Allison had looked upon her father after he had been delivered from his tomb, much of the superficiality of her former shell had fallen away. She suddenly saw clearly what was truly important. All those things in her father she had tried so hard to reject were in reality the very qualities in life which mattered. For so long she had shunned her family. Yet now she knew she would be lost without them. Her father, in all the commonness of his upbringing, his occupation, his clothes, and his unrefined speech, represented all that she had disdained. Yet none of them—especially her gentle and soft-spoken father—had ever done anything other than pour their love out to her.

How could she have been so selfish . . . so blind?

At this moment, however, she didn't want to burden herself down with all the questions and the guilt which they produced. Instead, now was a time to shed the superficiality of the past, start over, and try to make it up to them as best she could.

Hurriedly Allison dressed in her prettiest spring dress of pale pink. What did she care if she had to throw a white sweater over her shoulders to ward off the chill that continued to linger in the air? She felt like the earth must when the first tiny crocus pushes past the snow covering the stubborn spring sod, or like a butterfly breaking out of its cocoon. She didn't know what was coming or even what she wanted to happen next. All she sensed was that a new day in her life had come. The sun was shining, the old shell had fallen away, and anticipation fairly throbbed within her breast.

She hastened from her room, down the hall, and around a corner toward her father's recovery chamber. Whatever it was she had to do in order to make a new beginning, she knew it had to begin here. The door was closed, and as Allison stood there hesitating, wondering whether to knock or walk in, the door opened of its own accord and she stepped back. Dorey, moving with exaggerated quietness, appeared. He quickly put his finger to his lips when Allison began to speak. Then he stepped across the threshold and closed the door softly behind him.

He placed his arm around Allison and led her down the corridor before speaking. "I stepped in to see when he wanted breakfast," he said at length, "but he was sound asleep. Your mother said he had quite a restless night, so I thought it best to leave him be."

"I was hoping to see him," said Allison, "but I know he needs his rest."

"If I know your father, he will be up soon. Then the battle will begin to convince him to remain in bed for another day or two."

Allison smiled. Her father had never been sick a day in his life. He was up at dawn every day and continually on the move from that moment, riding, or driving all over the district tending his four-legged patients. He did sleep, it was true, but on many nights he was interrupted at all hours by emergencies large and small. He might grumble a bit then, but to be *forced* to stay in bed was quite another matter. No, she was sure he would not take kindly to a day in bed. Such thoughts reminded Allison of the boundless love in his nature that more than equalled his energy, and his hearty laughter, and his capacity to make friends with everyone. She had not allowed herself to notice such qualities of his character before, qualities which made of him no *common* man indeed, but rather a great one. How much she had missed!

"Oh, Grandpa Dorey, will he ever be able to forgive me?" she asked, as if her great-grandfather had been privy to all her thoughts.

"What are you speaking of, lass?"

"My father," she answered. "I've been so cruel and selfish to him, acting as if I were too good for him, when all along it was just the other way around. I wouldn't blame him if he hated me."

"Ali, dear, your father doesn't know how to hate. And I know that he has long since forgiven you for anything which may have required it. He is not a man to carry a sense of wrong. But it wouldn't hurt for you to ask him to forgive you if you feel it is necessary. He could not respond any way but with the loving arms of true fatherhood. And perhaps you need to do it for the cleansing it will bring to you. Then all the hurts you have been carrying can be put behind you."

"It couldn't be *that* easy."

"You can only ask to know for certain. I know your father, I think as well as I have known any man. But my telling you of his love for you can never take the place of your knowing that love for yourself—just as it is with our Father in heaven. That's why you are right to go to him."

"And you think he'd not be angry with me?"

"Oh, my dear, that's the last thing he'd be! A man who has known great forgiveness usually has a greater capacity to forgive. Your father has felt the touch of God's love in his own life. He'll withhold nothing from you."

"Oh, Grandpa, I hope that's true, because there are several others I must ask forgiveness from after him. I've been so foolish!" She stopped and looked up into his aged eyes of wisdom with the youthful eyes of entreaty.

He hugged her to him, then said, "Come, dear. Let's walk farther and talk."

They continued along the hall to the main staircase and then down, with Dorey leaning on Allison's arm, exiting the house, and emerging into the crisp spring morning. The sky was a brilliant blue, with scarcely a cloud except for two or three billowy white clusters—clean and sharply defined. Dorey breathed deeply of the fresh, cold air.

"Ah," he sighed, "there'll be new blossoms now. It is truly spring at last. How I love springtime! Lord, how I thank you for your seasons!"

They made their way past the leafless, flowerless rose garden, then down the slope of the lawn toward the rear of the castle.

"Tell me, my dear," Dorey said as they continued to walk at a leisurely pace, "what has been happening with you?" His voice was casual, conversational, but a tingle of something akin to excitement coursed through his aged body. "Am I right in sensing that there is a springtime of new birth seeking to blossom within your heart as well as in the earth all about us?"

"I don't know, Grandpa," she answered. "I don't feel very much like my old self lately. But seeing Daddy in such danger yesterday magnified it. Suddenly I didn't want to be that way anymore—how I have been for so long. Maybe I began to see myself as I truly was. And I found myself wanting to change."

She sighed, then went on. "But I don't know if I can. I just don't have the kind of nature that can be good and kind, like my mother or great-grandmother. I don't think I ever will no matter how hard I try."

"Have you talked to the Lord about this, Ali?"

"I don't think He'd listen to me," she answered. "I haven't prayed to Him much lately, and haven't been much of a Christian."

"Then, if you care to take the advice of an old man, it seems to me that you ought to deal with that before you go trying to do something as big as changing your nature. You see, Ali, it is God who changes natures. You'd not get very far on your own. Your mother, and my Maggie—they would never say *they* had good and kind natures either. They both had to come to this point in their lives when they laid down who they were on their own and began to let God remake them according to *His* design. That's why it's God you need to talk to first."

"But why would He listen to *me*—?"

She stopped short, for she knew the question hardly needed an answer. "Yes, I know," she said, more to herself than to Dorey, "He always listens. Maybe that's what I'm afraid of—facing God after so long. Grandpa, I'm not even sure I really am a Christian!"

By now they had come to a small courtyard. Dorey paused and pushed in the gate.

"Let's sit in here a moment," he said, leading her into the enclosure. "Look," he said, pointing. "There are new shoots on the oak tree. I shall be able to come out here next week to plant the annuals." The carved marble bench under the tree was dry, and he motioned for her to sit next to him there.

"May I ask you a question, Ali?" he said after a moment.

She nodded.

"You have a kind and loving father, do you not?" She nodded again, this time with more emphasis.

"And if you went up to his room this moment to ask, you believe he would forgive you and love you completely, don't you."

"It's hard... But yes, I do believe it."

"Do you think your heavenly Father, who sacrificed His Son for us, would have less capacity to love and forgive?"

"I wouldn't blame Him," she answered, tears welling up in her eyes. "I've been so awful! All my life I've wanted to be like mother, and like your Lady Margaret. All I ever see is how giving and kind they are. And everyone knows how much they have given their lives and the wealth of their heritage for the common people. Yet I'm nothing like that! I can't possibly ever measure up to what they must expect me to be like. I've been cold and distant and arrogant. Oh, how I've prayed to be like them, Grandpa! But down deep inside there's such a fear ... that I ... that I never will be. I feel like ... like I've let the family down!"

She hardly spilled out the words before a torrent of weeping assailed her. She hadn't realized what pain her confession would bring until it was at last spoken.

The sudden gush of tears and uncontrollable sobs did not surprise Dorey. He had seen the turmoil building for some time, and now, even as she wept, silently closed his eyes in thanksgiving to his Lord for bringing it at last to a head so the deep healing of her heart could begin.

He drew her to him, and quietly stroked her head as it lay on his shoulder. She cried for several minutes, until the surface of Dorey's jacket was quite damp. Then she lifted her head, sniffed, and dried her eyes on his offered handkerchief.

"Oh, Grandpa, what am I going to do?"

"Simply ask your heavenly Father to help you," he answered. "He wants nothing more than to help His children."

"But . . . I don't even know if I am His child . . ."

"Then let's take care of that first," said the old man, taking her hand in his. "Come, dear, let's pray. . . ."

43   The Prayers of the Righteous

Ian and Maggie walked hand in hand up their favorite little knoll near the house. Their shoes were wet by the time they reached the top, and they were nearly out of breath. But it was always to this place they came when they had a special joy to share.

Indeed, though the stillness surrounding them would hardly have indicated it, they each knew there were multitudes of angels rejoicing with them on this great day for the Duncan clan, when their dear child Allison had been welcomed into the fold of God.

Lady Margaret both rejoiced and wept at the news. Part of her, however, was saddened as well at what had oppressed the girl for so long.

"I knew she was troubled," she told her husband, "by some of the things she saw in the rest of us. It was clear her resentments and shows of pride were coming from her own insecurity. If only I had been more sensitive, how much pain might have been avoided. The dear child!"

"I won't have you blame yourself," Ian gently rebuked. "You did everything God gave you to do. You could hardly sacrifice what He wanted of you in order to shield another from a very necessary pain."

"How do you mean?"

"The Lord gave to you and Joanna the vision of what serving these people of Strathy means. To you fell the blessing of giving a portion of Stonewycke's heritage back to them. Allison felt she was supposed to live up to that tradition. But she couldn't. And therefore she turned that very thing into a false sense of pride that God had to break. You could not have avoided it for her. Your legacy, in a sense, proved the tool in His hands to break through into Allison's heart."

"All things do indeed work for good, don't they, my dear husband?"

"There are many things only He can do. And certainly one of those is knowing a person's mind and heart, and then doing whatever is necessary to open that heart to His love. Only the Lord could identify that something in Allison—whether it was rebellion or fear or insecurity—made her feel so oppressed by the rest of us. Only God could identify that, and then reach in and heal it."

"Oh, Ian, I'm so glad she's whole again! I remember how fresh and clean I felt when at last I released the terrible burden of unforgiveness toward my father. When at last I was able to give it up, even though I was not yet with you, I felt my spirit could soar!"

"I'm glad for her, too. But it will not be easy for her. She is with her father right now on one of the difficult errands God has compelled her to do. You had to forgive your father; she has to ask her father's forgiveness. And that can sometimes be even harder. I suspect she will want to see you and Joanna next. And that will not be easy for her either."

"But now she won't be alone," added Maggie, as if she were encouraging Allison herself. "With the Lord's Spirit now inside her, she will have a strength to face such challenges she hasn't had before."

"That is exactly what I told her."

"And a strength to grow into the new nature He has fashioned for her. When I look back on our lives, Ian, I marvel at that very thing—how the Lord gave us such new natures! Do you remember what we were like?"

He laughed. "How could I ever forget? I was so caught up in myself."

"We both were! And yet here we are, at least in some small measure, beginning to reflect Him. Oh, He has been *so* good to us!"

They walked along for a while, gradually making their way back down the hill toward the house, when Ian stopped and slowly bent his aging body down to the ground. With deft, experienced fingers, he pushed back a tuft of grass.

"Look, Maggie!"

When she had stooped down next to him, he indicated with almost a sense of joyful reference a tiny yellow primrose, so small that few casual strollers would have seen it.

"Winter is coming to an end," said Maggie, her words sounding oddly prophetic.

They rose and continued on.

"You know," said Ian at length, "there's another element in this change in Allison that I continue to puzzle over."

Maggie glanced up inquisitively. "You're not thinking of our new mechanic friend?"

"Aye," replied Dorey with a twinkle in his eye. "Somehow I think he has more to do with the unlocking of Allison's heart than even she knows. She mentioned him a number of times when I was talking with her. You do know whom he reminds me of, don't you?" he asked.

"Why, of course, Ian—you!"

He laughed. "I only hope he can be a better influence on Allison than I was on you."

"Nonsense! Don't you even think such a thing," she chided.

"But it just goes to show again how the Lord uses the most unlikely instruments."

"I know! Just imagine—old Digory's descendant."

"I was actually thinking of his background. It's as if he just turned up here out of nowhere. We really know nothing about him. I sometimes almost imagine him to be an angel, planted here at this time for the very purpose of triggering these changes in Allison's heart."

Maggie became silent for a moment. "He is a puzzling fellow," she then said. "From the moment I laid eyes on him, I could see Digory in him. His eyes drew me. Yet I've sensed something else, too—something I can't quite put my finger on. I don't know whether it alarms me or excites me. But it seems that there is more to him than we know."

"Of one thing we can be sure. He is intrinsically bound up in the Lord's present work in Allison—and, for that matter, of the whole estate!"

"We must remember to pray diligently for Mr. Macintyre," said Maggie solemnly. "Angel or not, there can be no doubt that God sent him to us, not only for Allison's benefit, but also because of the work the Lord is carrying out in him. Whatever his future at Stonewycke, I sense that he is troubled. We must pray earnestly, for there is no doubt but that he is among us by God's design."

44 Ramsey Head Again

Logan spent that same morning brooding over the events of the previous day.

The quest which had brought him here was becoming increasingly difficult to fulfill—not because he couldn't find the treasure, but because it was becoming harder and harder to keep his mind on its business. Suddenly all sorts of new emotions were bearing in upon him from many unexpected directions. Every time he thought of resuming his search, and then packing up and leaving town in the dead of night as a rich man, he could not help but cringe inwardly.

He threw down the tool he'd been cleaning, jumped up, and began to pace about the stable. He couldn't keep his mind on anything! True to the half-hearted vow he'd made with himself, he had dug out old Digory's Bible that morning and tried to read it. But he couldn't make sense out of it. Vaguely familiar passages from childhood occasionally stood out. But the rest of it might as well have been Greek. He was too troubled to concentrate on it, anyway. Whenever he tried to read something, the phrase Jesse had said to him kept coming back into his mind: *Things aboot God, things we've all heard from oor mothers but which we pay no attention t', till we get older an' wiser an' then we start rememberin'*... His brain was too full to read, to think ... to do anything. He had then thrown down the Bible and gone downstairs where he hoped some work would take his mind off his dilemma. But work proved as impossible as reading, and even cleaning up rusted tools turned out to be more taxing than his restive mind could cope with.

All his life he had looked out for only one person—himself. The instinct to survive was deeply ingrained, and with it a certain mistrust of others. Because his own motives were often self-seeking and larcenous, he naturally suspected the same of everyone else—and experience more often than not proved him right.

Yes, he admitted, this Duncan clan seemed congenial and hospitable enough—now. But they, like anyone, he tried to convince himself, had the capacity to turn on someone who proved a threat. What was to make him think they'd treat him any differently? The risk of revealing his motives was too great. Even if he hadn't done anything strictly illegal, people with the power and prestige of the Duncans could find some charge against him and make it stick.

Logan knew he was risking their friendship, which was, for some reason he could not quite identify, difficult to give up—not only theirs, but also that of Jesse and others. And to continue on his chosen course of action would mean to give up Allison, too. Whether she would ever accept someone from his station might be doubtful, but that made it no easier to forget the moments they had had together.

Did none of the last two weeks matter? Was it all a mere distraction, one of the obstacles he anticipated in seeking out this lost treasure? How could everything change so quickly? What Jesse had said kept coming back to haunt him: *I don't know why we willna listen t' truth till we get oorsel's int' trouble, or until some catastrophe smacks us in the face an' wakes us up.* But he didn't want to hear it! He had no time for all that now. And that old poet talking about bad boats and wretched crews and freedom. Was he one of the poor, foolish men who refused to be free?

No! He *would* be free. The treasure would give him freedom. With it he could help all these people who had been kind to him and have plenty left over for himself. It was his rightful inheritance anyway! It had last been in Digory's possession. It did not belong to anyone. It had belonged to an ancient people and whoever found it— well, possession is nine-tenths of the law. Everyone knew it. He would not listen to these doubts any longer, all these ridiculous religious fancies that somehow got stirred up in his brain.

Survival. That's what it amounted to. No more!

He had to survive, and he knew only one way to do it.

Logan sat down, picked up an oily rag, and began to wipe down the scythe he had been sharpening for Alec.

He could take uncounted chances with a deck of cards. He had done so for years. He was good at it. But he had never gambled with his emotions, never let his personal feelings emerge far enough to lay them on the table. The mere thought of giving up his quest for Digory's treasure in exchange for friendship, even love, was so unimaginably foreign to his nature that he could hardly believe such a thing was occurring to him. No, he was not ready for a risk like that!

The incident yesterday on Ramsey Head proved it. When he had been dangerously wedged between those crushing rocks, the only thing that had mattered was saving his own skin. Alec MacNeil could have rotted in that cave, with his daughter too, for all he had cared. Now was no time to start getting soft. He came here to do a job, and he had to stick with it. For the moment he conveniently forgot how in those tense moments of fear he had silently prayed for Alec's rescue, and how good he had felt when it was over, until Alec's praise had sent his conflicting emotions spinning.

" 'Each man for himself,' " Logan murmured to himself, quoting Chaucer, " 'there is none other.' "

He had picked up the words once in a pub, and though he knew very little about Chaucer, he did recall the bloke who had recited the verse. He'd been a dandy of a man by the name of Charles E. Franklin, rather good-looking for his age, which had at the time been about sixty. Extremely slick with dice, well-dressed, he claimed to have worked the Riviera and America for some years. He boasted that he had married and divorced a duchess and earned several thousand pounds selling real estate that didn't exist, and had once even sold a so-called gold-manufacturing machine to some gullible American.

Logan had admired the man from afar for some time, for he was not without a reputation, and it had been quite an honor to meet him that night. But later that evening, Logan had encountered Franklin again, passed out drunk in an alley where several street urchins were picking his pockets.

The sight of his fallen hero had been sickening, for he was fallen in every sense of the word. The self-reliant man had no one but a near-stranger to pick him up and haul him off to his dingy one-room flat, filled with dusty momentos of a life that was quickly passing.

When he had recalled the quotation, sitting there in Stonewycke's stable, he hadn't expected to conjure up the whole scene. He had hardly remembered how that evening had ended until just now as it flooded his mind. *Bad boats and wretched crews . . .* That certainly described Franklin!

"Well," Logan thought, trying to shrug off this newest wave of reflection, "you have to pay a price for everything, especially independence."

But was it independence or cowardice that was driving him? The question pierced his mind before he had time to hide from it. For the first time in his life, Logan Macintyre was truly confused. He didn't know the answer.

Out on Ramsey Head, when Alec had praised his courage, Logan knew how close he had been to running. Yet he had never before considered himself a coward. He had stood up to Chase Morgan, hadn't he? Was it the danger he had wanted to run from, or something else? Was it because he didn't care about these people . . . or because he *did*?

Logan threw down the scythe, and its point stuck in the dirt floor. He rose again and unconsciously began pacing. This questioning and confusion were too much! He should never have gotten involved. He should have stayed at the inn, found out what he could, retrieved the treasure, and then left. It had been a mistake to come live at the castle. He had to get out of here! He turned and headed toward his loft to pack his things.

Halfway up the stairs he stopped and closed his eyes tightly, as if to halt the careening assault of thoughts.

He had to get away from here . . . to think.

No! He had to *stop* thinking!

316

Frustrated, Logan spun around and raced down and to the bay's stall. He managed, despite his inexperience, to saddle her, opened the stall door, mounted, and rode off, having no idea where he was going or what he would do. He just knew he had to get away. *Perhaps I will never return,* he thought with a trace of a smile. Then horse stealing could be added to his many other indiscretions, and the Duncans could prosecute him on those grounds.

It was not really coincidence that his path led him to Ramsey Head. Its mournful awe drew him. In many ways it was similar to the moor he had visited days ago—lonely, barren, and dangerous. But where the moor had been dead and impotent, Ramsey Head seemed to stir with an energy and even a certain power. Perhaps it was from its constant contact with the life of the sea. And now Logan knew why he had come here.

He tied the horse where the path began to narrow. He could have ridden farther—in fact, it appeared that at one time wagons or carts might have traversed the Head. But today he wanted to be alone, to walk unassisted. He turned up the path along the grassy side of the promontory; he wasn't quite up to the challenge of the rocky seaward side today. It was the top he sought, where he could be alone—completely alone. The beauty all about him slowly muted his previous thoughts. He hoped that perhaps, in the midst of the grandeur of this place, surrounded on all sides by grass and wind and sky and sea, his confusion would be clarified. It was the first time in his life he had sought out nature for nature's sake.

The grass was still slick from the rain, and he did not negotiate the summit without slipping many times. But after a ten- or fifteen-minute hike, after which he found himself puffing lightly, with splotches of mud and bits of bracken clinging to his tweed work clothes, he stepped at last onto the crown of Ramsey Head's highest point.

As he crested the top and the sapphire of the sea spread out before him in all directions, he breathed deeply, and let out a silent exclamation of incredulity. It was a sight like he had never seen, and its impact on him was profound. He simply stood and gazed, his heart and mind at last quiet enough to receive the voice of peace that had been silently shouting to him through the created world all along.

Yesterday the sea had been gray and angry, but now it wore a completely new face. Rough whitecaps still beat against a shimmering blue. No boats were out yet, no doubt because of the strong wind which still lashed at the coast. Directly below lay the spot where they had been yesterday. Without the mist and rain to obscure his vision, he could see just how treacherous had been their position. Had he or Allison fallen when they were scrambling around on that ledge, they would not have survived for a moment. The mere thought sent a chill into the pit of his stomach, and he recalled again the tale of the murderer who had fallen, probably from that very spot. This was not a friendly place, nor a comforting one. Why had he come here? What sort of solace had he hoped to find?

At length Logan looked about for a rock to sit on. He'd have a short rest, then head back. There was nothing for him here, and he didn't want to waste any more time thinking. It was beautiful, and he could enjoy that. And it had helped to clear his head. He should have known all along what to do. It was simple enough. When he got back, he'd pack up his things, and when the house was asleep tonight, he'd slip away. If he walked all night he might make Fenwick Harbor by morning, and from there he'd get a train or schooner to Aberdeen and thence to London. The treasure had been a bad idea; it was probably just imaginary, anyway. At any rate, it would be easier to leave it behind, and with it any necessity for wearisome sensitivities and awkward confessions. He'd been a fool. He'd put too much into the pot on a bad hand, and it was now time to cut his losses, quit while he still had seed money for the next opportunity, and get out of the game.

But he would have to keep his mind off what he might be leaving behind. It wasn't only the treasure; there was Allison.

He couldn't dwell on that! It was for the best. He couldn't stop to consider what they would think of him sneaking away like a criminal. What did he care what they thought? He would never see any of them again, anyway. What did it matter what Allison thought? He'd never been good enough for her; she had made that clear from the start. She would probably breathe a sigh of relief to learn that he was gone.

Walking about fifty feet farther along the crest, he came to a large rock and sat down. As far as he could see in both directions the rugged coastline stretched into the distance. He had never thought much of the sea, but this truly had to be one of the rare high points of creation. Unconsciously his thoughts turned to the rock he was sitting on. For some reason it struck him as oddly out of place. It had a strangely sculptured look, as if it had at one time been chiseled toward some shape, then abandoned. He could not quite make out what the shape reminded him of. It was probably nothing, only an accident of nature.

As he rose to leave, his foot stepped on the matted bracken and weeds surrounding the rock and struck something hard underneath. Absently he kicked at the foliage and saw that buried beneath the surface of the tangled weeds was a smooth, flat board—hardly the sort of thing one would expect to find on this wild, uninhabited piece of earth. Maybe some children had dragged it up here with the intention of building a little hideaway.

Idle curiosity, coupled with a desire to divert his mind from its uncomfortable and confusing thoughts, made Logan bend down and scrape away the plants in order to excavate the board. When at length he was able to pull it free from the tangled roots and undergrowth, he found it to be only about two feet long by some six or eight inches wide. The edges had at one time been sanded smooth and the corners carefully rounded, but many years under the wet ground had caused some rotting, and Logan could pinch off small chunks of wood with his fingers. There were holes in the center where it had apparently been nailed to another board. Turning it over in his hand, Logan discovered the most curious feature of all— carved letters spread out across the length of the wood. This was no random piece of scrap. Someone had made this very carefully and had designed it as some sort of plaque or inscription. Logan brushed away the dirt and grass and saw that the letters were still almost legible, though time and the weather had taken their toll. With a curious finger Logan dug away at the encrusted buildup until the two names *Raven* and *Maukin* began to appear before him.

At first glance they struck no chord of familiarity to him, but he was certain this sign had to be a marker of some sort—for a grave, perhaps. But the names were hardly human. Had this been the burying place for some child's favorite pets? Two dogs, perhaps? A dog and a cat?

Raven and Maukin ... where had he heard those names?

Suddenly Logan knew it was no child who had dug a grave at the top of Ramsey Head.

"... I remember how he had pampered our horses, Raven and Maukin," Lady Margaret had once said.

It couldn't be! Yet what else could the plaque and this strangely crude rock signify? A grave for two beloved animals! If he had been anywhere else, Logan would not have believed such a thing possible. But at Stonewycke, where loyalties ran deep, where sympathies were out of step, where a hard-working vet was laird of the land, where the landowners gave away the largest portion of their once-vast estate to the poor crofters and villagers, where the heiress of the family lived forty years in a foreign land only to return to live out her golden years as matriarch of the family—this was certainly a place where anything could happen! Nothing at Stonewycke fit the expected patterns. So why not a grave on a high and windy promontory overlooking the sea?

Had Lady Margaret herself buried her favorite animals up here? No, that was unlikely. Surely she would have mentioned it. Her mother, the Lady Atlanta? Possibly. Could she have perhaps sought to enshrine the memory of her daughter after her flight to America with a loving tribute in the form of an honored grave at some place the young Maggie loved? *It could be,* thought Logan. *It would be just the sort of thing some mothers would do. Was Lady Atlanta the emotional sort,* he wondered? Would she have suffered the loneliness of her latter years in silence, or would she have tried to find outlets through which she could remember her Maggie?

Instead, a picture filled Logan's mind of an old man, the trusted family groom who had cared for these two beloved horses all their lives, perhaps with tears filling his aged eyes, bending over a roughly hewn hunk of wood, carving out the names of the horses he had loved as his way to remember the young girl he would never see again.

Was it possible, thought Logan, that the two horses were actually buried right here beneath his feet? It hardly seemed possible that the old groom would have hauled the carcasses of two huge beasts all the way up here. Yet it would be possible for a wagon to navigate the Head. And if Lady Atlanta had backed his scheme, with several of the hands assisting, it would not have been out of the question. He had heard of stranger happenings in London.

Logan tucked the board under his arm, turned, and began his downward trek off the small mountain to the point where he had tethered the horse. Maybe he should follow this one last lead, if not to the treasure, at least a little deeper into the past of Lady Margaret and his remarkable ancestor.

He'd give it one more day. He could not resist the challenge of a new set of puzzling questions.

45 Crossroads

Margaret, Joanna, and Allison sat around the large oblong table in Stonewycke's kitchen.

This was Joanna's favorite spot in the entire castle, for its homey warmth reminded her of the little kitchen in the cottage she and Alec had shared in the early years of their marriage. It also stirred the memories of her first days in Port Strathy with dear Nathaniel and Letty. They were gone now, but their memory was all the more special because in their home Joanna had given her life to the Lord. She recalled the quiet joy of that day as clearly as if it had only just occurred. She did not think there could possibly be another day so profoundly meaningful, though her wedding day and the birth of her children came close. Yet the moment of her own rebirth went beyond even these milestone events, perhaps because it enriched them and added still more to their meaning.

Yet Joanna now realized there could come another moment as significant to her as that memory of so long ago at the Cuttahay's— the day, after so many years of inner conflict and struggle, when her own daughter came to the point of repentance and new birth. Only parents can know the depth to which their own children can bring heartache or joy by their responses to life, by their growth, by their sorrows, by their victories. Suddenly mother and daughter became what they had never before been able to be—sisters, born of the same Father.

Joanna reached across the table and took her daughter's hand. She smiled.

"Allison," she said, "I just don't know what to say. I'm sorry for whatever grief I ever caused you."

"Mother, I know I don't need to ask your forgiveness," said Allison, tears welling up in her eyes. "I know now how much you have loved me. But Daddy said that though I wouldn't *have* to, I should anyway."

"Forgiveness is a healing balm," said her great-grandmother, "a duty that proves to be as much for our own good as it is for another's."

"That's just what Daddy said," replied Allison. "Mother, will you forgive me? I know I've caused you nothing but sadness these last several years."

"Oh, Allison . . ." said Joanna tenderly, weeping in the fullness of her motherhood. She rose and went to her daughter. Allison rose also, and Joanna embraced her gently. "Of course I forgive you, dear," she said softly, still crying tears of joy and healing. "And believe me, any grief you may have caused me is far outweighed by my love for you. I'm so sorry for anything I may ever have done to hurt you."

They clung to one another for some time, as if to make up for the past breach and in anticipation of their future together.

When the tender moment had played itself out, Joanna resumed her seat and Allison struggled to bring up the subject that had been nagging at her but which she knew she had to bring into the open.

"I want so much to change," she said. "I always wanted to be like both of you. But I felt that I failed. And Grandpa Dorey helped me understand that God could use that failure to help me depend on Him. What I guess I'm trying to say, again, to both of you is that I'm sorry. I'm sorry for blaming you for my own inadequacies. And I don't know how much better I can do, but with God's help I'm going to try."

"Dear," said Margaret, "God does want us to change—to become molded into the image and character of Christ. But what makes you think you must someday become like your mother or me?"

"You are the kind of women God wants. You are the kind of women Stonewycke has always had—generous, kind, loving."

"Oh, dear, your mother and I are nothing of the sort! Whatever good you may see in us is not *us* at all. It is His work in us!"

Allison shook her head. "I suppose I've used all the rest of you as an excuse not to take responsibility for myself and my own attitudes. I could get away with being a beast while blaming it on you. That's why I have to both ask your forgiveness and forgive you, too."

"And forgive yourself," added Margaret. "When I was in America I was able to forgive my father. But the time came in my life when I had to accept the Lord's forgiveness for myself, too. The healing that God is always trying to carry out in families, even through the generations, is a forgiveness that extends in many directions—out toward others, inward from others, and outwardly to God as well as inwardly from Him. Only by forgiving and receiving forgiveness in all these ways will true wholeness come to us. We cannot leave any stone unturned, any relationship unhealed, any person unforgiven, if we want God to have His full way with us. And it is through forgiveness and healing that God is able to extend His plan and purpose for a family down through future generations of time. I do not doubt for a moment that my forgiving of my own father is one of the reasons the three of us are sitting here today. God himself only knows what the impact will be, Allison, of the forgiveness now blossoming in your heart.

"But healing is never without profound consequences. I do not doubt that as the history of Stonewycke continues down through the years, Allison, you will play a vital role in it, and that this moment when three generations of Duncan women can join in oneness with the Lord will prove a pivotal crossroads time. Perhaps that is why the Lord has spared me so long, so that I could share this moment with you. Allison, in the name of our Father, I tell you that I love you, and I give you my blessing as you carry on the Duncan line. I do not know how much longer I shall be among you—"

Joanna reached across the table and took her grandmother's hand. There were tears of admiration and love in her eyes.

"—but however long it is, I will be praying fervently for the continued godly faith of this family, and for you, Allison, as you carry that legacy into the future. I bless you, my child. May the Lord truly be with you!"

All three were silent. As Lady Margaret had been speaking, an aura had seemed to come over her, her entire lifetime focused into that single moment when she passed to her granddaughter and great-granddaughter that life which had sustained her so long. She had been the Lady of Stonewycke, but seemed to sense that now the moment had come to transfer that heritage into their hands.

Joanna first broke the silence, though her eyes remained wet for some time to come. "So you see, dear, you don't have to be like anyone to please God. You are a unique creation. Whatever gifts and whatever personality you have, *He* gave you for *His* purposes. He will not expect you to be like either of us. Stonewycke will face challenges in your lifetime that we have not known. Times change; we live in a modern world. He wants you to be *you.* Of course He wants us to change where we have been self-centered. He wants to bring healing. But He will not change the special nature He gave you. He only wants it channeled for His purpose."

"You make it sound easy, Mother."

"Be assured," laughed Margaret, "it is *not* easy—far from it! Especially when you resist, as I did for many years. But in the laying down of self is true healing born. And in that laying down is the only path along which you will find true joy and peace."

The conversation was abruptly interrupted with a sound from the scullery door. Allison looked up at the instant when Logan Macintyre had just stepped across the threshold.

Joanna, on the opposite side of the table and facing her daughter, did not immediately see who had just walked in. But she noted a strange interplay of emotions cross Allison's face—initial surprise, as if his arrival was very unexpected though welcome, then a flicker of concern followed by a smile. The smile was unlike any Joanna had ever seen from Allison—shy, a bit awkward, even uncertain.

All these images flashed by in no more than an instant. But in that time, the discerning mother saw, before even the daughter realized it, that Allison was in love.

46   The Lady and the Seeker

Logan had not expected to find three women seated thus. And to the usurper, the man who had come in guile and deceit, they appeared not as three women merely having tea and pleasant conversation, but rather as the mighty first line of defense to their ancestral home. Indeed, his reaction was not far off the mark. For something of a delicate glow yet hovered in the air, which he could feel rather than see, a sense that he had stumbled unknowingly onto holy ground. As indeed he had. For where healing, forgiveness, and new birth are at work, there the Lord surely is. It put him immediately in an exposed position, and he hesitated momentarily.

His eyes strayed toward Allison. He quickly jerked them away, but not before he had caught a glimpse of her smile. There was something different in her face; that much he could see. In so many of her previous smiles he had detected traces of motive or cunning; today her face shone with a purity he had not seen there before.

Why had she chosen this moment to smile at him like that? It nearly undid his resolve to play out this last hand and get away from here. But he had to keep his wits and not melt, smile or no smile. These people were not going to get to him any more!

He yanked on his composure. He had business here. Nothing but business.

He had come directly to the house after leaving Ramsey Head. Entering through the kitchen, as was his custom now that he was accepted about the grounds as an employee, he had hoped to find a servant whom he might send after Lady Margaret, inquiring if he might beg a moment of her time. Though disconcerting, this unexpected turn would at least save time.

"Excuse me," he said. "I didn't mean to barge in."

"The kitchen belongs to everyone!" said Joanna cheerily. "There are plenty of places to go in this old house if we expected privacy. What can we do for you?"

"I had hoped to speak with Lady Margaret."

Allison's disappointment, though she tried to hide it, was apparent.

"Certainly, Logan, what is it?" the lady asked.

Logan hesitated. Somehow he would have felt safer if he could have gotten the old lady alone. She was cagy enough. But he wasn't sure he was up to braving a series of questions from all three. The women of this family, after all, were a pretty stalwart breed. He didn't like to cross them with unfavorable odds.

Joanna, perhaps sensing his misgivings, quickly rose.

"If I'm not needed," she said, "I have a few things to attend to. Please excuse me." Then turning to Allison, she added, "I could use your help, Allison..."

Allison moved back her chair and retreated with her mother. In the shyness of her change and the uncertainty of her true feelings, she had not uttered a word to Logan.

"Would you like some tea, Mr. Macintyre?" asked Lady Margaret when they were alone. "It's still quite hot."

But before he could say anything, she was on her feet and taking a cup and saucer from the cupboard. *Why did she have to be so hospitable?*

"Now..." said the lady, seated again, and pouring the steaming tea from the pot into Logan's cup.

Logan had carried the board from Ramsey Head into the kitchen with him, setting it against his chair as he sat down. He now picked it up and held it out to his hostess.

"I found this today on the top of Ramsey Head."

She took the wood and examined it with gradually dawning wonder spreading over her face.

"Raven and Maukin..." she murmured.

She laid it on the table, still gazing at the carved names. "Where on the Head did you find it?"

"At the very top, right on the crest."

"How very like him."

"You think it was Digory who put this up there?"

"Who else? It would have been so like him to do such a thing. And I think I even recognize a trace of his hand in the letters. He knew how Raven and I loved to romp along the beach and up and down the shore for miles. It was only natural for him to place a memorial to the animal where the view of the sea was the most spectacular."

"Of course! I see it now," said Logan, in a detached tone as if a great discovery had suddenly come upon him. He was just then thinking of Digory's letter and the reference to the girl Maggie riding along the sea.

"Pardon me?"

"Oh ... nothing ... it just makes sense when you put it that way. Tell me, Lady Margaret, do you think it possible that the horses are actually buried there? Could that be what this plaque signified?"

"Hmmm ... that would be something indeed. Quite an undertaking. But he was reasonably strong for his age. He and I dug big holes before."

"What?"

"Nothing of significance. I was just thinking out loud. I was just reflecting on how it would be the sort of thing he would do, the sentimental old dear! Did it for me, no doubt." She dabbed her eyes. Thoughts of Digory always brought tears.

"And in his mind it would be only fitting that Maukin should be laid to rest there also," she concluded.

"I don't mean to sound disrespectful of the dead, Lady Margaret," ventured Logan, "but the whole thing does seem rather bizzare. I mean, they were only animals."

"Very special animals. He knew what they symbolized to Ian and me. They were almost a symbol of our love. We rode those two horses everywhere. And too, it was our mutual love for horses that strengthened the bond between Digory and me."

She stopped and smiled that peculiar smile of hers, which Logan had yet to fathom. Filled with mystery, wisdom, and sympathy, it was always disconcerting to him, especially today.

"Digory was a man of hope," she went on. "Perhaps he felt that in keeping alive the memory of the animals which had been so dear to me, he was also keeping alive the hope that I might one day return."

"It seems rather an absurd and sentimental gesture for a man who was supposed to have faith in God. If he wanted you to return, why didn't he just pray for it instead of carrying dead horses around the countryside and erecting memorials to a life that was gone and past?"

Logan could see that his statement pierced the lady's heart. He hadn't intentionally tried to hurt her. Yet in his present mood, impertinence was but one more tool to insure his isolation, and thus his survival.

When she replied with gracious calm, he had to admire her, though it almost made him angry at the same time. Could *nothing* rankle this lady?

"I did not know you were an authority on the subject of how men of faith live out their hope, Mr. Macintyre," she said, with just the merest hint of a challenge in her tone.

"You know very well I make no claim to be!" rejoined Logan, prepared to accept the challenge. "But even to an infidel like me, it sounds like the good Digory MacNab had more faith in a couple of dead horses than in that God he was so fond of."

Suddenly Logan was sick of the whole lot of them, and their prattle about God. The new air of belligerence in his attitude felt good. It made what he was going to do that much easier. The religious sops! He'd had enough.

Lady Margaret smiled, only this time it was an open smile and filled with amusement.

"I have the impression, Logan," she said, the smile gone from her lips but lingering in her lively eyes, "that you are trying to strike up an argument with me."

"Why should I want to do that?" he replied rather too hastily. He was noticeably on the defensive, the cool aplomb of the confidence man wearing thin as his battle to hang on to his past identity increased.

"That's exactly what puzzles me. I sense that a change has come over you, but I don't know why." She fingered her cup thoughtfully. "You are struggling with something, aren't you?"

Logan barked out a sharp, hollow laugh. "I can't imagine what would give you that idea. I only want to understand my distant relative better."

"I only wish that were so. But there's more to it. Something else is on your mind." Margaret sipped her tea, then set the cup softly on its saucer. "If you were simply seeking to know your uncle

Digory," she went on, "then I think you would try to *understand* his faith and not ridicule it—for to understand Digory you must understand his faith. They are too much bound up in one another even to be considered separately."

"Then to ridicule his faith is to ridicule him?" queried Logan, "and that angers you?"

"You take me wrong, Logan. It doesn't anger me—rather, it hurts me. But not for Digory's sake, nor even for mine. It hurts me for *your* sake."

"Mine!"

"You are afraid, Logan. You are afraid to understand Digory's God."

She *was* challenging him! However sweet and charming, this was still a boldfaced challenge.

"I think you are running from God," she went on. "I once knew a man who tried to run from God. But he knew no peace until the moment he stopped."

"You've got it all wrong, Lady Margaret. But perhaps it is hard for you to understand someone who has no need for religious crutches. Your faith may be fine for people like you and Digory. I won't belittle you for it. But so far I've left God alone, and He's been kind enough to return the favor." Even as Logan spoke the words, the memory of his hastily spoken vow on the flooded road shot through his mind. He hadn't wanted to be left alone then.

Well, that was then—he had been caught up in the moment. It had been a foolish and sentimental reaction. *He could take care of himself.*

Yet the words reverberated through his brain with a hollow and foreign sound. He was lying even to himself. What about all the times in his life when he *hadn't* been able to make it alone? The time his mother had helped him out of the jam over the Fairgate fiasco, and later when Skittles had taken him in as a fifteen-year-old who knew no more about the streets of London than an innocent babe. And how many times when his luck had run sour would a friend lend him a quid?

But that had nothing to do with God! That was people—he had done the same thing for his friends! It had nothing to do with God or Digory or Lady Margaret or any of it!

But she was speaking again. "Many people consider religion a crutch, Logan. But that's because they don't grasp that what it *really* boils down to is a relationship, an intimate friendship. I have not chosen to live my life as a Christian primarily because I am weak and He is strong and I am unable to get through life on my own. Though of course that is true—we all *are* weak, and *can't* make it on our own, and we *do* need His help. And someday you will see those truths in your own life. But primarily, Logan, something even greater draws me: simply the fact that He is the God who made me, who knows me, who loves me ... and I can *know* Him intimately! Oh, Logan, I hate to think where I would be if He left me alone!"

"I haven't done too badly," he said steeling himself against her passionate words of truth.

"You are entirely satisfied with your life?"

"Completely!" His voice sounded firm and confident. Who besides Logan could have been aware of the stark hypocrisy behind it?

"You are a very fortunate young man," she answered, and Logan knew that she saw through him as if his very soul had been naked.

But rather than feeling a sense of conviction, he withdrew yet further into the fortress he was trying to build around himself. It angered him to sit there exposed and foolish before the self-righteous old woman! She had no right to do this to him!

"Yes ... *very* fortunate!" he repeated, glaring at her. Then stood quickly and strode from the kitchen without another word.

He didn't have to take insults like that from anyone, even the grand Lady of Stonewycke. For the moment the irony was lost on Logan that she had not insulted or belittled him in any way. She had, in fact, been nothing but kindly in her tone. It would have made it easier on him in that moment had she responded in kind and tried to crush him beneath her noble heel. He could have taken that ... understood it. But not this, not kindness in exchange for his rudeness.

The crisp air of the early evening jolted him like a slap to a man in panic. That was one thing he couldn't do—panic. He had to pull himself together. He had to think clearly. He had given himself one more day, and he needed to make the best use of it.

He crossed the lawn in the direction of the stable when a figure came striding toward him, arm raised in a wave.

"Logan, there ye are!" It was Jesse Cameron.

"Jesse," he said without enthusiasm. Here was a friend who had saved his life, to whom he had pledged his loyalty. But now he wanted no friends in Strathy, no ties.

"I've got a telegram fer ye." Her voice was grave and in her eyes was a look of deep concern.

"I suppose you've read it," snapped Logan as he whipped the envelope from her hand.

"That 'tisna my habit," she replied, and Logan could see he had hurt her. "Telegrams 'most always bring bad news, ye ken."

He wished he had the guts to say he was sorry. Her friendship had meant something to him. But he could not flinch now. This was no time for repentant deeds like apologies. No time even for smiles. He let her turn and walk away just as he had left Lady Margaret— saying nothing, giving nothing. As she went he watched her—sadly, but with resolve.

When she had walked dejectedly out of sight, he turned his attention to the telegram. He looked at it for a long and agonizing moment. No one knew he was here except his mother. And only one or two of his London friends knew how to get in touch with her.

With a shaking hand he ripped open the flap. He would not be able to cope with it just now if something had happened to his mother. But the telegram was not from Frances Macintyre.

LOGAN

CHASE MORGAN HAS LEARNED WHERE YOU ARE STOP HE IS STILL IN THE CHOKEY BUT THAT WILL NOT STOP HIM STOP KEEP A LOOKOUT AND BE CAREFUL STOP

BILLY COCHRAN

47   A Deal at the Bluster 'N Blow

At last something was starting to happen. Sprague had begun to fear he might just end up rotting in this hick town.

Sprague's contact at Stonewycke had just passed on an interesting report. Early that afternoon Macintyre had gone off alone. Although that was not altogether unusual in the context of his job, this time he had ridden by horse to a lonely, uninhabited spot called Ramsey Head—hardly a likely place for the services of a mechanic. The field hand from the estate said Macintyre had returned empty-handed except for a piece of wood he was carrying. Curious, Sprague had concluded that this excursion must have ended with the same result as the one Macintyre had taken several days ago to Braenock Ridge. Perhaps they were both wild goose chases. But the piece of wood was interesting; obviously Macintyre bore continued watching. It certainly indicated that he had not abandoned the hunt. If he was sticking to it after all this time, possibly he was on to something.

But sitting idly about was getting to him. For a diversion, after hearing what the man had to say, Sprague decided to have a walk out to the promontory himself. By the time he arrived dusk was approaching; he had no time for a thorough appraisal, but it looked as likely as any place to hide a treasure. But with no map or specific instructions, it might as well have been a needle in a haystack. Therefore, there remained no alternative but to watch Macintyre. He was still the one with the clues—whatever they might be.

Following his afternoon trek, Sprague returned to the Bluster 'N Blow. When Logan had moved up the hill to Stonewycke, Sprague saw no further reason to remain at Roy Hamilton's dingy place. The Bluster 'N Blow was only a step or two above it, but at least it was clean and the food was edible. He now sat at one of the rough tables in the common room stirring his coffee and waiting for his dinner to be served. He was also anxiously awaiting the arrival of the inn's two new guests. They had checked in while he was out. But sneaking a look at Cobden's register, he had learned their names: Frank Lombardo and Willie Cabot.

Sprague's boss had mentioned Morgan's interest in Macintyre. He definitely recognized Lombardo's name as one of Morgan's transplants from the Chicago crowd. It was only too bad they had found Macintyre before Sprague had finished his business with the London con man. If they got to him first, it would be the end of Macintyre, and the end of Sprague's mission. And his boss didn't like excuses. His motto had always been, "Get it done. Whatever you have to do—just get it done." Even if Morgan's men put an end to Logan, his boss would blame Sprague. "If you want to work for me, Sprague," he would say, "getting it done is the only thing I care about."

So he would have to try to handle these two somehow.

Sprague lifted his cup to his lips and drank deeply of the strong black brew. They never could make good coffee on this island.

But he quickly forgot the bitter taste in his mouth when, peering over the rim of his earthenware cup, he saw the two newcomers enter the room. Both were veritable hulks, typical of the thugs Morgan liked to surround himself with.

"Evening, gentlemen," said Sprague in an easygoing, friendly tone.

The two stopped cold, and a flicker of recognition crossed Lombardo's swarthy face. Sprague had met him some years ago, but he had not thought the younger man would remember. Not that it mattered.

"You talkin' to us?" answered Lombardo with an accent that combined Bronx, Sicilian, and a touch of cockney with a most curious result.

"None other," replied Sprague, though an answer was academic since there were no others in the place.

"Do we know you?"

"It's possible. Have you ever been to Chicago?"

"What'd you want?" Lombardo's voice grew menacing and his eyes grew wary. Sprague had never been mistaken for a cop before, but Lombardo appeared more blessed with muscles than with brains.

"Come on, Lombardo, do I look like a Fed?"

At that moment Sandy Cobden burst into the common room bearing a tray laden with Sprague's dinner.

"Here ye go, Mr. Sprague," said the innkeeper, setting the heavy tray down with a deep sigh. "Hope I didna keep ye waitin' too long. Ne'er hae acquired the knack fer kitchen work. My missus used t' do all that in years past. Noo that she's gone I jist dinna get much chance t' practice. We can go fer months wi'oot a single guest. It picks up a wee in summer, but here tis April an' sich a foul one at that, an' I've more guests at one time than ... than I dinna ken when."

He turned to his other guests as he emptied the tray of its burden, setting plates and bowls before Sprague. "I'll be bringin' yer supper in directly," he said. "Jist hae yersel's a seat."

He paused in his steady chatter, perhaps expecting a *thank you*, but since none was immediately forthcoming, he swept up his tray and bustled away.

"Sprague?" ruminated Lombardo thoughtfully.

"Five years ago," prompted Sprague, "Leighton Club, Chicago."

"That place was only open to a very special clientele."

"That's right."

"Well, if you really was there, then you'll know the maitre d'."

Sprague shook his head as if he were placating a child. "Benny Margolis. Do you want a description, too?"

"No, I guess you're on the level."

"Have a seat," Sprague went on, confident that his estimation of Lombardo's intelligence was not too far wrong. "Your silent friend, too."

The two hoods took seats opposite Sprague, barely squeezing their brawny frames into the narrow, high-backed bench. Cobden returned with their meal and the three spent the next few minutes engrossed in their food.

At length Lombardo spoke, his words muffled as he continued to chew a large hunk of meat pasty.

"Prohibition ... them were the days," he said. "I took it on the lam right after the crash—figured they wouldn't be able to afford it no more, and I was right—they repealed it lickity-split."

"You should have stuck around. As I hear it the mob doesn't need boot-legging to keep it going."

"Yeah . . . well, I had other reasons too," replied Lombardo cryptically.

"So," Sprague went on, pushing back his empty plate and pouring himself another cup of coffee, "then you migrated to England and hooked up with Morgan—?"

"What about Morgan?" broke in Cabot sharply, breaking his long silence.

"Relax," said Sprague, then turning to Lombardo, "tell your friend to take it easy. I've got a business proposition for you, but we won't get anywhere if you keep jumping down my throat."

"Okay," replied Lombardo. "Put a lid on it, Willie."

"Don't tell me what to do," growled Cabot. He was apparently beginning to feel the imbalance of being the odd man out as the only Britisher among these two Americans. "Don't forget who we're working for, Frank."

"You got me wrong," said Sprague, feeling the need to placate the Londoner. "I figured I might be able to help you out."

"What'd you know about us?"

"Why don't I begin at the beginning?" said Sprague, adopting his most congenial tone. "Here, have a cup of coffee."

"Ain't there nothin' stronger?" put in Lombardo.

"Later; I'll buy. In the meantime . . ." Without completing his sentence, Sprague poured out coffee for his companions. "Now," he began again, "as it happens we all have the same interest here in Port Strathy. And that happens to be a third-rate con artist by the name of Macintyre—"

"Macintyre!" repeated Morgan's men in unison.

"That's right, boys. I'm afraid this is a small country and word gets around fast. Morgan wants Macintyre's skin, and I know that's what you're doing here."

"What's your interest in him?"

"I want him, too. Only I need him alive and well."

"So what's this business proposition of yours?"

"Like I said, I need Macintyre in one piece. So it seems that at the moment, we are somewhat at cross purposes. When I'm through with him, you fellows can do what you please. Now, I'm willing to make it worth your while to hold off for a spell—say one thousand pounds apiece?

"What do you want with him?" asked Cabot, determined not to let his guard down so easily.

"The specifics aren't important. Let's just say he has some information I need—that is, he will have soon," answered Sprague.

"Two thousand pounds ... that must be some information he has!" said Lombardo, stuffing a thickly buttered bannock into his mouth.

"Not the sort of thing that would be of interest to you or me," answered Sprague evasively, "but there are some highly placed individuals who are anxious to have it."

"I don't know," said Cabot.

"Aw, com'on," prodded Lombardo, "it ain't like we're not going to do Morgan's job—we'll just tell him we got delayed a few days."

"Exactly how long?" asked Cabot.

"That's the rub," replied Sprague, "I can't pin it down exactly."

"Two days," said Cabot, answering his own question, "then we move in."

"I'm afraid if we pressure him, he'll bolt. Then neither of us will get what we want—and you'll be out a cool thousand." Sprague directed this last remark to Lombardo, whom he judged as most sympathetic.

"We got Morgan to think of," said Lombardo, almost apologetically. "He's not a man you try to con. And if we don't bring him Macintyre's head, he'll have ours."

Sprague leaned back on the bench to ponder his dilemma.

Even if he withheld Macintyre's whereabouts, this town was so small that they'd locate him in an hour if they put their minds to it, however vacant that part of their anatomy was. His only chance had been to deal with them, and that would have worked if it hadn't been for that hardnose Cabot. There was no way of knowing how close Macintyre was to finding the loot, if it existed. He might even have already found it and was only sticking around to avert suspicion.

Sprague knew he now had no choice but to force Macintyre's hand! If he had nothing, well, they were both out of luck. Sprague knew his boss would be none too pleased. But in part it was his fault, too. Hadn't he said he would take care of Morgan? Obviously his slick manuevering had not worked too well in that arena, so he couldn't blame Sprague.

"Give me three days," bargained Sprague, "and you get *two* thousand each." It wasn't *his* money, Sprague reasoned to himself.

The two hoodlums looked at each other, then nodded toward Sprague. Lombardo appeared much more satisfied with the deal than his cohort, who looked as if three days was an interminably long wait for his sport.

48 Digory's Clues Unfold

Logan stared once more at Billy's telegram.

Somehow he had let himself forget about the threat of Morgan, which had been hanging over him for weeks. As he reread the words he felt as if a heavy boulder were resting on his shoulders.

After receiving the telegram, Logan had climbed the steep, narrow steps to Digory's room. Now he slumped into the coarse, straight-backed chair that had probably been there when the groom had occupied these same quarters.

He had just told Lady Margaret what a lucky man he was, spitting the words out defiantly.

Some luck!

This turn of events left him no alternative but to get out of Port Strathy as fast as possible. If Morgan knew he was here, no doubt a couple of his thugs would be hot on his tail, if they weren't here already. His own sense of panic was dulled by the events of recent days, but suddenly Logan thought of Morgan's hoodlums tainting the quiet peacefulness of Port Strathy. These were dangerous and merciless men—look what they had done to Skittles! And now they were coming to Port Strathy . . . and Logan had brought them here!

Even if he left immediately, the men looking for him would cause trouble. And these locals would be foolish enough and loyal enough to stand up to the thugs. They could be hurt trying to protect him, never realizing that he had double-crossed them himself.

As much as Logan wanted to convince himself that they cared no more for him than he cared for them, he could not do so. Jesse Cameron had saved his life at the risk of her own. Lady Margaret would no more turn on him than his own mother would. He had little doubt Alec would stand up to anyone who threatened one he loved. And Allison . . . that look he had seen in her eyes an hour ago could not quickly be erased from memory. She *had* changed after Fairgate's visit! She cared about him. And she too would protect him.

How could he put all these people in danger? Yet the only other alternative was to confront Morgan's men, possibly even give himself up to them, or perhaps draw them away from Strathy. That's what he'd have to do: set up some kind of decoy to lure them out of town. Then if they got him, at least it wouldn't have to involve his new friends.

Friends! He could hardly believe he'd called them that. He desperately wanted to believe that he didn't care about what happened to the people in this town. He had lied to them, cheated them, was about to steal from them and put them in grave danger. Yet he still cared about them. Were they indeed his friends? If so, how could he be so dishonest with them?

Evening shadows now darkened the room, but Logan had no heart to light a lamp. He leaned forward on the old pine table, resting his head in his hands.

He *did* care! It made him cringe to think of any one of them being touched by Morgan's evil. He hated himself for what he was doing. He was in debt to these folks, just as he was to many others in his life.

He remembered Lady Margaret's words: *I hate to think where I would be if He left me alone!*

Was he not only in debt to these people but to God also?

Then as Logan raised his head, his eyes fell upon Digory's old Bible on the table. Instinctively he touched the worn cover. It reminded him of the promise he made on that flooded road: *If we get out of this mess, I might even read that old Bible . . .*

He had opened it a time or two. But he had done just what Lady Margaret had said—he was not trying to understand, he was trying to pick it all apart. He was as false in his halfhearted attempt to carry out that vow as he was with everything else. He was doing just what he despised others for doing—trying to use God to get him out of a jam when things were going sour, like some benevolent magistrate in the sky, without getting personally involved, without any relationship with Him as Lady Margaret had said. He had always considered such an attitude hypocrisy, and yet he was guilty of the same thing. Well, neither Lady Margaret's words nor the earnestness of her voice mattered. He wasn't going to do what he did when they were out in the flood and go blubbering to God now.

Yet what if she was right? What if he was running from the only person who could help resolve this dilemma and rescue him and his friends from terrible danger? What if all this was happening, as Jesse would no doubt say, just as a way of God's getting his attention? What if the only way out of his confusion was through the one door he was refusing to open—the door of his own heart?

"Oh, God. . . !" he cried, but nothing else would come. He laid his head softly down on the table, and in the quiet stillness of the evening, Logan Macintyre began weeping tears of bitter remorse.

When he lifted his head a few minutes later, his eyes were red, but he felt no healing balm. His tears had been acid on an open wound, for he knew nothing about him had changed. He was alone and in a despair of suffering, seeing for the first time in his life the sinner he truly was. But he would not give in.

Logan sighed a comfortless sigh. His eyes strayed back to the Bible and he again thought of his uncle. Logan had never before truly envied another man. When he had said that he had been satisfied with his life, on the surface he had been speaking the truth so far as he knew it. Yet now he found himself envying old Digory. Here was a man who had been the picture of simplicity. It was evident in this very room where he had dwelt. Logan could almost feel the impact of his unpretentious life in the soul of the place he had inhabited.

"He loved his horses and his Bible," Lady Margaret had said.

A man without struggles, without the complications of modern life, without people chasing him, without the sham of a false personality tearing at him—it must have been easy for him to follow his God.

Yet ... was that true? Is it ever *easy* to lay one's life down? Though every man's sacrifice is different, does not every man truly sacrifice when he lays his *self* on the altar and chooses to follow the path God has laid out for him? Is it ever *easy*, even for a man like Digory? Was he not wrapped up in the struggles and heartaches of those he loved? Did his heart not ache for his little Maggie? Did not the decision he had to make about the treasure tear at him, too?

All at once Logan caught an image of the old groom bent over his Bible, agonizing over what to do, forced in the end by his love for the girl and his loyalty to the family he had served to hide a priceless treasure in order to keep them from further heartache, evil, and self-generated suffering.

He loved his horses and his Bible. . . .

Digory had sacrificed at least some of his natural simplicity for those he loved. But Logan knew even in his present confusion that if his life had become too complicated to cope with right now, he had only himself to blame. With a frustrated gesture he shoved Digory's Bible aside. If peace was to be found there, he deserved none of it. He would never be like Digory. He could never be devoted to others. And he deserved none of Digory's peace. Fatigue began to wash over him. He rose to his feet and shuffled to the bed where he stretched out, fully clothed, on the straw mattress. His eyes drooped and sleep seemed but a moment away, yet his mind continued to race in confused, anguished disarray.

I deserve no peace, he thought. If he had promised to read the words in that old Book, he had lied.

He was a liar! That was how he lived. He had no horses, no peaceful stable, no Bible. He had nothing—but himself! And a rotten self it was. The old poet, Mac—something, whatever his name was—had been right. *Low souls, weak hearts . . .* That was certainly him! A bad sea-boat with a wretched crew—none other but himself. He was low, weak, and wretched! A poor, foolish man, made to be free but running from the very freedom Lady Margaret said was the source of Digory's peace—and her own. He was a fool, but he couldn't help himself. All he had to keep him going was the hope of a treasure—a dirty, stinking treasure.

Maybe that was what he deserved. He had given his heart to this mammon, so his reward would be the anguish of seeing his lust for riches fulfilled while his soul remained tormented in the hell of his own selfishness. There would be no peace for him, only the suffering of the rich man whose tongue could not be cooled amid the flame. Digory had given up the treasure for love. Now his wretched and selfish descendant would turn his back on love, for the treasure . . . would unearth that which had brought evil . . . and would loose more evil into the world and upon himself.

No horses, no Raven, no Maukin, no peace, no quietness of spirit for the descendant. He, Logan Macintyre, whom no doubt old Digory had prayed for without knowing his name, was about to undo what this man of faith had done—he was about to dig up the pain, the heartache, the self of mammon which Digory had tried so hard to banish from the reach of any hands but Maggie's.

No horses . . . no Bible . . .

Suddenly Logan jerked out of his groggy, half sleep.

His body trembled from the abrupt awakening from a much needed rest. But words tumbled wildly through his brain . . . *it was not the first time he'd dug a large hole.* Where had he heard that?

He leaped out of bed. Groping in the darkness, his hands fumbled over the table and fell onto the Bible. He flung it open to the spot where he had replaced the letter after loaning it to Lady Margaret, the very page where it had been hidden by the old groom. Still trembling, now for other reasons, he took the letter out. What had Digory said? It had been a long time since Logan had read it. Groping farther, Logan found the lamp and matches. He lit it. The bright glow pained his eyes momentarily, but he forced them to study Digory's scrawl.

I hae moved it, Maggie, and hidden it where I pray none will discover . . .

No, thought Logan . . . further . . . where did he move it?

To see ye with auld Raven . . . lonely Braenock . . . the sandy beach . . . I hae put it in a spot I thocht ye loved . . .

There was the mention of Raven again!

. . . that cliff and ye both got stuck . . . sand . . . the other direction . . .

The other direction from the sand! Of course! It had to be Ramsey Head! It was in the other direction from town than the sandy beach. What else could the cliffs mean?

Ye loved that path to the rock bearing yer name.

That's it! That's it! cried Logan—the rock bearing your name . . . *Ramsey* Head! He buried the treasure on Ramsey Head somewhere near, or in, the very graves of the beloved horses. No one but Maggie could know those secrets the two of them shared—the horses, the love for the path, the time she got stuck riding there. He had done it! He had located the treasure! Unconsciously his eyes continued reading, *I pray one day ye will read this and return to us . . .*

He folded the letter hastily, wanting to hear no more. Not now. Not when he was on the verge of unearthing what might be millions! He would not condemn himself for being the one to keep Digory's prayer from being answered, for being the one to keep the letter hidden from the one whose eyes it was intended for.

He began pacing the room, a cold sweat breaking out over his body. How could he have known, at that moment, that the last line of the letter was the most important of all, the line he had not allowed himself to read: *But 'tis all in oor dear Lord's hands, and his will be doon.* The direction the bad boats of men's hearts sail is not always dependent upon the temporal plans of their wretched souls, but instead on the direction of the winds of God's Spirit that blows upon the waters, guiding them toward the harbor their blind eyes cannot see.

Even as his mind was racing with how to carry out the final stage in his long-awaited scheme, Logan found it incongruous that he should discover the location of the treasure just at the moment he had almost grown to detest any further mention of it.

Yet he could not stop himself. He could not leave it buried as Digory had. He was compelled to go on. But another compulsion, one whose promptings he was altogether unfamiliar with, told him to go back to the table and look again, this time at the Bible rather than the letter. Reluctantly, he obeyed. The book was still opened to the page where the letter had rested all those years. Then his eyes fell on something he had not noticed before. The Bible was opened to the sixth chapter of Matthew. He had never paid any attention to that fact before. And there on the yellowed page, seemingly for the first time, yet he knew that could not be the case, he noticed that one certain verse had been underlined. How odd that Digory would mar this book he so loved, that one—and only one—small passage would be so marked. Carefully Logan bent down and read the fine print:

"For where your treasure is, there will your heart be also."

Logan snapped the Bible shut. He knew he had not been intended to find peace or comfort from these pages. Digory, a man of peace, had left his final admonition to anyone who would seek that which his letter revealed—one doomed to tear Logan apart.

He turned away from the table and clasped his head between his hands in a fresh turmoil of confusion and indecision. He *couldn't* stop now! To do so would mean to relinquish so many other things! Maybe they were things he was not even sure he wanted anymore. And if he had thought deeply about it, he probably would have admitted he loathed them now. His past life was fading into a mist behind him, and with many backward glances of longing he watched all he had once loved retreat from him. And as he looked to the future, he was afraid of the unknown, afraid as Lady Margaret had said, to understand Digory's God. He was afraid to depend on Another, even though his own attempts to help himself had failed so miserably. He was afraid to go forward, but realized it was almost too late to go back, stuck at a crossroads of life's journey. He realized, without framing it consciously in his mind, that to repent of his past now would mean a complete changeabout, would mean to turn on the path and begin moving in a whole new direction. But making that turn was something he could not do ... not alone ... not yet.

Logan grabbed his heavy coat from the hook behind the door and ran down the steps into the stable.

49 The Turn

The air was oppressively warm and the evening was so still that Logan could hear his heart thudding within his chest. He hardly needed his coat. The wind and chill of the morning had been almost welcome compared to this. It foreboded more ill weather to come, though that fact hardly mattered to Logan at this moment. He would be gone from here before the storm broke. All this mental turmoil would be behind him. He'd be rich. And he'd be gone.

He had descended from his room with a resolute determination. His mind cried out for him to stop, but he refused to listen. From the tool rack he grabbed a shovel, then walked past the stalls of horses. He would not risk the commotion it might cause to take out a mount at this time of night. When he stepped outside, intuitively he clung to the shadows as he crept stealthily along the sides of the buildings. *'Tis only fitting,* he mused, *that I act the part of the thief for this, my final job at Stonewycke.* Looking over his shoulder, he crossed an open space to the point where, he recalled, a breach in the great hedge surrounding the courtyard existed.

In the morning, early, he'd go into town and leave specific instructions with the innkeeper that he had to leave for Aberdeen immediately, and then Edinburgh. He'd say he was expecting friends and they could be directed to follow him. He would give him the names of two hotels in each of the cities. Thus when Morgan's hoodlums came looking for him, they would follow his trail south and would not have to *force* any information from anyone. His one final favor to these people would be to avoid a confrontation or bloodshed in Port Strathy. These arrangements done, he would return to Ramsey Head, retrieve the treasure, or as much of it as he could reasonably take with him, and make his way on foot along the coast toward Fraserburg and then possibly Peterhead. He would lay low there for a long while; he'd have left no trail to lead anyone to him, and eventually he'd catch a schooner bound straight through for London.

The face of Allison kept intruding into his mind, but he forced it from him. His plan may have been foolproof. But inside he was miserable. He walked steadily faster, as if tiring his body would keep the voices of conscience and old ladies and old grooms and old poets at bay.

But he could not keep the words and images from that day out. Something had begun to open within him, and now that the door was ajar, a torrent of unwelcome thoughts pressed to find entrance.

"I think you are running from God," the lady had said.

If she could only see him now! Half walking, half running along the road, shovel in hand, his motives hidden by darkness, on his way to steal that which was rightfully hers. What a picture he made!

Was she right? Was this flight symbolic of his running away from truth ... running away from God? Was he using the treasure and the supposed threat of Morgan's thugs as just another excuse not to face up to himself—who he was, what he was doing? Was he trying to bolster his cowardice with noble-sounding gestures, thinking what a brave man he was to save the town from Morgan's men and put them on his own trail, when in reality he was afraid to stand up to the most basic truth of all—the truth of his own sinfulness, the truth of his need for God? Afraid ... that was all he was. A coward.

"I knew a man who tried to run from God ..." Lady Margaret's words echoed in his mind. *"But he knew no peace until the moment he stopped ..."*

What was his life—what had his life *always* been but a sham? A giant con game played upon no one but himself. What he had taken for contentment had been nothing more than a thick protective wall to enclose his fears and insecurities. He had seen that very thing in Allison and had been quick to identify it. But in himself he had been blind to it—until now. He had been hiding ... running ... covering up the truth of his ugly nature.

Did he want to stop running? Did he want to stop the sham, the con? Did he want to break down the walls with which he had been trying to protect his heart?

Logan was physically running now, gripping the shovel so tightly that his hand and arm muscles ached. His whole body was drenched with perspiration, but even he—self-reliant, calm, cocky Logan Macintyre—could not mistake the tears streaming down his face for sweat from his forehead. He was crying, and he knew it. Yet somehow in the anguish which precedes new birth, he could not be ashamed. They were tears, if not of comfort, yet of healing, and it felt good to unleash them.

What would it be like, he wondered, just once, to make the kind of selfless sacrifice that his uncle had? After all, Digory MacNab's blood ran in his veins also. Could it ... be possible that ... perhaps he *might* be able to know the peace and freedom that the old groom must have had? Again the words of the old poem came into his mind, *Thou hast to freedom fashioned them indeed.* Had he been made for freedom, and refused it all along?

Could he make the necessary sacrifice? Could he lay down his self? Could he give up the treasure?

He would gladly do so to have the joy in his heart that Lady Margaret had. But would he have the courage to face them, to expose himself for what he was, to face their rejection, and possibly prosecution? Would he have the courage to make amends for the life he had lived, to repay those he had swindled? Could he make such a gigantic change?

Gradually Logan's pace slowed, and he came to a halt. All was still and silent around him. The only sound he could hear was the breathing of his own lungs, and the distant call of the sea where he was headed. Silent tears of decision continued to flow.

He could go on like this all the rest of his life—blindly running and hiding, seeking one elusive treasure after another, playing con after con on himself, always trying to convince himself of what Lady Margaret had known was a bold-faced lie from the beginning—that he needed no one else. But now that his eyes were open to his true self, could he continue on in that way? Could he go back to his former life and ignore what his heart was prompting him to do?

Logan sank to his knees. "Oh, God...!" he cried, throwing the shovel from him and burying his face in his hands. "God, help me! Forgive me for what I've been ... help me become ... a true man!" And with the words Logan broke down into an impassioned fit of penitent sobbing.

———

It was ten minutes before he rose. The tears had dried and the prayers of his heart had soothed his agitated spirit. He picked up the shovel, took one last look down the road on which he had been headed, took a deep breath, turned, and began walking in the opposite direction. He had a more important treasure awaiting him at Stonewycke.

As he retraced his steps back toward the estate, the awful burden which had been bearing down upon him all day lightened by degrees. Yet he knew in one sense he had only begun. For the first step in beginning to live differently would be to make reparations for the wrong he had done. For a life such as Logan's, that would be no easy matter. And the first step might be the hardest of all—to come clean before the people he had been trying to hoodwink.

But he did not have long to think about these things, for before he was halfway back he saw a figure dart behind a thick clump of broom.

"Who's there?" he called, stealing cautiously forward.

Then two men, large and imposing, stepped out from the cover of the bush. It was dark, and on first glance Logan registered no recognition. Then gradually it began to dawn on him. He had sat between them, long ago it seemed, in a fancy Rolls Royce. Here were Chase Morgan's henchmen, sooner than he had expected. He did not have long to ponder, however, when another voice yelled behind him.

"It's time we talked, Macintyre!"

Logan spun around.

Though he had seen Ross Sprague in Hamilton's pub, Logan did not now recognize him. What he did recognize was the pistol Sprague held in his right hand.

Logan hardly thought about his next act. It was generated instinctively, from panic rather than logic. Remembering the shovel he still held, he swung mightily at Sprague's arm. The impact knocked the gun loose and into the heather and Sprague into the ditch on the side of the road. But the other two were on him in a moment. Logan barely had time to hope that if they had guns they might be reluctant to use them this near the house. Clumsily he wielded the shovel at once as a battle-ax and lance. He thrust forward, clipping Cabot in the head and knocking him temporarily unconscious. Lombardo, left alone in the attack, charged Logan. Had the thug gotten a firm hold on him, Logan would surely have been finished. But the big man, thinking through his attack none too clearly, simply rushed at Logan angrily, with all the deftness of a wild bull. Logan let him come, then at the last moment, stepped aside, shoved the shovel into Lombardo's oversized torso, and pushed with all his might. The uncoordinated goon was taken completely off his guard, stumbled over a rock, and crashed off the road somewhere near his cohort Sprague.

Logan did not even wait for Lombardo to land. The last thing Logan wanted was to bring danger to Stonewycke. But for the first time in his life he realized—with a humility that was new to him— that he was in over his head. He could handle this alone no longer. He needed the help of his friends.

He threw down the shovel and ran for the house.

50   The Confession

Though the evening was well advanced toward night, Lady Margaret and Joanna were sitting alone together in the kitchen. Ever since their talk with Allison, Joanna had felt a growing urgency to find out as much as possible from her grandmother about the family's history and her own life. She had long been gathering what information she could and writing it down, knowing that in her grandmother's memory lay the wealth of the Ramsey and Duncan heritage that might someday be lost. In giving her blessing to Allison, and passing along of her legacy to the two younger women, Margaret had, Joanna sensed, released something of the energy of her life, sending it into the future through the lives of her descendants. Now her time was coming to move on into that next phase of her life with God, which only death could bring. Heartbreaking though this realization was to Joanna, she knew of its necessity. Yet she could not look into her grandmother's face, seeing there a gradual fading of the embers of life, without tears rising in her own eyes. It was a crossroads which must come, but God would help her to live through it with victory, for it would bring a sadness to her greater than any she had ever known.

Their quiet conversation was interrupted by a knock on the door. Logan had gone to the only place in the castle where a light was still burning.

Despite the late hour, the family gathered immediately in the drawing room upon his urgent request. They were all there except the younger children.

Dorey reclined on the divan, Joanna took a seat in one of the great winged-backed chairs, her face displaying clear anxiety over whatever Logan's plight might be. Lady Margaret, clad in a quilted, satin dressing gown, took her place next to her husband. Alec stood easily by the hearth, his arm resting on the high mantle. Logan admired the calm and utter peace in his expression and wondered if he'd ever possess such a quality. Allison sat stiffly on the stone skirt of the hearth, a trace of fear showing out of her blue eyes but also a brave attempt to appropriate a calm like her father's, whom she resembled in so many other ways.

Part of Logan had wanted to flee after his attack. Yet another side of him knew he needed help.

But more than that, at last he knew he had to make right the terrible wrongs he had done, and even planned to do against these people. He had struggled too hard on the road out there to come to this decision, and now he must not turn away from it.

Now, however, as he stood before them, he had no idea what to do or say. It was rather an imposing array of lairds and ladies, representing a span of four generations in the Ramsey and Duncan line. He felt more than simply foolish. He felt low, insignificant, petty. And worse, he had probably brought danger right to their doorstep, though it was unlikely his pursuers would breach the security of the estate.

Logan's glance moved from face to face, resting momentarily on Allison's, where he could not keep from lingering a moment longer than he wanted. Their eyes locked for an instant, during which a hundred unspoken words—apologies, pleas, explanations—passed between them.

Logan jerked his gaze away. She figured strongly in why he had come back, but he could not think of that now. It would only confuse the more urgent issues.

"You must be thinking I have gone crazy," he said, in a voice that was taut and thin. "Perhaps what I want to say could have waited until morning. I only know that *I* could not have waited. I may have brought danger here, but it is too late for me to bemoan that now— I only hope I can make you understand how very sorry I am."

His words were met with puzzled looks all around. Then Alec spoke.

"I'm afraid we're a bit in the dark, lad," he said. "That is, ye might do best if ye started at the beginnin'."

Logan nodded, then took a deep breath. "I have presented myself falsely to you," he began, each word spoken deliberately as if to insure they were not misunderstood. And though Logan felt none of the release he expected from the confession, he went on. "I have spent my entire life in lies and cheating. Honesty and dishonesty have all been one to me. When I'm not gambling, I swindle innocent folk in any other way I can. That's how I make my living, not in investments, as I tried to make you believe."

"We appreciate that you have seen fit to tell us this, Logan," said Lady Margaret, to whom it came as no surprise. "But it changes nothing in how we feel toward you." She looked at him intently, with the same penetrating gaze he had encountered on his first day in Port Strathy. But now for the first time he felt from the look what had been at its root all along, a great heart of compassion and understanding.

"How can that be?" said Logan, both astonished and frustrated. "I know you people detest dishonesty. I'm a thief; don't you understand that?"

"I understand," she replied with that mystery in her voice which he had yet to fully grasp. "And we do detest dishonesty. But I see honesty in you now, and that means everything. What can we do for you?"

Logan shifted his weight on his feet, flustered and uncertain what to say. He had expected rejection, and possibly could have handled that. But he didn't know what to do with *this*! "You don't understand," he began again more firmly. "That's why I came *here*— to Stonewycke. It was no accident that I met you. I planned it. I intended to swindle you! All of you—but you in particular, Lady Margaret."

He looked around, the old part of his nature almost defying them to accept him now. But just before his eyes turned toward Allison, they faltered and looked away. He couldn't bear to see the changed expression he knew must be on her face. Instead, he forced his gaze back to Lady Margaret. He knew he had wronged her more than any by presuming on her love for Digory.

"And Digory ... the Bible?" she asked.

"Oh, they're real enough."

"Then if you have committed some crime against us," she replied, "I am quite unaware of it."

"I lied to you! That ought to be enough. I didn't come here to research my family roots. I never gave a thought to anything like that until I found a letter written by my great-great-great uncle Digory—a letter written to you, Lady Margaret. The letter mentioned a treasure, and I came here in hopes of finding it—a treasure rightfully belonging to you—and to steal it from under your nose."

At the mention of the treasure, Margaret's face turned pale. It was as if a ghost out of her childhood had suddenly reappeared. Ian perceived the change and reached out to take her hand.

A long, silent pause followed. Logan stared down at the Persian carpet, for he could stand their eyes upon him no longer.

"And though it's too late to undo my falsehood to you," he said at length, "I want to apologize ... to say how sorry I am." It was not easy to get the words out. The attempt was a new one for him. "I want to try somehow to make it up to you. You have all been ... so ... kind—you have treated me like I was one of the family when I did not deserve it." He stopped. If he said more he would likely break down again.

Finding her breath again, it was Lady Margaret who spoke next. "And did you complete your plan, Logan?"

He shook his head in reply. "But can you forgive me?" he blurted out, almost like a child.

Joanna stood and walked toward him. She led him to a chair, then sat down beside him. She rested her hand gently on Logan's shoulder while she silently prayed that the Lord would give them the words with which to comfort and show the way toward healing.

"Oh, Logan," said Lady Margaret, "do you know us so little yet that you do not know that our hearts are overflowing with love toward you? Of course we forgive you!"

"A confession such as yours, Logan," added Dorey, "is from the heart and is a clear sign of repentance. Believe me, I know about the need to repent. I ran from God for years before I accepted His forgiveness. So not only do we forgive you, so does God."

"How can you both say that!" This new outburst came from Allison, who looked ravaged with hurt and indignation. "How can you forgive him so easily? We believed him and he *lied* to us. We thought he was our friend and he deceived us. How can we trust him now? How do we know he hasn't just come to us because he's in some kind of trouble?"

"Oh, Allison ... dear," Joanna began, but before she could utter another word Logan broke in.

"I am in trouble, but that's not why I've come to you—"

"How can we ever believe you again!" said Allison.

"I know I don't deserve it."

"I trusted you!" Allison exclaimed tearfully, the hurt clearly evident in her voice. "How can I be expected to forgive you now, Christian or no Christian? I just don't see how I can." She turned and fled the room.

"Logan," said Joanna, sensing the pain in his heart as he watched her go, but knowing he was unable to reach out to her, "you must try to understand Allison ... she's young, and—"

"But what she said is right."

"I should go to her now," Joanna added, "but I know she didn't mean those things. Her heart will be able to forgive you, too. Just give her time." She gave his shoulder a motherly pat, then turned and left the room after her daughter.

"Come o'er here an' sit ye doon, lad," said Alec, drawing Logan to an overstuffed chair opposite the divan where Lord and Lady Duncan sat. Alec pulled a straight-backed medieval chair next to him. "Lad," he said when they had settled themselves, "do ye think forgiveness has anythin' t' do wi' merit? Wi' whether we *deserve't*? Weel, it doesna. It has t' do wi' only one thing—a contrite an' repentant heart. Where do ye think any o' us would be if God took the attitude wi' us that He'd forgive us if we deserved it?"

"I can imagine you forgiving me much easier than I ever could God," said Logan.

"It is from Him that we learn forgiveness, Logan," said Lady Margaret. "The first step of all is to accept *His* forgiveness."

"The first step of what?"

"Of committin' yer whole life t' Him," replied Alec. "That's what He wants from us. An' only by givin' Him yer life can forgiveness an' peace an' healin' come."

"I know now that I do want to be different, to be honest, to be upright. I want to be forgiven for all I've done. But it's hard for me to think of God as wanting anything to do with someone like me. I already told you. I'm not good, like you people. I've done dishonest things, *illegal* things."

"We ha' all been there t' one degree or another. Before God no one's free from sin. The Bible says that 'God commends his love toward us in that while we were *yet* sinners, Christ died fer us.' Dinna ye see, Logan. *Sinners* are His chief interest!"

"Calling all people sinners is just a religious way of talking. But nobody really believes everybody's just as bad as everybody else. What could you have done *really* sinful?"

"I strongly doubt, young man," put in Dorey before Alec had a chance to reply, "that you've spent any more time in the jails than I have—London and Glasgow both. I'm not proud of it. But God reached out to me, and I was in as despicable shape as anyone could have been at the time."

"And Logan," added Alec with an intensity in his voice, "I once killed a man."

Any argument that may have been posed on Logan's lips melted away to nothing, and he gaped in silence. The thing couldn't be true—surely he had misunderstood! Yet he could see in Alec's earnest blue eyes that it *was* so—beyond all reason. And yet despite such a crime, Alec still spoke about God as if He were his friend. It hardly seemed possible.

"The court exonerated me, but it made it no easier t' live wi' such a thing, knowin'—"

Alec closed his eyes and swallowed hard. It was still heart-wrenching to discuss it, and he wouldn't have except for Logan's benefit. "—Knowing that wi' my own hands I had destroyed a human life. I'm only tellin' ye this so ye can see jist hoo great God's love is fer us. When I came t' Him, He didna look at my deed an' say, 'Sorry, 'tis a bit too much fer me t' forgive!' No, Jesus had *already* died for that deed. He was merely waitin' fer me t' realize it, repent o' what I had done, an' let His love come int' my heart in place o' my old selfish nature. His love had nothing t' do wi' what I had done. His love's great enough t' cover the worst an' the best o' us. But we *all* need that love abidin' in oor hearts equally."

"I've never really heard it said like that before," confessed Logan. "But how did you know it was true—I mean, really *know*?"

"A dear friend first told me," Alec replied. "Then one night I knew in my heart that He *did* love me an' had answered my prayer an' had forgiven me. I guess ye could say He spoke t' me in a quiet sort o' way. Once ye take the step o' askin' His forgiveness an' invitin' Him t' dwell wi' ye in yer heart fer the rest o' yer life, He'll not leave ye alone."

"I've never thought of God like that before—so close."

Almost as if by common consent, the three older persons laid their hands on Logan and bowed their heads. Feeling both a slight embarrassment, yet at the same time the warmth of their love, Logan closed his eyes. Dorey was the first to speak.

"Father," he began, "we all thank you for bringing Logan here to live among us. Thank you that his heart is open to you."

He stopped. After a moment Alec prayed, "Oh, Lord, keep yer lovin' hand on oor friend Logan. Reveal yer love t' him in a special way. An' show him the way through this present trouble in his life, usin' us, yer servants, in any way ye see fit. Help him t' accept yer forgiveness in his heart. Thank ye fer yer great love, Lord. Amen."

"Help me, Lord," said Logan simply. "Help me to live as you want me to. Please dwell in my heart like you do in these people's. And thank you for forgiving me for what I have been ... Amen."

He looked up just as Joanna came back into the room. She smiled at him as she approached. Alec held out his hand for her, and she took it gratefully.

"Hoo's oor daughter?" he asked.

"I couldn't find her," replied Joanna. "I looked all over the house. She must want to be alone. She's probably gone for a walk outside."

She sighed. "Maybe the cool evening air will settle her emotions."

"She has every right to hate me," said Logan. "I talked about being friends—but I've proved myself nothing more than a liar to her."

He looked solemnly at Allison's parents. "I want you to know that whatever happens, I never meant to hurt her. I..."

His voice faltered. He wanted to tell them that he cared for her, cared for her more than even he was sure he wanted to admit. But he left unspoken the words of his heart, rose, and began to leave the room.

"I'm going to pack my things," he said. "I'll leave in the morning. I appreciate all you've done for me. I appreciate what you've said and done this evening, and your praying with me. But it's best that I leave. There are ... some men ... looking for me. Men from out of my past. It would not be fair of me to stay. Lady Margaret, I will leave you the Bible, with Digory's letter. I know it will mean a great deal to you. His memory—and yours—will always be special to me. But it is best this way..."

He paused and tried to look up at the four of them where they stood watching him through eyes of love. He felt the filling of his tear ducts and would have to make his exit soon.

"If only ... if I could do all this over again, I ..." but he left his words unfinished, turned quickly, and fled from the house.

51   Abduction

The sliver of a moon had broken through the clouds, but it shed no light on the deepening night. As Logan crossed the yard, the quickly moving clouds rolled past, obliterating it once more. The air was heavy. In the distance he heard a faint rumble of thunder.

Was he running once again—this time perhaps not from God, but from people? Why had he been so afraid to open up and tell them everything? He knew they would have accepted him with open arms, would have prayed with him, would have done whatever they could to help. What made it so difficult to receive the help and love of one's fellows?

Suddenly a sound arrested Logan's attention. He stopped and listened again. Was it Allison? He wasn't sure he wanted to meet her right now.

He glanced all about, but saw nothing. It was just as well. What could he say, anyway? As he walked on he reviewed all their times together. They had made no promises or commitments to one another. But then they were both too self-centered for that. He immediately rebuked himself for thinking ill of her; he knew there was more to Allison than that. He had seen glimpses at first, but then after that day when Fairgate came to call she had seemed genuinely different. Was she fighting a battle within herself—just as he was?

He walked on. He didn't want to leave. But what else could he do? He and Allison had merely had a brief glimpse of what might have been. What was he thinking, anyway? He could never settle down—even for love. The very thought of the word sent an electric charge through his body. It was not something he had encountered much of in his hard life on the streets. He had not even sought it, nor wanted it—until now, when it seemingly lay so close within his grasp. And yet his chance for love was all but gone.

Logan reached the stable door and opened it wide enough to let himself through. All was pitch black and still, except for an occasional snort from one of the horses in back. He had never known until now what a comforting sound that was. No wonder his uncle had so loved his animals and his little world here!

Before he had a chance to secure the door behind him, he again heard a sound, like the shuffling of feet. Again he thought of Allison. But before he had the chance to wonder what she might be doing in the stable, another voice broke through the silence. Logan froze.

"Don't do anything funny, Macintyre," it said. "I have a .38 aimed right at your head." It was the same voice he had heard with Lombardo's earlier.

So, the walls of mighty Stonewycke were not impenetrable after all!

"Who are you? What do you want?" Logan struggled to keep the tremor from rising in his voice.

"Sprague's the name," said the intruder coolly. "But it won't mean anything to you. You have something I want—at least I hope you have it. If not . . . then I'll be *very* disappointed. You see, Macintyre, I have a fondness for buried treasure."

How could Morgan have found out about that? Logan wondered. But it hardly mattered now.

"Where is Allison?"

"You mean that sweet young thing that was roaming around out here an hour ago?"

"Where is she?" was Logan's only reply as he started to spin around.

"Hold it!" barked Sprague. "You turn around real slow and keep your hands where I can see them."

Logan complied. "What have you done with her?" he shouted, feeling a mixture of rage and self-derision for getting her mixed up with men who were likely murderers.

"Don't worry. She's safe and sound—*for now*. You cooperate and give me what I want, and you'll have your little mistress back." Sprague's threat needed no further embellishment.

"And what is it you want?"

"I told you. I want that treasure."

"That's all?"

Something didn't fit. If this man were from Morgan, settling the score against him would count for far more than some elusive treasure. He might want the loot anyway, if it chanced to come his way. But Morgan was the type who would want Logan's blood. Morgan would want revenge.

"I'm not a greedy man," Sprague was saying, "nor a violent one. I can, in fact, be most conciliatory."

"I won't tell you a thing until I know the girl is safe."

Sprague clicked his tongue in mocking rebuke. "It hurts my feelings, sonny, that you won't trust old Uncle Ross."

"You'll get nothing until I see with my own eyes that she is alive and well and will go free unharmed."

52   The Abandoned Cottage

Allison squirmed against the rough stone wall of the deserted cottage.

Except for the blaze in the fire pit, there was no light in the single room of the hut. But it showed enough to reveal the cruel, menacing faces of her abductors. They were strangers, and, though she had heard them refer to one another as Cabot and Lombardo, the names meant nothing to her. Logan's name, however, had come up once or twice.

They had grabbed her in the courtyard behind the house, hustled her out through the gap in the hedge, shoved her into the backseat of a car, and driven her here. They were about half a mile from the moor, as close as any automobile could get to it. The old cottage had not been occupied for years, and though so many of them were alike and it was difficult to see, she was sure this was the same hut where she and Logan and Fergie had taken refuge. Now, it seemed it had become Allison's prison.

She shivered, as much from fear as from the descending cold of night. An icy wind had started to blow down from the moor, stirring up the stagnant air of the last several hours, portending a new storm.

"Cold, little lady?" asked the man named Lombardo gruffly, but not without a flicker of genuine concern.

Allison nodded, but she would never tell them she was also scared. *Oh, Lord,* she prayed, *please give me courage. I need you now more than ever!*

Lombardo slipped off his jacket and laid it roughly over her. She knew she should acknowledge the gesture, but with her hands numb from the cords that tightly bound them, and her arms still aching from their rough handling when they captured her, she could muster up little thanks.

"You're a bowl of mush," jeered Cabot to his comrade.

"Well, we don't want her to croak on us."

"No one ever croaked from a little cold."

"Aw, shut up!" growled Lombardo as he lumbered back to his place on the other side of the fire.

The jacket didn't help much, but it was something.

"What do you want with me?" Allison asked. "My family doesn't have any money."

"Hmm, that's a thought," said Cabot ominously. "Too bad we don't have time for a side venture."

"Please just let me loose, then go away—no one will come after you."

"You're awful generous," laughed Cabot.

Allison slumped back and fell silent. This seemed a harsh way to test her new faith, especially after she had failed so dreadfully when Logan had been confessing to her parents. If she hadn't run out acting so stupidly, none of this would have happened. She prayed once more, and continued to pray for help until she fell into a restless sleep.

A sudden rush of cold air awakened her. The door had been pushed open, but in the distorted light of the flames and the haze of sleep, she could not make out the newcomers. At last her eyes came into focus.

"Logan!" she cried, relieved and exultant, forgetting all past anger.

"Allison!" He rushed forward, stumbling over a piece of wood in the darkened room, and falling to his knees. She could see that his hands were tied. He made his way toward her, and, raising his hands to her, brushed her cheek as if to make certain she was real. Then, closely examining her from head to foot, he asked, "Are you all right?"

"Oh, yes. I'm so glad to see you!"

"I'm sorry to have gotten you into this. I hardly deserve your forgiveness, but I *am* sorry."

"Oh, Logan," she said, "all that's behind us. I treated you so rudely!"

Sprague interrupted before either could speak further. "Sorry to break up this warm little reunion," he said sarcastically, "but I don't think we're quite finished with our deal, Macintyre."

Logan turned. He had little faith that Sprague would spare them once he had his precious information, but Logan had few options.

"Let Allison go. Then I'll tell you."

"What kind of fool do you think I am?" laughed Sprague. "Once she's gone, you might tell me anything! She's my only insurance that you'll tell me the truth."

Logan looked at Allison and sighed. Well, it had been worth a try. But Sprague was no dummy.

"There's a place called Ramsey Head," he said.

"Yeah?"

"It's buried at the top."

"How will I find it?"

"You'll see when you get there. It's under a large rock, part way chiselled to look like the head of a horse."

Sprague grabbed Logan by the shirt and dragged him to his feet. "I'll see, because you're going to show me!"

"Then Allison comes too."

But Cabot stepped forward. "No go, Sprague," he said. "You start moving them around and you're asking for trouble. There might be people out looking for the girl by now. I'm not letting Macintyre out of my sight. You go check it out. But believe me, my friend, if you find it and try to double-cross us and skip town—we'll find you!"

"What if it's not there?" asked Sprague.

"We won't have at them till you get back."

"That's going to waste time," argued Sprague.

"You're not running this show anymore. We've done our part and I'm taking no more chances on losing Macintyre. You've got two hours. If you're not back by then, I'll just assume you don't need Macintyre anymore."

"Two hours! You must be crazy! I'll need help. Who knows how deep the stuff's buried."

Cabot gestured with his gun toward Lombardo. "You go with him. I'll watch these two."

"Don't tell me what to do!" grumbled Lombardo. "This is your idea. So you go!"

Cabot eyed his accomplice intently, then rose, apparently thinking it fruitless to push the point. Where could the two kids go, anyway? Even Lombardo should be able to handle that. But Sprague just might try to skip. Maybe it was good for him to go, to keep an eye on Sprague—and the loot.

There was at least some comfort in the fact that they had some time to spare, and Allison tried to be thankful for that. Logan had come. Perhaps the Lord had sent him. She was no longer alone. And when Lombardo pushed him down next to her, she felt a warm peace from his nearness.

"Logan," she said softly, "you're not the only one who has things to be sorry about. I haven't treated you fairly either. From the very beginning I judged you. When you hurt your foot, I knew it was fake."

"You did?"

"Yes. But believe me, I didn't keep quiet about it for any noble reasons. I planned to wait till the right time, then use it against you. Don't ask me why. I'm not even certain myself. Let's just say I was a different person back then. Not a very nice person. Everything was so twisted in my mind."

"I asked for it," Logan replied. "I badgered you—"

"It's enough that we forgive each other," Allison interrupted. "And I *do* forgive you. Something's happening inside me, Logan—"

"Hey!" broke in Lombardo's sharp voice, "what're you two whispering about."

"Just passing the time," Logan replied.

"Well, no funny business, that's all!" He waved his gun in the air to add emphasis to his words.

"We can't do any harm talking, can we?"

Lombardo grunted and fell silent.

Logan said nothing for a few moments. Allison wondered what he was thinking. She wanted to tell him that what she had felt that day in the rain was *not* mere accident, as she had said earlier. But she didn't know how to begin. Then she noticed that he was working his hands, within his bonds, back and forth. Quickly she jerked her gaze away, not wanting to alert Lombardo's attention.

"Logan," she said at length, "you know all those things I said earlier about our time together, you know, coming home from the Bramfords'?"

He nodded.

"I was wrong to try to make so little of that. It *was* a special moment for me. I didn't mean what I said later."

"You mean if I tried to steal another kiss from you, you wouldn't slap me?" he teased.

"Logan ... please. You'll embarrass me," she replied with good-natured chiding in her tone.

"Now," said Logan more softly, "how are you at acting sick?"

"Maybe as good as you," she answered with a coy smile.

"Well, give it a try—and make it look good."

Allison doubled over and let out a terrible groan. She repeated it over and over several times, but still Lombardo paid no attention. Finally Logan intervened.

"Help her!" he cried in a most convincing tone. "She's in pain . . . please."

"That's an old dodge," said Lombardo callously. "I wasn't born yesterday."

Allison rolled over onto her side, still moaning.

"Come on, lady," said Lombardo, "it's the oldest trick in the book."

"You can't just let her lie there!" yelled Logan. "What if your friends come back and she's dead? They'll feed you to the cops, while they make off with the loot."

"This better not be some game." Lombardo hitched his frame to its feet, then motioning with the gun at Logan, added, "You get way over there."

Logan complied, and still Lombardo had taken no notice that the cords binding his hands had loosened considerably. The big man bent down beside Allison and tapped her shoulder.

"All right, lady, what's wrong?" he asked.

"My stomach," gagged Allison.

Lombardo had been careful to keep Logan, who had moved to the far end of the wall, in his sight. But for the single moment while he took Allison's arm to pull her up from the ground, he let his gun hand drop.

Logan's next move was so quick and unexpected that even the split second it would have taken to raise the gun was not enough. Logan sprang across the space between them, his weight momentarily stunning the hoodlum.

"Ali . . . run!" he shouted. He knew he was no fighter, and this man was nearly twice his size. There might be only a few seconds for her to escape.

Allison scrambled to her feet, but instead of taking flight looked about for a way to help Logan. In the meantime, Lombardo had regained what wits he had, and tried to aim his gun. Logan caught his arm and flattened it to the ground. They struggled for another minute, until, with a horrifying crack, the pistol fired.

For a frightening instant everything stopped. Then Logan raised his hand, the weapon gripped tightly between his fingers. Lombardo stared, shocked both that he had fired and that this amateur had been able to wrestle the gun from him. Then he backed slowly away. Pale and trembling, with his right arm pressed against his side, Logan steadied the gun in his left hand toward Lombardo.

"Ali, go!" he repeated.

"Are you all right?"

"Yes, yes! I'm fine," he answered with a weak smile. "You have to run for help."

"I'm not leaving you."

"You *have* to. Don't you understand? There's no one else. I'll keep him here. You're the only one who can do this."

"But you're hurt!"

"It's nothing much," he lied, thankful that his jacket hid the spreading red beneath his shirt. "I would only slow you down. Just go. I'll be fine."

Then he turned to his prisoner and said, "Untie her, Lombardo."

With hesitancy Allison at last approached the door. With her hand on the latch, she turned and looked back, her eyes pleading with Logan. Reading her unspoken, "Are you sure?" Logan nodded and said, "Now, make a run for it."

The moment she cleared the rickety wooden step of the cottage, she broke into a run, a prayer on her lips, and an ache in her heart that she might not get back with help in time.

53   Looking Death in the Eye

Pain seared through Logan's side as if a red-hot iron had been thrust through his chest.

Sitting on the ground, he had to raise one knee in order to rest the arm that held Lombardo's pistol. When the slug had first hit him there had been no pain, only a jolt and an instant feeling of weakness. That's how he knew he'd been hit bad. He'd seen flesh wounds; they were the worst of all. The deeper the bullet, or so he'd been told, the greater the shock, the less the pain. But the stabbing throb had followed soon enough, and if the slug didn't kill him, he'd no doubt faint eventually from sheer agony and loss of blood, and then Lombardo would finish him off. In either case, he was a dead man.

He had never been hurt like this, never knew this kind of physical torture. Already his vision was blurring and his hand was so weak it shook. Then Lombardo stirred and Logan tensed.

"Don't, Lombardo," warned Logan in a voice thin and dry.

"You're not going to make it, Macintyre. You're half gone already."

"I can still pull this trigger."

"You don't have the stomach for it," taunted the hoodlum.

"Maybe not. But I'm beyond caring, so I might be able to do what I don't have the stomach for."

Lombardo sat back quietly. Logan's point made sense, and was well taken. What was the hurry? He would faint soon enough anyhow. Lombardo's chief worry now was what to say when his cohorts came back. If they found no treasure, and discovered the girl escaped and Logan dead, they would be none too pleased. True, Morgan's mission would have been accomplished. But then the girl was loose to point the finger at them, and Sprague would be furious. He did not relish a tangle with that man. If the kid died, maybe he should split and try to get back to Morgan first, with his side of the story.

Meanwhile, Logan sat with his own thoughts. He knew Lombardo was not far wrong. He could never pull this trigger. Here he was again trying to be something he was not. He had always hated guns and had never used one in his life. But something else was also operating within Logan at that moment, which Lombardo could not possibly realize—a stubborn determination not to let Allison or her family down again. He didn't know if he could take another man's life. But he did know that he had to keep Lombardo here long enough to give Allison enough time for a clean escape. The thought of this hulk getting away too soon and catching her was enough to make Logan think that he just might be able to kill. He hoped it wouldn't come to that.

Perspiration dripped into his eyes and he dashed it away with his free hand, a hand as cold and clammy as death itself. His eyes began to droop and he forced them open. He had to hang on!

As the minutes ticked away, Logan had to work harder and harder to keep his brain from freezing in a jumble of fog. His head already felt too light, as if it were three or four feet above his shoulders. Every once in a while Lombardo would appear distorted and distant, like the view through the wrong end of a telescope.

How long had it been, he wondered? Where would Allison be? But all perception of time was gone. It felt like hours, but it might have been only minutes. His wounded body screamed out for release, but he steeled himself against surrender. He could not lie down and go to sleep, though every fiber of his being cried out for rest.

Oh, God, help me!

Suddenly his head jerked up. His brain had begun to swirl about as consciousness started to leave him. Seeing his advantage, Lombardo inched forward. Logan thrust out the pistol.

"I'm warning you, Lombardo. I *will* use this." But Logan's voice sounded hollow and far away. He wasn't even certain his finger any longer was touching the trigger.

"You're a goner, Macintyre."

No! Logan tried to shout. But it was a wicked dream. He heard no sound come out of his mouth. His tongue and lips were so dry they felt glued shut, and the room spun sickeningly around him.

How long ... how long had it been ...?

Allison, I'm sorry ... I tried ... I love you ... but I can't ...

When Logan was next aware of anything, he was sprawled out on the hard, earthen floor of the deserted cottage. He lifted his head long enough to see that Lombardo was gone; then he let it fall in despair. The fire had burned low. He had no sense of time. He did not even bother to wonder why the hoodlum had left him alive. Could it be that even a criminal like him had no stomach for cold-blooded murder? His friends would hardly be so kind.

He was alive. But barely. He knew it would not be long now.

Logan had not often thought about death. He was young and it had always seemed so distant. He had always scorned deathbed confessions. He thought of his last conversation with Skittles. His dying friend had said, "You're a bright boy, and you can make somethin' better of yourself."

Well, Skits, he thought feebly, *guess I let you down again.*

They had never talked about religion. And now Logan regretted that, for it seemed a shame that it should have been missing from their close relationship. But of course, he had not been interested in God, not seen so many things clearly back then.

Deathbed confessions... Now Logan understood what they were all about. They had to be real because a man could not be insincere when he was dying—it was no time for lies or games or false promises. Skittles had tried so urgently to get him to listen, but he had brushed it off.

Now it was his turn, and there was no one for him to talk to. Was his life passing before his eyes? Was this what it was like? He knew what he wanted now, and only wished he had time to prove he was worthy of the same faith as Digory's and Lady Margaret's and all the rest of them. He only wished he had time to make amends to all those he had hurt, to those he had swindled, to Buckie and Jimmy and how many others. If it took a lifetime, he wanted to undo the results of his former lifestyle. But now it was too late ... there was no time left ...

Logan drew a ragged breath.

"God, forgive me for what I have been, for what I have done," he prayed in a hoarse whisper. "Forgive me for ignoring you for so long. Let me die with the peace I know only you can give—"

He stopped suddenly with a fit of coughing that sent renewed pain shooting through his body.

Then he was silent. He could hardly think. But in those moments that he knew would be his last, he recalled Alec's words: "*One night I jist knew in my heart that He did love me an' that He had forgiven me.*" With the thought Logan felt the peace he had yearned for.

Logan knew the same voice that had spoken to Alec. In some mysterious and miraculous and unfathomable way, God had accepted to His heart a liar, a thief, a swindler, a no-good, self-centered young man who had lived his entire life for no one but himself.

It was all Logan needed to know.

He closed his eyes. He had seen into God's heart of love—and was ready to die.

54 The Stretching of Allison's Faith

Allison ran hard the entire three miles between the deserted Krueger place and Stonewycke's gates.

Had she taken the road, the way would have been easier, but longer, and she feared she might run into the other two men. She had therefore struck out over the moor and, despite the darkness of the night, had miraculously made it without breaking her leg in a peat bog. Even as the imposing walls of Stonewycke's outer perimeter came into view, she was not sure she could make it. Her chest heaved frightfully and a painful stitch tore at her side. But the rain did not begin until she was in sight of the castle.

The ever-present thought of Logan forced her to keep going. *Please, God,* she prayed over and over as she ran, *please don't let him be hurt seriously. Protect him, Lord … keep your hand upon him.*

She pushed open the ancient gate and paused a brief moment to catch at least one more breath with which to go on. Glancing up at the house, she found two or three lights still on. It must be nearly midnight.

The kitchen door was still unlocked. She entered, frantically calling for her mother. Footsteps hurried along the corridor above, then down the stairs. More lights flashed on. As her mother reached her, Allison collapsed into her arms, crying and trembling. Alec was but two paces behind his wife, the anxiety of the night etched clearly on his face.

"Lass," he said, "oh, lass, what's happened? I've been oot lookin' fer ye this last hour."

"It's awful, Daddy!" she cried, now finding his strong arms enfolding her as well. "It's Logan—"

"What's he done?" exclaimed Alec, his proud Scottish blood on the rise.

"He's hurt, Daddy…" replied Allison. "There are some men, bad men. They kidnapped me. Then they brought Logan. We were both tied up. Logan got loose and overpowered the man so I could escape. But he was shot—he wouldn't tell me how bad. Oh, I'm so scared!"

"Shh," soothed Alec, concerned by Allison's disjointed explanation.

"What men?" asked Joanna.

"I don't know, but they wanted Logan. They made him tell where the treasure is. Two of them left. I think they had orders to kill us once they found the treasure. If they get back before help comes, I'm afraid—" She burst into tears.

"Where is he?" asked her father, his mind clearing.

"At the old Krueger cottage."

"All right, we'll go fer him," said Alec, springing into action. "I'll get the truck from Fergie an' gather up a few men on the way. We'll be there in no time."

He started down the hall, but Allison ran after him.

"I'm going with you," she stated.

"Lass, there's no tellin' what we'll find."

"I don't care. I have to go. I can't let him think I didn't care enough to come back."

"Let her go, Alec," Joanna said with an understanding smile. "This is something she has to do. The Lord will protect you both."

"Ye must do whate'er I tell ye."

"Of course I will," replied Allison earnestly. "But let's *go*!"

Within twenty minutes, the truck was brought out and the farmhands who lived on the estate were awakened, and they set out for the deserted cottage. On the way Alec tried to get what additional information from Allison he could. He sent Fergie into town to gather assistance in order to apprehend the men who had gone to Ramsey Head, if they were still there.

The truck bounced and clattered over the old, rutted dirt road they had to use for the final leg of the short journey. Allison sat on the edge of the front seat, clinging tensely to the dashboard, trying to peer through the rain.

Suddenly she saw something, a dark and shadowy figure, moving toward them.

"Look!" she exclaimed. "Daddy, stop . . . it's Logan!"

Alec ground the truck to a halt and jumped out, Allison at his side. They ran forward.

But it was not Logan, only Frank Lombardo trudging heavily through the rain, soaked to the skin, utterly lost. In spite of the certain disaster awaiting him, he was actually relieved to see a sign of human life through the dismal night.

"It's him!" cried Allison. "That's the man!"

Alec needed no further explanation. He stepped forward, grabbed Lombardo's arms, and pushed him against the truck. With two other burly crofters now backing Alec and ready at the first sign of a struggle, Lombardo surrendered without a fight.

"Where is he?" screamed Allison. "What have you done to him?"

"If you mean Macintyre," replied the subdued Lombardo, "I didn't do nothin' to him. He just died, that's all—at least he's dead by now. You saw for yourself. He's the one who attacked me, and the gun just went off."

"No! Daddy . . . no!"

"Dinna ye give up hope yet, lassie," said Alec. "Ye jist keep prayin' hard."

But Lombardo scoffed at the words. "It's too late fer prayin'. I tell you, he's a goner. But it weren't my fault."

Without further conversation, Alec took the prisoner toward the back of the truck and made him climb up. "Can you handle him?" he asked his men. One of them, sitting in the back with his hunting rifle on his lap, wielded it knowingly and nodded.

As they approached the cottage, it looked more deserted than ever. Nonetheless, Allison was out of the truck even before it had come to a full stop and racing toward the door. *Lord*, she prayed, afraid for what she might find, *help me to face this with strength.*

The fire had died to all but a few pitiful embers and it was almost dark inside. But the next moment Alec came up behind her holding a lantern. Allison saw Logan lying on the hard earth, deathly still, his skin ashen as if the fire of his life, too, had died. She rushed forward and fell to her knees beside him.

"Logan!" she wept, gently lifting his head. "Oh, Logan . . . please don't be dead."

For several agonizing moments there was no response. She grasped his hand. It was still warm with life. With tears of anguish and love in her eyes, she leaned down, kissed him, and laid her head on his chest. "Logan . . . Logan . . ." she said, softly this time. "Logan . . . I love you!"

A flutter, though faint, stirred in his chest. She looked up at her father helplessly, then back to the prostrate form.

Slowly Logan's eyelids opened, but the merest crack. A pathetic, crooked smile bent his lips.

"Ali . . ." he breathed. "Ali . . . is that you?"

"Oh yes! Logan . . . yes, it's me! Oh, thank you, Lord!"

". . . told you I was a lucky fellow . . ."

"Oh, Logan! . . . hush now . . . please . . ." rebuked Allison with joy in her voice.

Alec knelt down and gently lifted Logan into his arms, and, with Allison beside him, murmuring words of love and encouragement into his ear, carried him to the truck.

55 The Fate of the *Bonnie Flora MacD*

Frank Lombardo was securely in the custody of the local authorities. But the search party that climbed Ramsey Head found another kind of justice had been meted out to Willie Cabot. He was found lying next to a hastily dug hole with a bullet through his heart.

Ross Sprague it seemed had escaped justice altogether. A search for Ross Sprague was mounted, but to no avail. No one had thought to look north toward the sea until it was too late—although the rising storm would have discouraged even the most tenacious pursuer.

Sprague, meanwhile, had hired a thirty-foot fishing vessel, one sentimentally styled *Bonnie Flora MacD* after the prince's daring lady, under the name Albert Smith. Even that did not arouse suspicions until a day or two after the escape. Port Strathy's law-abiding community was simply not equipped to deal with crime at this level—a fact that worked to Sprague's benefit.

Sprague was no seaman, but he thought his cursory knowledge would suffice him for the short distance which would be required of him. When the rain began to fall and the wind rise, his confidence began to wane somewhat. But he knew he couldn't turn back. The once sleepy little burg of Port Strathy was wise to him by now, no doubt. So he steered the crusty old boat due north against the gale, cursing the cagy yokel who had rented him the craft. The five-pound rental fee had been highway robbery, for the vessel was barely seaworthy. But the fellow owned several boats, and this one had been equipped with a radio—its chief selling feature, as far as Sprague was concerned. Anyway, Sprague could not complain too heartily about the fee since he had no intention of returning the crazy old tub.

The minute Cabot had decided to tag along, Sprague knew there would be trouble. Not only was the Englishman surly and disagreeable, he was also greedy. The moment he had laid eyes on the cache of wealth buried underneath the rock on Ramsey Head, he had gone wild. No court would ever acquit Sprague on the grounds of self-defense, but he knew instinctively that had he not taken care of Cabot, he would never have made it to the mainland alive.

But he had made it, and nothing would stop him now. His boss had better be there to meet him! He didn't relish the idea of a submarine, but it was the safest means of undetected escape. His boss's connections in Berlin had paid off; this was, after all, the surest getaway. They'd be looking for him all up and down the coast, probably watching all the roads, and he'd be safe and sound where none of those yokels would ever think to even consider—under the sea. He didn't like Germans, and never had. But he could put up with them for a few days if that was the price for becoming a rich man.

A fifteen-foot wave crashed against the side of the boat, sending a column of spray over the deck and lifting it dangerously starboard. Sprague grabbed the wheel and forced the vessel around a few degrees in order to break away from the rough water. The compass told him he was off course. It was almost midnight. He better get her going right if he planned to make his rendezvous.

He would never have considered himself greedy, but then he had never had much to be greedy about. So why was he risking his neck on this stupid little boat in the middle of the night? Couldn't he just as well have paid off some farmer for a wagon and a couple of horses and hightailed it away on some back road to Aberdeen or Inverness, and then by way of some freighter to a nice safe South American country where he could spend the rest of his days a wealthy man?

Why, then, was he out in this storm?

Sprague answered his own question, although this time it was not the safety of the sub which convinced him, but rather the memory of his boss's face. He was not the kind of man who would let a man like Sprague get away with a double-cross. His boss had the kind of resources that could ferret out a traitor in the most remote lands. He was not the kind of man you betrayed, if you wanted to stay alive. It probably would have been next to impossible to fence the loot he had unearthed, anyway. He was being well paid for his services, and now he had also arranged some insurance for a bit of a raise from his boss. So in the end he reached the same conclusion as before—he may not like it, but this was no doubt the best way.

Sprague glanced at his watch. It was the time to make contact. He flipped the switch on the radio, turned the necessary dials, and began tapping out the appropriate Morse Code. After a few minutes he received a response, though faint. At least someone was out there. Sprague knew his boss wouldn't back out if he smelled money. He tapped out another message: "difficult to read ... repeat message." If only he knew German, he thought, and could talk to them.

A minute later came the reply, still choppy, but he got the vitals. The rendezvous sub was three miles offshore, north by northeast.

Sprague looked again at the compass. He was still way off course. Cursing, he struck his fist angrily against the panel. Then he gaped with disbelief. The instrument needles were spinning wildly.

It was broken!

The no good piece of junk was broken! How long had he been steering blindly? Where was the sub?

Perspiration beaded on Sprague's forehead as the cold dread of panic seized him. His hands shook as he grabbed the wheel. But he had no idea where to steer. He didn't even know in which direction the land lay! He could have been heading anywhere—

Suddenly he heard a sickening crack.

The craft lurched and shivered. Sprague was tossed off his feet, struck his head against the bulkhead, and knew no more. Perhaps he was better off that way, for the old fishing trawler was taking water fast.

56 The Guest of the *Admiral Mannheim*

"Herr commander," called the young lieutenant as he removed his heavy headset.

"Ja, Lieutenant," replied the commander of the *Admiral Mannheim* wearily. It was already midnight, and he had been up since before dawn maneuvering his submarine to its present locale some three miles off the coast of Scotland in the North Sea. He hadn't liked the assignment from the first. It was dangerous in such shallow water. But his superiors had made it clear: *This man is worth keeping happy. Do whatever he says.* And the commander was one who could follow orders, whether he happened to like them or not. That was how one got ahead in the German navy. So he would carry out his duty and ask no questions.

"It's been half an hour, mein Herr, and I have not been able to raise our contact again. Shall I continue to signal?"

Commander Von Graff sighed and, as if he planned to ignore his officer's query, ordered the periscope up. Leaning heavily on the horizontal bars, he scanned the storm-tossed seas above. On nights like these he was thankful for submarine duty. The other-worldliness of traveling fifty fathoms below the turmoils on the surface never failed to thrill him. And to do so in this craft, one of the Fatherland's finest, equipped with all the newest technology as part of the newly revitalized German military, only added to the dreamlike dimension. Of course, even if Hitler were elected and, as some predicted, poured three or four times as much into more sophisticated equipment, that would still not enable him to see more than a few yards on a night like this.

Von Graff stood back from the periscope and turned toward his subordinate. "The wind is blowing twenty to thirty knots up there," he said, "and he probably has nothing but a fishing radio. But ... you had better keep up the signaling, if for no other reason than we shall have trouble from our *guest* if we don't."

"Ja wohl, mein Herr," replied the lieutenant obediently, but there was a smirk on his lips that the commander could hardly miss.

"You do not approve?" asked Von Graff with a knowing smile.

"Are you asking my opinion, mein Herr?"

The commander nodded.

"Then I would candidly say," the young officer went on, "that the German Reich could do well enough without *American* financiers getting involved in it."

Von Graff laughed, though without making a sound.

"Someday that *will* be so," he said, turning suddenly serious. "But in the meantime we will have to suck in our pride and kiss the boots of men like our *guest*. We are still paying for the foolishness of 1918, but it shall not be so much longer."

"What were you saying?" came a caustic voice from behind the two men.

The commander swung around. "Ah, mein Herr," he said with an air of cool politeness, "we were discussing the status of your associate."

"Which is?"

"We have had no radio contact for the last thirty minutes. In this storm ... anything might have happened."

"Well, you just better find him," retorted the newcomer. "I'm paying you good money for this excursion."

"The *Reich* is paying me," rejoined the commander with just enough emphasis on the word *Reich* to give it added, sinister meaning.

"I'm pumping enough money into the Reich to make it all one to me," said the American.

"Be assured that we will do everything possible to reach your friend, Herr Channing."

Jason Channing turned sharply and strode from the bridge. Those arrogant Germans! You'd think losing a war would have taught them some humility. But fourteen years later they were still strutting around as if they owned the world. Well, maybe this time they'd make it—at least that's what Channing was banking on.

When he had lost nearly everything in the crash three years ago, he had been despondent. It was not easy for a man of sixty to think about starting over. But he'd never been the type to jump off a ledge because of a little setback. Thus he hung on to a hope that something would come along. And it had, during a trip to Munich at the invitation of some friends. While in Berlin he had heard Adolf Hitler speak to a crowd of union workers. Channing had found himself almost caught up in the frenzy of the gathering—the man was mesmerizing! Admittedly some of the things he said, if you listened closely enough, bordered on insanity. But Hitler himself had such a depth of charisma that he could get away with it. After the speech, Channing met the upcoming Nazi leader at a cocktail party. He was again struck with his absolute command—here was a man, he had little doubt, who *could* carry out his wild schemes. And since Channing was tired of his recent defeats, and the system that had brought them about, he decided to hitch his wagon to the brilliant rising star of Adolf Hitler.

It took Channing a year or so to recoup his losses, which, when he began liquidating his properties, proved to be less disastrous than at first report. Soon he was again able to wield the kind of power he craved. It didn't quite compare to the old days yet. But it was a start.

This business with Sprague had taken him off course for a time, but it was a long past-due debt. And after all, revenge was as sweet as power. The moment the name of Stonewycke had surfaced in his life again, he knew he would not be able to let it go. He did not like to lose.

He had lost only twice in his life. The crash had been the most recent loss, and he had switched national allegiance because of it. The other had been some twenty years before, when a pretty little bit of nothing by the name of Joanna Matheson had denounced him to his face. He had lost to a frail, stupid woman, and that fact had goaded him all these years far more than the loss of any fortune.

Now it was beginning to seem as if he may have been defeated again—this time in his attempt to settle the debt with Stonewycke. But he'd bury them for this—he'd not rest until every one of them was a dispossessed pauper.

Channing came to his cabin door, kicked it open and went inside. Lying on the small desk was the flimsy paper, Sprague's last communication. It wouldn't acquit the Duncan clan in his mind, but Channing reread it nonetheless. "Am aboard boat. Our package is secure. Rendezvous at midnight."

It did not seem possible to have come so close to such wealth and lose it so quickly. Had Sprague's boat indeed gone down in the storm? Sprague was too cold and calculating not to have covered all his angles. Was there a hidden meaning in the message? First of all, the specific use of the word *our* was not in keeping with their boss-employee relationship. Being a calculating man himself, Channing was well able to guess his intent. He was no doubt planning to cut himself in on the action. His lackey had seen the wealth and had decided that his boss should share it. What did he mean by "secure"? If he was planning on striking a deal, had he only brought aboard part of the loot, to insure his own continued safety? If so, what had he done with the rest of it?

Of course, he didn't want to give Sprague too much credit. He was not exactly a brilliant man, Channing noted. Before, he had always done what he was told. Perhaps the message meant nothing more than it said.

Channing refused to admit complete defeat.

If Sprague had gone down with his boat, so be it. But it didn't mean all was lost. Channing might still get his hands on the treasure. The only obstacle was to figure out just what Ross Sprague might have done with it.

A knock came to the door.

Channing rose and answered it.

"We're unable to reach your colleague," said the commander. "What would you like us to do?"

Channing thought for a moment, then replied. "Hold your position for another hour, and keep trying the radio. If there's no contact by then, head back out to sea."

57 The Legacy Continues

Three weeks passed.

The first had been agony for Allison as Logan semiconsciously struggled against death. Fever, delirium, and pain marked the slow passage of days, while Allison attended him faithfully, leaving his side only when she herself could ward off sleep no longer. She had been stretched and tested in her new faith beyond the capability of her tender years. The strength of the bloodline of her ancestors rose up from within her, and both Ian and Alec marveled silently at the resemblance she had suddenly taken to their own two wives—in both the look in her eyes and the depth of her character. She had indeed, in a short period of time, stepped fully into her heritage as the next in the proud line of Ramsey women.

Even more significantly, through her late-night vigils of prayer next to Logan's bed, she stepped fully into her heritage as God's child, as his woman of valor. More clearly and personally than ever did she at last grasp the truth of the words she had heard since infancy: "Though I walk through the valley of the shadow of death, I will fear no evil, for thou art with me. . . ." Never had a darker valley loomed before young Allison MacNeil and when it was over, a lasting glow of maturity flashed in her eyes from within.

At last came the morning when Logan awoke from his travels in the netherlands. Allison had nodded off to sleep where she sat. He looked up, saw her, and closed his eyes again, content to know that she was near him. When she awoke she saw that a change had passed. He seemed to be breathing easier, and the trace of a smile remained on his lips. With her heart beating anxiously within her breast, she rose and approached him. Her presence awakened him again. He smiled up at her. Though welcome beyond words, the sight accentuated all too clearly his pale, drawn complexion and his thin, wasted frame. She saw more clearly than ever what a terrible ordeal had passed.

"Oh, Logan. . . !" she said, weeping tears of joy.

"It seems I am a patient here once more," he said softly.

"Yes, but this time I think you'll remember which foot to limp on," she replied, laughing through her tears. She felt such an exuberant joy she could not contain herself.

"I wish it were only my foot that hurt." He winced as he tried to move. "I thought for a while I was going to receive *new* life and *eternal* life all in the same package."

"Logan, I'm so happy for you. Mother and Daddy told me about their talk with you, and the prayer you prayed. I'm so sorry I ran away."

"I think we'll both be learning about this new life for a long time to come," he said. "I tell you, Ali, on that night I didn't think I had much of a life to give to God. But I learned something since—God knows a man's heart, and you can't fool Him. And when you think you're dying, you don't *want* to fool Him any longer."

"I'm so thankful for all that's happened."

"Yes," he agreed. "But I'm afraid I've just caused more trouble for your family."

"Oh no! You are already like a son to them. You know how they are—it gives them pleasure to serve you. It does me too, more than you know!"

As the first week had been agony, the following weeks were bliss for Allison. Logan was strictly charged by the doctor to remain in bed, and had not the strength to argue the admonition. Allison was with him most of the time. She read to him, often from the Bible, frequently, too, from the old Scottish poet whose poem about the man-boats so tugged at his heart during his days of indecision. Usually they wound up discussing what they'd read. Sometimes Lady Margaret or other family members would join in, gently opening new insights to both of them concerning their new faith. Dorey quipped that he had a captive audience and likened the atmosphere, more philosophically, to that of his greenhouse. God was providing them a time of respite through which to grow and become strong and extend their roots down. But soon, like Dorey's precious plants, they would be transplanted into the harsher elements of life outside the greenhouse, where wind and rain and snow and sun would beat upon them, helping them to grow stronger yet.

As wonderful as such discussions were, even more memorable were the long talks between Allison and Logan when they were alone, sometimes lasting until late at night. They poured out their beings to one another, as each had never done to another before. Both, in their own way, had hidden their deepest selves for so long. Suddenly there was so much to say, so much to share, so much to try to understand. Their spirits linked together inextricably and the love that had begun between them solidified upon the strongest foundation of love a man and woman can have—the love of God.

Thus, when Logan was at last given leave for an outdoor excursion, the turn of the conversation was not altogether unexpected by either of them.

They walked to the wild and tangled walled garden at the back of the house which Ian and Maggie had loved so much. Summer, as early as the spring had been late, had come full force to Stonewycke. The great old birch was heavy with fresh green foliage, and the untrimmed rhododendrons and azaleas lent splashes of vivid orange, red, and lavender to the woodsy surroundings. Tangled ivy wound around the feet of the bench where Logan and Allison sat. No more perfect setting could have been dreamed for what followed.

"Ali," began Logan when they had finished talking about the lovely garden and the warmth of the weather the past several days, "now that the direction of my life has changed, I've tried to think what I will do with myself. I have no education, no money, and very few talents that could be marketed in an *honest* world."

"You have more to offer than you think," said Allison. "And I know your position here will always be open to you."

"Yes..." Logan said, drawing out the word thoughtfully, "and I am grateful to your father for it. But there's not a great deal of future in repairing another's tools and equipment. I had hoped to have more to offer—that is ... were I ever to settle down, it would be nice to have better prospects."

"Settle down?" Allison cared nothing for prospects. Those days were past for her. All she wanted was the man she loved.

"You know I've never been one to worry about position," Logan went on. "I never thought any nobleman was better than me in any way. But now I'm seeing—"

"Logan, *I'm* not making you feel awkward about your background, am I? That part of me's dead and buried. I don't care about class or distinctions anymore."

"I know. But still, opportunities for someone like me are ... well, limited. What can I do other than work with my hands for a few quid a month? That's no way to ... I mean, I could hardly expect ... well, that would hardly be a suitable life for a man with a wife ... like you."

"Oh, Logan!" exclaimed Allison in tearful and joyous frustration, "you dear, dear fool! I love you! Do you think that matters? It's different with us. We don't need position. Besides, there is a family precedent we have to keep up, you know. Such things did not stop my mother and father."

"Your father is a different man than I," replied Logan. "I have things hanging over my head. Things which make me far less worthy."

"I love and respect my father," Allison replied passionately. "More than ever in my life, now that I truly see him for the man of truth and integrity and courage he is. But you are every bit the man he is, Logan Macintyre."

"Oh, Ali, I don't know how you can say that ... how you could believe such a thing. But I thank you, and I love you from the bottom of my heart for it. I do so want to marry you ... if you'll have me. I will wait ... or you can have me as I am."

She threw her arms around him. "I would not take you any other way, Logan, than just how you are. Because that is how God made you. And it is the person you are that I fell in love with!"

He winced with pain at the exuberance of her embrace, but quickly recovered and drew her to him, kissing her tenderly. "Thank you, Ali," he whispered in her ear. "Thank you! Thank you for accepting me. Thank you for loving me."

"God has been good to us, Logan—seeing us through all that has happened and bringing us to this."

They were silent a moment. Then Logan spoke again; this time his voice registering concern. "But your parents—" he began. "What will they say?"

"Oh, Logan, they love you! Social barriers mean nothing to them. I should know that better than anyone. Remember, they've been through it themselves."

"Then I should talk to your father," said Logan.

"My parents will be happy for us," said Allison gleefully; "I know it!"

"I wish I had your confidence just now."

"They love you already—as I do," she replied.

"Logan," she went on, "we will always be together—imagine it!"

"That brings up another matter," Logan began, then hesitated. He had not been looking forward to this part. "As soon as I've recovered, I must go to Glasgow to see my mother and give her a personal invitation."

"Of course."

"And after that, to London."

Allison frowned. "I've told you about Molly," Logan went on. "She's been like a mother to me, and I must see her—I want to share with her . . . well, all the changes in my life. And especially tell her about you."

"Are you certain you have to go to London?" asked Allison, her voice quivering. "I don't think I could keep from worrying about you."

"This is not the sort of thing you tell a dear friend in a telegram or a letter. But I will be very careful."

"I want to go with you, then."

"Your parents are gracious and perhaps progressive," he replied, "but that would be asking too much. Besides, I won't be gone long."

"I'll hate every minute of it."

Logan took her hand in his. "I still have a few more days to recuperate," he laughed. "And I'll need you beside me every minute!"

———

Later that evening, when Logan was alone, he heard a gentle knock on the door. His welcome was followed by the entrance of Dorey, looking more solemn than Logan had ever seen him. He walked in, clearly with some purpose on his mind, and sat down next to Logan's bedside.

"I want to talk to you, Logan," he began.

"Certainly," replied Logan.

"Alec has told me of your conversation with him. I want first to offer you my congratulations, and to say—on behalf of Lady Margaret and myself—welcome to the family. We could not be more happy for you and Allison."

Somehow, thought Logan, *his face and tone do not indicate great joy.*

"But I would be gravely remiss if I did not warn you that I think you are making a serious mistake by wanting to return to London alone."

"Because of the danger?" asked Logan.

"More than that, because of the separation it would mean between you and your future wife. You know, I believe, something of the story of my past?"

Logan nodded.

"We all know the Lord has used it for good," Dorey went on, "but I was so young and foolish. It was impetuous of me to send Maggie to America while I remained behind myself. Good . . . yes," he sighed; "the Lord used it to strengthen us. But I just don't want to see you make a mistake you might regret."

Logan nodded again, receiving the words of wisdom from this man he had grown to respect.

"Take her with you, Logan," he concluded. "Now that the Lord has brought you together, do not let anything happen to interfere with your love."

"I will think about what you have said," said Logan. "You may be right. Thank you."

Dorey rose and extended his arm. The two men clasped hands and shook them firmly. "The Lord bless you, son," said Dorey at last. "I meant what I said. Welcome into this family. I have no doubt that great good will come to Stonewycke and its descendants through the virtues you bring to the line. I pray the Lord's fullest blessings on you and your marriage."

It was now Logan's turn to fight back the tears rising in his eyes. God had indeed prospered him beyond anything he deserved by bringing him into the wealth of this heritage.

The following afternoon Logan and Allison once again walked

in the walled garden. Circumstances had kept them apart the entire morning.

"I spoke to your father last night," said Logan quietly.

"And?" replied Allison expectantly.

"It was just like you said."

"He smiled and shook your hand . . . am I right?"

"Well, yes . . . in a way," said Logan with a smile. "He smiled. Then he gave a great roar of laughter. Then he embraced me in a huge bear hug that nearly burst my wound open again. When I winced, he jumped back, a pained look of apology on his face. Then he laughed again. And then . . . finally, he *did* shake my hand!"

Allison laughed. "That's just like Daddy! So warm . . . so boisterous!"

"And I had a visit from Dorey too, late last night."

"Yes?"

"We talked about several things. He welcomed me into the family, and gave me his blessing. He truly is a remarkable man."

They walked on, hand in hand, saying nothing for several minutes. Finally Logan broke the silence.

"Do you still want to go with me to London?"

"Oh, Logan, do you mean it?" exclaimed Allison.

"If you want to. I've already spoken to your mother. She said she would be free to accompany you."

"How wonderful. I can't wait!"

"We'll have a great time. I'll show you all the sights of the big city! Molly will love you both!"

Turning, they walked back toward the garden gate. "Oh, Logan," Allison said, "I've never been happier."

"Neither have I, Ali," he replied, bending to kiss her forehead. "God has given me everything. What more could be left?"

"Only more of the same!"

They left the garden and, laughing like two children, walked toward the great castle where they had found treasure beyond compare—not only each other but also the fullness of God's love.

Lady Margaret, having seen them approach, walked to meet them. She reached out, took each of their hands in one of hers, gazed deeply into Allison's eyes, then turned to Logan and did the same. She needed to speak no words. The love which she felt and the prayer of her heart for their well-being was written all through her face. They saw, received, and understood.

After a moment, she turned with them, and the three, still hand in hand, walked into the house to join the rest of the family.